PRAISE FOR *A TEA-DARK BEARING*

"Janice Kidd's *A Tea-Dark Bearing* opens in 1801 and is set in the then wilderness of the Adirondack Foothills. From the start it reads as if that wildness is being channeled through the rugged energy of the tactile, vivid prose itself. This is an historical novel in which one of the pleasures is the skill of how both place and the past have been authentically recreated. The conflicts of its complex characters are forerunners to those of today: race, class, gender, personal freedom, greed versus the preservation of the natural world. To Kidd's enormous credit those themes don't seem imported from the present. They arise from deep within the time and place she has so artfully recreated. *A Tea-Dark Bearing* is a rich, ambitious, and powerful debut."

—Stuart Dybek, author of *Ecstatic Cahoots*

"In the early 1800s hinterlands of the Adirondack Foothills, men blast dangerous rock to build a tourist resort, yet it is the lives of the female characters in *A Tea-Dark Bearing* who are in even greater peril. Georgie, once a wealthy Englishwoman, is now subject to her husband's physical and mental abuse as he literally brands her and requires her to tend to his mistress, while Black Vy, a former slave, is similarly entrapped. Only strong women can possibly survive in this rugged environment dominated by unscrupulous men rife with prejudice. A deeply researched and resonant historical novel, *A Tea-Dark Bearing* offers memorable heroines who we cheer for as they struggle together to escape to freedom."

—Virgina Pye, author of *The Literary Undoing of Victoria Swann*

A TEA-DARK BEARING

Janice Kidd

Regal House Publishing

Published by
Regal House Publishing, LLC
Raleigh, NC 27605
All rights reserved

ISBN -13 (paperback): 9781646035755
ISBN -13 (epub): 9781646035748
Library of Congress Control Number: 2024943763

Regal House Publishing, LLC
https://regalhousepublishing.com

Printed in the United States of America

To Michael

For man has closed himself up,
till he sees all things thro' narrow chinks of his cavern.

—William Blake

JUNE 1801

UTICA, NEW YORK

In the fire room of Auntie Wemple's Tavern, two kettles hung boiling inside the hearth. The pigs' heads churned, one to each pot. Georgie floated pigs' feet into each kettle. A snout, an ear tip, then a trotter arced and broke the surface of the bubbles as if the animals were pawing for air on pronged clothespin legs. The bubbles would later slow, swirl to milk, splash lazy wax, and Georgie would cool the pots overnight until the pink jowls and snouts and knuckles gelled in the risen fat cap.

The men had returned, outside knocking open boxes of charcoal, saltpeter, and sulfur.

"Spoilt!"

"Wet!"

"This 'ins dry!"

There was the thump of separation, dry boxes from ruined. Every few weeks, the men walked and rode the fourteen miles from the falls to Utica for a meat supper at table and to gather fresh supplies for black powder blasting. The men who came in before separating supplies were the ones injured: a spray of rock blast to the face; a rod driven into a knuckle; a knee bashed against a slippery crag; a numb and cold-blackened forefinger. Once, a charge had been left unexploded, forgotten, then busted alight at close range. Dirch Maas had entered the tavern that week with a spray of ripe berry scabs across his cheek and neck. Yet the men, Dirch included, had rejoiced for the victory of busting apart rock.

But no injured men stumbled in this night. A box crashed, and the men's voices erupted. Another week of unexploded charges, soaking rains, no progress blasting away rock for the trail.

The foreman, Noord Boorsma, booted open the dining hall door, sacks slung over both shoulders, arms wrapped around a box at his chest, a bundle of cloth fuses in his teeth. Men behind him carried more boxes.

Mr. Boorsma nodded to the far table. "Mix the cakes thitherto. What 'tis dry needs must remain so."

The men dumped the boxes. They could not have free hands without shoving each other, elbowing for space, grappling for the tender, defenseless sidebellies, floating ribs, shins, flanks, collarbones, jaw hinges, sternum bumps, throat guggles that were sure to take the other man down, the younger men testing, tussling the older men for the dominant stations at the foreman's sides, palming jaws to catch another's guard down.

"Off!"

"Git away!"

Boots scuffing. Chair legs scraping.

Mr. Boorsma grabbed two of the young sprawlers by their collars to separate them against the hearth. "Meal!" he called.

And Georgie's daughters ran with platters and bowls from the fire room into the dining hall.

There were too many men. They walked in cursing as if to knock down the fust and whiff of a week's work; they walked in regarding their red swollen eyes in tin reflections behind candles on the walls, announcing, "Him returned from an Irish wedding!"; they walked in with arms raised, smiling. "Do 'im look braw?" These young men months in the woods, clearing, blasting, hauling, reverently checking for new muscle and the crosshatches of scars upon scars mounding over their boyhood frames. The low-timbered eating hall was not warm. They wrestled for space at the cramped, long table. Fistfights flared, men rearing, heads bent for butting, hands choke-holding, then backing down from hunger and fatigue. In the stink, in the cold crowd, men would wait for a hot bowl of oily broth and pig's ear or trotter and warm bread. Mr. Boorsma might haul out an unruly man, then hold open the door to let another man replace his seat. But Mr. Boorsma allowed the men with subdued fight to beat each other until they collapsed, all spent, onto the supper table. Men opened the door every few minutes to relieve themselves or shout down the belligerent South Pocket workers, the second round of diners who waited, stamping their feet in the mud and thumping their hands on the door for space inside at the table.

They waited for the notices of the coming week's work assignments to be posted. Some men stood reading the other postings: the escaped slave notices, advertisements for local sempstresses.

When Mr. Boorsma posted the work assignments, he shouted each one, "Adams, Amson, double-jack! Bullfinch, hammer! Knecht, Murphree, axes! Smyth, single-jack! Syphur, wagon haul!"

No man dissented. This night after supper, they would form the black powder cakes from the raw materials in the boxes, working the measurements with tight lips and serious care, packing gently, then tucking the wads into the pouches slung from their belts.

They smoked at the hearth, gulped ale, clasped a hand on another's shoulder. This one hot meal at table transformed them, the men now warm-bellied, studying with open grins the cuts and bruises on each other's faces from the past week's fights, the space to venerate the week's handiwork. "Look what I have done to you, brother." They laughed and touched foreheads, chirping-merry, grasping each other, leaving white fingertip prints in the backs of sooty necks.

The men were fed. The hall filled with smoke and bellowed with stories. There would be more folk traveling through and trotters to pack for the men's journey back to the falls in the morning. Georgie stooped at the crock set aside from the morning's boil. She lifted the still-warm sow's head, heavy and dripping, and carried it, stuck with tines beneath each ear flap, to her worktable. She would leave aside the jowl and spit fry this later for her daughters' supper. The girls were permitted back in the dining hall after the men ate. Clara and Poppy cleared dishes in the dining room and lighted men's pipes, curtsying if a man gave her a "good lass" or a smile.

Clara, the younger, waited for a man to stack black powder on the hearth, to watch its slow burn and dark smoke lift and trace over the men's heads.

"That will be a grand trick for your wife one day, sir!" Clara laughed after this made the men laugh.

When their faces were red and tired, but tearstained from laughing, she looted one or two powder wads from their pouches and tucked them in her apron. But the foreman was stern, kept the fuses close in his vest pocket. There would be no lifting wicks off Noord Boorsma.

At her worktable, Georgie scraped off downy hairs from the pig's chin. She slapped her palms on its steaming cheeks to reckon the heft of the meat inside. The lips were set to a boiled, sleepy smile, the eye sockets tattered-edged and bruised. The eyeballs were sooty, dark smoke caught against lantern glass. Dirt caught in the pores around its snout, at the tips of its ears. She dug out wet hunks of hair and grime from inside the ears. Grasping the tine handles, she flipped the head over to the mosaic of meat and bone, the ragged, careless cuts of the butcher's dull blade at the animal's shoulder girdle. She turned the pig face-side up again, her rag-wrapped thumb hooking the base of the skull, the rough, abraded bones of the chine embedded in the neck, packed in by thick neck muscles. She slit up the throat, pulled back the rind, exposing the jawbone and teeth. The pig's teeth were clenched tight, row upon row.

She yanked another pull on the hide, her elbow cocked high, bits of fatty meat falling off the flat cranium. She tapped the bone with her knife as if to call up the animal's thoughts. Thoughts boiled clean, memories flayed away. She sliced out the sow's tongue and whacked it like a trout onto the cutting board.

Mr. Boorsma would come to her that night to say her husband, Hugh, bade her back to the falls. That she and his daughters were to depart by wagon in the morning. That he didn't know why she was ordered back. That she was to leave her workspace tidy. That he didn't know who would cook for the tavern now. That Mr. Bell would escort them. That she was to leave fripperies, such as slippers and ribbons, behind. That she should salt and pack as much pork as the wagon could bear from any carcass the butcher had hung that morning. That she should bring along her butchery cleaver, for the crew was behind with the slaughter and dressing of hogs running about the woods.

But Georgie didn't know this yet as she cleaned her night's work, soaking liquid from the worktable with salt and rags, setting aside a few trotters for what she thought would be the men's journey back, clearing space for more dishes the girls would retrieve from the dining hall. She denuded the skull of its ears and lips and snout. She thought she would boil the skull in the morning for stock and gelatin.

Most of the men left her alone. They couldn't understand her speech.

"Proper-like."

"Bluestocking."

"English bitch."

"Leave it. S' heavy baggage of Kettle."

The men called her husband Kettle. He had once nearly drowned in a kettle, a deep, swirling hole on one of the High Falls's ledges, after he and the men first started blasting away rock. The men had let him flounder and spin awhile before lifting him out, mostly to measure his mettle and worth and his physical stamina, the sand of his lungs, and because this was the first they had seen him knocked sideways from the river's power. But somewhat because he was the boss, and even early on there were petty grievances over pay and duties. The night Hugh almost drowned, one of the drunken men stood and squealed that Hugh looked like one of his wife's boiled hogs, and she might be conjuring spells all the way from Utica for Hugh to slip to a watery grave. That was the night Hugh began pairing the men to fight, and he chose this man for himself.

Most of the men left Georgie alone because they saw Hugh's brand on her forearm. At this, some men paled at her ruined skin; others blinked, their eyes wandering the rest of her body; and others ground their teeth in disgust, the smell of burnt hair and hide filtering up from memory of so many livestock brandings at their own hands. A few recalled their first brandings as boys, cherished calves bawling from the roots of their tongues at the pain and betrayal. Some men left her alone because a rough tack was gummed onto her dress and forearms. At the hearth's boiling pots, the rendered oils escaped with the steam, coating her. When a man grabbed her by the wrists, expecting a female softness, he recoiled. But there was something else, a forbidding demeanor. August Knecht backed away first for the sad hang of her eyes, then for the stony challenge in her posture, *What have you in this capacity?* They all felt the thunderclap of her gaze, but they had different ways of explaining it, some receiving it as a benedictory squint, others as a baleful reproach; in others, deep memories surfaced. Rye Syphur backed away under her scowl, bowing with sudden reverence for her station in the kitchen. He retreated in whispered veneration for the reliance on her for dear, hot meals. Quill Stibbens backed away having recently learned about ill-considered impulses, eating an entire basket of pigs' ears intended for the crew, the lesson freshly imprinted on his broken rib. One glance from her to his middle cavity flooded him with the gravity of the whipped-dog lesson. Derk Arendshorst recalled the spoilt spring on his land east that he wouldn't pay off for another eighteen years and that siphoned his horse cash to pay for land tax, which he used as extenuation for having his way with her, but her sensible advice on the matter of debt shamed him soft for its obvious pragmatism. Ham Key said he had smelled vinegar and onions on her breath and backed away, disrupting tin plates in his wake, which further rattled his nerves and quickened his escape. "Who was she to entreaty me to bring skills to the entanglement," he later huffed. Noord Boorsma left her alone because her jackbooted poise reminded him of his grandmother's on mornings when she fed him cold cabbage instead of warmed cornmeal.

Most of the men's hearts were soft, dripping and friable as honeycomb. But a few men were lumpen, embittered, and those men did

not last long on the crew. There was Cager Bullfinch. At first sight of
Georgie, he had bowed and left her alone. But he watched her, and she
guarded against looking at him, spooked by his distance and gaze, the
first time in her life without protection of her uncle or husband. Then
one night after dinner service as the girls slept, she wiped clean her
cleaver, stropped its edge sharp, and stored it away between soft cloths.
As she swabbed pink butchering juices from her worktable, another
man, Cuthbert Cuddy Smith, pressed behind her, the table edge a
fulcrum trap as she grabbed forward for leverage away, disrupting the
bucket, sloshing pig water onto herself, spilling it over the table onto his
boots as his hands sifted through layers of skirt and she felt dread and
revulsion as he palmed her flesh. She could not turn around. He was
too mud-headed to stop. She did not cry out, for her sleeping daughters
were near. Then Cager was beside Cuddy. And she withered and rasped
out a cry, mistakenly foreseeing a gang-up of men. But Cager shoved
Cuddy away, and Georgie stood gripping her worktable in disbelief as
Cager told Cuddy to leave. Cuddy did not obey, slurred a protest, found
an iron poker, and with a guttural cry swung the poker sideways for
Cager's face, but it stuck fast in the planked wall. Cager punched him
once in the throat. Cuddy coughed and swore and spat, and Cager made
him clean it up, then elbowed his windpipe and hauled him outside
of the tavern. Cager that night slept at the fire room door guarding
anyone's crossing into Georgie's hearthside bed.

After that night, Cuddy worked one more day on the crew. Cuddy
and Cager were on the same double-jack drill team along with Oepke
Bonnema. Cuddy held the rod as Oepke and Cager each swung
hammers, alternating strikes as Cuddy rotated the rod, drilling a hole
into the rock. Cager did not utter a word to Cuddy, but Cuddy thought
Cager's hammer strikes bore down more breakneck than usual, swiping
close to his hand. Cuddy saw Oepke glance at Cager, urged by Cager's
hammer pace to keep up. Cuddy braved a few twists after their hammers
beat down the rod, then he lost his nerve, walking off the site for good,
clenching all ten uncrushed fingers. Cuddy's finger bruises remained
like wax knurls on Georgie's thighs for some time. Cager never became
more than another man to cook for, yet he continued to sleep outside
her door.

Mr. Boorsma entered the fire room, nodding as Georgie sat with a
bowl of broth. He told her. Tomorrow. With Mr. Bell. The wagon. To
the falls.

Her hand dropped, her spoon splashing broth. "Where are those girls with the platters?"

Did she hear? Tomorrow. The falls. The wagon. At Hugh's bidding. Clean up. Pack.

"Yes. May I eat?"

He left her alone to spoon her broth.

Before America, she had been served four sweet cakes each day along with venison steak, porkpie, wings of partridge, steamed cabbage, cherries, pears, and plums. Most of her food was discarded to the hog pens. She picked at the best bites: the rounded cleft of a plum, the stickiest charred point of a wing, the swirl of cream and candied marigolds atop a cake. In the evenings, she lifted each cake off its tray and lodged creamy cake into her mouth, then discarded the rest into the fire to the giggles of her maids. The maids had grown tired of the sweets and often used them to bribe young grooms into sneaking a newborn puppy or kitten or small pig into their sleeping quarters.

Georgie drank her broth, listening to the men's voices, booming ever higher as the ale and night and fire wore in, and the high laughter of her girls and the clatter of dishes shifting in their arms as they lingered for as long as possible with the men.

A year priorly, when Georgie had first arrived at Auntie Wemple's Tavern, the butcher hung a carcass in the back shed. He did not deliver quarters. He advised her to serve ale, not spiritous liquors, for that would attract and keep an unsavory lot. The carcass was headless, but the butcher held a twill-wrapped bundle under one arm that was stained pink. He set it on the worktable, removed the twill. He nodded to the head. She was to dress the meat and salt or dry as much as possible before the high summer heat spoilt it. "Sous the ears and cheeks and be quick about it. Pot the tongue."

She did not understand his instructions. The carcass spun round on its rope. Its belly was open in a great slit with all the insides removed. She was to cut off and stuff the knuckles and score the crackling of the fore loin and chop off the leaf fat. Or was it to the score the leaf fat and chop off the crackling? Was she to put up much lard from the leaf fat or the rind? What was she to do with so many pots of lard? The butcher was not amenable to her requests for clarification.

The men were direct with complaints after two bad meals. For the first, she served salted pork straight from the crock without scrubbing or soaking the meat. For the second, she fried meal in leaf fat that had not been rendered for lard. Thereafter, Oepke Bonnema taught her to plunge the ears and feet into boiling liquid. Chute Littlejohn trained her to let harden overnight the leaf fat, then cut it into a pot of water over the fire. Dirch Maas sat four hours stirring until the water evaporated, then showed her how to smear a bit of lard over a pot of salted pork to seal it well. Jantjen Meijer tutored her to cut out the chine so it was free of rind and to roast it in a dry pan with sage. She knew enough to look forward to learning more; the men promised to show the curing of bacon and the smoking of jowls.

The men intended to eat well through the work season. They brought her vegetables, sliced them paper thin, strung them on cords, and showed her where to hang in the coolest and driest spot of the cellar. They showed her that the brine to store pork had to be strong enough to float an egg. When the tavern's root cellar flooded, they showed her a decent replacement could be dug out of a hill, which was the very spot where the village of Utica had posted a sign: *This Spot Do Mark Withal the Boundary that Forbades the Digging of Cellars, Privies, Wells, Graves.* But the men said it was prime because no one would disturb it. And no one did. Sometimes the men brought back from the woods acorns and wild fruits to scatter in the butcher's pen, for that was the sweetest mast. They told her to oft drop a snake in the pen, and she did. After the small pigs ate and grew and were slaughtered, boiled, and served in the dining hall, the men would give her a nod, and this nod meant they could taste the snake in the meat.

From the fire room she would see the fire in the dining hall spark and glow. And feel the golden heat of the fire room at her back. She built and stoked these two fires in the tavern each day. Nights after the men settled, she would draw hot water to bathe the girls, pouring jug after jug to rinse their hair, listening to their recitations of a poem about a freshly killed turtle whose heart still beat. And Clara would dramatize its swimming and its capture and its seizing final breaths. Clara would still her body in the shallow tub and cup her hands, bellowing to mimic a heartbeat. Georgie would wipe her down, thinking ahead to when her girls would marry the sons of the upstart merchants setting up stores in town. And Georgie felt the largesse of her spirit, the warm spread of her being. This was a high point in her life, a life she did not believe possible after Hugh banished her from their home and dumped her at the tavern.

Georgie spooned her broth and sputtered and wiped her mouth and sat shaking. Why was Hugh calling her back to the falls?

New men sometimes mistakenly addressed Georgie as Auntie Wemple as if Georgie were the tavern's proprietress. If a man did so without the other men hearing or noticing, she would smile and let him think she was a woman of means and great tenacity for building such an establishment. There had never been word from Hugh about how long she and their daughters were to stay working at the tavern. She might slog there over the boiling kettles for the rest of her life. She sat at her table, the comfortable confines of the fire room already falling away. No bolt, nor door, but the space was hers, the tasks were hers and hard learnt.

The girls had not brought back the next round of dinner plates. Then Clara entered the kitchen, dumping a stack onto the table.

"Why haven't you more plates?"

Clara did not answer. She puffed her chest to show off the blue embroidered flowers on her bodice.

"That dress is too big for you." Yet Georgie did not notice that the dress was different from the one Clara had been wearing all day. Georgie gestured toward the worktable. "And the bones have boiled out of the pettitoes. Now tend to the meat before it's ruined."

The older sister, Poppy, entered the fire room, her arms loaded high with plates. Georgie addressed her. "Wipe them quickly. We're to pack and head north in the morning."

Clara cast her eyes to the boiled, pinked pigs' feet on the worktable and rolled them under her hands like wooden blocks.

There had been rain in the night, and they hung back from the mud in the street. The lantern lit the calf-skin shoes they each wore for the hard terrain of the falls. Georgie did not permit the girls to pack their cloth slippers. She held one oilcloth satchel. In it were the cleaver and bloody dresses from the night's butchering and a noonchine of cider and salted pork. They had been up all night salting and packing the dressed pig parts, and those barrels stood alongside them. Georgie had made the girls change into their hog dressing clothes after dinner service. Clara had stepped out of the embroidered dress; Poppy had claimed it for wearing later. After the hog was dressed and packed and they knew they were to forgo sleep, Georgie told them to change back into their service dresses to await Mr. Bell's wagon. Clara remained in her butchering dress. Her service dress could not be found. Clara didn't tell her ma the man in the gangway had taken it. Georgie scolded and rolled the barrels of pork streetside and fretted about the bloody dress Clara would appear in before her father. Their dawn departure was near.

They waited for Mr. Bell outside of the tavern. The lantern lit the buds of the new embroidered dress. It fit Poppy well. Her ma did not notice. Poppy had packed her old service dress deep into the satchel. How had her ma not noticed? Poppy did not help her ma roll the barrels. Their ma never paid them enough mind. Poppy calmed her breath, an uneasy quaking. Why had the traveler changed her ten-year-old sister's dress? Poppy fixed her posture. She was four years older than Clara. Why hadn't the man given her a dress too?

Their slippers were left lined up at the tavern's hearth, the only sign they had ever been there.

Mr. Bell bumped around the dark of the lean-to harnessing the horses. He had been up all night with the men drinking. The other men were to stay at the tavern to wait for an extra shipment of goods; they were behind schedule clearing rock and Hugh intended to double up on blasting powder.

The horses were hitched to the wagon, a pair of heavy draught brothers named Balor and Brace with sound feet and bright bay coats. Mr. Bell said nothing in greeting. He lifted the lantern to the high wagon bench, and when the light passed his face, Georgie saw his puffy scowl.

He scanned the girls first, then the barrels, the satchel, the girls again, and, seeing no win, stiffly hoisted the barrels into the back of the wagon. He bore the loads without sound though his knee once buckled. He hefted each girl as if stacking tree trunks alongside the barrels. He lifted the satchel onto the driver's bench, picked up Georgie by the waist and perched her on the bench, and she allowed this without protest because of the early hour and his fragile bearing. Only later in the day would he feel embarrassed and at the same time try to recall the feel of his hand on her ribs, but it was so many hours ago, in the dreaming of predawn and his head still gummed up with spirits and his back shooting pains, he would have no remembrance or imprint of feeling.

The log-and-frame houses and stores were dark as the wagon jangled through town. Two lanterns glowed alive, faces at windows. The night watch sentinels drifted through the dark street. It was their last hour scouting for fires before sunrise. Francis Bloodgood touched his finger to his hat brim as he burned trash in the street, tidying the ash into a kettle before the burn curfew of daybreak. The men who ran the mercantile house, Archibald Kane and Jeremiah Van Rensseleer, mounted their horses but waited for the wagon to pass. They followed toward the river to collect any goods arrived by boat during the night. Mr. Bell held a tight rein on Balor and Brace as they crowded past street rubbish—hogsheads, slaughterhouse offage, standing wagons—but they soon cleared the village.

Until they climbed out of the valley, Mr. Bell spoke only to the horses, "Hold" or "On." As the horses stretched their necks and blew breath and bore down for the ascent, Georgie looked back toward the tavern, the town bobbing with lantern lights on wagons delivering goods, the tavern still dark, the other crewmen still asleep. Black smoke rose from a few chimneys in households rousing fires for the morning cooking. She turned forward. The road was now a rocky trail, and the horses' ears pricked at each bright bird call, the leaves flecked with rising light.

Mr. Bell's head cleared, and as he looked back to the girls as a ruse to read Georgie's face, he saw for the first time Clara in her bloody dress. "The litl'uns a proper butcher now."

Georgie glanced sideways in scant acknowledgment. He gave slack to the reins, at which the horses brisked pace. Georgie caught the side of the wagon for balance. He didn't think her beautiful. She was worn in the face, slight of figure, her tension and tiredness popping out in swollen eyes and the veins that roped across the tops of her hands.

Her mouth was rarely alive, an inscrutable thin line. Yet her hair sprang with dark, glossy curls escaping her cap. Her forearms were often bare, sleeves folded for working, and they were well-formed, tapering to elegant, though chipped and chapped, hands. All was exaggerated in the morning hour. He knew to be kind with people in the mornings when they were at their most vulnerable and aggrieved. He would set the conversation to himself to unburden her from having to initiate polite talk.

"At the next payout, 'im take Mr. Post's packet boat down the Mohawk."

Georgie turned to him. "Down the Mohawk River?"

"Yes, to Schenectady, mistress."

"And which direction is that?"

Like most of the crewmen, he strapped a powder horn to his side. He tapped a spot on the horn, unslung it, and passed it to her. The men engraved their horns with maps of the Mohawk Valley, extending from Lake Ontario to Albany. Mr. Bell's horn named the West Canada Creek, Wood Creek, and the other tributaries feeding into the Mohawk. His horn was flourished with flowering vines and brickwalled forts and the oxbows of rivers. He had carved the detailed spires of the churches that dotted upriver. Other crewmen carried their father's and uncle's horns from the Revolutionary battles, and those horns were marked with crosses indicating where comrades had fallen along the waterways, where windsails stood to power gristmills, where navy ships had run aground. Georgie had learned that the men's maps were mostly sentimental, the navigable details reserved inside men's heads, for she had stolen a powder horn to escape from the tavern soon after Hugh banished her there. The map led her downstream only to nudge against the mire of a dried-up creek thickly barricaded with a tangle of fallen logs, the dense forest beyond, and she was forced to turn back. She had not been gone long enough for her daughters or any of the men to notice.

"Pardon, mistress? Say again?"

Georgie repeated her question, and his eyes moved to her lips.

Mr. Bell nodded to the expanse of forest as if a specific direction were evident. "Mr. Whetmore needs a crew. Rebuild the church steeple. Wood rotted. The belfry mayhaps is salvageable. But I will get me time piecing a new spire."

"Do Mr. Post's boats run one way only?"

"Whyfor he would carry a cargo of ruined onions?"

"The direction. Of his boats."

His confidence was tarnished at her lack of engagement with his charms and her disinterest in his ambitions. Georgie could see he had only used his allure on young ladies. It must have worked many times for him to have beamed like a crow upon his wagon bench. But he was now chapfallen, working through the first crush of its failure.

He became somewhat cross. "Those boats is not for ladies. Cussin' and drinkin' in the presence of passengers and clergy alike." He withdrew from looking at her.

"How much does Mr. Post charge for passage?"

"I am not accustomed to women pursuing a single-mind of questions about worldly interests." He tried a scolding tone on an older woman. He had only ever before clutched his hat and bowed his head to his mam and grandmam. But he was now driving in unbroken country, in charge of these women, and he sat tall again for the spank of his words.

She wished to tell him that she would have him whipped upon arrival at the falls. But she folded her hands.

He resolved once more to be obliging, it being forenoon. "Now this section of the river here," he began.

"Are we nearabout the river now?" She could only see trees.

He nodded to a point in the distance. A rise of more trees.

"Me paps in the battle at Oriskany high summer of '77 carried the litter for General Herkimer and laid him out in the boat that was rowed sixteen miles down the Mohawk to Fort Dayton."

"And in what direction is Fort Dayton?"

He prickled at her stubborn lack of interest. "If'n your Regulars had been present, mistress, the good general might not have been struck down mortally."

"Then you would not have so grand a story to relay about your lineage, sir."

He understood her tone but had stopped trying to make sense of her words. "At least we show to a fight."

She tried to pick out distinguishing features of the landscape. As they drove into denser country, it would become more confusing and closed. She remembered her long journey from England after she and Hugh were first married, a voyage she had imagined as an unencumbered line westward. She had paid no care to navigation as Hugh ferried them out of London to the harbor nor after landing on the American shore as he arranged a string of northbound ships. Now retreat from the interior of upper New York seemed impossibly difficult, the route wiry and overgrown with so many creek bodies dead-ending at deeper and murkier points of swampland and forest.

Mr. Bell persisted. "I mean, your Regulars are scum, but they wouldn't have planned an ambuscade like did the Loyalist militia."

He took her silence as his victory for the exchange and a reconsideration of her own brash questioning. "If'n I was to duck out of here, I would not pay Mr. Post's high toll on his filthy boat. I would secure myself a private rig."

"And how would one so motivated acquire a private craft in these parts?"

"Croft?"

"No, sir, obtain a private bateau."

"Anyone can borrow or steal or hire a bateau. You need men to pike the thing down river. And men to portage at Little Falls and down again. And that's in a good season with full water."

"And Wood Creek leads to Lake Ontario, which then leads to the seaway and the Atlantic harbors?"

"Yes, traveling to the west, Wood Creek will take you to trade posts with the Natives 'round Upper Canada. You planning on taking up the peltry trade? I believe you're all turned about. I presume you intend to travel homeward, make your way to a ship at the New York harbor Atlantic-bound? You need to travel east down the Mohawk to the Hudson. The reverse way you came to the falls with your husband. Traveling west and north to the seaway is a longer and more dangerous route even for a man."

Years ago, she had been flummoxed at her first sight of the wild land. Men had piked their boat against the currents for the entire journey: up the wide Hudson River to around Albany where the Hudson met the Mohawk. More piking upriver on the swift Mohawk with a substantial portage at Cohoes and another at the place called Little Falls. Hugh had paid men to hitch sleds to the fore and aft of the bateau. The men hitched a wagon tongue to the front sled, and a team of oxen pulled their boat and supplies overland along a swampy path. Much of their journey had been portaging around falls and water too furious to paddle against before they landed at the homestead. The man whom Hugh had paid at Little Falls to unload their supplies and portage their boat had offered to buy the goods from Hugh. They were Georgie's household goods. She had refused to part with them, so Hugh paid a dear price for the carrying and restowing of her china and furniture, most of which was still packed in crates at Hugh's small shanty except for the china, the display of which had been her first household task. She thought grimly of her foolishness then. She should have packed heavy woolens and a few good knives. If she could secure a smaller boat, could she portage the craft herself to get back to the New York harbors? There was a rowdy tangle of wilderness and rivers in her mind.

"And how do I undertake such a journey without protection nor manpower nor funds nor a sense for navigation in these wilds? And with vulnerable daughters in tow? You foreguess too much about my intentions, sir."

"Yes, but you put much thought to the matter. I see that. It's best for you to stay close to the protection of your husband."

She was quiet again. How would Mr. Bell present without clothes, a rope slung over his shoulder as he hauled with long, slow strides a boat through a shallow, swift section of the Mohawk River, with her dry and shaded by a parasol, seated in the boat?

Poppy huddled her head and knees against a barrel and looked at their backs seated on the wagon bench. Clara leaned against the barrel, and she soon sagged like a sack of feed. Poppy cradled her sister. The town was dark, and the lurch and jangle of the wagon pulled the girls into sleep.

Poppy woke at the slowed pace of the horses as they started to climb out of the valley. Mr. Bell was looking at her ma, but Poppy couldn't hear what they were saying. Poppy rested her cheek against the barrel and put one arm around its middle girth, fingering the metal bracing. She studied the side view of Mr. Bell's face. He had black hair that grew almost over his ears but was not long enough to tie back. His face was full, and when he smiled, he held his lips together, but his cheeks and eyes rose and crinkled pleasingly. His eyes were dark gold capped by thick black brows. He was unshaven as most of the men were, including her papa. One time, the men had come back to the tavern, and all were freshly shaven. This had been after the momentous first blast had split free five loads of limestone. Now she could not see Mr. Bell's mouth through the heavy beard. Before, his mouth looked quite fine despite the pink nakedness and nicks of the blade. Once she had put both

hands on either side of her papa's beard and kissed and pressed her
palms against the thick bristles. Some of the other men had beards so
scant they reminded her of the hairs her ma scraped from the hogs.
And these beards she did not like, for those wispy hairs were like the
hairs around the nipples of the hog's underbelly.

Mr. Bell sometimes looked at her ma a long time, but her ma mostly
did not look at him. Poppy knew how that felt, a lowdown numbness
like wiping clean a stack of plates taller than herself. If Mr. Bell turned
his neck back a mere click, he would see her listening. She was eager to
hear about any matters he spoke of; she wanted to know what he sought
in this world; she could be a perfect teacup to receive his thoughts. She
swore he said the word *church*. She imagined him as a sexton, ringing the
church bell each morning and evening, and she a sexton's wife. Mr. Bell
was likely confused, and she could offer to sit between them to translate
what her ma said.

Mr. Bell did not wear an overcoat, only a linen shirt with the sleeves
pushed up. His skin was tan, and his hands held the reins in a bunch,
like flowers, to his chest.

Poppy had seen a man the night before in the tavern, before Clara
went into the gangway. He was not a man on the crew, but a lone traveler.
He had a full crimson mouth, and if he spoke or sang, the sound would
be low and beautiful. His beard was trimmed, he held his fork palm-
over-handle, the manners of a man from Philadelphia or even farther
south. His overcoat was not homespun, but a dark blue wool weave
cut close to his body, a contrasting shine on his satin cuffs and lapel.
But buttons were missing—a gold one hung though still functional. He
looked travel-worn, perhaps frail, his color ashen. Yet he tipped his chin
to catch the attention of Mr. Boorsma, and he spread his elbows and
legs to occupy the most possible table space. Mr. Boorsma had nodded,
and the man rose stiffly to shake hands. She had tried not to stare for
too long, working her rag over the cutlery.

The next time she had looked up, Mr. Boorsma was speaking to
another man. The traveler's seat was empty, his plate showing the track
mark of the last swipe of crust. She took away the plate to her ma for
washing. When she came back into the dining room, Obadiah Bray had
met Clara at the front door. She was wearing a new dress and a new
ribbon in her hair and was shy to enter at the raucous burst of laughter
that was cresting. Mr. Bray fought a lot, always had crusted knuckles.
But Poppy knew he hadn't been responsible for the change in Clara's

clothes. It must have been the traveler. The traveler had changed Clara's dress.

Mr. Bray instructed Clara to hold out both arms as he stacked them with dirty plates, then patted her bottom to send her off.

"Sir, did you chase that man away?" Poppy asked.

"Why would I chase me crew mate away, miss?" Mr. Bray had not seen the traveling man. "Tell sister to stop flying out of doors bothering the men as they pump ship at the privy." Mr. Bray sat back at the table.

Poppy had picked up her rag, wiping out mugs for the next round of dinner.

In the back of the wagon, Poppy decided the traveler had been lonely, unwell, likely a landowner, but a man to be pitied. Mr. Boorsma had clasped the traveler's forearms upon first meeting him, affirmation that the man must've been harmless. Poppy studied the new dress, fine cotton with tiny blue cornflowers embroidered at the bust and wrists, work that not her ma nor any sempstress in Utica could stitch up. Her ma still had not asked where the dress had come from. Poppy delighted in the borrowed time until her ma understood the dress did not belong to them.

Clara was still asleep. Poppy draped her white skirt over Clara's slate-colored, bloodstained skirt. Its drab relief to the new white dress made Poppy draw her arms around her sister. The wagon jolted over a rutted patch, and Clara shifted in her arms. Poppy wore the man's ribbon too, tied around her cap. It was a silky grosgrain, a soft green. Poppy lifted the ribbon from her back to lay over the front of her shoulder. She fingered the ribbon. The man had not handled it much for there were no snags or smudges. The ribbon's face had the soft, uncrumpled plush of a sage leaf. How considerate of the traveler to keep the ribbon and the dress clean. Poppy didn't expect ever again to see the man. She and Clara had received a few gifts from their ma and pappa, small treasures at holidays. But the girls had never given back gifts. Poppy rocked in the wagon, recalling how the crewmen gave her coins if she poured ale with a generous hand. She could not imagine the traveler wanting something in return for the dress. She thought him a generous soul, one satisfied to bestow her pretty sister with a new dress without expecting anything in return.

There began endless breaks and ruts and fallen limbs in the trail. The wagon staggered sideways, sliding in the mud. Georgie gripped the wagon's side and for a moment quit the worry of having to greet Hugh.

"Hold, mules!" Mr. Bell shouted. Balor and Brace, stoutly elegant and glossy, were not mules though their stubborn tendencies had earned them the appellation.

He stepped down to drag fallen branches from the road. Georgie and the girls climbed out of the wagon, lifting their heads to the treetops, yawning, tapping gloved fingers onto their cheeks to restore color. Mr. Bell limped and stiffly dumped the tree debris. He backed into a large, moss-covered boulder and rubbed the length of his spine up and down, squatting with his knees. His shirt was open at the neck, and black hairs spilled over the notch, visible all down his torso through the linen. As he rubbed and squatted against the rock, Georgie turned her back to him, and turned the girls so they did not see this display.

"The wagon I was driving tipped in a rut and crashed near a month ago."

They heard the scraping of his shirt against the rough moss and the jagged catch of pain in his breath.

"To calm the lead pony, I leapt down astride her back to untangle her from harness and rein." He worked up a steady, deep squat, evident in the rise and fall of his voice.

Poppy tried to turn toward him to show she was listening, but Georgie redirected her.

"So short was that pony that me toes dragged on the dirt once it got trotting along. Durn thing pitched me over, and something in me back jarred loose. People asking if I fell from a roof for the way I limp about so."

The scraping ceased, and they faced the man. In front of the girls, he tried again to win Georgie's favor. "Have you heard the summer will end sooner this year?"

"I have not."

Mr. Bell cast his gaze onto Poppy. She bore her eyes onto him. *They are bright fireflies lit up just for you, Mr. Bell.*

"I had a sweetheart from Little Falls, Lorna, from when I was a much younger man. Do you know her?"

Poppy started to reply, but her ma turned toward the wagon. "We do not."

"'Tis about the only reply I can make out from your mam because of the fact that she oft repeats it."

"If you like, sir, I am at your service to decipher her more formal expressions and inflections."

He smiled with surprise and tipped his hat to Poppy. "Well, me lady, we shall gets along fine, shain't we then?"

Poppy looked toward her ma for approval of the arrangement, but she was already seated in the wagon, her back sternly against them.

"Where's your girl?" he called to Georgie's back.

Georgie stiffened and grasped the wagon's side.

"A lady like yourself will need a girl in this wilderness," he persisted.

"I did not bring her," Georgie faltered. "I did not bring her because of the tragedy with Verna Lenox."

She closed her fist over her heart in reverence to the dead woman. He nodded—everyone between Utica and the High Peaks knew the story—and took off his hat in respect. Verna Lenox had been carried piggyback by her lady's maid the previous summer down the treacherous pathway to the High Falls. The maid had slipped, sending Verna into the churning water to drown. The maid had survived.

"Who will carry you to the falls then, sister?"

"If you please, call me madam. No one chaperones me. I make my own way."

"It is a dangerous business for ladies." He squatted up and down again against the rock.

Her daughters ran for the wagon, not wanting the scolding of being near this spectacle.

"Mama, are we getting a servant girl?" Clara asked.

"No."

"This gives me some relief," Mr. Bell called from the rock.

Georgie pressed the lace of her day cap against her eyes. "We must be going, please. My husband has expectations for our arrival."

She could not think with the rubbing and the questions. Should she attempt to memorize this turn and that clearing, or not? Was this the way of escape but going backward? Should she drop a ribbon or tear off lace to mark a trail? Her thoughts swam low and frantic in her guts.

As they trundled onward, Georgie dropped into brief sleep, lifting above the rutted, wild road to almost above the high, dense trees. She looked down to the wagon, saw Mr. Bell palm the top of his hat to cant the brim forward, saw her daughters huddled together in back. She rose higher, out of the shadows of the trees, into full daylight, and without having to scan the horizon, the golden flash of the river beamed the right side of her face. Mr. Bell slapped the reins, and she was thumped back to the wagon bench, jolting awake, grabbing to stop from pitching forward. She regathered her bearing, and he knew not to look at her.

They neared territory Georgie recognized but in the disorienting way that memory papers over present day. She had last been there before Hugh sent her away to the tavern. She had missed late summer, fall, winter, and spring in the woods, cooking long days inside the tavern. As the trees broke open to a sunny glade, she was delivered back to the same place in the same season. She was not yet ready to face Hugh.

"May we stop here?"

Mr. Bell squeezed the reins back. She slid forward as the horses slowed.

The wagon stopped in the clearing, and Georgie jumped onto a carpet of cedar needles. The air was much cooler and the ground more wet. There was the high thrash of insects and branches. "Shall we take noonchine?"

"Yes, then. What have we?" Mr. Bell cupped the horses' noses in his palm, into which they blew greetings.

"Salt pork and cider."

Mr. Bell led Balor and Brace to shade, the wagon clattering. He wiped a rag along their shoulders and muzzles. He blotted the sweat underneath their collars and spoke low in their ears that soon he would return them to town to unburden them of their harnesses and bits so they could forage their meadow. He would let them cool down before watering them. He walked back toward the women. Squat apple trees hedged the thick forest.

"And apples." Mr. Bell picked from low branches heavy with blushing green clusters.

Georgie unfurled a blanket and arranged the food. Poppy knelt alongside her ma, drank long from the cider jug, fixed salt pork between two biscuits. Mr. Bell gathered apples in the crook of his arm. Despite his injury, he had the strong bearing of a man who worked outdoors sunup to sundown. His forearms were thick and tanned against the white of his rolled shirtsleeves as if he cleared trees all day, tearing at limbs and roots, flinging them in his wake.

He gripped an apple in each hand, alternating bites from each one. In a few chomps, they were both down to the cores, and he lobbed the cores aside, grabbing for more fruit. He tossed one to their picnic area. Poppy caught it, wrapped both hands around it. The juice ran down his chin. Mr. Bell kept slinging apples, and they landed all around her.

Clara slept in the back of the wagon.

Georgie called a few sharp words, but the child would not rouse. "Do as I say at once."

Clara stumbled off the wagon, one eye bloodshot. Her surroundings were foreign and she fussed.

"Quiet. This will not do. Take your sister to water and soak her face."

As Poppy caught her hand and led her toward the woods, Clara quieted.

The girls wandered deep into the woods. Poppy held branches aside so Clara could advance. The branches snapped shut behind them like cellar wickets. They hurdled the crisscross of colossal trees, scraping their ankles and skirts against the mass of greenery curling over the decay of logs. They peeled back thick hunks of rotting bark, and it crumbled in their hands like soil, the smell dank and acrid, but not unpleasant, like what they cleaned from between the sow's teatlings' feet. They ducked and scrambled and found an opening where wind had crashed down a chain of trees, the debris piled in a long sweep, with pale, splintered wood spiking upward from where each tree had fractured. Away from their ma, Poppy hiked her white skirt, tucking it under her arms. They rode the fallen trees as if breaking wild ponies. They whooped, then hopped to their feet, skipping across the expanse from one trunk to the next, keeping their feet dry of the black, wet earth below.

There were standing patches of water, and Poppy held her sister still as she wet her matted hair and dabbed at the blood stains from the previous night's butchering on her skirt. The blood stains spread across the fabric, her skirts muddied from the mire. Poppy ran her fingers through Clara's hair, gathering it back. The water was cold, and Clara had enough. She plucked her sister's fingers away. She spied birds to follow, but they scattered low then fluttered high out the opening of the treetops. Clara squalled again, so Poppy led her to dry ground, rolled a few branches before finding a leathery black salamander with yellow spots. Clara squatted and watched it a long time, touched her finger to its different spots. It rooted beneath leaves, even tucking away the tip of its tail. And Clara pressed on the leaves, felt its slithering, but then it bedded farther through the layers, vanishing. She cleared away to black dirt. It had not left a hole in its wake. She lifted her bottom, shuffled forward on her hands, the dry top leaves scattering at her elbows, her hands ploughing through the wet leaves beneath. She stood and admired the path behind her. Within the clumps of earth in her hands, she saw critters wiggling in the light and other creatures unmoving in the light, their hard backs shining. She dropped the clumps free and wiped her hands on her skirt.

There was a shaft of light through the trees ahead, another wind-damaged section. They passed through the ray, and Poppy blinked at her dirty dress. They would not look pleasing for Papa. They picked their way, crawling over limbs, slick and green with moss. One giant tree had tipped over at the roots and left a hole in the canopy of treetops. When it had crashed, it took down many other trees with it, and the mess looked like a wrecked ship, a concentration of hashed trunks and knotted chaos of branches. The upturned roots of the great tree that had caused the collision looked like a shield, and the root shield was much taller than Poppy. There was a large depression in the earth where the roots had once held. The hole was filled with dead leaves.

At the upturned roots, Clara picked up a stick, beat the hole in the earth, and commanded, "Come out, devil." Clara waited, but nothing came, so she traced the tangle of roots, knocking off dirt and stones. Poppy knelt. Clara set her eyes intently on the hole, the chatter of birds overhead interrupted by the low, distant call of a crow. Something had been traveling in and out of the hole, had burrowed a narrow opening in the depression of earth. The dirt was eroded but there were no paw prints or tracks except for what might be the long, wide trace of a tail or cape.

"Come back with me." Poppy ran off.

There were rustlings all around. Clara kept her eyes on the hole, not wanting to miss what would come out. Mist or a cloud or rising smoke might precede him like the trick at the theater she had once seen. As the phantom had appeared onstage, the great flourish of his cape had cleared the fog that filled the stage, spilling it into the audience.

Clara turned in a circle. The forest's cavities were dark, and birds dove in chutes of light.

"Poppy!" Her voice was sharp and loud, and she jumped as the birds scattered.

Near her feet at the hole, she heard a hiss. She grabbed the front of her dress, her feet frozen in place. The leaves at the top edge of the hole slowly sank, disappearing into the depths. A wedge of black dirt buckled.

"Clara!" Poppy's faint call came from the edge of the forest.

The dirt stopped moving, and Clara let her skirt fall. She dropped the stick at the edge of the hole and ran toward her sister's voice.

There was silence between Georgie and Mr. Bell as they ate. He bit another apple, nibbled the scant flesh around the seeds. Sunlight filled the narrow clearing of the road, and translucent wings lifted from the grasses, tumid with light. Mr. Bell scanned the sky. There would be a warm afternoon ahead. He would drive back to Utica, bed the horses, bathe in the Mohawk, savoring a quiet pool by himself, drink another night with his fellow crewmen at the tavern.

The girls returned. Clara, on her hands and knees, grabbed for apples and pork. Georgie gave a firm tug. "Sit."

"She, the lass whose mam sent her to wash and upon returning appears to have done an afternoon's work grave digging." Mr. Bell laughed.

Poppy settled on the blanket between Clara and Mr. Bell and raised her hand to her mouth as a lady would giggle.

Georgie turned from the jest and allowed Clara to eat with a dirty face and hands. "We must wash properly before greeting your papa."

Mr. Bell reached for another hock, but Clara stood and faced him down like a bulldog. Poppy and Mr. Bell both recoiled.

"Clara! At once, offer Mr. Bell a hock. Use a clean hanky." Georgie pulled Clara by the wrist and stuffed the cloth in her hand and laid her large hand over Clara's small hand to extend the hock in his direction. Mr. Bell hesitated, then reached for it, but Georgie drew it back and dropped the hock to the blanket. "Now pick it up yourself and offer the gentleman his meal."

But Clara sat and drew from her pocket another bite of pork that she had squirreled away overnight. She let the hock sit in the middle of the blanket, and as she chewed, fat filled her mouth, and her tongue probed for the bits of meat buried in the creamy morsel.

"I do so truly apologize, sir." Georgie cast her dark eyes upon her daughter.

Poppy mumbled in echo her ma's apology and sought to briefly read his face. Had they forever lost a chance with him?

Mr. Bell held up his hand as if to settle the matter, then claimed the hock and sat in his own silence chewing. He fought inwardly to regain composure, burning with confusion for retreating from a little girl. It was as though a weasel had been booted from its nest onto the noonchine blanket.

Poppy was silent with shame, and her ma was remote and cross, scanning the tops of the trees like when she fixed on the rafters in the tavern when she was trying to convince herself out of a dark mood. Poppy wanted to say, *Ma, do you see how many apples Mr. Bell has provided?* But she did not say this out loud, only a few times in her head as her eyes bounced between the cores scattered on the blanket.

Mr. Bell bit into another apple, his mouth taking half the fruit in one bite, his hand wiping away juice from his beard. Another bite, juice dribbling down his shirt. As he grasped another apple, Poppy waited for his mouth to take the fruit. She flinched when he instead offered it to her. She buried it in her skirt, glanced to see if her ma noticed, but her ma's gaze was still deep in the trees. Poppy bit into her apple as Mr. Bell bit into his own. How long could she indulge in staring at him before her ma noticed? He nibbled his apples down to the last possible sweet bits, denuding them of flesh. He stared off into the trees, too, or into the apple he was devouring, and when he was done, he groaned and lay on the ground, letting his fingertips tent about his heart. His legs eased and his boots angled outward. Poppy wanted to say, *Ma, look at this man who pulls a whole bushel of apples into our noonchine blanket and chomps with such grace and falls back with such contentment.* But she did not say it aloud. She leaned toward him, imagining his hand outstretching for her hand, grasping it as he gazed at the sky. But soon his fingertips relaxed and flattened to the curved planes of his chest, and he tipped his hat to cover his eyes and rest awhile. Clara lay down, still chewing pork fat, and drew her overskirt to cover her eyes for napping.

Poppy grew excited at the liberties she might take while Mr. Bell dozed. She stared at his body, his clothes, his mouth. His chest hair did not curl or puff out the split in his shirt; it grew in long streaks as if he lay in riverbeds at night, the current washing flat the black floss. She considered his willingness to wait out her ma's foul temper, lost in a retreat of his own pleasurable thoughts. He was in no hurry for her ma's mood to change. He held a reserve of patience until she came around. Poppy decided then she loved him.

He awoke awhile later with all three of them staring at him.

He sat with a feeling of having napped too long. He cleared his throat and asked if the horses had been checked on. Poppy jumped to volunteer. Clara lay down again. He tried once more at courteous conversation, to gauge Georgie's present disposition. "You been gone from your husband for some time?"

Georgie straightened. "I have."

"Is it the family business you run there?" He lifted his hat and ran his hand through his hair and pressed his fingers into his eyes.

"It 'tis."

"And who was Auntie Wemple herself, then?" He knew, but he hoped his questions distracted from his sleepy appearance and the vulnerability he felt at collecting himself and standing to wakefulness.

"That was my mother-in-law. But that wasn't her name. Her name was Margaret. Wemple was her old family name."

"Ah. I do remember a small, gray woman for some years at the tavern."

No one had rolled Margaret in the last days of her life because she had gasped so hard for air no one dared disturb whatever force she had left to heave in breath. Hugh had not been able to bear the rasping, so he pursued errands in Boston to secure more supplies for the blasting endeavor and to foster his business associations there. Georgie had stayed with Margaret in the homestead at the falls.

Margaret's lower spine had melted into the bed sheets and yellowed them. But no one had seen that until Margaret was lifted from bed and carried out of the house on a flat board. Her head was wrapped in cloth, her body lowered into a grave, and the first shovel of dirt stonily hit the canvas pall shrouding her body. She was buried on a sharp rise in the forest, the torrent of the falls dim though near.

Georgie had heard that Americans were bumptious, that they

embraced strangers with odd hospitality. A cousin had described it as a fellow-feeling and benevolence that made one suspicious of their intelligence. Yet Margaret had been practical, a woman to solve problems. She was sensible and tough as Georgie's aunts who acted on authority for her family's estate, but Margaret did not conceal her control from her son, her neighbors, anyone. She was not one to act behind closed doors. Had Margaret not fallen ill, Georgie would have asked her to join the board of women trying to save her family's Shropshire estate.

When they had met, Margaret grasped her daughter-in-law by the arm. She wore a white lace cap with a strap of oxblood leather hanging down her forehead to secure a single glass lens over her right eye. She clenched her eye socket muscles to firm up the hold, and when she relaxed the clamp to free the lens, white rays of deep wrinkles burst like a corona.

Margaret had provided Georgie energetic mentorship until her decline. Margaret, before meeting Georgie, only hearing about her through Hugh's letters, had heartily endorsed the union, beholding from Hugh's letters the opportunity for the family to own land that they had, for the years after the war, tried to claim and also to welcome a sturdy and spirited daughter-in-law. The marriage was his mother's decision, so Hugh rode the ship back to America with his new, contrary bride. But the Georgie in Hugh's letters had been bolder and more inured than the Georgie whom Margaret met in person. On the day she met her, Margaret spat on the ground, said to hell with her landed aristocracy and to hell with her monarch's tyranny. Georgie retreated into a simmering silence. Margaret declared that Georgie indeed had a temper, but she had no backbone, and that Hugh had not provided a plainspoken nor veracious rendering of his bride. Yet Margaret redoubled her commitment to school Georgie in the fundamentals of surviving in the wilds. Georgie had to be strong enough to stand up to her son, for a man was only as strong as his wife. And she had to be self-governed, for many women were widowed early in these woods.

Georgie had been overwhelmed by the wild forest, the immense canopy blotting out light, the cacophony of one hundred thousand insects, the almost-perceptible upward creep of new growth, green vines, flowers, fungi, tree shoots, impossibly dense and lush with noise, the soft sucking mud underneath that threatened to swallow her whole whenever her boot fell through the scaffolding of fallen branches. Margaret first showed Georgie the bogs and sloughs, the water sources no longer useful, "being full of frogs." Margaret showed her where to throw refuse and filth: around the dead trees standing in shallow water, the trees' roots long rotted from accumulated flood rains, filling the bogs higher and higher over the years. In winter, Margaret skated on the bogs and rivers, dragging fresh kills of deer behind her in red arcs. She showed Georgie how much more efficient their work could be in winter, for the bogs were snow-packed, hard and smooth like roads, and they could travel straight through instead of wandering a mile around the wet mud of summer.

Margaret held up squealing young pigs and noted the contrast in color between them and their sires. The young were white-lipped and dark-skinned from acorns and the tea-dark, mineral-rich water of the West Canada Creek. Hugh had brought pen-raised hogs from Utica, and when let loose in the woods behind the shanty, these first pigs blinkered their domesticated eyes, timid, and seemed to construct mental pens for themselves, shying abruptly when they trotted too close to an imaginary border. But their offspring were wild, snuffled their snouts low into the game trails, kicked up their heels, squealing, let loose, ran, tore up the growth, and rutted hollows in large patches of ground cover. The old boars took comfort foraging in the sweet mush of fallen apples, and the oldest sow trotted one apple at a time in her mouth to build a store of them in her nest.

Margaret led Georgie through the high points in the forest, narrating as they walked, pointing to the minuscule salsify and cattail spikes carried on the wind, the pollen grains that the Natives would make into bread. "They used this pollen, not that pollen." And Margaret would wave her hand over the light shafting down. Georgie stumbled behind, trying to see; at first, seeing none of it, only blazes of light, then adjusting to the umbra cast by trunks of trees rising out of the fallen tangle of limbs, lurching her gaze skyward to the great waving green arbor, fields where there should have been sky. It was disorienting, but Margaret persisted, firm in her belief that her new daughter-in-law learn the land, not spend so much of her day stitching.

One day, Margaret steered Georgie to the level in the woods where the mist from the river rose to meet the detritus on the wind, where the moisture from the river wicked the fluff floating on the air. This day, Georgie saw tiny, tufted seeds sailing upward. Caught by the damp mist, the seeds dropped like wet moths. The women picked their way down the steep, wet rockface to watch the seeds carried by the swift water.

That night, they sat by the outdoor fire with the men who were bent over their mending and knitting, the fire high and crackling, and as the sparks flew, Margaret's instruction intensified. Margaret was energized at Georgie's breakthrough for seeing the tiny fodder of their forest. Georgie thought her botany instruction would deepen, and her initiation to the groundwork for grasping its entire system would get underway. But Margaret instead introduced entomology, stirring the dirt at their feet and glomming onto her finger pads tiny pincers and lobes and proboscises, recently disjointed mouthparts. "For chewing, for siphoning. Maxilla, mandible." And as the men put away their mending and picked up their fiddles and mouth harps, the women kept their heads close and considered the bird whose bite was not plenty quick to devour the whole insect, the bird only swift enough to chomp and sever at the prothorax, losing the mouthpart delicacies as they strewed to the dirt.

Margaret decided her a worthy pupil. So Georgie was sedulous and hoped to reach the depths of what Margaret knew and was willing to share. They became immersed in a few short months of closely bonded study until Margaret grew frail.

Margaret schemed delights to lure tourists to the falls: she asked Georgie to recite the Latin names for wildflowers. Georgie delivered flawlessly, so Margaret gathered the men one night and instructed Georgie to perform her recitation. Georgie repeated the wildflowers: "*Impatiens capensis, Caulophyllum thalictroides, Barbarea vulgaris.*" Georgie paused after each, providing the common names: "Spotted jewelweed, blue cohosh, yellow rocket."

Margaret frowned afterward. "Your voice was not limber. And I anticipated you would recite something of your own choosing, beyond what I instructed you before."

These words hung like a wet cape on Georgie's shoulders as she that night went into the forest and sat to identify new ornaments in the herbaceous layer that Margaret had not yet disclosed and made obvious. A couple of the men had been moved enough by her performance to lay handfuls of lemon-bright bellwort and wild oats on the porch in the morning, the flowers long-winged as squash blossoms.

During the time Margaret was hale before falling infirm, she raced her beautiful mare Amaranthus across the low meadow by the creek, talking of attracting tourists with a show of horse and rider. Georgie declared people would not be interested in watching a woman ride through a meadow on a horse, but Margaret was convinced the folks traveling from the cities to the falls would have the discernment to appreciate the springing pasterns of Amaranthus's Spanish bloodlines.

To build Georgie's fortitude, Margaret urged her to perform with an injury, instructing her to recite to an invisible audience with a raw throat, her glottis inflamed, while Margaret rode Amaranthus with a broken ankle, her lower leg lashed to the mare's belly. Margaret also pretended to have a broken arm, hooked it tight to her belly with a rag, reining Amaranthus one-handed. Margaret had tried to amend Georgie's timorous nature, for the security of the family relied on resourceful, bold initiative. Even weeks after her death, Georgie had seen the earth stirred up by the hooves during their practices.

When in her sick bed, no one had thought to roll Margaret, and Georgie still repeated silent words of contrition.

Georgie had wandered alone for hours after Margaret's burial into the fall's cataracts, the winding chasms of rock the only succor for her grief. She had heard Margaret's voice bouldering downstream in the shallows. Margaret always knew which tree root would be the next to collapse from the soft clay bank into the current and for how long boat and oar splinters had been lodged to an acclivity. Georgie's grief had drawn her to the deeper chutes until she had sunk to such a depth in the earth she felt closer to Margaret, in the subterranean otherworld to which Margaret had flown from her deathbed. Not a heaven nor a hell, but an unexcavated strata of earth.

Georgie gathered the noonchine blanket. "Yes, that small, gray woman was Margaret. We must set off again."

"This is about where I must leave you," said Mr. Bell.

"But we are not yet to the homestead. How much farther?"

"Near ninety rods in." Mr. Bell pointed.

Georgie walked to the edge of the woods, the fallen cedar trees knitted high and dense. The fringe of woods was familiar, but Hugh had always led the way.

"There is no farther from here lest you start rolling away logs, mistress. Or madam. Or you sit astride a horse as it picks its way along a game trail."

"Game trail? Where?"

Mr. Bell pointed to a slivered parting in the undergrowth.

"Sir, you must shoulder the barrels and accompany us on foot. I will carry the satchel."

"A'compny?" He looked to Poppy, agasp for the chance to step into her role as translator.

The woman and the girl spoke over each other, one in steady fury, the other smothered in a raw smile, simplifying her ma's lathered words, parroting with lilting cheer.

"No, I must get these horses back. They require rest before hauling up here again tomorrow."

"Who is to help guide our way and assist with the supplies?"

"That would have been your servant, mistress." Though he knew the rest of the crew would travel through the next day to carry the barrels to camp.

"That would have been your servant, ma." Poppy overeagerly translated from both sides.

"I hear what the man says."

Mr. Bell spat and turned toward the horses. He felt tired of these women.

"Did he pay you extra to leave me and my girls here to fend for ourselves, then?"

"Seeing as how you have not employed me, mistress, there is no reason to slander the man who has."

Poppy stepped back, unable to keep pace with her ma's words. Mr. Bell's words overlapped and confused the exchange.

"Are you aware of my place in my homeland's household? Sir, I am not accustomed to ungentlemanly treatment and discourtesy."

"We are a free and independent land, mistress, and it matters not if you wiped the arse of your queen and tied her ribbons. I am not bound by your tyranny and codes of conduct."

Georgie faltered. She had lately sat in the tavern's fire room and reflected on her prior duties in her family's estate as fussy and meaningless. "I was not a petty servant. I had a distinguished role." She felt obliged to defend herself in front of her daughters.

Mr. Bell heard the lack of conviction in her voice. The mules knew their way back to Utica, and he looked forward to giving them rein and drinking his whiskey on the ride. He jumped into the back of the wagon, wrapping his arms about one of the barrels. He squatted to lift. A jolt of pain seized him. He immediately regretted the jump. It had been to impress the women. He half stood. His back stiffened, spasmed. He leaned against the barrel, grasped its rim, tried to budge it. His breath shortened. He wouldn't be able to lift the barrels off the wagon, and he couldn't roll them off without breaking them apart.

Georgie gathered the satchel from the wagon and secured Poppy's cap. They would go on by themselves. The barrels would stay in the wagon. Mr. Bell would have to ride Balor back to Utica with Brace following by lead rope. But she hesitated. "Sir, are there not Natives in these woods?"

"Hereabouts, not for near on ten years. Gone west to the lakes and Canada."

"All of them? How can that be so? Did they not have strong connections to the land?"

"Some sold off their lands, others were run off. A few Oneida farm, but they keep quiet. I've not seen Iroquois in these woods to bother you." He did not say he had encountered Iroquois traveling through, searching for the displaced remains of their ancestors from the Revolution. The Loyalists had dug up Native graves at the Oriskany battle site. The surviving but dispossessed descendants still tried to recover the bones, to bury their dead in their new lands.

Clara woke from her nap, drawing the skirt from her eyes. Her eyes were ringed yellow, haggard from the night's work and journey. She dropped her head. The child was exhausted.

Mr. Bell wiped his mouth. "I will walk you the roughest first rods," he conceded. "From there, you will have to pick your own way, but the path is evident. You will have to hike up those skirts. Little one, on my back." He took Clara by the forearms and bent down, turning her over his shoulder. He groaned.

They climbed over the green growth and fallen logs.

"Mind, the ground can be more water than dirt if you fall through the timbers," Mr. Bell called.

Their shoes sank into black mud, soiling up their pale stockings. For a long mile, they picked their way up and down timber-scattered hills.

When the terrain opened, Mr. Bell said, "Little miss, off now."

He winced, and she slid down, her small feet landing on a patch of dry ground. Her face was rosy. She had loved the game of pony with Mr. Bell who had enough thick, damp hair under his hat to sink her hands into like a real mane.

"I am dirty like ma," Clara said, pleased.

"Like *maman*," Georgie corrected. And indeed, the child had drawn more dirt to her skirts even while being carried upon Mr. Bell.

Poppy tripped and fell behind them, not clearing one leg over a log. Her face and palms were flat to the mud, her skirt bunched past her knee. She yanked the skirt down to cover her underlayers. Mr. Bell turned away.

"Get yourself upright, and come along, Penelope." Georgie strode ahead.

Poppy brushed leaves from her dress. She clutched something at her backside.

Mr. Bell called, "Right yourself then, miss?"

"Yes, I am coming along presently."

She stood, her front wet and dark with mud. She held the back of her skirt and heard a crumple of paper. She wrenched around, the crinkle in her hand, a flat square pinned in the layers of skirts. How had she not felt this before when dressing in the cold, stark morning? She thought of her sleepiness that morning, the urgency with which her ma had prepared for their departure. She sifted through the fine skirt layers. The paper was delicate, a thin parchment, barely discernible from the gauze of the dress. Was it a message or a curse? Her backside prickled, and she ran toward her ma's call.

"You both are a mess for your father, and we are so delayed. There is a waterfall ahead where we can wash."

"Are you well and unharmed, then, miss?"

"Yes, quite fine, thank you, sir."

Clara stood in a dark cloud of exhaustion, sensing the adults were tense and about to change something about the situation again. Her eyes shone like the toe caps of black boots, casting the familiar vacant stare that foretold wailing. Last evening at the tavern, Clara had been out of doors for so few minutes. What had the man pinned inside this dress? Poppy startled. Her ma had been scolding her to translate.

Her ma's words were clear and loud. But Poppy looked to Mr. Bell. "I do not know what she says, sir."

Mr. Bell looked away from the women in irritation. He bowed slightly. "I bid you leave, mistress." He tipped his cap, waiting for Georgie's reply before turning back for the wagon.

Georgie fixed her eye on him and nodded curtly. She could not muster polite words.

He turned to make his way back through the bramble.

"I thank you," Georgie called.

Poppy took a few steps after him. "We thank you," she echoed.

He raised a hand in reply but did not turn. "I thank you, *Mr. Bell*, if you please."

Georgie retightened her jaw. "Come," she instructed the girls. "There is a long way yet."

Clara yowled.

Georgie squared her shoulders. "Enough. Walk now." She strode forward.

Poppy took her sister's hand, and Clara quieted. Poppy replayed their exchange of words, the high trees amplifying their voices, her own voice still crashing inside her head. There was a church quiet in the hardwoods, but her emotions would not dampen. Her fever of shame at their behavior reverberated in the trees. Their unlikeable qualities were clear to Mr. Bell, and those had made him leave.

Georgie led her girls away from the distant whistling of Mr. Bell. He would be gone, too far to hear their calls if they needed him. She let down her heavy skirt, the path easier as Mr. Bell had promised. They were dirty and wilted.

"Come." Georgie seemed to follow Mr. Bell.

"Are we going for him?" Clara chirped.

"No. We will wash at Buttermilk Falls, in the same direction, but Mr. Bell will not be there. We must clean ourselves for your father."

"What if Mr. Bell needs to clean himself too? He will join us at the water."

"He will not. He does not bathe. He drives mules."

"But they are horses. They are fine horses. Did you not see their velvet mouths?"

"Stop this. You will learn not to wail over gentlemen. There is no greater nonsense." Georgie knelt to Clara's face. But Clara would not stop crying.

"I want to go back to my bed at the tavern." Clara's sobs broke wide open.

"You will learn new chores, be of use to Papa," offered Poppy.

"I do not want to learn new chores. I want to watch the men light the black powder in the dining hall."

Georgie picked up her daughter, carrying her like an infant across her body. She stepped into the wild growth, striding over the mass of tangled trees and branches.

Her ma's rocking steps settled her crying. Her ma was perspiring, and Clara rest her lips near the wet triangle at her underarm. Her ma's bodice was salt-puckered from the brine the night before, and because her ma had taken more care with the dark organs when dressing the hogs, she smelled of minerals, of the wood planks where people sat in the necessary house.

Clara lifted her head at the last memory she had of her papa, when he had carried her through the dark woods and she clung to him against the brace of his ribs. He had bent over the wagon bed, and her feet had dropped in. Her ma was so much smaller than him, but she was strong and would not tire. She might grow taller than her ma, and this might be the last time she was ever carried.

"Candle-lighting," Clara said, the lambent interior of the woods aglow like the time right before bed when her ma led her with a warm drink and candle to her straw ticking. Her ma nodded in agreement and latched Clara more firmly to her body. Clara knew her ma could scale a mountain with Clara strapped in front and a pig carcass roped to her back if she had to.

Buttermilk Falls gushed over milky white rock. Georgie opened her mouth at the spray. She steadied herself from stumbling as the girls clasped onto her skirts and leaned, thirsty, into the falling water. She wet her hands and ran her palms along each girl's hairline. They stepped back from the slippery rock and sat, slicking back their hair and shaking the dust from their caps. Georgie wet their skirt hems, but they were too soiled, and the water cold, so she resigned to a disheveled reunion with Hugh.

There was a wet mound of what looked like the matted fur of a carcass. Clara, wobbly, started for it, crossing the narrow stream. Georgie grabbed for her, missed, and Clara crisscrossed swiftly to the pile, sinking both hands in, then examining the clumps of rot, spilling more filth onto her dress. Georgie cursed, dropped her head. Clara drove her hands further in and drew out a length of something blue. It was not the blue of putrefied meat.

Georgie splashed across to Clara and the pile. Then she rasped a wondrous cry. Next to where the stream flowed from the waterfall, there lay in a heap a skirt, hat, boots, redingote—all where Margaret had disrobed and left them. Georgie had long ago given up on finding these. The items were drab, damp, moldering in with the leaves. The redingote had once been a brilliant pale turquoise, the full skirt a gorgeous sail billowing as Margaret, when still robust, had raced Amaranthus in the yellow field between Partridge Hill and the creek. Georgie had not remembered Margaret as strong in a long time. When Georgie thought of Margaret, it was of her elderly form during her wasting before death.

❧

Hugh was often gone once Margaret had fallen infirm. On one of his trips, Margaret had asked Georgie to help her die. But it had not worked. Georgie discussed with Margaret about whether to wear her riding habit or evening dress. Before setting out to her death in the snow, Margaret had decided upon the riding habit, the turquoise redingote.

Margaret's hands had started to shake; at first, only when she ate, the fork clinking against the pewter plate. Then the shaking became constant. Georgie assisted her with smaller tasks like brushing her white hair, suggesting they cut it off when Margaret woke most mornings bewildered from its strands wound round her mouth. But each time, Margaret would slowly, firmly push away the knife, dragging back with knotty fingers the errant hairs. The shaking became so bad that Margaret could not hold a fork to her mouth; she kept missing, lurching too far left, hitting her ear. Her sense of balance and space diminished.

Margaret's decline advanced. She could not focus on anyone's face without tearing into a rage. Then she would lapse unresponsive; Georgie had to sponge her down, tend to her like a child, take the broom from Margaret's hands after she had swirled and swirled the same dirt pile on the porch. Margaret revived some, but she never returned to her previous energy and command. Her already-silver hair turned pure white, her skin dried to chalk, and milky nubs spoored up in the whites of her eyes.

Margaret had asked about her husband Samuel's return, and Georgie had stopped repeating that he had died in the war because it made Margaret cry fresh each time.

She was often nauseated, yet painfully costive, leaning against the walls to shuffle from the table to the fire. There was a brief time during which Margaret was aware of her own decline and had the long sight to see an imminent anility, a void from which she would never return.

"I do not want my son to watch me become a demented yard animal." Margaret persisted with the plea to help her die despite Georgie's words of encouragement and deflection to carry out what Margaret saw as her daughter-in-law's responsibility.

"It's only a spell, Mother. You must rest and not take on so much of the household."

But Margaret had long stopped any household chores. Georgie meant to say stop fretting. Or unburden your worries. But she could not. She held Margaret's hand through two days of lassitude. On the third morning, Margaret sprang awake and lifted the sheet as if to tend to the fire or a crying child or a loose hog. She had snapped back to her old self. Yet her brain was drying up, leaving a frostwork of crystal-hard truths as the memories, angers, and pleasures cleared out. She gained one grim clarity. She thought she was done with certain relatives after burying them years ago, but she now knew she would have to face them upon her own death. It wasn't reuniting with Samuel that worried her. She did not want to hear the bleating of her other relations, the liars, the money-grubbers, the drunkards, the victims of bad weather, the malingerers of hard work. She imagined in the afterlife that her dead relatives hectored the angels to defend why they had lived weak and corrupt lives. Margaret was inconsolable at having to rejoin them, but her confusion swept in again soon enough as a mercy for forgetting these new misgivings. Her hands lay palm up on her lap, curled inward like dry husks.

On a day when her hands flexed and warmed, she lifted from a box a chaplet of red Hobblebush berries and placed the dried garland around baby Clara's neck. It was an idol that a Seneca had dropped at the Battle of Oriskany, and as Margaret had stripped fallen militiamen of weapons and clothing, she found it along with a thin circle of silverwork. She saw the man who had dropped the chaplet and the silver; he ran with speed, unwounded, over the hill. He had discarded the totems on purpose among the dead bodies. He would later fast, dream, sweat, and be painted with fish needles and bloodroot to inspire the choice of a new idol, the old ones abandoned for having been ineffectual at the battle. Margaret knew the ritual, but picked up the chaplet and silver anyway, regarding them as luckless for the retreating Seneca but fortunate for herself for having survived the ambuscade and the hours of battle afterward. And now at death, she would pass them on to her granddaughters, Clara and Poppy.

On a good or bad day alike, Margaret remembered her horses, each one since girlhood.

"When I was younger and would rake for salt at the shore, my horse Oxenstierna used to help me by dragging her lips and collecting the crystals on her muzzle." And she would stop and dream on this a while.

"No, Mother. That was the cold of winter. A rime on Oxenstierna's lips, not salt."

"She was a horse, not a balladeer. She spoke no rhyme from her lips."

"A rime of frost about her lips."

But Margaret waved her hand impatiently and dreamt on. "And she so war-exhausted. My next mare, we sent for. She rode a ship alongside barrels of Madeira wine."

If Georgie were to give her mother-in-law mercy, it must be when Hugh was away. And she must do it when the cold was killing enough to seize Margaret quickly. It was a long time before such cold arrived.

But the cold did come, one early winter day when the chill in the cabin perked Margaret for a brief lucidity. "This day," she said with bright eyes.

"How shall I dress you?"

"Properly. With a cap and cloak. No, the redingote."

Georgie dressed her, her skin so thin she had sores from the pressure of sitting. Before putting on her hat, she braided Margaret's white hair and pinned the braid atop her head.

No snow had yet fallen; all that was bare and brown was crisp and edged with frost. Georgie sat the girls in bed to suck on milk-soaked rags. The women walked into the woods, holding hands, caps tied under their chins with wide satin ribbons.

"To Buttermilk Falls," Margaret instructed. She soon became breathless and wheezing, the cold too much for her lungs. Vapor rose weakly from her mouth, drifting to Georgie's face as Margaret sagged her weight onto her daughter-in-law.

"This is the spot." Margaret let go of Georgie's hand. She sunk, her skirt filling with air, her drop to the leaves a ship with foundering sails cruising into a shoal. She unhooked her eyeglass lens, passed it to Georgie. She would meet her death purblind. She slipped her thin hands into her fur cuffs. "Leave me with one maple sugar candy," she ordered.

Georgie gave her the candy, which Margaret tucked into her cuff. Margaret mustered a bit of strength, the old iron back in her eyes. "Leave me now."

Georgie obeyed, turning only once to see Margaret, her mouth hung, her frozen breath suspended like smoke as if her body was already starting to smolder from its last respiration, a final, long exhale.

Georgie returned to the shanty, nursed her daughters, drew them close for warm sleeping, but she lay awake, mentally ticking through the group of cottony seeds, briefly dipping into sleep as the floss silk floated in the strands of her light dozing. Her body jerked awake. Her daughters shifted. She sat at each neigh from Amaranthus who paced in her shelter and tested her weight against its boards. Georgie fell hard into dreaming: Amaranthus carried Margaret across a swift river but was shot out from under her and died a hero's death like one of General Washington's mounts. Margaret and Amaranthus sank into the depths, the dark stripe down Amaranthus's rump and spine swallowed up, then Margaret's redingote and plume sucked under as the tea-stained river buried them.

"However your thoughts race, do not come back for me," Margaret had said.

Georgie had woken the next day to the trees, the ground—everything—blanketed in thick snow.

Margaret could not have survived the night: the cold would have taken her to a sleepy death within hours; the coyotes, ripped away at whatever warmth and flesh she had left; the snow, buried her as solidly as shovel and dirt at a proper gravesite. Then by spring, the ground would shift and the waters rise to flood away any remaining hide or bones.

It snowed all morning, past noon. Margaret must be dead and gone, having had the courage for a slow, cold death. Amaranthus still fretted against the boards of her shelter, her whinnies high and frequent. Georgie would walk back to retrieve Margaret, drag her back to the house, undress her body, unlace the tiny black boots, small enough to fit Poppy in a few years perhaps. Hugh would return to his mother laid out in the cold of the cabin as if she had never left. Georgie would fold the riding habit on the bed, ready to dress Margaret for proper burial, and tell Hugh there had been nothing she could do—Margaret had died in her sleep. In her bed. These were the details the women had discussed beforehand, during the fleeting moments of Margaret's clarity. But the women had argued. Margaret wanted to be left in the woods. Georgie could not face Hugh's response to allowing Margaret to wander out of doors, finding her body torn apart by wolves. Margaret's final instruction was for Georgie to walk back to cut off the braid from her corpse, for the silver braid would be a telltale sign of what she had committed and could not be mistaken for any other creature. Margaret would not let Georgie cut off her braid at the house; she was to walk to her death with her hair.

In the pink afternoon light, doubt plunged a leaded line straight to a cold sinkhole in Georgie's conscience. What if she could not drag Margaret's body back? Margaret was a slight woman but still dead weight that must be heaved over the fallen logs and tangle. What if bandits had robbed Margaret of her fine riding habit and boots, and Georgie could not account for the items when Hugh returned? And how could Margaret not have the forethought to help her sort out these difficulties in advance of her dying? Georgie could only sit, hamstrung by worries. Then young Poppy started to howl. Then infant Clara burst out indignantly, matching her sister's intensity.

Georgie sat each daughter upright, but after a few quieted hiccups, the wailing resumed, wet faces, slobbered fists and elbows. She offered milk-soaked rags, but they were batted away, red, toothy faces turned. She tied their day caps under their chins since this usually delighted them by marking the start of an outdoor journey, but this time it only increased their pitch and fervor. She could not withstand this. She sat with them on the bed and wept openly herself.

There was a great crack outside, and dark shadows played against the crannies between the shanty's wall boards. Amaranthus had broken free of her tether.

Georgie hurried after the mare. But the mare had stopped short in the yard, huffing her nose to the white drifts. Georgie started toward her, but the mare shied. Georgie stepped forward, tripped, flying face down, whumping in fluffy snow. She picked herself up, turned, and saw Margaret's silver hair, undone, loosely splayed, barely distinguishable from the snow piling on top of it. Margaret was face down in the snow, her body naked, not even wearing her boots, the afternoon's fresh snow collecting on her hide like feathers.

Margaret had crawled back during the night, tucked into a hog rut in the yard, and Georgie had tripped over her. Margaret had survived one frigid night and half a day on one maple sugar candy.

Georgie dragged her inside, wrapped her in blankets, set her before the fire. After hot liquids, Margaret roused to consciousness. She was forlorn. "I am sorry. I could not think of anything but salt pork and the warmth of this fire." She had stripped her clothing to speed her own death, but she had been too strong. Death would not come.

The next day, Hugh returned home. Margaret was propped up, her hair re-braided across her head. She sipped hot cider, her eyes bright.

"You look well." Hugh kissed the braid. "Your color is rosy again. And look how steady you hold that cup. You've been resting as I told you to."

Margaret had given him a small, obedient smile and sipped more steaming liquid.

But it was not to last. The next day, the shakes returned, and Margaret whispered to Georgie that she regretted being unable to sufficiently instill fortitude in Georgie. Margaret rattled her hand on Georgie's and said it was her fault, not Georgie's. This trounced Georgie to her core, but she rejected the notion, citing Margaret's feebleness of mind. Though over time, in moments of introspection, Georgie had brooded over the declaration. She thought Margaret would respect her reprisals toward Hugh, but Margaret had regarded them as undignified tantrums. Margaret had noted Clara's insolence toward Georgie, predicting her son would use it as an excuse to spurn Georgie from the house. Margaret said Georgie would deserve it because no child should run roughshod over its mother. Margaret's final malediction marked a stunting of Georgie's character. Georgie was wracked, retreating to the small burrow holes of herself, where she could barely acknowledge the disinheritance of what she had gained under Margaret's mentorship. A few days after Margaret had announced her regret at Georgie's tremulous spirit, Margaret died in her sleep. Georgie had searched to retrieve the redingote and boots, but the snow had been too deep. Hugh never asked about the riding habit. He had asked Georgie to sponge Margaret's evening dress to prepare it for burial.

And now, many seasons after Margaret's death, Georgie was at Buttermilk Falls with her girls, Margaret's riding clothes in a heap right before her. Georgie lifted the sodden petticoat, bright wings and coppery bodies scattering then reburying themselves in the tucks of leaves and mud. Georgie startled at the thought that Margaret was hidden in the pile of clothing and still presented specimens to her for examination. Clara had already lost interest in the pile.

"Ma, where does the water come from?" Clara found the ledge over which the water fell too steep and slick for climbing.

Georgie searched for the maple candy paper, but it was long gone.

"Ma, what do you search for?"

Georgie's head shot in the direction of her daughter. "It burbles from the ground a far ways up, then falls over this ledge. Do you not find the white rock beneath pretty, Clara?"

"Yes, Ma. It shines pretty." Clara picked up a stick and beat the torrent, splashing and disrupting it.

Georgie draped the redingote across her arms and picked up Margaret's tiny black boots. They might fit Clara in a couple years. The boots were already too small for Poppy. Georgie recrossed the stream.

"Clara, sit here." Georgie held the bottom of the tiny black boot against the sole of Clara's foot. The boot appeared large in comparison against Clara's foot, but the leather was mostly sound.

Poppy had been kneeling aside, hunched, her hand grazing the note. It was still there. She had seen bunnies encrusted about the eyes and ears with ticks. A rabbit's eye fixed in place looking askance, unable to focus forward as a swollen tick latched at the tear duct. An ear bent in half from the weight of what looked like a cropping of burrs. She had wished to relieve the bunnies of these pests. And she itched to rip the note from her dress. She stood to slip away, but her ma called.

"Ma, you tickle." Clara squirmed. "A man has undressed a tiny lady and left shoes for me? Am I to wear those fine skirts to the theater?"

Georgie eyed the length of the shoes. "Gentlemen do not undress women."

Poppy looked over in interest.

"Well, now, indeed they do, Ma." Clara's voice rose with authority.

But Georgie would not have it. "No, indeed not, child. Only the devil himself undresses a lady, mind. Now cross yourself and put those wicked thoughts away. A lady has obviously undressed for bathing right here and forgotten the clothing long ago. We will not waste them." Georgie made a bundle of the garments, rolling them tightly for carrying.

Clara gasped with a firm realization. "The lady came to him dressed in her fine skirts and cuffs. No lady goes bathing in fur cuffs, Ma!" Clara faced the white rock. Her chest heaved. She beat the rock, again splashing water and displacing its fall. "She came to him at this rock." She whacked using both hands on her cudgel. "Come out, devil!"

Georgie grabbed over the water, but Clara was too quick. "That is enough, child. You will only recite stories about God and good men."

But Clara would not stop. "The rock beneath is the white, grand doorway to his horses. They wait beyond the rock, ready to burst forth when he pries open the rock with his fingers. The horses leap through the water and scatter into the night woods. And the devil is the last to come out, driving a silver carriage with the best horse pulling. And he grabs for the lady to force her down in the carriage. But this time, they took the lady so quickly she could not reach for her clothes."

Georgie stepped unsteadily across the water and clamped her hand across Clara's mouth. Clara looked up, unblinking, to her ma, not so much defiant but daring her ma to deny the likelihood.

Georgie removed her hand. Clara's lips were pulled tight. "You are overly tired, girl. Now you will stop."

Clara dropped her stick, her mind still knitting vivid skeins of her tale.

"Now, Poppy, let's get some of this filth off," Georgie said.

Georgie wet the inside of her cloak, then sponged at the mud smeared down Poppy's front. The water was cold. Poppy shook.

"Turn 'round." Georgie grasped her daughter by the waist, dabbing at the skirt. Then she stopped. "This isn't your dress. Where have you gotten a dress such as this?"

Poppy dithered.

"Did you lift this? From the woman traveling through last month with her stacks of luggage?"

"She left it. Behind."

"What is this?" Georgie caught the note pinned underneath the skirt.

Poppy wrested the skirt away.

"Do you play games? Penelope, mind." Georgie unpinned the note.

The paper was ink splattered as if the person did not have enough time nor an adequate ink supply to compose a coherent message.

"Who pinned this note to you? Did that driver? Mr. Bell?"

"No, Ma, not Mr. Bell."

"A demon pinned it!" Clara cried.

"A demon, then? Where is she? We have been here all this time, yet we have not seen her? Only you can see her, Clara? A demon with an oval frame? And haired pulled back like this?" Georgie pulled her own hair tight. She bent down, drawing her face close to Clara's.

Poppy was silent, the note made more troubling now that her ma was angry. Poppy could not sort events to explain about the man from the gangway. She looked away, waiting out her ma's rant. How had her ma not noticed Clara in a new dress and ribbon at the start of the second dinner service? Poppy kept her eyes diverted; she was too tired to hide her unguarded disappointment and knew it could spark up her ma's crashing tirade. If her ma had not kept to herself so often, Poppy would not have to explain now.

"Yes, Ma, it was a demon." Poppy had no way to untwist what it really was, but even if she had the words, her ma was not of a disposition to hear them.

"Where? When? When you and Clara played in the woods? You must show me."

"At the tree upturned by its roots."

Clara smiled at this.

"But how?" Georgie asked.

"At the tree. Clara called the demon, and it rose from the hole in the ground, all that dirt torn up by the roots."

"And he happened to have fine parchment and ink on hand?"

Clara was eager to make stories. "The roots tore up so much dirt when the tree fell. All that was left was not even mud. It was fine sand. And the demon had no trouble wriggling up through it when I called. And he was not even choking from the dirt. He breathed it like fish breathe water. And he looked like he had just taken a long nap, a little puffy in his eyes but ready for chores."

"He?" Georgie asked. "Or she? A person appeared at this tree?"

Clara looked to Poppy. She hesitated, but went on. "He asked us to go down the hole with him and play. He had teacups and biscuits. He said he did. We wanted to go but, Ma, you called us back."

"Poppy, why do you stand there and allow your sister to tell stories?" She clutched her hand to her throat, eyeing their muddy fronts. "There are no demons. Some who pass through here are too fond to leave us peaceably alone. We are leaving this wood right now." Georgie marched ahead, Margaret's clothes bundled underneath her arm, the note tucked within the pile.

They walked for some time, wending their way back to the path where Mr. Bell had left them.

"Ma, what do the ink scribbles mean?"

Georgie was preoccupied. She felt lost but not yet willing to admit it. She stopped and laid her hand on a cedar trunk, looking in all directions.

"Ma, when can I wear the boots?"

"Hush." Georgie cocked her head.

The girls were still. They all heard the wind clatter through the overhead branches. Insects woke, swarmed, lifted in throngs from the bore holes of tree trunks and ground nests toward the late golden light. Then there it was, a far-off voice.

They made way toward the voice, stopping now and again to correct course for it.

"It must be Mr. Bell!" chimed Clara.

"It is not. He is long gone back to town. It must be your father calling out for us at the point where the forest meets the path."

But it was Mr. Bell.

They saw only the back of his black hair, his hat knocked off, his head tipping in a spasm to one shoulder. He had collapsed at the base of a tree.

"Mr. Bell!" Poppy called.

The girls ran ahead and knelt by his side. They didn't touch him.

"We are here. Whatever is the matter?" Georgie reached the tree where he lay.

He was pale and sweating, his eyes ringed pink. His breath came wheezily. His jaw set rigidly, and his labored breathing snuffed out any words he was trying to muster. Georgie bent to lift him, but he swatted at her grasp. His boot heels dug a few tries at the leaves to right himself standing, but he seized again as if a tight cord was strung from his neck through his trunk.

"Mr. Bell, we must lift you and take you to the homestead. You need assistance and cannot stay out here. Girls, get on his side."

He resisted with reflexive, vehement grunts, but he was too weak to fend them off. They lifted him, and he squalled, both girls jumping in fright, but Georgie held him fast.

"Whatever happened to you, Mr. Bell?" Georgie asked. "Did you reach the horses and wagon?"

He tried to speak but could not. His breath smothered, his fingers rigid.

"Put your weight on me, sir."

He briefly lost consciousness, sagging onto her, and the girls rushed to keep him from falling, but he did anyway, hitting with his knees first, then tipping sideways with full force onto his ear and chin. Georgie righted him onto his back, put her ear to his mouth, slapped his face, smacked his chest, lifted the linen of his shirt, and felt the warm skin of his abdomen. She slapped this too. Her hands searched and found spots of cold flesh and warm flesh. She sat back on her heels.

"The man is racked by feverish insides." Georgie rolled her sleeves.

"No, Ma. His back bleeds into his legs. See how they swell." Poppy straightened his legs.

Clara laid her hand on his ankle.

"See how the skin beneath his beard and on his neck is blue. Does he choke on more apples?" Georgie palpated his throat.

"Does an apple lodge in his throat?" Poppy gasped.

"His fingers twitch. He seizes like he's palsied."

"Keep back. His stomach wambles."

"But he chills and sweats like a consumptive."

"Ma, will he die? How must we save him?" Poppy's voice grew high in alarm. "His back pains him from the old fall off the horse. Will he survive this?"

With a great gulp of air, Mr. Bell sat, winced, curling sideways, coughing and spitting into the leaves. The women moved toward him again, but he held one hand in protest.

"How will we get him through these logs and growth?" Poppy asked.

"We must get him through. Put thoughts of his pain out of your head."

Poppy drew his shirt closed. "Perhaps if I stay with him while you and Clara fetch Papa."

Georgie drew away her daughter's hands from Mr. Bell's shirt. "No. Mr. Bell knows the way. We do not." She smartly slapped Mr. Bell's cheek as his lids fluttered. "Mr. Bell, you must stand."

They supported his weight when they could, but he mostly scooted over the fallen trees on his own. At the break in the forest, they went under his armpits. His heavy arms fell on their shoulders as if encased with lead sleeves. Clara, on the far side of Poppy, grabbed Mr. Bell's hand.

Mr. Bell muttered about leaving him in peace, about how his mules needed feed and water.

"Hush, now. You do not have all of your wind back." The brunt of Mr. Bell's weight crushed Georgie as his legs buckled. Georgie righted him, felt the strength of his carriage return. The sweat from his body had seeped onto her cloak.

"Ma was scairt. But we found you," Clara reassured him.

"Hush, girl. The man cannot walk one foot before the other hearing your nonsense."

They walked onward, steadying the man.

"Ma, he chills," said Poppy.

They all lay their hands on his face, and he moaned pitiably. He tried to shake off the women like a hoard of deer flies. They dispersed then buzz-circled right back to cling to him.

They found the rutted path the men traveled with their heavy loads of black powder. The pain kept knocking out Mr. Bell. The women dragged him under the arms as his boot heels hitched at roots and his bottom scraped over fallen trees. They made slow headway. He came to and crawled on his own. Georgie suggested they leave him for the men to carry back later. Poppy insisted they stay with him and not let bandits or panthers claim him. The light was fading. Clara first heard the rushing roar of the falls. The sound guided them in the last half mile. They followed the cool, wet air. Clara remembered when the sun was about to set, the safe space for play was this bank of air, where the river sprayed and drifted up the rock face. They were nearing the homestead, a shanty built atop the falls, at the edge where the water boiled over flat slate slabs.

In the yard, embers from the spent remains of a cooking fire dimly lit the cleared site of stumps. The sweet hickory smell of the yard fire smoked, and strips of meat hung on a rack over the coals. At the shadowy edge of woods, pigs chewed mast and rooted in cedar needles. This was where the crewmen made their crude camp, the same men Georgie fed at the tavern each week. Oil cloths were strung from cords to tent against rain. There were a few four-sided cloth tents with roofs, the worn and patched leftovers that Margaret had kept from the Revolutionary encampments. Warm light glowed from within the shanty.

They eased Mr. Bell onto a stump.

"They are still awake." Georgie straightened her cloak and tucked pieces of her hair underneath her cap.

The door opened before Georgie climbed the steps.

"Oh, jiminy. Ya come. We thought you might camp overnight." A woman of no more than eighteen held open the door. She wore no cap or bonnet or corset, and her feet were slippered. The candle she held glowed close to her face as if to showcase her welcome. She made the impression of an unlicked cub but tried for a lady's dignity with her shift in posture and the height of her hair with its sweep of length in back. She dipped a little girl's curtsy and announced her name, Mathilda May Starr. "Call me Hildy." Her spine curved, limbs branching, relaxing into what Georgie scrutinized as a slattern's bearing.

Georgie expected she would be a beauty, but in the first moments of studying her, she decided her only power was beauty, and she had not the sense to have earned any other authority.

"Yes, indeed. We are here to see my husband."

Hildy closed her lips in a half-smile. She lowered the candle and examined Georgie. "Did you fall out the wagon?"

There was not a hint of derision; Hildy had decided her place in the household, and her question was sincere. This upset Georgie's sensibilities. She laid her hand on the porch railing. "Would you be so kind as to tell my husband that his wife and children have arrived?"

"Oh, he know. He scoot me out the bed to come fetch ya."

Hildy swung a hip and stood solidly in the doorframe, beaming an uxorial ease at her post receiving guests. She tipped the candle to light a lantern at her feet, and her gown glowed, its hem furbelowed with lace. Unlike other American women, whom Georgie regarded as frail, this one was ample. Her gown didn't have ash marks or black pin holes from spitting cooking fires. She wore no apron. Her frock was white with a dark pink sash tied underneath the bust. Her fore and upper arms were bare. She did not have bruises. She was clean and fresh as an apple. Hugh must have hired a cook. Georgie grew flustered at what her own role in the household would be now if not cook.

Hildy looked beyond Georgie. "Them's your girls and man." She called out with her fingers fluttering, "How do!"

Clara and Poppy curtsied but knew better than to call back.

"That is your man. Hugh's man. My husband's man. He is hurt and needs physicking." Georgie smirked at Hildy pretending not to know Mr. Bell. The crewmen had known Hildy since they were children, had sprunted after her in the fields and the woods. Georgie had heard the men wonder out loud at the tavern if Hugh, Kettle, was to marry Hildy, Old Boots.

"Look at how they bob like little dolls!" Hildy clasped her hands together, impetuously crouched, extended her arms forward, inviting the girls to run at her for an embrace. The girls did not understand and hung back with Mr. Bell.

"My, they's shy lambs." Hildy removed her slippers and strode barefoot into the yard. The girls smiled as she came near, and Hildy plucked each of their chins with her fingertips, then drew them close and turned toward Georgie, triumphant. Poppy was nearly as tall as her. Clara sifted her hands through Hildy's sheer dress layers, held the sash tied under her bust, stared up at her creamy bosom. Georgie's composure crumbled at this violent intimacy. Then boot steps approached from inside the house.

Hugh bowed. Georgie turned away and loudly scolded Clara to drop her hands from the lady's skirt. "Child, you will catch contagious effluvia with your hands in there."

Hugh looked the same, if a bit thicker through the shoulders. His curly shock of auburn hair rose atop his stout sun-reddened forehead and cheeks. He strode past the doorframe, donning his hat with his broad, snub-fingered hand, and into the yard.

"Gid. You were paid extra to not escort them all the way." Hugh addressed Mr. Bell.

Mr. Bell rose to answer but collapsed in the mud. Poppy lifted her head at hearing his first name. Gid. Gideon. Gideon Bell.

"Lord, where are the horses? Fetch whiskey. He must bed down." Hugh knelt to listen for Gideon Bell's breathing.

Poppy and Clara ran to their father, curtsied shortly before him, then stooped to check his pant cuffs for the ticks and walnut husks they remembered caught there.

Georgie went inside to retrieve whiskey. She heard raking coals. Someone else was there. She walked to the back fire room where Hugh kept the spirits. An aproned woman bent over the fire. She stood upon hearing Georgie. She did not bow or nod but turned her back to tend again to the embers.

"Who are you?" Georgie asked.

"Black Vy."

Georgie stiffened. "Whiskey."

Without turning from her task, Black Vy pointed toward the cupboard.

"Fetch it outdoors. There is a man needs tending."

Black Vy turned to face her. "I's occupied. You not so engaged." She shoveled more ash to bank the fire for the night.

Once Georgie's uncle had beaten a servant for disobedience, then packed her an egg and cider noonchine, two days' pay, and a shawl, ordering her back to her father's croft. The housekeeper henceforward held daily drills, rapping knuckles when any of the servants' responses were slight or mumbled.

Hugh entered the fire room. "The need for whiskey is urgent."

Georgie nodded toward Black Vy. "Refusal to provide it."

Black Vy did not turn around from the coals. Hugh grabbed Georgie's arm and roughly marched her to the spirits cupboard. "There shan't be idle hands in the house."

Georgie resisted him, tried to throw off his grasp. He shoved her face inches from the cupboard. "Fetch the whiskey from the cupboard."

She angled away from him and opened the cupboard, burning with shame to understand her position.

Georgie and Black Vy set down the straw tick in the fire room. This was where Black Vy slept. Visitors bedded with her. The women hung a sheet to make a partition for Clara and Poppy who were already down, curled into bags of corn husks. Their bedding smelled of cooking smoke, of the bitter hog's oil Black Vy rendered from fresh carcasses. There was one more task to finish before sleep. Hot broth dripped down Black Vy's forearms as she lifted the steaming pig's head out of the kettle by the corners of its lips. It slid greasily across the worktable until it snagged on a wormhole in the wood. She peered into the kettle, fishing with her ladle in the cloudy broth for neck and jaw bones. They clattered like necklaces onto the workspace, and she set her hands into the meat of jowls, tearing it away from the skull in chunks. The hide of the pig's face lay like a deflated mask alongside the bones.

Georgie cleared her throat. "I know well that work and can assist if you'd like."

"This here my kitchen." Black Vy sorted splintered bone from fat.

Then more hospitably, Black Vy said, "I crisp some jowl meat in the morning to let the girls crunch on after their chores."

"In the pig's rendered fat," Georgie instructed.

"Stop." Black Vy pointed a glistening finger at Georgie. "How else I crisp jowl? Only one way to crisp jowl."

Georgie gripped the edge of the work table. Black Vy wrapped a handful of bones in a muslin and tucked them underneath the straw tick. In the morning, she would rouse the fire, go outside to the thick moss at the edge of the trees, and roll the bones to understand her dreams. Black Vy claimed her place on the bed. She would sleep hearthside; Georgie close to the wall. The hearth fire embers glowed, ready to be stoked in the morning for bread.

They had fixed Mr. Bell outside in his tent, two fires on either side to loosen his pains. Georgie heard his whiskey-loud singing, the fires glowing through the loose planks of the house. In warm weather, Hugh removed the chinking between the boards to let in air. Georgie looked out between the wall boards. The men's empty tents were amber in the firelight, and the trees' dark shapes moved above. Mr. Bell lay on his back, singing to the trees. Amaranthus stood inside a rebuilt shelter, and

Georgie heard her blow and snort into her straw bedding, rub her neck against the boards. After Margaret's death, Hugh had used Amaranthus as his primary working mount, and she had piled on endurance muscle, no longer a show sprinter. Georgie was overcome by sudden weeping and buried her face in the bedding. She tried to keep quiet, but that resulted in wracking sobs.

Black Vy muttered, "Ain't no man keep to one woman." She thought Georgie wept for the loss of her husband, not for the loss of Margaret.

Georgie curled into her weeping and looked beyond Amaranthus's lean-to. The slumped frame of Margaret's sugaring house stood in the shadowy trees. Margaret had planned to tap the sugar maples but fell ill before harvesting the sap to boil down for syrup. She had lined the floor of the sugaring house with clay jars, the vessels for storing the final product. Bees and wasps had hovered at the jars' openings and soon built their spit-chewed nests in the rafters of the house, a prime vantage to watch what would happen with the jars. The bees and wasps sailed down with purpose to the lips of the jars, dipped inside the dank cavities as if cave exploring, then crawled to the daylight at the lips again as if frustrated by spent lanterns. They worked their legs and tongues over the jugs, trying to divine the meaning of the ordered rows. When winter came, the spiders and mice nestled into the pleasing dark pits of the jugs, but none of the pests tipped over the heavy-bottomed vessels, even when their spindle legs and bud noses peeked over the edges toward the spring warmth. The sugaring house roof had not held up against the past winter's heavy snows. The roof bowed, the small shack already dilapidated. The men avoided repair because there wasn't anyone to take up the work of Margaret's intention for it. But it was the best shelter they had for storing black powder.

Georgie was aware of the sounds above her, of Hugh and Hildy in their sleeping garret, the loose-fitting floorboards casting blots of candlelight down onto her and Black Vy. The lovers whispered. Georgie set her mind against hearing them.

Black Vy removed her sooty apron and overdress. She did not wear the coarse dress of other slave women, but a sheer cotton one tied underneath the bust like Hildy wore. Black Vy's underbust ribbon was a fine satin, brilliant blue. Underneath the dress, she wore a white homespun shift. She was a young woman, slight of build, but with the dropped breasts of motherhood that bobbed underneath the shift. She smoothed the lumps from the straw tick. The neckline of her shift fell

forward to reveal raised scars that trailed across her breast and shoulder, a jumble of white lines like the confusing wanderings a slug leaves
behind in the dirt. Yet Georgie thought Black Vy pretty. She was dark
with sharp cheekbones narrowing to a small chin. Her lips were equal
in size, very full, and they met in the middle in a pink splotch when she
closed them together. Her eyes were flashing black, wet and blinking
with thought and energy. She was named after her eyes, not her skin.
Her face and neck and arms were badly pitted with smallpox scars. Her
palm bore a brand. This made her left hand appear larger than her right,
for the BB initials branded there had healed badly, so this hand splayed
open.

Black Vy settled lightly onto the bed. She wore a cloth head wrap.
She secured and smoothed the tucks and ties about her head. Black
Vy had no pretense or impatience for sharing the space, and the ease
of her movements, which suggested she was either a guest or relation,
confused Georgie. She didn't behave like bought property, but how
had she come here? She didn't behave like a paid servant. Hugh hadn't
ordered her to do anything as they set up Gideon Bell's fire and tent
bedding. Black Vy saw tasks to complete and did them herself. Black Vy
paid no mind to Hugh, neither seeking his approval nor busying herself
with meaningless work to avoid his reprisal. She completed chores thor-
oughly, not taking more time than needed, then allowed herself a seat
and a smoke and didn't have to be asked to rise for the next duty. It was
as though the household were hers out of pride of efficiency. Black Vy
soon fell into the heavy soughing of sleep.

Georgie rolled to her back and stared at the ceiling boards. Hildy
must have jumped into bed, for there was the cushioned sound of a
heavy landing and a soft squeal. As their voices muffled above, a feather slipped through a floorboard crack and sawed downward toward
Georgie's face. She caught it and drew its soft baby down between her
fingertips. Georgie grabbed the straw tick beneath her. She sat upright.
She and Black Vy were sleeping on her and Hugh's bridal bed of straw.
Hugh and Hildy were sleeping on a new feather bed. It was the straw
bed Georgie had been asleep in when Hugh had dragged her out of the
house over a year ago. Georgie clutched the straw ticking, rooting there
in the smoky fire room.

❧

Hugh had dragged her out in the middle of the night. He had been deliberate about it, gun shy of his past underestimations of her strength. He had taken his sleeping daughters first, wrapped them in blankets, made each hold her shoes. He had slung the girls bandolier-style to his chest, and walked through the dark cedars to the waiting wagon and driver. He laid the girls in the wagon, and soon after his retreat, the cold and the night sounds frightened them. They whimpered for him, sounds he heard the entire walk back to the shanty to retrieve Georgie. The driver had hunched bitterly away from the crying children. And when an hour later their mother was set insensible into the wagon, the driver regretted the agreement.

Five years before that, upon first seeing her in England, Hugh had decided to claim her. Then he became intimate with her simmering reserve, but it was too late for he had been persuaded to marry her. The marriage agreement bound the two together along with her uncle's funding for the Buttermilk Falls property. Georgie had been obedient to the arrangement, seeing the necessity of the gamble for securing her family's estate in Shropshire. Poppy was born. Then Clara. Hugh met Hildy and hired the crew in the same week. He had ascended to his fate. He was the luminary he and his mother had struggled to make him for years. It was time for Georgie to leave.

Before entering the house, Hugh had paced in the yard and rehearsed the struggle that was about to happen. She would first ask about the girls, and not seeing them anywhere in the house, would fly into an excited temper, the physical force and verbal fusillade both of which Hugh was familiar. Her furor had caught him unaware on previous occasions. He bore two scars: one depression in his skull over which hair grew back patchily, the result of a flaming log that she had hurled. His head had caught the log's blow sidelong, sending him reeling into the stone hearth, which he had slid bumping down, unconscious. The other scar was a bloom of black powder embedded deep into his side belly, billowing up his pectoral, the consequence of her close-range pistol misfire. The ball had impotently dropped out of the barrel after the smoke cleared when she tipped the pistol down to examine the firing mechanism. Both occasions had been the blowback of when she caught him with two different Oneida women who did not understand her notion that she had sole rights to this man. A caprice Hugh did not understand, either. He still carried the misfired ball in his breast pocket and fingered it as remembrance of Georgie's irascibility whenever he caught himself admiring her small shoulders or hands.

Before entering the house, he had braced himself. He would have to catch her before wakefulness took hold. He had not much time to get her tied and bound.

He busted into the house, the rope pulled taut between his hands. He paused at her sleeping form, her face buried in curls, the blankets snug at her neck. Then he sprang. He pinned her with his body and forced the rope between her teeth, trapping her flat with his hips. "Now, Georgie, it must be this way."

Her eyes were wide and wet with fury. She thrashed, but she was overpowered. She was then quiet and still, her teeth clamped onto the rope. He would have to first remove himself and the blankets if he was to pry her out of the bed.

He peeled the rope from her mouth and lifted off her, keeping one hand on her wrist to nail her down. He snatched off the blanket, and in her white shift, she began to writhe. She kicked and screamed, hoarsely, weakly from the early hour. No one in the yard would come to her aid. The men were all new hires, early in their relations with the man, before a series of his bad judgements piled up a briar patch of disregard for his leadership. She spat and cursed and crashed the bedside lantern. She cuffed him on the ear, which stalled him for a second, but she did not run away, for she was pulled in two directions: to stay planted in her bed to claim her rightful place or to run. She grabbed a handful of the straw tick. Her moment's hesitation was too long. He flopped her roughly onto her belly, catching her low back with his knee. She choked into the bed sheets.

Hugh tied Georgie's hands, did not force stockings or shoes onto her feet. He pulled the rope like a leash, roughly tugging. The girls would need her awake even if she were hysterical. He avoided her sensitive spots; he dared not pull her by the hair. It would set off a fit of mad-dog biting. He re-gagged her with his hanky, dug his fingers into her shoulder, and led her outside.

At the door's threshold, he licked his lips. He had bested her. If he could cross the threshold, he had a chance of ousting her. Now to get through the woods to the wagon. She garbled words, probably asking where the girls were. Georgie's sweet mare, Glory, was saddled, and Georgie balked, realizing a journey ahead. He grabbed one thigh and forced her onto the horse, swinging himself behind, but the reins flailed, and Georgie, her hands tied low behind her, grabbed his crotch, and he tumbled off the horse. Georgie kicked Glory's belly with her bare feet, but without the balance of her arms and the reins flailing, it was not but a few skittering steps before Glory tripped off the path, sending Georgie sidelong to the dirt. She raised her head, staggered to her feet, hurling herself a few steps toward the woods. But without shoes, Hugh caught her. He cuffed her upside the head, and she lost consciousness.

He could have dragged her then to the wagon. But his temper was up, and a few of his men looked out from their tents. He knew they did nothing because they had seen worse done to women. Hugh's thoughts raced to how he would contain Georgie at the tavern. He couldn't very well ask the driver to chain her alongside the hearth. As she lay knocked out cold, he kindled a fire. He spun the branding iron over the flames as if roasting a ham joint. She roused and ground her cheek into the dirt, coughing. He straddled her, bent one knee onto her back, and set the iron sizzling onto her forearm. She jerked alert, unable to wrench free from his weight, screamed against the back of her throat, then registering the hiss and sear of her own flesh, passed out again.

She woke cold and jolting in the back of the wagon, already miles into the journey. Her forearm radiated pain up to her shoulder, her flesh welted with his initials. The rope was gone. Her hands were free. The girls huddled, staring. A bare, pink dawn rose, arcing across her girls' dark eyes and soft cheeks. There were buildings and houses. They were in Utica.

The driver slowed the wagon at the tavern. "I am to drop you here." He unlatched the back of the wagon, handed Georgie a folded note, written in Hugh's sprawling hand. She did not read it. She already knew. She and the girls were to earn their keep working the tavern. Hugh was done with them.

Georgie tightened her clutch on the straw tick. Black Vy's leg pinned Georgie by the hem. Why had Hugh fetched her back to the shanty? Red embers pulsed within the hearth's ashes.

During the first nights at the tavern, her girls had tended to her fever and to the festering wound. They had held bread-and-milk poultices to the brand mark. They had sweated her feet. Georgie pulled back the sleeve of her night chemise, the scar silvery in the moonlight. She made a fist, flexed the thin muscle, listened to her girls stir behind the curtain.

Clara woke in the night. She missed her bed at the tavern, but the length of Poppy was near, though she was sweating in her sleep. Clara felt the emptiness of everyone asleep except for her. She covered her head with the pelt, crawled away from Poppy's damp side, tucked into a dry hollow, and drifted back to sleep. She was outside. She knew how to open a door without waking anyone in a household. The trees voided the moonlight, but at the great drop of rock, the moonlight flared onto the rushing river. She followed the High Fall until the water slowed, and the slabs of limestone descended like steps. A man lay floating in a deep kettle of slowly circling water. He wore armor, and his eyes blinked to the moon. The armor tapered at his wrists, the chainmail sleeves full at the shoulders like feathered wings. He drew his arms out from his body to keep afloat, and she watched this fallen angel swim in her dream. He opened his mouth, and ink scribbles spooled into the water. When Clara woke, the embroidered dress hung from a rafter, lit from the dawn.

Black Vy shrugged off the pelt. She smoked her pipe in bed awhile, her legs and feet splayed out. In the yard, she rolled the bones of a pig she had watched for weeks, a pig that roamed deep into the hemlocks, fat on acorns and mushrooms, its bones fresh, still warm from the muscle boiled off, the oils not yet rancid. This pig had tottered up the steep, muddy hills to root out the undergrowth and hearty tree shoots. This was the pig to tell a secret, a loner with strong neck muscles pulling at dense neck bones, a constant rooter. Its bones had clankered to the bottom of the kettle like shipwrecked ceramic jugs. Black Vy shot the bones onto the slant of moonlight. They scattered across the moss, and she prayed for peace and rest.

Noord Boorsma parted his tent flap and extended his hand. Black Vy flitted across the moss, took his hand, and he wrapped her in his arms, his heart swollen as a tremoring crater.

It was past daybreak. The whole house was awake: the girls had folded their bedding to the corner and were already in the yard leading a young pig around by its ear. One group of men, the South Pocket, had returned. They kindled breakfast fires to cook the pike they had caught on the ride up from the tavern. Smoke rose from Gideon Bell's night fires. A wasp crawled in and out of the wall boards, and Georgie noted its globiferous antennae, swelling large and round at the joints sprouting from its head, as did the spurs of its back legs. Its antennae and legs tapered to spare tips, which trolled the crannies of the wood.

The men grew flinchy and superstitious the longer they tried to light black powder and the charges failed to go off. Each man wore a talisman tied to his belt, a turtle shell or marten head. They berated men who didn't. These were protections each man guarded and wore in earnest for strength against the forces in the woods: contagious effluvia, trees falling, frostbite. When Noord Boorsma was the only one who didn't get leeches between his flanks when wading through the southern slough, being the only one wearing a salamander claw around his waist, all the other men threw off their turtle shells and hunted down salamanders, overturning rocks. They would all face this workday with newly strung salamander claws around their waists, like foot-clappers all dressed in the same spangled beading.

They had succeeded in the early days of blasting, alighting the powder and exploding rock and overgrowth. The black powder created such smoke that the men followed its drift downwind to the river, and watched it float on top of the water, carried by the current's updraft. The smoke would ride along the top of the flux, then lift from wind or dissipate at rough mist sprayed from the swift, rocky patches downriver. The men hauled the blast debris to a central dump pile, a reserve to stabilize future roads. Then a blast was imprecise, and another. The men's bore holes were not deep enough, eager as they were to stuff the rock with explosives and make further progress. The rains came, an uncommon wet season, and nothing would alight no matter how dry they kept the powder. The rock itself held onto rainwater. The bore holes wept and splintered the rock with tiny, wandering cracks that darkened and dripped. Hugh had swung at the rockface with his sledgehammer, heaving and striking for days, chipping away mere bits. The men set fire to the overgrowth, dousing the choke vines and rotted logs with turpentine. They tied rags around their faces and trudged in advance of the flames, directing the spread of the burn with trowels and shovels. It was slow work, and some men dropped from the fumes, being already weak from stubborn consumption. The fire flamed out easily once it combusted the topmost layers and sunk to the pulp of the forest floor, black and damp as tobacco. After the first successful explosions, they never gained another momentum, but Hugh's mood and ambitions had thrived. Yet now, progress toward carving a pathway was stuck, the area blighted, unordered ruin.

Hugh stockpiled a collection of broken-up fossils. He kept them as penance to his and his mother's deception of the Oldenbarneveld villagers years ago, a scheme of counterfeit fossils for which he and Margaret had been caught. When Hugh had successfully blasted away rock, he ordered the men to sort rubble and scavenge for organic materials, the Mollusca whorls flat to the grain of the limestone; the bulging, onyx-smooth carapaces; the tumid dorsal shields and thoracic joints thrusting out from the surface of the rock's pressure. The men knocked the limestone to free whatever ancient nubs and convexities swelled out. Sometimes they tossed what they found onto Hugh's pile of collectibles, but as many times they purloined the treasures to rub like amulets by lantern light inside their tents.

Sometimes the fossil fragments were not separated from the blast rubble. When the blasting had stopped, Hugh had given some of the rubble to Isaac Coe who had used it as ballast for a hot-air balloon he launched in the just-harvested corn field of Cromwell Fetters. To urge the balloon higher, Isaac jettisoned overboard handfuls of rubble, reducing the balloon's weight. Fossilized parts plummeted and hit the earth, scattering and half submerging in soil with solid whumps. As Hugh watched the balloon rise and drift northward, Isaac heaved more debris overboard. Hugh regretted giving away the rubble. Fossil hunters in the decades to come would mistakenly think the Leperditid had made its home outside of the West Canada. Hugh lamented that these men of science would make faulty conclusions. This was when doubt of his own judgment had begun to kill his intuition, initiating a string of weak decisions.

Isaac's balloon drifted fifteen miles north to Kayuta Lake. The balloon's long respirations, exhales echoing across the treetops, drew the lake's residents out of their homes. They gasped at the sight of the beast scraping against the blue sky. The only flying conveyances they had ever seen were manned by demons in their dreams. The fragile silk balloon popped a leak and withered like burning paper, crashing on the shore. At the pop and freefall, the residents ran to it, not seeing Isaac Coe bail headlong into the lake. As the balloon flopped on the beach, the men shot and stabbed the deflated silk as though harpooning the bladder of a sky monster. Isaac swam to shore and tried his best to convince the residents of the concept of manned flight.

Hugh and Hildy walked around above stairs. Black Vy dressed as she heard Hugh bounding down. The lower half of his body, clad in dark breeches, filled the stairwell.

Before ducking his head to enter the fire room, he asked, "Ladies, might I?"

"Yes, you might." Black Vy set the kettle on the pivot crane.

He entered and looked at Georgie, sitting on the straw ticking in only her shift, unbraiding her hair. "Come along. Hildy needs dressing."

So that was it. She was to wait on Mathilde. Georgie narrowed her eyes on Hugh. "May I have a word?"

He was impatient. "Don your gown. This is a busy household."

Georgie dressed and followed him.

He walked outside and turned to her, but his eyes roamed from the yard to the hogs to the splintered rail of the porch.

"What is it then?"

"My uncle would not…" Georgie began in a low voice.

"Calm down."

She folded her hands and tried again. "My uncle would not approve…"

"Collect yourself. You're hysterical."

She blinked, unruffled. "My uncle would not approve of you using his money to purchase a slave. The agreement is quite specific about disbursal of funds."

Hugh kneeled and tested how much life the railing had left. "You abandon your dignity." He looked around the yard. There was movement in Gideon Bell's tent. "Keep your temper, and mind me, Georgiana." Hugh belabored the syllables, george-ee-AH-nah, horsewhipping the name, which she pronounced jor-JAY-nah.

Mr. Bell crawled from his tent, staggered, roused his fires.

"You must answer to this, or I will write to my uncle, and he will demand repayment of funds for this endeavor."

"Black Vy is not my slave. She was a gentleman's from Virginia. I employ her as a free woman."

"How did she come to be in your employ? Did you steal her? You cannot do that, Hugh, not even as a man born in this country of no laws."

"There was no pettifoggery. She fled. And needed protection."

"She fled? By herself? To these woods from Virginia? Is that not hundreds of miles?"

Hugh sighed. "She ran from Virginia to Georgetown. Still, a great distance to travel by foot. I found her in Boston."

"I don't believe you. No woman travels alone. No slave woman flees by herself through the night without escort or currency."

"This one did."

"Was she not completely conspicuous as an escaped slave? Does her master understand her to be employed and free? I should think not."

"She travelled by night and covered herself by day. As for her former master, I should not begin to know how to find him. Black Vy would never tell me, and I will not ask her to."

"Lord, she walked." Then her anger flared. "Let your hired girl wait on your hussy."

There was movement beyond the yard, shouts of greeting. The second group of men returned, the North Pocket, bearing the new crates of black powder. Hugh called out if they had seen the horses and wagon on their journey up, but they said no. They had camped all night but did not see or hear them. Hugh ordered two more men to measure back to search, instructing them to leave the wagon if they must but to return with the horses and barrels of pork. And if they did not find Balor and Brace in the woods, he told them to travel back to Utica to inquire and post notices around town.

Gideon Bell limped toward Hugh and Georgie, holding out a dried-up poultice. Two sows, drawn by its sour milk smell, trailed, their snouts tipped to the rag.

"Are you still in pain, man?" Hugh asked.

"I am." Mr. Bell gripped the railing.

"Stay on and rest here. I've no man to spare to guide you back."

"It did help some, but could I trouble you for 'nother?"

Georgie threw the rag in the dirt. The sows squealed, stepping over each other, grunting as they chewed off bits of the muslin.

"That one is spoilt. Go inside for a fresh one," Georgie told him.

Mr. Bell removed his hat and walked up the porch steps, eyeing Hugh, letting the door slam behind him.

Hugh spat in the dirt and laughed. "He with that look to me? In defense of you?"

"The glare does not defend me. It comments directly upon your conduct."

Hugh held her arm. "I will let you work in this household to keep our daughters well and hale. But you are to understand your role now."

"Off!" Georgie snatched away her arm. "Raised right here in these woods no doubt. Can Hildy read? Can she play music aside from drumming twigs on her knees? Whatever domestic tasks does she know? None that I can so far tell."

Hugh rubbed his hair. "She cannot be trained. She is not of the mind. She must learn to sit still in obedience. Needlework, perhaps."

"Did the household in which she was raised not need feeding, nor heating, nor comforting? You could train one of your sows to carry in firewood and drop it in the hearth. And if she doesn't have that sense, then you have ways to persuade." Georgie clutched her arm.

"She does not respond well to that." Hugh adjusted the seam of his breeches.

Georgie sank to the wall. The loiter-sack had figured a way to handle Hugh. Georgie had only seen other women submit. Georgie had fought back, but to no end. Hugh had always overpowered her. Then Georgie's mouth shut in sudden understanding: Hugh loved Hildy. He had been more kind to Hildy. There was nothing Georgie could do differently to repel Hugh. Georgie was bound in their marriage, a dump field for his coarser impulses.

"Surely any woman feels a responsibility in the household? Her character is poor. You must instruct her to perform labor. The domestic arts are of no use here nor be reading nor manners. A woman proves her worth filleting eels and hauling water rather than mending hankies. You cannot hire servants with my uncle's money when there are able bodies to perform household labor."

"The terms of the agreement allow my discretion toward payout of funds. I need an able housekeeper. Black Vy will stay on. You will train Hildy toward refinement and tend to her needs."

"She is too old for learning. Criminy! Her ways are set. Her mind is formed."

"Lord, you whine. That is to be your role. You have no other choice."

She knew there was no more speaking with him that day.

He would not divorce her. There was dishonor in publicly renouncing his responsibility. Moreover, divorce would dissolve her uncle's agreement to fund his blasting effort. He would have to repay the money. He would keep Georgie under his protection until his daughters were raised and married off. By then, Hugh figured his tourist lodging would be built, thriving, his funds self-sustaining.

"Go upstairs," Hugh ordered Georgie. "And attend to Hildy. Then heat water for laundry. The girls' dresses are filthy." He followed her inside to where the girls were napping. With his large hand, he brushed back the hair from each sleeping girl and drew Clara in his arms. Clara clung sleepily to him, and Poppy stretched her arms as they walked down to the river. Hugh swung Clara under the arms as he dipped the soles of her feet onto the rushing surface, and Clara squealed awake.

In her old life, the one she had back in England, Georgie had assumed a position of prominence in her uncle's household. She had not been raised to wear an apron, much less attend to anyone. From the time she was old enough to require a cap to cover her head, her uncle had trained her to one day assume the position of a baron's wife. This meant honing a singular talent in the household. It did not mean managing a staff for laundry day nor organizing meals nor overseeing the finer points of shining pewter and scrubbing surfaces. These were lesser duties, the logistics of which would never clutter her energy for reading about animal husbandry in Latin and Greek.

She had practiced each day the facility of her household contribution—raising a novel bloodline of pig, the first litter sired by a wild boar, the breed provisionally named the "black breed of the Old Forest," even though their mother was a White Lincoln, docile and heavy with milk. The strongest of the first litter favored her in looks with creamy, curly locks sticking up along his spine, but he rooted at the crevices of the stall, hungrily snorting at the cattle hooves nearby like his wild, omnivorous father. It was the job of the stable hands to ensure the young pigs did not develop a taste for meat, so they lined the stall crevices with ash, and when the men slopped the mother and mucked the stall, they touched geranium leaves to the young pigs' noses, and the little ungulates dropped onto their bottoms, so intoxicated from the perfume.

Georgie did not feed, bathe, nor clean up after her drove (she did not know where the dunging area was located); nor did she chase any errant escapees. Her eye for detail of the breed mattered; she trained to run a hand along each swine's back to judge exceptionality of form. She dressed the part: she wore a grey wig, a tall black hat, a dark overcoat and shirt, and snug veil of black lace that rose over her mouth and nose. She wore gloves on the walk to the stable which she removed and handed to a stable hand after settling onto a stool atop a wooden platform, her position of authority over the pen. Another stable hand passed her each tiny pig, and as she ran her hand over the baby, the stable master, Nevin Chudleigh, stood in the center of the pen shouting descriptions for her to repeat. She recited the remarks of assessment about skin thickness, width of forehead, the spacing of ears, the point or curl of ears. A third stable hand wrote down her parroted remarks in a ledger. When she gained confidence, she elaborated on the stable master's assessment. At first, this resulted in his sharp corrections: "No! Its nasal disc is indeed lovely, yet my lady mistakes relevant attributes with inappropriate observation." Mr. Chudleigh thumped disapproval upon the brass knob of his cane, which caused the pig pen to collectively jump and scatter to the shadowed end of the stall, a huddled chorus of alarmed squeals and nervous twitching pink backsides. This was to be her sole function in her future household as duchess, the virtuosity of a singular talent. Her cash-poor family banked upon prize money as sorely needed income.

Dinner tables across Shropshire tittered about Georgie's lack of female deference, for neighbors had observed her purported appraisal talents in the hog pen. Despite an audience, she was focused, had no time for greetings beyond curt nods to a dusty hay bale offered as a seat. She was absorbed in her task, breathing deeply as though in preparation for sport. And when gentlemen and ladies sat upon the hay bale without receiving from Georgie so much as an inquiry about their health or condition, and when they realized Georgie would keep her mouth pursed and her eyes averted, without any submission to their need to be asked about themselves, they glanced with outrage at each other. Who was this young woman in odd funeral veiling to completely overthrow social dictates? And if any gentleman dared to break the hush and verbally assert on behalf of the void of good manners, Georgie turned away, signaling a pig to be carried forth, even before he could form a stuttered indignation. If he continued disruption, she would command, "Kindly mind your movements, sir, and keep to your seat."

Despite any social misgivings, most of those who attended Georgie's performance were charmed from the moment the stable hand lifted the stall bolt and the first blinking pig trotted forward. The audience was rapt with Georgie's natural eye and ability and conceded praise to her, though it was expressed dubiously by most heads of families as lessons to their own daughters and nieces: "She lacks female submission, and though skilled, her mastery shan't be a tentpole upon which to build the foundations of motherhood and marriage."

Still, these daughters and nieces saw in their fathers and uncles true admiration for Georgie. And forks across Shropshire dropped onto plates as young women bristled at this shred of praise for Georgie, the confirmation from their paternal authorities that one of their own had a gift. These young women scanned over their short pasts, the burden of being a compliant and pretty-cheeked female suddenly merely acceptable, not remarkable. They all fought quietly for favor but within the precincts of accepted tactics: impeccable grooming; a bright, smartly selected ribbon; a plumly chosen moment for silent, composed derision at someone else's rash or fevered comment. Upon the revelation that the standard for favor had shifted, these young women glowered with resentment that it might be too late for them to cultivate a skill. They fell into existential brooding over whether or not their own estates needed a young woman upon whom to place its hopes and aspirations for elevating the household reputation. The young women became furious there might not be enough resources nor indulgent attitudes throughout Shropshire for more than one female to rise upon her own developed expertise. Angrily forking up chine of mutton, some of the young women resolved to apply their needles in earnest instead of daydreaming and inattentively stabbing at the linen. Others decided Georgie stank and time in a barn would harden any soft maternal love she had in reserve for future children, not to mention the rumored erosion to her conversation and poise and manners with which to lure a young man. Any admiration for Georgie would be fleeting, crumble away after people saw her bereft of marriage prospects.

Yet one aspiring young woman, Cressida Orry, had asked Georgie to show her the swine trade so she might take the skill back to her own estate, but Cressida fainted after trampling a suckling under her heel. The stray baby fled in circles, squealing, and Georgie scooped it to safety next to its huffing mother. The other animals shat out more liquid than usual in Cressida Orry's presence, their stomachs sour as she flailed about the pen. The whole pack was on edge. Cressida Orry could not comprehend what to judge in the animals. She could not keep fetlock and forelock remembered straight. The swine were not like vases or paintings. She could not discern any aesthetic merit in the animals. Even so, Cressida Orry returned to her estate, her family casting the future of its prestige upon the light of this one girl. She tried her hand at breeding, the beams of her family's expectations following her all summer like grasshoppers spraying from her step.

Cressida's first litter grew moundering under layers of fat, standing only after mustering a huff to heave off the ground then whump back down, buckling at the joints of their bowed limbs and slumping sideways with a fart. The sow lay on her side for sleeping, her belly spiked with an arc of teats, and the corpulent babies lay with their noses tipped to these points, toes tucked in milk-soused dreaming. Some of them suffocated in the night beneath the folded layers of their cheek fat that buried lips and eyes in slumber. The ones that grew older were clearly knocked-kneed when viewed from the back, with not quite deformed hind leg structure but certainly poor, one leg canting, both legs squat and straining to undergird thick hams. The Orry family was crushed at not having a young female maestro of animal husbandry to meet the standard Georgie had established. Other Shropshire families saw the failure and scrambled in a bid to keep pace.

Meanwhile, Georgie had mastered her skill and after besting in show for her first competition, she was appointed hog mistress over her prize swine herd. Mr. Chudleigh quit his position of stable master, his pride too fragile to bear Georgie's accolades. It was a boost in prestige to the household, and the family hoped to the county, which for a century had not bred nor raised any beast of note. Georgie showed off her handsome, sound stock to people who traveled from as far away as Cannock to see the distinguished herd. But those in Shropshire were annoyed that their place on the social rung had been bumped, so they began devaluing the endeavor of swine rearing by gossiping in the shops and salons that one family's undignified pastime reflected so poorly upon the whole respectable bearing of Shropshire. This talk swept into Georgie's family's ears, her uncle and the matriarchs agreeing that Georgie's talent was too disruptive; they could not bear such social snubbing. So Georgie was told to stop, and she obeyed and packed away her veil and costume.

The remaining stable hands assumed sole responsibility of Georgie's swine herd. In one breeding, the stable hands had fallen into the clumsy ways of amateurs, creating stock fit only for butchering. Georgie had no appetite for the beefy chops that became the animals' fate. Her uncle carved the first beast, the family not accustomed to eating such fatty joints, white ribbons of adipose glistening, curling, ringing the pink loin. Their guests for dinner, neighbors from the county, sopped up every bit of juice and fat with their bread, relishing the meal, assuming the patterns of ease and familiarity that had defined their acquaintance prior to the prize hogs.

Georgie understood that if she didn't become extraordinary, peace in the county would reign. So she embroidered and looked out the window and accepted young men who called each week. The matriarchs regarded Georgie's quick conformity as a sign—she wouldn't have been able to withstand the pressures of prominence. She hadn't a mind of her own, was inherently submissive, consented without question to orders. Hers was not a decisive nature. She was wifely. Georgie overheard the matriarchs' assessments but did not believe them. She had folded away her stock pen garments so her family's position would suffer no more harm.

One week as a young man sang to her, dark storm clouds rolled in, boiling low. The dogs and ponies riled from the cool change in wind, the minutes before bursting, cold rain showers. There had been spectacular storms that summer. Nearly every afternoon, Georgie had endured some young man reciting poetry, skreeking a violin, recounting a lecture he attended on the continent. This afternoon, as the storm clouds tippled toward the estate, over the hill and ahead of the clouds rode a man on a white horse, galloping hard toward the house, trying to outpace the downpour creeping at his back. Georgie sat, gripping the windowsill.

Her suitor stopped his pitchfork singing and tried to reassure her. "Just another summer storm. Come away from the window."

But it was too late: Hugh was in view, the first sheets of rain pouring off his open, ecstatic mouth as the stallion Spumador shied from the grooms' leaping hands.

Georgie climbed the narrow stairs to the sleeping loft. At the top, she was met with the full-on stare of Hildy in the mirror. Hildy sat at the large dressing table that Georgie and Hugh had brought over from England. Hildy brushed her hair with Georgie's gilt paddle brush. There were a matching hand mirror and comb with several fillets and coronets for hairdressing. Hildy had nothing of her own on Georgie's table.

Hildy offered Georgie the brush.

Georgie picked up a section of Hildy's fine blond hair. She worked through the end knots, checking the mirror, disbelieving Hildy could be so lovely. Delicate brows and bones framed her pale gray eyes. The natural flush of her cheeks sat low toward her jaw, where the last pockets of adolescent fat pooled. Her mouth had the hue of a downy peach with a cleft puckering the lower lip. Though when Hildy smiled, she made no effort to conceal bad teeth, her flushed skin and fine china bones and rotted teeth a fascination of contrast.

Hildy did not look at herself in the mirror but kept her eye on Georgie. "He told me you were a maid for Queen Charlotte."

"Not so. I never was. My cousin was a woman-of-the-bedchamber, not a maid."

"Woman-of-the-bedchamber," Hildy repeated. "She were a tucker-in. Or she were a knocker-upper? Did she put her to bed or wake her up? How many did she own?"

"Her Majesty held fifty-five ladies in her service during the time my family served her court."

Unlike Mr. Bell, Hildy was not going to punish Georgie for her English. "Who all did what? That be many servants."

"They were not servants as you know them. My cousin was invited to court as a lady of good breeding and high standing. She received the privilege of her position. She was provided her own ladies to attend her needs."

Hildy laughed. "The servants had servants? Lord. You Englishers." She winced, and Georgie held the hair near its roots to blunt the pull on her scalp.

"My cousin fastened her Majesty's necklace before her evening meal."

"Did the queen have fine hair? Was it powdery? No, it was a wig. What was the true color withinside?"

"My cousin was not one to touch her Majesty's head." The soft bristles were not stiff enough, so Georgie sorted the mats with her fingers.

"She told secrets?"

"Certainly not."

"The queen was a shut face. Oh, your cousin told you the queen's secrets, you just cain't tell!" Hildy's lips curved with marble seduction.

"Even English common life and conversation are much more refined and reserved than you know. There is protocol to every step of the queen's day."

"Mayhaps I sha's start telling you my secrets."

"Only if you wish so."

"I have no friends here, and besides, we two share a common lord." Hildy waited for a rise, but Georgie methodically stroked the brush, lifting Hildy's head up and back. "Well, you sha's to wait for my secret. The next time. Tell me your cousin did not have to empty the queen's soil from the night?"

"No. Her job was to converse with the queen, to help improve her English."

"She wern't educated? She were simple-minded? Sure must her English was better than anyone else's, her being the crown?"

"The queen is German. My cousin was in her attendance to accompany her from place to place."

"She is a crippled German?"

"No, dear girl." Georgie addressed her with impatience but had not meant to let this casual title slip. Her eyes flicked on Hildy's in the mirror. It was an endearment Hildy did not seem to mind, having no notion for what she should be called.

"She were oft busky at court?"

"Lord, no. Never." But Georgie thought of her cousin's report of the sleeping laudanum stupor through which the queen stumbled regularly, especially in the dreary winter months.

"She was unmaggy, then? Why have someone follow her 'round?"

"I suppose it was a show of her importance. Her position afforded several attendants around her at any time."

"And your cousin followed behind her, then? Or walked apace? No, your cousin walked ahead to guard against smugglers?"

"Always behind."

"Well, I wish you to companion me reg'lar. But you sha's walk ahead of me."

Georgie ran her hand from Hildy's crown down the length of the strands, checking for more knots.

Hildy reached underneath the dressing table, withdrawing a short blade. "Here, you be my first line buckler. Ain't it be fun?" She held the knife like a torch, an empress of liberty.

Georgie did not take the knife. "That's a man's job. A husband's duty."

"Well, seeing as how I's thupsupon without a husband, you ought step to." Georgie kept her eyes on Hildy's scalp, her face impassive. "Why's you come here?"

"He ordered me to."

"Would you not come back elsewise?"

"A father must see his children."

"Yes, those be hissen. Fine beauties they are." Hildy paused. "Though he seld time speak of them."

Georgie gathered the hair into a simple back knot. So the girl did have some acid in her heart. "Shall we bathe you, then?" Georgie's head cocked toward the copper tub.

"No, he don't like that. Just wipe me down. Soon we sha's ourn own."

It took a moment for Georgie to understand. "But your children won't be entitled to anything. A man can only have one wife and the children bound to their lawful union in the eyes of God."

Hildy unstrung the ribbon holding together the front of her chemise. It fell loose, exposing the topswell of her bosom and shoulders.

"Why you think the code book of your country make to mine? We free-think, we free-reason. Those men who framed us, who wrote our freedoms, they thought of everything for us. You have girls who are 'titled to nothin.' I sha's bring boys. I sha's bear little presidents." She drew the chemise off her shoulders. Her breasts draped alluringly. Like bunting unfurled on a spring day of celebration.

Georgie scanned her shoulder blades for pockmarks from disease or fingerprints from Hugh's grip. There were no marks. Her back and spine flexed pure white. She appeared as though sculpted from ivory. She was beguiling.

"Sponge," Hildy said.

Georgie squeezed the cloth soaking in the basin. Hildy cocked one elbow in the air. Georgie wiped at the armpit. Georgie didn't know the laws of this country, yet Hildy's wooly interpretations of her young country's rule of law felt true enough. Male heirs could upset any legitimate place Georgie held in the household. She did not remember any ironclad proviso in her marriage agreement to keep her protected. She had thought all along her daughters' husbands would inherit the tourist enterprise Hugh was trying to develop. Now she was not sure.

Georgie wrung the cloth, ran it under Hildy's breasts and between them. She drew the cloth along Hildy's upper back then down her spine. She wiped dry the damp spots and tied the chemise around Hildy's shoulders.

"Ya grow'd so quiet. What be your thoughts?" Hildy asked.

"I think my husband will enter soon. I must be downstairs for the butchering and breakfast." Georgie turned for the staircase.

"Don't forget this." Hildy bore the knife.

Georgie drew the knife close to her heart, lightly running her palm over its edge. It would need sharpening. She slipped the knife into her apron and tied the pocket closed. Hildy rose from the dressing table.

"One moment," Georgie said. Hildy's gaze latched onto her in the mirror. Georgie reached for a mother-of-pearl comb and swept up the girl's loose strands.

They ate meals at Black Vy's worktable in the fire room. Black Vy warmed salt pork over the spit and slid it onto plates. Georgie set teacups, saucers, and a pot of hot tea in the center of table. This was Georgie's china, her wedding gift from distant London relations.

"Do we not has fine things? Do you not think so?" Hildy asked. She wore another gauzy gown, this one the palest lilac with the same crimson sash tied below her bust. Hildy moved freely about the fire room as Black Vy and Georgie worked, unencumbered by guilt or sheepishness, touching things with authority without performing any useful task. She was airy and feckless as French nougat.

"Black Vy, whey's the other dishes? The too-reen and the joint platters?" Hildy asked.

Black Vy nodded to the shelves. On tiptoe, Hildy grabbed for the large serving pieces. Georgie closed her eyes and set her jaw. These were her belongings, the ones she had arranged to set up the household of her early marriage.

The serving pieces were out of Hildy's reach. "You can see them up high for yourself. They's pretty and we use them by snaps for Sunday suppers."

Georgie poured tea.

Hildy crouched and opened the mesh doors of the cupboard. She retrieved two glasses, grasping the stems in each fist, holding them before Georgie. "Ain't they's clever and pretty?"

Hugh entered the fire room, sitting down to his breakfast.

Georgie sipped tea to conceal her face. Each glass was etched with a frosted *T*.

"A family her-loom," said Hildy. "*T* for Tepper."

"Indeed," replied Georgie. "Quite pretty." It was coincidence that Georgie's grandmother's maiden initial was also T, but for Tempest. Hugh registered no awareness of the wedding gift from her maternal grandmother. The glasses had been sent after they had arrived in America. Hugh had helped load the crate into the carriages and boats, barking at the men to handle the fragile items with care. And when Georgie had unpacked the crate, full of wood shavings, each glass wrapped in leather, Hugh had remarked happily that the set of six glasses had survived the journey intact without a crack.

But now Hugh sat, stirring his tea; all that was once her own, he felt entitled to as his. He dismissed entirely the record and remembrance of the glasses' provenance.

"Listen." Hildy clinked the rims of the glasses together, which made a musical tink and resounding chime. She turned one of the glasses over to read its base. "Newcastle-upon-Tyne. Is that north of here?"

There was not a ripple of recognition in Hugh's face. He had taken Georgie there when they were still courting in England. It was on the streets of Newcastle-upon-Tyne where an old gentleman had tipped his hat and said to Hugh, "Hold fast to that one." At the time, Georgie thought he had said that because of the flush in her cheeks or the fine gown she had worn. But she recognized now the man had seen complete devotion in her for Hugh.

Hugh kept his eyes on his food. He had erased their past together. Georgie sipped her tea. Over a pan of cold river water, she would flay the leaflets of his heart.

Hildy shrugged and took her place at the table. Poppy and Clara bolted inside, slopping water buckets. Black Vy sat at the head seat opposite Hugh. Jantjen Meijer and Rye Syphur, the men sent to Utica to scout for Balor and Brace, stood in the doorway then knocked on the frame. Hugh stood. The men removed their hats and nodded to the women but did not enter the house.

"None in Utica has seen hide nor hair of them," reported Rye.

"Not hide nor hair," echoed Jantjen. "But we posted a notice at the tannery, and the semptress and the butcher said they'd pass word."

Hugh paled. "No word or trace?"

The men shook their heads and returned to the yard.

Hugh sat but didn't eat.

Clara held her salt pork with both hands. "I know where the horses are, Papa."

Hugh hooked his boot onto her chair leg and slid her closer. "You do, child? Tell me."

"They are behind the rock in the devil's p'session."

Hugh addressed Georgie: "How do these girls not know the value of horses and a wagon?"

"I know the value, Papa," Poppy offered.

"No, you don't. If you did, you would have taught the lesson to your sister already." Hugh ate, and they all knew to stay quiet.

Clara stared at the portrait hanging on the wall. It was of her and Poppy, much younger. Clara wore a chaplet around her neck, and Poppy held a silver coin, gifts from their grandmother Margaret, who had hired the portraitist soon after bestowing the objects in hopes of capturing the girls' excitement. But Clara had never liked the painting. She had been an infant, Poppy a toddler, yet they both looked like grumpy adults in babies' swaddling and caps. Clara was unable to see herself in the image. What bellied up from the canvas was her ma's face on a tiny, shrouded body. It was her ma's face on a severe day framed by the white linen cap. Chubby arms and legs poked from the embroidered cuffs of the infant's gown. The infant's hands incongruously held an embroidery needle and an apple with a fresh bite mark. Poppy looked like their grandmother, a serene though weathered beauty. She held the coin with the graceful dexterity of a woman, not a nursling, balancing the silver between her thumb and forefinger, holding it up for the viewer. Clara did not remember posing. She only remembered the paint that had been smeared on the walls of the artist's studio. Paint smeared upon his clothing, his apron, his hair, the floor, every surface mucked wet or spiky with dried paint as if the walls and sideboards grew sedges.

Clara understood the chaplet and the silver coin to be valuable inheritances. She often asked Poppy to retell the objects' origin because she loved to hear of her grandmother snaking on her belly across the battlefield to gather what she had seen a Seneca man drop as he had retreated from the scene. Their grandmother had told the girls the objects were powerful charms for them even though the man had discarded them as luckless for himself. But other than sitting for the portrait, Clara and Poppy had never been allowed to handle the items. Clara eyed the spirits cupboard where the chaplet and coin were stored out of her reach. As Clara chewed a knob of fat, she burned a little as she thought the right thing was to let her cradle the chaplet and the coin, to sleep at night with their protection.

The rest of the family ate, wordlessly occupied about the day's work ahead. Poppy wore the dress from the tavern gangway, now laundered. She traced the raised buds of embroidery, hopeful the trim dress would allow her to sit and stitch instead of the hot and heavy work of cooking and keeping the fire.

Hildy smiled at Poppy. "That is a fine dress. A real fine dress. When I first see you in the yard, I thought, jiminy, what a fine dress."

Poppy sat straighter, in the way her ma had instructed her to.

"I should think mayhaps I would like that dress for my own," Hildy said.

Clara stopped chewing.

Poppy looked to her papa then to her ma. "But, Papa—"

"Quiet. No words at the table," Hugh said.

Hildy's eyes grew hard, flints of stormy sky beneath heaped white clouds. "But she must wear a work frock, not such fine clothing."

"Yes, she will need a work frock. But she will put that fine dress away for her wedding one day," Hugh said.

"Surely she will have outgrown it by then," Georgie said.

"Yes, outgrowd it. 'Course she will. The dress sha's be put to use now. By me."

"But it fits me now and…" Poppy glimpsed Hildy's dumpling soft figure.

"Of course, if Hildy wishes to have it, she should," Georgie said. "Perhaps you have a dress in trade until I can sew a replacement?" Georgie knew Poppy still had her work frock from the tavern, but Georgie wanted to make Hildy give up something.

"Oh, I have me a work gown put away." Hildy held out her hand to Poppy.

Poppy touched the sage green ribbon in her hair. Hildy had not coveted that, at least. Poppy climbed the staircase with Hildy.

There was the wisp of slippered feet on the upper floorboards, the twirl of the fine white dress between the cracks, Hildy spinning in her new frock.

Clara sat unmoving in her chair, her eyes following the dress like a signal flag through the floorboards. Her papa nodded in satisfaction of their obedience to Hildy's wishes, rapped his fork on the table, then resumed eating. Clara burned. The dress was hers. The traveler had gifted it to her in the tavern gangway.

In the tavern gangway, the traveler had borne the embroidered dress in his arms like a limp child. He called Clara's service dress "shabby," unpinned her apron, and plucked free the service dress laces. Clara shrugged off the dress, standing in her petticoat, jump, and shift. He declared these underpinnings "unremarkable." She followed his movements, unable to make sense of him. He acted like a dressmaker, particular, though he fussed out of doors, not in a shop, and it was well past shopkeepers' hours. She blinked, and the embroidered dress fluttered to life in his arms, a night moth drying its wings on a porch rail. He shimmied the new dress over her head. She studied his face. He admired the dress on her even though the fit was too large.

The traveler was shy, as if he knew Clara understood him to be something other than a man. He did not appear surprised when she said, "You are the devil," though he scoffed. As he tied the green ribbon in her hair, he tried to explain the idea of second cousins, common grandparents, generational relations, but it confused her.

"We, the devil and I, are family like any other," he concluded. He introduced himself as Baron Saturday.

Then she understood him to be related to the devil because her ma's side of the family held titles, like baron, and duke, and earl, one more important than the next until you could trace the highest title to the king. Clara knew titles were inherited, like she had inherited the chaplet of red Hobblebush berries from her grandmother. Though it was still a knotty concept for her to grasp; the whole idea of family was counter to Clara's notion of the devil as a lone wicked force.

Dried pale-green foam streaked across Baron Saturday's jacket hem, a sign of a horse wiping its workout exhaustion upon its dismounted rider. Baron Saturday told Clara about his horses. He started drawing her a map to see his horses, but Obadiah Bray called out for her. Baron Saturday hastily pinned the half-drawn map to the back of Clara's dress and disappeared into the night before Mr. Bray found her in the gangway and led her back inside the tavern.

Her papa finished his breakfast, so Clara was allowed to leave the table. Behind the partition to where she and Poppy slept, Baron Saturday's map lay atop the bundle of the old clothes her ma had pulled from Buttermilk Falls. Her ma had called the map a "note" when she had unpinned it from the embroidered dress when Poppy wore it. Clara unfolded the map. The scribbles looked like madness, but the map was only unfinished, and it could get her partway to Baron Saturday's horses if she were keen to remember where to start.

At the breakfast table, Georgie felt Black Vy's stare and abruptly looked up. Black Vy tapped the rim of her teacup. The women did not yet know how to read each other. Black Vy picked up a black ledger and quill, shoving her dishes aside to make room. She nodded to the mess of plates. Georgie gathered the dishes. Black Vy wrote in the ledger and ticked off numbers. She asked Hugh, "I's to take off for the lossin' of Balor and Brace, the wagon and pork?"

"Not yet. Give the men more time to find them." He put on his hat and went outdoors.

Black Vy wrote a few brief entries, then closed the ledger and went into the yard for butchering.

Hugh had never given control of the accounting to Georgie even though all the money they had was the trust payments from her family's faltering wealth and Georgie's prize swine money. Hugh and Georgie had stayed in England long enough to garner three trust payments. Other family members were to keep receiving life-long allowances, but Uncle William had written Georgie a letter indicating that the parting sums would stop soon after she landed on American shores because, "I presume the life expectancy of any Englishwoman in the wilds of the New World to be no longer than eighteen months." Uncle William would divide and direct Georgie's remaining allowance to other relations entitled to the trust funds. After more than a century of spending with a history of ill-chosen tenants to farm the estate, the family cash reserves were low, so one of their own leaving the country was reason enough to cut her out so other family members could increase their annual incomes. Georgie conceded losing the cash because Uncle William was funding the launch of her new husband's land venture in America out of his own allowance and savings as well as loaning the prize swine money to Hugh.

Uncle William had provided provisional funding for Hugh's land development in America outwardly as a gesture of good will for the newlyweds. He sought to prove himself as magnanimous. It would be the foremost talk among other gentry in Shropshire for the better part of a year, the risk and novelty of investment in New World land ventures regarded as a fashionable sophistication. After the American War of Independence, Georgie's family were among British citizens whose land grants in Florida became null. It was a point of pride and nationalism for her uncle to get a piece of North America back in the family, to reclaim land he felt they were owed. This was a respectable scrim for defending his decision to invest. William beamed to fellow gentry that his short-term investment had direct bearing on the influx of coin in the isolated New World. Inwardly, William fretted for ways to earn money for the family and having no skills for doing so was easily persuaded by this brash American woodsman that if successful, the development would prove a rich source of tourist revenue—income for Hugh and Georgie and extra to send overseas to repay the Christie side of the family and boost their coffers for years to come.

William's ancestor who built the Shropshire estate, Goat Willow Hall, in 1586 was the last family member to earn an income, he a prominent lawyer also having the good fortune to not only inherit land from his family but to marry two heiresses. The surplus inheritance of land and money passed down the line until heirs bungled the management of funds and overspent. The family's welfare now depended on the success of the blasting effort at the falls.

Georgie stacked the last dish, dried her hands, and heard Poppy and Hildy still above stairs. Black Vy was outside, elbows deep in a pig carcass. There was no sign of Hugh in the yard. Clara had wandered off. Georgie sat at the table and opened the ledger. Before Hugh had discarded her to Auntie Wemple's, Georgie had snuck looks at the accounting ledger. Hugh had used most of the money to pay wages to the crew, and now he was using the same money to pay wages to Black Vy. She remembered Hugh as a profligate disburser of her uncle's money. The first expenses were paid to the saddler and the lorimer for leather and iron horse tack—bridles, saddles, whips, brushes, combs, collars, cruppers, surcingles, breastplates, reins, riding boots, crops, harnesses, four-in-hand reins, longlines, snafflebits, martingales, spurs, and from the lorimer also a half hogshead of Madeira. The next purchases were fees to the farrier for pulling thorns from and repairing cracked hooves, to the apothecary for liniment for inflamed pasterns, to the wainwright for the acquisition of a gig and wagon and cutter, and to the curer for several ropes of tobacco. Hugh reserved the rest of her uncle's money to pay the regular buying of household consumables, candles, tools, cider. But these expenses were few.

Hugh was an expert at bartering; most Americans dealt that way because no one claimed to have coins. There were hardly any coins exchanged. Most people stored away coins they acquired because of different monies in circulation: shillings; Dutch rix-dollars; Russian kopecks; silver dollars, halves, quarters, eighths. No one knew the worth of anything. Some passing through New York called a shilling a Spanish reale—and the locals pretended not to recognize the coin as having value even though it was identical to what they held in their hand as a shilling. Some shopkeepers reckoned their wares and wages by the English system of pence, shilling, pound. But there was a shortage of money, and Hugh traded with almost everyone. People simply walked off when demands for cash were made.

Hugh could not trade with the men for wages, though. Georgie ran her finger down the wages column. Hugh had not shorted the men's wages to pay Black Vy. And he had doubled up on purchases of black powder. He would expend her uncle's payout money by the end of the season, at the brink of winter. It was plain in the entries. She paged through the ledger. There wasn't a notation for the purchase of Black Vy, only wages paid to her, the same rate of frequency for each man on the crew, but less than half the amount. There were no miscellaneous entries, so Hugh was not trying to conceal her purchase within the bookkeeping. So how had he obtained her?

Georgie reached blank pages. The last entry was Black Vy's of that morning, notes on the extra black powder. In the back of the ledger, there was a sleeve that contained the deed for the land. Behind the deed was a letter. It was addressed to Mrs. Georgiana Christie Tepper. Georgie blinked at her name. The letter's seal was broken. She unfolded the letter and recognized Aunt Emmeline's penmanship—widely looped vowels and narrowly spaced words—stating if Georgiana returned to England to the family estate by a certain date, her allowance would be reinstated, but she must show herself in person; written replies signed by Georgiana herself or her husband would be presumed forged, thereby invalid. The letter was dated October, 1800, the previous fall. Hugh had received the letter while Georgie had been at the tavern.

Emmeline was a respected figure in the Christie family, the most plainspoken of the matriarchs. The family line had passed for centuries through the females after a male heir had spawned a curse by wrongly accusing a valet of murder. After the trial, the family had a wobbly year of conspicuous spending—new chimneys, five hundred head of deer in two large game preserves. Then they suffered years of retrenchment—letting staff go, lighting their own fires. Before the curse, the family name was Chichester. Then, instead of having to sell the estate, the family used the wife's inheritance to pay off debt, so her son, the male heir, took her name. The family name became Christie. The Christie women took charge, winning a jointure for the freehold estate, owning Goat Willow Hall outright even after the death of the male heir. The women's possession would never expire. And the descending Christie women took seriously the management of Goat Willow Hall, nodding obediently at male figureheads as they bloviated in public, but quashing them in the private dens of their family trust meetings. For generations, no male had finished a complete sentence when closed-door discussions of Goat Willow Hall were conducted.

When Hugh and Georgie's marriage agreement had been drawn up, Hugh had demanded the conditions be sorted between men. He had ignored the Christie women. Despite Hugh's disregard, Emmeline had agreed with her brother William to fund the New York venture with limited payments. Yet Emmeline's letter spelled out great unrest in the family, a split of decision between the matriarchs and the men. As a conservative faction, the matriarchs voted to recant all funding for Hugh's land development in the New World. The men supported further payments, smoked in their chairs at night mentally stamping flags in the dirt of the American wilds. Emmeline aligned with the males; she saw the payoff of the risk of sending more funds to further civilize American land. But her stance seemed shaky, easily persuaded to the other side with any whiff of indication to do so from Georgiana. The matriarchs intended to block more of the family money unless provided with validity of a flourishing enterprise. All of them, Emmeline included, wanted a detailed report of the progress of the blasting. And they wanted the ledgers of accounting audited, down to every last dribbet. Furthermore, Emmeline hinted that the matriarchs had staunchly decided for calling back money already paid. Someone had seized the crow-quill from Emmeline's hand and written in a slantwise, bold script: *Were the falls now accessible for a visit of inspection?* The matriarchs were writing to land development agents and inspectors in Virginia to gauge their available dates for travel to New York. The letter closed with a desire for her aunt to be reunited with her dear and loyal niece, an implicit plea for a female family member to align with her in solidarity and to alleviate her doubt. Emmeline was foremost concerned for sound decision-making regarding the family fortune. Her aunt said surely by now Georgiana had had enough of the squalor of the New Wilds, but did not state an outright lack of confidence in Hugh's character or efforts.

Georgie worried the matriarchs had every intention to make Hugh provide clear testimony of progress. Any prudent financier would do the same. Though the matriarchs seemed primed for attack since Hugh had disregarded their authority for deciding terms for the original binder. Emmeline's letter hinted that William's voice in the matter was diminished to the point of having no vote. The estate was in additional decline, the family money further depleted.

Why hadn't Hugh sent her back to England to claim the allowance? The cost of passage would've been worth the sum received. Perhaps he thought she would stay, would never return to him and their daughters in America, would take a controlling seat in the family interests, establishing herself free and clear of him, thereby dooming his blasting efforts.

Georgie had collected few coins at the tavern. When she first worked there, she had hopes of running off with a sack load, but the men were fed and given ale as part of their work agreement. The men never had a bill for food or drink, so Georgie rarely transacted cash. The locals bartered with her for food and drink, bringing in baskets of apples and berries and eggs. Noord Boorsma reconciled her books each week to account for any tourist revenue. Sometimes the men gave Clara or Poppy a coin for a smile and a dance, but that was infrequent. Georgie gave up hope of access to a cash stream. She had written her aunt for money but suspected Mr. Boorsma had intercepted her letter on Hugh's instruction because she had never received a reply. And now Georgie saw that Emmeline's letter did not acknowledge Georgie's plea for cash.

Georgie leafed through the earlier pages of the accounting. Black Vy could form symbols and numbers. Black Vy had managed the ledger, kept it current, for almost a year. Hugh had taught her basic accounting. Georgie ran her finger down and across columns, figuring the arithmetic. It was mostly accurate; in the earlier months, Hugh had notated a few corrections with his hash marks and initials, but as the weeks progressed, these amendments became fewer. The early entries used crude symbols for wages, taxes, salt, whiskey. Then words began appearing: *black powder, wicks,* and *bed.* Hugh had taught her to write. Black Vy had kept the ledger detailed and current to prove the solvency of Hugh's blasting effort. But any inspector would demand to see blasted pathways and piles of rubble to justify these expenses no matter how accurately the books had been kept.

Clara followed into the woods Jeptha Buell and Isaac Coe, another pair of men sent by her papa to retrieve Balor and Brace and the wagon. The trail cut a downward spiral, so she hung back at the turns, crouching then darting ahead, making no more noise than the birds scattering skyward from the men's loud song. They didn't know she followed them. They laughed and smoked. They weren't truly looking for the wagon, and they would keep the horses at a distance with their noise. But they did stop and take off their hats and turn around a few times at the narrow wagon trail between heavy bands of forest, their faces peering low as they crouched to the dirt. They exchanged a few words, picked up a broken leather strap, walked to the far edge of the trees and examined several fresh breaks in the branches, as if the wagon had been whipped loose and dragged a few rods before the horses broke free of their harness. At the picnic, Mr. Bell had not unharnessed the horses.

The men didn't follow the evidence further. She waited until they were out of ear shot toward the homestead until she emerged from hiding. There were wheel ruts and drag marks and hoof prints on the road. She tucked into the woods, near a moss-covered clearing ringing a black bog. On the bright green moss were the two barrels, the staves broken open like fallen petals from a flower. The pork was mostly scavenged. Some of it had been dragged, the glistening oil trail winding across the moss. There was a fallen tree, the roots lifted from the ground, cakey with dried mud. Her back prickled. She backed toward the wagon road, keeping her eye on the bog—its surface as still as spent bathwater. She jumped as a pinecone the size of a leather shoe plopped into the vat, the ripples fanning. Then the dark scum of the bog came alive. Skaters stalked their legs from above, and fish trolled their lips and frogs blinked their eyes from below. The surface poppled as if a light rain were pattering down, the creatures resuming motion, any threat they had sensed now gone.

There was birdsong, and the moss was sweetly green. A few more steps to reach the wagon road. There was a glint in the leaves. It was not the wet oil of the packed hogs. She ran forward and scraped away leaves. It was the side of her papa's wagon but edged in gold and pale lavender and garnet-dark red stones. Someone had tucked it away as if to resume the repair and embellishment later. A sound in the distance skipped across the bog. Clara jumped to see Balor and Brace—bridles and girths and straps loose, slapping their hides—dash into the far trees.

"But where did you see them?"

"Mayhaps I did not see them after all."

Hugh sat Clara at the table, slapping the Bible in front of her, paging back and forth to find the exact verse of obedience he had in mind. "You will sit and read until you decide to state where you saw the horses. Then you will state—in thoughtful, artful sentences—the value of a wagon and two horses to this family." He left her alone at the table.

Clara slid both hands down each page of the splayed book. She stared at the words for some time then slumped in her chair and rested the side of her face in her hand. Her throat stopped up as if her papa had set two pails full of supper before her and her chore was to fork each bite into her mouth until the pails were empty. She walked outdoors to find him at his wood splitting. "They were near the new moss and the bog, off the wagon road, in the part of the trees that glow red in the distance."

He capped the top of her head with his palm, then slammed his axe into its stump. "Walk with me to the water and we'll drink. And you can tell me the value of horses and a wagon."

They walked, and her papa waded into the river and drank several scoops from his hand. Clara stayed on the bank, forming her words. As her papa dunked his head into the current, Clara saw the seat of the wagon bob down the river.

Her papa stood, water dripping off the spikes of his hair, beading off his beard. "Tell me the value of the wagon and horses, child."

The wagon seat floated behind him, bumping out of sight across the rocky shallows. She did not say anything, and he wiped the water from his face.

He pointed to the shanty. "Back to your seat and Bible until you can tell me."

Jeptha Buell and Isaac Coe sat inside their shared tent. They had taken one of the jars from the sugaring room, leaving an obvious gap in the orderly rows, and smuggled the jar inside their tent. Isaac overturned the jar, and out spilled a few dead bees. The two men had built a small collection of found items, mostly teeth and bones and shells. They added the broken harness piece to the pile and stashed the jar beneath Jeptha's bear pelt. They agreed to decide later if they would halve the harness fragment to wear as phylacteries from their belts to shield them from misfortune.

The yard was clear of men. They had left their tents and cooking fires, scattered into the woods for lumbering and clearing. Poppy peered into Gideon Bell's tent. There was nothing personal or revealing about the effects: a lantern, a chest, heavy woolens, a camp bed. But these were objects he lay upon and held, and she sat reverently on the chest, breathing in the tang of a man who didn't often wash, who didn't feel well. The odor buffered against the sagging, yellowed tent roof. When she had been riding in the wagon behind him, a different smell had trailed off him, one of smoked woodcock, the strongest flavored game bird she had ever eaten. She lifted the lantern glass, dusted its smoke splotches with her finger. This is what he lit for warmth, for comfort. This was not a place he planned to stay. How long until he was well enough to venture back to his own home, to wherever he kept belongings he treasured, that held memories?

A wandering pig nosed behind her, and she startled. It lifted its nose, snuffled the dirt, and trotted off. She quickly exited Gideon Bell's tent.

After wiping clean the breakfast dishes, Georgie moved to tidy Hugh's refuse, the objects left in his wake: books, hankies, walnut shells, a brass-handled eye scope. Then she stopped; they were no longer her concern. She stood on the porch staring at the top of the falls, then walked toward the pull of the water's heavy roar. It spilled white and frothing, a wide channel bloated with the recent rains. She hiked her skirt, descending the rugged trail to the river. The cool spray from the water soaked her bodice and arms. The rock was slippery, and she hung onto its crags.

The first sight of Hugh had made her eyes water. His spirit was sheer

fire. She had submitted to the habit of unattached ladies who sat their
free afternoons with prominent bachelors of Shropshire. The dreary
nibblings of drawing room tea, politely attentive as the men eagerly
demonstrated their talents. One afternoon, Wesley Tracey Taylor
addressed her with plaintive song. Yet Georgie's focus lapsed out the
window. There was movement on the hill. A runaway horse with rider.
No, there was control through a barreling gallop, one of her uncle's
white stallions, racing long strides across the green slope. The rider wore
no coat, was bareheaded, his hair loose, his chest and forearms brown.
He held the reins in one hand, slapping the neck of his mount, urging it
to full speed. She walked to the window for a closer view. This situated
her alongside Wesley, which made his voice submerge to plummy bell-
ing. He dropped to one knee, head tilted heavenward, sending his song
in divine thanks at what he read as her gesture of surrender. The horse
drummed closer, the thwack of mud flying, the night's rain not yet dried
up in the gardens. The horse was Spumador.

The rider called out to spectators on the lawn as they stiffly watched.
The rider was all barbarous verve and brawn. A wild man turning,
galloping away to the edge of the distant horizon, tearing up the lawn
in his wake. Wesley had not broken song, his voice aimed laterally at
Georgie to engage her attention. But Georgie held her gaze, waiting for
the speck of the rider's form to return.

The rider raced back at terrific speed, hair and shirtsleeves punched
back by the wind, storm clouds roiling low. He stopped at the crowd,
touching his heels to Spumador's flanks, eliciting a pawing rear from
the animal. The horse was spent. Foam dripped off its muzzle, and
dark patches stained its flanks. A groom rushed forward, grabbing the
reins below the bit. The rain splattered down. But the rider drove his
heels into the horse's sides at which Spumador reared, snorted, and the
reins tore from the groom's hands. The wild man was not a horse thief;
he urged Spumador to circle the gardens, roots and mud at the hedges
flying, spraying. He was not a servant; he had no formal coat nor boots.
He was not a grocer delivering goods to the kitchen; he bore no cart
laden with greens. He was not a soldier taking goods for the cause; his
bearing was hunched. He was not a farmer; he was bold. He was not
an escaped prisoner; his chest and shoulders and legs were well-formed
and robust. He rode every ounce of power in this horse, goaded the
animal against its training to show that it knew more than control and

comportment. He was not British; he didn't have to speak for Georgie to know that.

He was, in fact, not responding to the tense shouts of the grooms circling him. He stopped the animal and grinned and spoke to the grooms just as Wesley closed his song on a full-throated, protracted note. In the blessed silence that followed, Georgie heard the man. He was not of this kingdom or hillside. Was he of the jungle? Was he a circus performer? The grooms lunged again for the reins, but the man struck his thighs against the stallion's belly, and Spumador with front-ward strikes of its hooves fended off the grooms' lurching hands. The horse was no longer white. Its coat was spotted, blackened, soaked with a sweat crude erupted from its ancestral memory of wild, winged moth-ers. The rider wailed a guttural cry, and the horse leapt away, dashing through the circle of stable hands toward the hillside. The gardens were torn up as if by badgers. The man was American.

One of the grooms shouted, "The American has stolen a horse!"

Hugh became known as the American who taught the Christie's horse to perform Iroquois pony tricks. For months after Hugh had departed, the grooms had to slap Spumador's muzzle to curb its tenden-cy to break into a loose canter, show the whites of its eyes, and veer toward the horizon.

In his days at Goat Willow Hall, Hugh had conducted himself without formality, busting into rooms unannounced, grabbing the arms of other gentlemen in greeting, interrupting with his loud voice and entirely sun-browned and radiant face. He expressed all of his joy and seriousness in his features, not having a scrim of reserve for polite interaction. There was not a railing, bench, nor chair back upon which he did not rest his boots. He had an unfiltered, exuberant appetite for food and drink and for engagement with others. He had no manners, but a rowdy grace that commanded every room. He seemed not aware of the construct of English aristocracy. He was ungovernable. He had no thought to alter his behavior for them, and this charmed Georgie as her pale suitors continued to practice chamber music in the corners.

Hugh had been earnest and plainspoken when requesting funding from her uncle. He sat across from William at his writing desk, and instead of speaking, he handed William a letter of intent:

Monies. For men. To blast through Rock and Logs. A crew of Dedi-cated men to Forge a way through the wild terrain of Buttermilk

Falls, New York, America. Sustenance, medicking supplies, horses,
woolens, pelts, shelter. Powder. Black Powder. For Blasting. Monies
to hire and keep Strong, Reliable men. Men of Service and Health
and Fortitude. Let there be no Obstructions to inhibit any king's
carriage from pulling right up to the gloried High Falls so the king
may thrust his hand out the carriage window to feel the fall's mists.

Hugh had anticipated the question of why he didn't request provi-
sion of capital from his own government. And when William asked this
very question, Hugh handed him a second prepared note:

The American ambassador to France has for years tried to fund
Expeditions Westward to find Routes by Water to the Pacific. Any
resources shall fund Westward Expansion. The ambassador has no
mind for our Northern Outpost.

It took little to persuade William, though he restrained his response
to conceal his desperation. There were family relations of all ranks for
whom William was responsible. None of them had benefitted from
Georgie's cousin's place at Court. Many men in the family remained
ship hands; they had not been promoted to masters of their own ships
as the family thought they might after the niece's appointment. The
Court position would not save the family estate; it would bestow honor,
relief from the swine-rearing scandal, but scant material gain. The
family was left to innovate ways to increase its income by any means
possible, including risky ventures in the New World.

On the ship passage back to America, Hugh had returned with the
warm body of Georgie, a stolen brick from Goat Willow Hall he had
chiseled off the front gate, and an agreement of funding. As he held
the swaying bunk ropes to keep balance from the pitch of ocean swells,
Hugh spoke long conversations in his head with Ledyard and Michaux,
the explorers funded by American statesmen to penetrate the western-
most continent. For weeks in the dark steerage deck, Hugh huddled as
Ledyard would have as a prisoner in Irkutsk, his overland route denied.
Hugh touched the wood of the ship, imagining Michaux's ship running
aground and wrecking apart, Michaux flailing to save his botanical specimens from ruin. These men had failed. Hugh sang to keep his new
bride cheerful and to keep faith in his blasting endeavor buoyant.

Georgie walked among the high walls cut by falling water. All sky was blotted out. She was enclosed in the cathedral sanctuary of crashing water, crouched on the flat rock lining the river's edge, water sheeting down the cascades of graduated rock. Mist hung suspended over its flow. A voice called from the ridge. It was Black Vy. A wood-swine appeared at her skirt hem, its snout tracing a scent on the rock, its ears falling forward, bobbing lightly over its eyes. Loose stones disturbed by its hoof patterings showered down.

"Fetch some eel for supper. Hurry on, now." Black Vy threw an oilskin bag to Georgie. It landed heavily, weighted with something. Georgie unlaced its neck and peered inside: a small baton, evidently her weapon for clubbing supper.

Black Vy shooed at Georgie. "Go on, woman. Get to some use." She turned from the ridge. The hog lifted its snout and followed.

Georgie tied her heavy skirt between her legs and walked downstream past the white-tipped current to where the amber water slowed. She waded into the creek's lazy tug. She slung the limp bag over her shoulder, griped the baton, minced her steps in the shallows to shuffle out the eel. She curled her feet onto the palm-sized rocks as she proceeded, teetering unsteadily. The eel scattered at her steps, and she bashed the baton several times splashing herself, striking only rock.

The water was cold; she waded back to land, sitting on the cedar needles blanketing the banks, cupping her pink feet for warmth. The sun lit the tawny water. There was a low haze of darting mayflies and the frequent rise of trout. Where the sun sliced to the river's bottom, she spied inky black flashes of eel.

She lay back, her dress hem and toes grazing the water. She thought of Captain Lewis, their friend from the Whiskey Insurrection seven years ago. They had heard rumors he went to Lake Erie, traveling in Great Lakes territory, more vast and wild than upper New York.

"And what were your comforts and nightly rituals, sir?" She asked the question out loud.

He might answer *fire and hard tack and picking bones clean from fresh meat* and maybe *tobacco*, but they probably ran out on their return home. Maybe he had found someone to talk to on the trail or a star to fix his gaze upon as it wandered its seasonal course.

Captain Lewis had been recently appointed the new president's secretary, marked by a distinguished portrait in the newspaper, the stiff coat and jabot about his neck. He must have changed so after his voyage back from the Great Lakes, scraping off scruffy whiskers and shedding buckskin acquired from a Native. She ground her back and legs and hair into the cedar needles. Any spell she might have cast over him during the Whiskey Insurrection would by now be broken.

She spied a deep pool underneath a tree, its trunk tipping low over the water, the bank partially eroded from its roots. Water seeped down the hillside, meeting the river's flow, forming the pool. The water eddied slumbrously. She inched sideways out the tree's length, then laid on her belly. Her fingertips disturbed the water's surface, and she peered closer. She couldn't see far into the depths but knew the eel must favor a spot like this, the shadows, the fresh influx of spring water. Her eye caught a flash of metal in the pool. She plunged her hand into the cold, stretching over the top of a tin. She pulled, but the tin was weighted, anchored. She could feel a ridge at the top; it had a lid, but it was fastened tight, or so long submerged it was rusted shut. She was not strong enough to maintain her balance on the tree and haul up the box with one hand.

Before Hugh had dragged her out of the house, she had been stashing away coins, storing them in a tin cache buried near the riverbank. It had been only a handful of coins, but a start to gaining freedom from Hugh.

The location of her cache had been considerably downriver, buried in soil several rods from the water, but it wasn't uncommon for seemingly stable banks to sink and slide. The men in the tavern had talked about the rains and flooding displacing sugaring kettles and a whole litter of pups upstream. Things weren't always supplanted downstream. She recalled the weather of the last year, inventorying the freeze and melt cycles. Through the spring, the men had provided detailed reports of the weather damage at the falls. The grounds had been saturated by the rains, and embankments had washed away. Low fields had been underwater for weeks, and even trees rooted into high ground had been dislodged. Her tin could have shifted by the rains. Yet someone could have thrown the empty tin into the river after pocketing its contents. She slid herself backward toward the bank. She would have to return later by boat to retrieve it.

She continued downstream to a stone bridge that cast a shadow over shallows, a promising spot to snare eel without their having the advantage of a hiding pool.

The water hushed as its flow diminished, a bare trickle through the river stones. The rocks were dried pale, exposed in the sun. Georgie approached the bridge, a graceful arc over the river, framed on either bank with sturdy rock-studded buttresses. At the shadow cast by the bridge, the water deepened to Georgie's ankles. She crouched and over-turned stones, uncovering ghostly white crayfish that scuttled under new rock havens. The shiny blade of an eel back broke the surface of the water. She stumbled forward with her club but lost her balance before striking.

Behind her, she heard a splash. She shielded her eyes against the sun, blinking upstream. Then something whizzed over her head. An apple bounced on the rocky riffle. The apple rolled, caught in the deeper water, and floated toward her.

"Is someone there?" she called to the stone arc. The wall of the bridge was high enough to hit most men at hip level. But someone could be crouching, out of view to anyone down on the river. The current pulled against her ankles. She had to move soon or her feet would be too numb to move at all.

She waded to underneath the bridge where the water crept up to her calves. The dark stone underside of the bridge danced with reflected light from the water. An apple dropped, splashed, bobbed, then floated past her. She emerged into the light.

"I will never catch eel if you continue to frighten them away, child. Show yourself, and let this prank be done."

Another apple sailed toward her face, hurled with considerable force. She dodged it then stumbled toward the dry bank, the club clenched in her teeth. This side dropped precipitously into a deep pool, and she was soon swimming. But it was not a far distance. She threw the oilcloth bag high onto the bank, then grabbed a root to haul herself to the full view of the bridge. Water sheeted off her skirt, tightly binding her legs. She wrung out her sodden skirt, her feet stinging with cold. She looked down the empty length of the bridge. No one was there.

There was movement behind her. She curled her hand around the club still between her teeth.

Something struck the back of her head. She pitched forward but caught herself. Then her head was jerked back. She was clapper-clawed to the ground, but she whirled to face the man, twisting out of his grip. She staggered back, her feet and legs slow with cold. She did not recognize him, his red face, the wild black hair that hung untied. His eyes glittered green then darkened. He lunged for her, but she thrust the club, smacking him hard between the eyes. He fell to the dirt.

She was stunned when he got back up for more. "Whatever could you want?"

"You hunt my property." He roughly pulled her close, stripping the club from her grip.

He had been swimming, though not in stream water. His hair and shirt were caked in bog mud, and he stank of it.

He yanked her head back by the hair, pinning her jaw to the sky. His breath traced her throat.

She rutted her elbows at his ribs and tore away, stumbling into the woods, advancing a few steps before her wet skirts tripped her. He caught her bare ankle, flipped her over. Her legs scooted, heels digging into the cedar needles. But he had his whole body on her now, and he bit into the side of her neck. Her sight pinholed black as he latched onto a chokepoint of vessels. He bit into another spot, the pain jolting her, and she felt sickness as his body relaxed onto hers, his face buried into her neck, his hands like manacles on her wrists.

There was an approaching sound of barking. Rifle fire split the air. The man pinned her pelvis with his hips, but he raised his head, scouting for the direction of the noise. The dog barreled in and leapt at his throat, the force pitching him off Georgie. The dog straddled the man, its jaw clamped on the man's windpipe, a low steady burble in the dog's throat. The dog's tongue stuck against the man's whiskered neck.

The man choked for breath. He gripped the fur of the dog's ruff, and the dog let out a sharp warning, its teeth dancing on the man's neck. The man set his fingers on the dog's gums, pried open the dog's jaws, unwrenching its bite. He struck a blow to the dog's ear, and the dog rolled away.

A man with a rifle ran toward them. The attacker was on his feet, his arms hanging, palms spread as if ready to grapple. He faced the rifleman, locked eyes with him, blood from his neck soaking his shirt. Georgie backed against a tree, the dog barking between her and the attacker.

The rifleman packed his gun, fiddling with the powder flask, spilling most of it. He wet the rod on his tongue—and the attacker ran off, the dog close at his heels. Then the dog stopped, hearing something in the trees, and ran after it, abandoning its chase of the attacker.

The man and dog disappeared in separate directions. The man had an easy path through widely spaced cedars. "Who goes?" the rifleman asked Georgie.

"Who goes you?" Yet she recognized him. The man with several dogs guarding his shanty.

"Name of Dewitt Otis Lipson." He eyed her without a tip of his hat. "I own this land, m'triss."

"Yes, I know you, sir. Then who was he?"

"Naught seen him 'afore."

"Aren't you going to pursue him?"

"Say again?"

Georgie thrust her hand in the direction the man had fled.

"No, Jacks will serve him up."

"But the dog ran toward something else."

"Yes, I seen that. Damn dog. But Jacks'll scent back." He eyed her neck. "Are you well, m'triss?"

"No. Yes. I suppose I am well." She clamped her hand to the blood.

"He bit you? And was to have his way with you? Is that all?"

"Is that not enough?"

" 'Tis enough. I meant the blood." He untied his cravat. She pressed it to her neck, her pulse throbbing through the cloth.

"What be your business on my land?"

"I was to fetch eel for supper." Georgie felt a wave of nausea and bent over.

"What is your name, m'triss?"

"Mrs. Georgiana Tepper."

"Ah, Tepper from upriver at the top of the falls. I remember. I have not seen you 'round for a time." Mr. Lipson whistled a low, short peal for Jacks. He tipped his hat to her. "Mrs. Georgiana Tepper from the top of the falls, I shall escort you back to the safety of your family."

He whistled again, and Jacks came racing at them. The dog panted and wagged his tail, looking into his master's face. Mr. Lipson ran his hand along the dog's coat, checking for injuries. He took the dog's mouth in his gloved hands and touched a red gape on his gum.

"Bastard took a tooth."

"But the man did not flee that way."

"Must've turned course and pursued the dog. Damned misget."

Jacks drew his face away and licked his lips then resumed his open-mouthed pant. He glanced at Georgie then to his master's face. He trotted to Georgie and nudged her hand with his nose then thrust his nose against the knife in her apron pocket. She had forgotten about the weapon.

She grabbed a handful of the dog's ruff. "Where is he, boy?"

The dog whined and lay at her feet, his tongue sideways, white-flecked.

"Jacks," Mr. Lipson addressed his dog. Jacks rose, ears pricked. "This lady must fetch back supper." He swung his arm toward the river. "Hie!"

Jacks dashed to the water, returning with a wriggling eel in his mouth, and dropped it at Mr. Lipson's feet. The eel writhed its head and tail, thrashing in the needles. With the stock of his rifle, he stunned it lifeless.

"Am I invited to supper?" Mr. Lispon asked.

Georgie nodded. "Why, certainly, sir."

"Hie!" He again threw his arm toward the water, and Jacks tore off to retrieve a second eel. He thread their heads through a sharpened twig, and they walked the path upriver, Jacks nosing the slippery tails jiggling lifeless at Mr. Lipson's hip.

Jacks led them into the yard, the hogs squealing and running for the forest cover. The yard was empty of men though it was time for making supper fires.

Clara ran out, eyes bright at the sight of Jacks. She knelt before him, burying her face in his chest fur. "Oh, Ma, a hound dog come to visit."

"Let him be, now," said Mr. Lipson. "He's to rest. Fetch him water, kitling."

But Jacks had already started lapping in the hogs' water trough, and when he had enough, he settled on the porch, laying snug in the corner, his nose on his forelegs, his ears alert toward the woods. Clara sat by him at a distance, not taking her eyes off him.

Hildy leaned in the doorframe. "Stars, we has visitors for supper." She dipped into a playful curtsey. "Mr. Lipson."

He tipped his hat then raised the eel for her to see.

"Mother," Hildy addressed Georgie. "Mother, you mus' come fix me special."

Georgie cast her an icy stare. She peeled away the cloth dried against her neck. "I will tend to myself first."

"Lord. Those woodland beasts." Hildy's eyes twinkled at their visitor. "Mr. Lipson, do takes a seat on the porch. Himself and the men will be along." Then to Georgie: "Fetch out some whiskey."

Georgie took the gig of eels from Mr. Lipson. Black Vy was in the fire room, heavy-handing bread dough. Poppy lay tinder to build the cooking flame.

Hildy breezed past them, climbing the stairs to the sleeping garret. "One more for supper, and he's thirsty for a dram."

Georgie held the eels and the bloody cravat. The hearth blazed, and Black Vy mopped sweat off her neck.

"They's warm water for washing." Black Vy shot a look to Poppy. "Child, fetch the dram." Poppy carried the flour-dusted cup to the porch. "He do this to you?"

Georgie lowered her head and shook it. Her eyes filled with tears and her throat closed.

"Which one then?"

"Didn't recognize him."

Black Vy lifted Georgie's chin and wiped her eyes with a rag. She licked the rag and dabbed at Georgie's neck. "The bleeding stopped. Now you stop. It be done."

"Take you a nipperkin." Black Vy poured two more cups of whiskey and handed one to Georgie. She sipped, its warmth hovering in her throat, its vapor floating to her head.

"They best if not skinned." Black Vy stuck the eels onto a metal spit, chucking the twig onto the fire. "You let the skin crackle." She reached into the hearth, setting the spit across the hot spot.

Georgie dipped for water, filling a basin to wash herself and Hildy.

"Woman. Where my club and sack?"

Georgie had no answer.

Black Vy punched her bread dough. "And you come back right fine enough to walk and speak and blink back tears. Yet you be without my club and sack. What you do when harm hits you direct?"

Georgie climbed the steps to the sleeping garret.

Hildy pinned her hair, tying it low and loose, undoing it and sticking it high, pulling at the wisps about her temples. She had already changed into the white dress with blue embroidery, her upper arms and bosom bulging. Georgie strung the laces of a corset, but Hildy waved it away, touching the ribbon tied beneath her bust.

"Mother, which do you like?" Hildy's fist of hair switched between high and low knots.

"Did he tell you to address me that way?"

"He did. How you know, Mother?"

Georgie secured the hair low on the nape, tucking pins close to Hildy's scalp.

"You may call me missus. Mrs. Tepper, not mother. And you will address my elder daughter as Miss Tepper and my younger as Miss Clara."

"Sister, then." The low, flattering knot pleased Hildy, and her eyes shone in the mirror. "And as sisters, we sha's share secrets."

"There is no need."

"Oh, but do you remember the secret I was to tell you last?"

" 'Tis sisterly to share companionable silence."

"You sha's want to hear this secret." Hildy's hand covered Georgie's. "You know'd of the spirits in these woods?"

Georgie stopped pinning. "Yes."

"It be the story of how the spirits came to these woods. And my secret be thus."

Georgie touched her neck. It wept pink water.

Hildy frowned. "Oh, but your necks cannot fester. Come."

Hildy led Georgie to the bed. She wrung the cloth in the basin and cleaned Georgie's neck.

"Many ages ago—maybe more than one hundred!—the king of the Canadas half-Mohawk daughter married a full-on Indian, and they…"

"There has never been a king of the Upper and Lower Canadas."

"Yes, there were. Listen to the story. The king's daughter and her Oneida husband run off, and they hid right here, in the gorge in these rocks. This was Oneida Country, and they were well protected by the clan that adopted them."

"How could they hide there when the water levels rise so dramatically?"

"Hush, now, if you keep contrayin' me, I sha's not tell you my secret."

Georgie pressed the cloth onto her neck.

"Well, so's, the king never stopped fretting over his daughter gone and all, so he sent his troops year after year down here to search. Some tracker would send back furs to the king and would right say he seen a near-white looking woman. So the king kept his hopes alive, sending search parties. They destroyed many an Oneida village. But the country was so thick and winding, and the rock spaces tucked up so good for hiding, it took years for the daughter and her husband to be cornered by rifle warning. They hid up in Buttermilk Falls gorge all that time. And now, this is the secret part I sha's tell."

Hildy lifted the cloth and wiped the seepage from Georgie's neck.

"They hid in the rock ledge down the path from the house. There are scratches on the rock. And someone made a little pile of snail shells. Some nights when the moon is bright, I sneak from Hugh and climb down there to lay inside the hiding ledge. And from the inside, you see the curtain of dripping water, and I let it run over my hand, imagining the two of them hiding out together."

"Someone recently made a pile of shells?"

"No, they be leftover from the lovers hiding."

"That is not possible."

"Yes, 'tis. I say 'tis so." Hildy ran her fingertip over the abrasions on Georgie's neck. "Did he drag you? He take a rasp to your throat?"

"No, he did not drag me." She thought of when Hugh rasped his mount's hooves to roughen the surface before shodding. She shuddered.

"You sha's not tell him to spite me? About me sneakin' off?" Hildy took hold of Georgie's wrist. "Because he has no reason to believe you against me. I 'es his darlin'."

Georgie stiffened. "No, I would not want Hugh to worry for you. What happened to them? To the man and his wife?"

"Her father's men finally caught them unawares, and the woman flung herself in front of her husband's body to protect him, knowin' they would not shoot her 'cause she was the one precious thing to the king. So's she, with her hair a-bedraggled after years without a brush, she like a wild cat guarded the vital parts of her man, pressed against his heart and lungs and digestive coil and such, and climbed high to the very secret hiding holes the Oneida had carved out centuries ago, the gunfire from the king's men pinging alongside her husband's head, but he with his quick reflexes, being of wild blood, dodged them good, and the king never saw his daughter in the flesh and so's died soon after his troops returned with this story."

"She was a brave woman. Or loved him much. Did she not ever want to reunite with her father?"

"I believe she did. But she made her sacrifice to her husband as a woman should."

"Sometimes love is such a spell that the woman fights to stay. She forsakes any attachments to the past, no matter how dear. And the woman was not kidnapped, as you say, but fled and willingly kept to her husband's side."

Hildy squeezed the cloth, excited as Georgie opened to the story.

"My heart does break for her father," Georgie mused. "What a devoted man to send troops year after year for his daughter. Because only an old man would know how desperate she would be if love grew sour." She fingered the small tears in her flesh. "Might you have a shawl so I may cover this?"

"Yes, and you should 'cause it grows considerable much purple."

In the looking glass, Georgie saw the darkening bruise. "Has Samuel appeared to you?"

"Who?"

"Samuel, my father-in-law. Hugh's father."

"I not never heard the name nor Hugh speak of a father." She draped a shawl about Georgie's shoulders.

Margaret had followed Samuel, her husband, in the battles of the Revolution, washing soldiers' clothing. At Ticonderoga, she boiled the Green Mountain Boys' britches; at White Plains, she scrubbed stockings in the freezing swamp; after defeat at Fort Washington, against the shouted orders of the commanding officer, she ran onto the battlefield to strip weapons, belts, and boots from the dead as the bloodied and stunned surviving men watched her crawl back with the gear, the heavy smoke of gunfire volley rising blackly. Hours after, under the cover of night, Margaret sponged jackets in the Delaware River.

At Oriskany, Samuel was killed in the first strike of gun fire, an ambush. His body lay facedown in the brook where he and fellow militia had knelt to drink water. It had been a hot morning. Before retreating with the others to speed the wounded General Herkimer to safety, Margaret had rolled Samuel's dead body into a hollow in the ravine, obscured his corpse in rotted wood and leaves. Later, Loyalists uncovered him, stripped his clothing. His remains were ravaged and dragged by predators. As Iroquois returned to claim their dead and remove them from the battle site, they mistook Samuel's badly wrecked carcass for one of their own. After realizing their mistake, the Iroquois returned him to the battlefield among the putrid remnants of the fallen dead, the ruined crops smoking in the distance, the grain fields black ash.

Samuel's spirit was restless, and it wandered the forest at Oriskany.

The night after the battle, his body had been facedown in brush as his spirit gasped upright, the night chirping thickly. The wet downpour of the thunderstorm from the day steamed off the nettles. The other soldiers' ghosts lifted from their bodies, some hovering over the stream. The men coughed into the mud as their spirits pulled free. Others stayed low, calling out. Their leadership had retreated hours ago. Some of the dead men called heavenward and wept when no answer came down. They hummed in anguish as no one came to bury their bodies. Those men rose and ran into the woods, burrowed into wet leaves waiting to be claimed by any force. If not by God, then any stake to their soul was better than being forgotten and alone. The men who tunneled into the leaves dove deep, burying themselves head first so the flats of their feet were turned toward God, a message of supplication to other powers, these men who before death knew only life as labor for hire. The waters that had drowned them at the ambush gushed from their noses and mouths, tainting that section of the woods—the dirt morphed coppery; the evergreens gone orange like pumpkins ripening. The men were easy to find. Roaming dark entities roused them like flailing, half-choked fish, claiming them. Samuel did not join these men. He hid near where the Iroquois had returned his body, flew above the trees with a band of Native spirits who had also died at the battle.

As Margaret and Hugh settled in Utica and scouted land for purchase, Samuel's spirit inhabited the confluence of creeks in Oldenbarneveld. Hugh built the shanty at the falls, and he and Margaret slept underneath an overturned wagon. Samuel tried to join them but suffocated there. When Samuel had been alive, when Margaret still had her strong mind, even then she had never admitted to Samuel's generous character. She had a blind spot for her son's weaknesses even as he was a little boy. So each man, her son and her husband, had a hard time understanding themselves, their good and bad qualities filtered and distorted through Margaret's notions. But they became the muddled truths of each man's perception of himself. Even in death, Samuel fussed in the same space as his son. Samuel fled back to Oldenbarneveld to inhabit a makeshift grist mill without Hugh or Margaret ever seeing him. Georgie had been able to speak with Samuel's spirit since she had first arrived at the falls.

Georgie pulled the shawl higher, covering her neck. *I will go to Samuel,* she thought.

Voices gathered in the yard, men's bellowing laughter, and the squeal Clara made only when her father lifted her high to spin around.

Hildy checked herself in the looking glass. "Oh, he's want to dance and smoke tonight. We sha's have a time." She took Georgie's arm, and they climbed down the stairs. They heard the merriment rising, which would peak early then turn to heavy drinking and surly blows between the men.

Samuel had always called Georgie daughter, never held her English breeding against her even though he had fought Regulars at Ticonderoga. Georgie had only ever known him as his ghost. When she and Hugh had banked on the West Canada Creek after their long journey from New York harbor, Samuel stepped from behind a tree. Georgie yelped, blinking at him, frozen in place. Hugh snapped at her to calm down, to keep moving, to not startle at every twig snap. When she realized Hugh did not see anyone, Georgie fainted. She recovered to Hugh berating her. "You're a woman of the woods now. Get up." Samuel stomped to Hugh, flapping in his face like a bird trapped against window glass. Hugh waved his hand as if to swat a wasp. Hugh spoke through Samuel, ordering Georgie to stand. She wobbled to her feet. Samuel lamented to Georgie that his son would not see his ghost. "You used the word *ghost*," Georgie mustered to Samuel. Hugh told her to stop talking, for they had a long walk ahead. In that walk, as Georgie calmed with Samuel beside her, she had the clarity that Hugh did not want to see his father's ghost any more than he had wanted to be in the same room with him when alive. Which meant a force Georgie did not know in herself called Samuel's ghost forth. She plumbed for what that could be, determining the peals of her loneliness when near Hugh.

Samuel gripped her forearms, squeezing as if to determine her health after the long passage, assessing her reserve of strength for the rough life ahead. Georgie grabbed him back, pressing the brawn of his forearm, feeling the bony armature within. He was not gossamer or vapor, but a flesh-and-blood man. She had never before seen a ghost, didn't know if she believed in them, but her instinct told her Samuel was a ghost indeed. Everything else about her new home was disorienting, so the appearance of Samuel became another ruffle to accept. She was sad and rattled early in her marriage, understanding the saddle of loneliness would only spread—she and Hugh would not have even a few happy years together, and her closest attachment was a battered spirit.

Samuel did not enter the shanty that first night or ever, shy as he was of Margaret. As Georgie settled at the falls, Samuel would appear, fetching her a shawl when she spent cool evenings in the forest gathering beechnuts; pushing the last potato toward her with a wink when she had not conceived after six months of marriage; holding her as she shivered on cold sleigh rides; rising from the river and cuffing Hugh in the throat after Hugh doused her with cold river water, making her cry. And causing Hugh great confusion as he whirled about trying to locate an invisible attacker.

Samuel was kind toward Georgie's reserve, never chiding her formal manner. He ate heartily, grunting with pleasure as he tipped large mouthfuls of pumpkin and pork into his mouth with his knife blade. He seemed to swallow the whole blade with every bite. The crewmen ate like this and Georgie wondered how they managed not to slice open a cheek or tongue. She would admonish Samuel, push a spoon toward him as if he could suffer injury, then they would both remember that he could not, and they would somberly finish supper. This was before Margaret died, before Hugh forced Georgie away. Samuel had not visited Georgie at the tavern.

When growing up in England, her uncle William had been more of a business associate to Georgie than an uncle or paternal figure. Her uncle was remote, but she did not realize this until her evenings with Samuel. Uncle William bore a stern carriage with many trappings to insulate himself from others—a starched, tall hat that added a cubit to his already imperious height; gloves he did not wear but that he batted the air with; unruly thistles of hair in his ears; a walking stick that struck the legs of persons who leaned too close; two hounds milling about and weaving barriers at his knees; brass buttons sticking out like burrs from his overcoat.

At the docks when she and Hugh had departed for America, she looked down on William from the deck and saw for the first time his vulnerabilities as an old man: stooped shoulders, slack cheeks. He still stood with dignity and command, holding his walking stick before him as he witnessed their sendoff to America, unflappable among well-wishers crowding the dock who tossed ivy wreaths and peony bouquets and pennants to the ship's decks, objects uncaught by passengers pelting back down around his boots. His face twitched once after departure at the widening gap of water between the dock and the ship.

Georgie's mother died from typhus when Georgie was only a year old, then her father died months afterward, so Georgie was given the title missus and wheeled in her shell-shaped carriage to seat a place alongside the command of her aunts at the family meeting table. She was tended to by a loyal nanny, but Nanny was a member of staff and Georgie treated her as one. When Georgie came to the shanty in America, she had tried to assume the same manner, but Margaret swiftly rapped her knuckles and told her to sit. Her tutelage in plants and insects soon followed.

Margaret never spoke of Samuel, only of her duties on the battlefields. Margaret and Samuel did not reunite in the afterlife. Samuel seemed forever tethered to the fringes of this place, anxious about any talk of establishing foundations for the family; Margaret had been determined to stake roots at the falls. And she had, being buried there. The morning after Margaret's burial, Samuel had appeared to Georgie soaking wet, his clothing and skin black with soot. He had burned the crops near the Oriskany battlefield, afterward soaking the heat from his skin in the creek where he had fallen dead over twenty years ago. Margaret's death had upset him. To console himself, he milled about with the other militia ghosts, but he could not tolerate their chatter, which was a whisper for nearly ten years after the battle, then pitched and whined as the land was later subdivided and the hardwoods felled for farming. Samuel still joined the ghosts of the Iroquois who avoided the spine of the Mohawk Valley, the Oriskany battle site the center of what had been their trade route for centuries from the western Niagara waters leading to where the Mohawk met the Hudson in the east. The Iroquois ghosts flew north to their living relatives who called them down with smoke and ceremony, and Samuel trailed after them, lurking in the forests of their reunions.

Georgie did not know how to help Samuel, but urged him to stop burning the same field at the battle site—this was not the first time his ghost had raged with fire. It was Hendrick Lake's farm, and he blamed it wrongfully on the Welsh. There were hardly any Iroquois peoples left in the area to reproach.

Samuel confessed to Georgie about accidentally starting another fire after the Oriskany fires. When Ham Beeuwkes had the quinsy, he had followed the crew practice of sleeping away from the yard. Samuel would sometimes sleep alongside a quarantined man. The crewmen carried a new generation of rifle, and Samuel would sit up handling and studying the firearm while the sick man slept. Ham had a spider of nettle syrup over the low fire, and as Samuel saw Ham shake with cold, he built up the wood to warm the man.

Around midnight, Samuel startled from a flash of lantern light on the shanty porch. It was Margaret roused awake, sleepless from her dementia, but Samuel had not recognized his wife in her stooped, elderly form. With Ham's rifle, Samuel aimed for the silver of Margaret's braid wrapped across her crown, recalling the braided cordage looped about the uniforms of British officers. Margaret heard the rifle blast, but Samuel didn't think she saw him shoot at her. She turned back inside to continue her night wanderings.

The rifle ball glanced and pinged from hardwood to hardwood, careening back to strike Ham in the meat of his shoulder. Ham bolted awake from the jolt, then the pain seized him. He was for a moment clear of his fever fugue, alert, then gasping as he reached for the wound. The pressure of the bullet split through his bone like a beetle had hammered its way to bore and nest there, the scrap of Ham's shirt punching back out the ball hole like wings. Samuel fled as dark smoke rose off the syrup, and the fire overtook the spider, bubbling, blackening. Samuel had not meant to start this fire; he had only meant to warm Ham by building up the fire heating the nettle syrup. The flames whooshed alive and licked sparks onto Ham's pelt and boots and the dry carpet of cedar needles surrounding him.

The trees ignited to shooting orange columns. Against the snap and wind of the flames, Noord Boorsma was the first to run with his shovel toward the boughs cracking down, and the other men followed to pile dirt against the flames' spread, ducking the raining litter of fiery branches. The fire lit the night, but the men were soon choked and blinded from billowing drafts and roundels of smoke.

Obadiah Bray shouted, "Rouse Kettle and his family from the house!"

Charles Boudinot punched sideways into a pouch of rolling smoke to alert them. Yet the family had been awake since hearing the gun shot and Margaret bumping around the shanty. In the confusion and smoke, the crewmen had not seen Hugh running from the shanty with buckets. Hugh directed Charles to the river to bring up water, but it was a treacherous descent in the dark, and the fire spread too fast. The crewmen clambered to dig a long trench around the perimeter of the shanty, to mound up fortification from the fire, and it worked.

The men had just dropped their work shovels before sleep. No one had checked on Ham for two days. They had waited for him to emerge when he was well and able to work again. They had all borne the extra work from the sick man's absence. And now they would work into the night and the next morning to redirect and quell the fire. They coughed and threw down their shovels and ran hands over their faces. Chute Littlejohn spit, cursed. Mr. Boorsma snapped at another man to fetch the shovels, for the fire might be diverted, but they needed to bury Ham with the tools they had lain down.

They dug Ham's grave, rolled his charred remains into the pit, no evidence of the bullet hole in the ruined flesh and blackened bone. The lead ball round was a shiny puddle from the heat. Georgie never told anyone what caused the fire on this night. The men assumed that Ham had been casting ammunition while cooking his supper, not shot in his sleep, though they had all heard the rifle shot. It was not uncommon for them to be woken in the night by a gun report; the crewmen often picked off catamounts prowling the swine herd. Willie Brister and Jantjen Meijer agreed that whoever had been setting the Oriskany fires was here on their territory targeting one of their own. Charlie Daubrey and Cotter Wilkens argued if an outlaw had killed Ham on purpose or by accident. They said burial prayers for Ham, ate breakfast, lifted their shovels again for work at dawn, toiling until sundown. Each man chipped away at rock and overgrowth, figuring numbers in his head, the math of labor division, days, men, his own share, the burden of losing Ham and how many extra axe fells and shovel heaves this meant for the weeks ahead. They figured math poorly and bitterly on scant sleep, the longest day of work the men could remember. Each man guarded the steps of the next, scorning even a moment's pause.

The fire burned for a week, but the men's tents and the shanty were protected by the dirt bulwark and the favorable direction of the wind. The smoke choked them all, and the sooty cloths tied around their faces were suffocating. They would remember the fire, but they would recall foremost this dry season as a time when the blasting had worked, fulgent days before the sucking wet season dampened their efforts.

After this fire, Samuel, with shame and remorse over Ham's death and almost killing Margaret, had retreated to Oldenbarneveld, this time to the footprint of the new construction of Braam Hall. The foundation of the estate was staked out, the ground leveled, the outline of a placeholder for its grand size and intent. Samuel had hidden against the earthworks as he watched the builders, cooling himself in the nearby bulrushes of the confluence in the hottest part of the afternoons, isolating further from his family.

Instead of joining Hildy and the others in the yard for dancing, Georgie snuck away. She first checked the grist mill, but Samuel was not there. She wandered to the Braam Hall construction, hoping to find Samuel in the half-finished walls. She called and whistled, but he did not answer. There were no signs of him. She sat surrounded by the partially built walls, uneven as ruins, and looked to the stars pricking dense static through the trees. There was light from the windows of the church next door and from the home built against the creek. The dirt was marred with divots of men's boots from the workday. She regretted not bringing a scrap of supper to lure Samuel out. He was not going to appear that night. He might have forgotten her, away at the tavern for so long.

The events of the attack recreated in her mind. She laid her fingers over her neck. The man had been hard against her but had not attempted to lift her skirts nor fumbled with the laces of his breeches. He had been intent on something else, leaving his mark on her. His arousal had been secondary, a consequence of his adrenaline. He had not meant to rape her. Otherwise he would have. She spied a honing stone among the builders' tools. She slid Hildy's knife from her apron and ground its edge sharp.

After the Battle of Oriskany, Baron Saturday had heard thrumming in the timbered walls of the silver mine he inhabited in Bolivia. He had first been confused at the source of the sound, not thinking it could be so far away, separated by continents of forests and an ocean. He had been deep underground for weeks, gathering the silver filings left behind by miners after they ascended to the surface each evening. It was easy collection. The flecks of metal shed off the miners' hair and coats like bubbles raining off deep sea divers rising toward their boats. Baron Saturday had plans to travel to the River Uruguay to melt down the silver specks, learn the trade of silversmithing, acquire a high-temperature furnace, adorn with handsome buckles the tack of the horses belonging to the viceroyalty. But this plan would be blocked by the sound rattling his hibernation chamber. He was capricious, easily distracted from the trades and arts he aimed to master, silversmithing not being the first hobby he had abandoned.

To follow the call of the racket, he had burrowed and crawled through rock, rode the molten lava rivers of the Earth's mantle, swam the depths of the Atlantic, and snaked up the interior North American rivers and springs. He surfaced in the middle of Lake George, shooting upward from the water, gasping for breath, water flinging off his black hair. He sank back down, his head and shoulders riding the calm lake like a buoy. He treaded water, watching the families on the shoreline shade their eyes as the sun dipped crimson against the mountain peaks. The water was cool. Hills. The Adirondacks. This would do. It was fresh, picturesque.

He swam to shore, dripping naked past late summer bathers, stumbling, disoriented from the quick change in hemisphere, the sun tracing left to right in a different part of the sky. The heavens had reversed motion. The gathering storm clouds spun anticlockwise. The drain of the lake pulled counter ways too. The long shadows of trees traveled offset across him. He lay on a rock for some time, aligning his bearings to the Northern orientations. His teeth burned, and his skin itched all over. His ears sealed then burst. He could not breathe for the high pressure in his sinuses. He passed out.

Over the centuries, he had taken the form of different men, reveling in taunting men to injure him, and throwing his broken body onto the path of other unsuspecting men for their aid. This playacting never grew dull to Baron Saturday, for men's responses to these scenarios were endlessly varied. The wear and tear of his antics necessitated the frequent discarding of an old body for a new one. Yet he never animated corpses; he assembled with hotchpotch materials a new body, the sturdiest combination so far being foam from a horse's muzzle, kettle water, the tatters of dead soldiers' linen shirts, flakes of slate, and the leathers remaining of deer carcass decay.

When he woke on the shore of Lake George, he saw stars he had not seen in centuries, not since his time in New France. His hearing was blunted, but the noise drummed his insides. He stripped clothes off a sleeping man and untethered a horse, rode toward the still-larruping sound to Oriskany, where the cries of agony from fallen men had directed his journey. He had inhabited the area ever since, nearly twenty-five years, content to bask in the reverberations of the bloody Revolutionary battle and the banquet of unburied men. Over the centuries, the vestiges of other skirmishes had rooted him at Thermopylae, Cannae, Kadesh, Persia. But the echoes of their violence had muted, had never fixed him to one location as long as Oriskany had.

The crewmen did not enter the house. They ate and slept outside and visited around their fires each evening. But when dinner guests came, the family migrated outside after dining, and they all made one big revelry. This had been the practice when Georgie lived at the house from their first year of marriage, and it was so now as Hildy took Hugh's arm. Kit "Stanhope" Smith sat before his fire, tuning his fiddle. The low whine and high plucking roused the crowd to chatter and the women to grab each other around their waists.

Black Vy pulled Poppy close. "You know the reel, sister?" Black Vy raised both of their hands high in the air. "Is a high-stepper!" Black Vy twirled Poppy toward Georgie. "Don't you be showing off with them courtly steps, sister. This here be Foothills stompin'."

Georgie closed the shawl at her throat and walked to sit on the porch.

Hugh's idea of being a gentleman included bare-fisted knuckle brawling after the women and men danced and smoked and sang. He chose his opponent days in advance, keeping track of who had bested him at riding or joking or chopping. But his opponent didn't know he was to fight until Hugh squared right up behind him, silent as a cat, and the crowd would holler and point, and the chosen adversary would turn around, head collapsed to his chest and slowly roll up his sleeves in acceptance. The man he picked this night was Charlie Daubrey, the newest and youngest crewmember. He faced Hugh with a smothered grin, spit into both palms and made fists, and raised his red face, acceding to the blows of his initiation.

Charlie knew to wait for the clang of the official "start" pot, which Cotter Wilkens gonged with ceremony. To the roar of the men, Charlie struck the first punch, a hard right aimed at Hugh's eye socket—which Hugh was quick enough to dodge, but just. This made Cotter laugh so hard he squatted and gripped the front of his breeches, falling over. Two men helped Cotter to his feet, and they clasped in raucous laughter.

"The tenderling has stones!" Cotter staggered back and drank long from the whiskey bottle.

Hugh and Charlie circled each other, fists raised. Hugh had a powerful shoulder, could take down Charlie with one swift blow. But the boy had determination in his eyes. He spat to the ground. Hugh liked to develop a man with pugilism. Charlie was a little fat and small, a pap-hawk fresh from his mama's hearth cooking. Working in the woods and nightly brawling would put hard layers on him.

The men shouted. "Put some mustard on it, Charlie!" They moved in unison as a troop of drunken geese around the fighting pair, ebbing and flowing to every dodge and deflected cuff. Stanhope bowed high notes, keeping *con spirito* pace with each strike and scuffle. The men loved a good show, and Hugh was a showman. He danced and nimbly dodged blows without raising his hands to protect his face. He sprung side to side, tucking his head back as the wind of Charlie's fist glanced the air where his nose had been mere seconds ago.

Hugh charged forward, driving his shoulder into Charlie's abdomen, muscling him to the dirt, straddling him, unsheathing his knife, holding it high for all to see. The crowd murmured low in anticipation. Hugh bit the knife and playfully drove mock blows to Charlie's kidneys. Stanhope lifted high his bow, conducting time to the blows. The crowd tittered and laughed to the irritation of Charlie who grabbed two fistfuls of Hugh's shirt and roughly threw him off balance, the knife knocked free like a long tooth. On his feet, Charlie let fly threats and invectives. The crowd quieted at the new seriousness.

Amused and energized, Hugh tested a half-hearted left at Charlie's chin. Charlie dodged it, grappling both arms around Hugh's knees, upending him in one fell swoop. The men roared again, and Noord Boorsma approached to help Hugh to his feet, but Hugh waved him back and poised his fists to guard either side of his face. He stepped lightly, resuming the rhythm of the wind-up. Charlie's arms hung at his sides, but Hugh would not allow him to make this a tussle. He motioned for Charlie to approach. Charlie raised his fists and fell into the pace of Hugh's quick mincing steps. Hugh bounded forward and landed his ham fist between Charlie's eyes. Charlie staggered, then fell in a heap. The men cheered; Hugh kissed both fists and raised them, bowing, turning around to beam at all his men.

Gideon Bell extended a hand to Charlie, clapping the boy on the chest. Poppy watched Gideon Bell, the firelight glowing on his loose white shirt, his long fingers around the neck of the whiskey bottle. He had a relaxed way, his eyes alight with warmth as he spoke words of reassurance. His mouth formed the words, "Good lad." Hugh embraced Charlie, pounding his back. Charlie clapped back, and as the men parted, he reached to shake Hugh's hand in formal concession. Then Charlie snatched away his hand, and he and a lineup of men bent over, lowered their trousers, wagging their bare bottoms at Hugh. Before covering her eyes, Poppy noted that Gideon Bell's was the hairiest, thick tufts on his rump. Hugh kicked dirt and booted their bare asses. He laughed helplessly, falling to the dirt.

Stanhope played a jig, and Black Vy made her way into the crowd, clapping her hands. The men bowed before her, keeping a respectful distance, but lifting their legs high, their shoulders swaying in time with hers. The fire shone on her joyous face. A few men circled her, and she lifted her skirt to her ankle, working lively steps, her toes and heels clicking in time with the fiddle. Mr. Boorsma stepped forward and drew her into his arms. Clara and Poppy rushed into the crowd of men, choosing partners by curtseying before them, and the men obliged, twirling them round and round. Jacks rushed in, dashing through tents and legs, barking.

Mr. Lipson gripped Hugh's shoulder, pressed Hugh's knife into his hand, and the men spoke to each other with mischief, recounting the fight. Georgie could see no evidence that Mr. Lipson had told Hugh of what had happened to her earlier in the day. She stared long into the crowd.

Hugh grabbed Hildy by the waist, pulling her close to dance. He whispered and bent his knees to lash a kiss on her neck. Sweat ran down his face and chest, plastering his shirtsleeves. Hildy traced the cut on his eye, ran her finger down his face, and pulled aside the collar of his shirt. Georgie noticed a scar on Hugh's neck. Not a fresh wound, but a scar. She was struck with how long she and Hugh had been separated, long enough for a scar to form. She knew of his other two scars, had in fact inflicted those upon him herself. But those had been years ago when she still cared that he slept nights away with other women.

Georgie recalled hearing the men laugh at the tavern that Kettle had suffered a blow from Hildy who had mistaken him for an intruder. Hugh was protective of Hildy, but frequently had to leave her in the woods so he could attend to errands and business. Hugh had given Hildy a bludgeon, an iron cable that had been used to fortify a bridge truss. He had shown her how to draw it hidden from between her skirt and her apron. He had even sewn two loops for securing it there. He had demonstrated where to strike a man, to the collarbone, the shin bone, the temple, the eye. "Don't go for the balls," he had advised, "because any man expects that." They had practiced in slow motion a few times with Hildy protesting she didn't think she could strike a man, that she would be too terrified. But Hugh had returned home early, and Hildy, having heard the door open, sprang on him, flaying his neck open. Georgie didn't expect the scar to be so raised, so thick. Hugh was truly another woman's now. Georgie's scars were no longer the only ones. Georgie watched Hugh and Hildy turn in the center of the crowd, and she felt the lead weight of being alone.

From the crowd, Mr. Bell smiled. Georgie didn't hold his gaze, and he didn't approach her to dance; she radiated her remote cool and had no armor against hiding her raw anger from the day. Jeremiah Schuyler ran to Mr. Bell, yanked the whiskey bottle from his hand, spread his legs in a wide stance, cocked his head, and drank deep. He thrust the bottle back into Mr. Bell's hand and ran off, knocking him around to no longer face Georgie. Poppy floated by, too shy to look to his face, but then in a bolt of audacity, she piled her hair on top of her head and shot him a glance over her shoulder. He looked for a long moment after her, her hair springing loose down her back as if she had dropped fistfuls of hillside meadow.

The fiddle pulled one last high, triumphant note. Black Vy stopped, her arm raised. She sopped her neck and cheeks with her apron, staring dreamily into a fire. After a few moments, she walked to Georgie. "Those girls need to be taught dancing manners if they's to attract husbands here."

The crowd milled in the lull between songs. Clara flung from man to man, pulling at their knees and jumping for more music. Poppy tiptoed a solitary waltz.

"They are children," Georgie said. "And they know how to behave in parties of men."

"You, children. Get up here!" Black Vy shouted.

Jacks ran to her voice, and the girls scampered not far behind. The fiddle started again.

"Ma, come dance." Clara twirled a stumbling circle.

Georgie closed her eyes. Clara walked to her and put her head in her lap. Georgie smoothed the soft, downy curls, tightening her ribbon.

Poppy sat next to her ma, wrapping one arm about her waist. "Look, Clara."

Jacks, ears pricked forward, whined and bowed to Clara, his rear end high. Clara ran to him, and the dog lifted his front paws onto her shoulders. "He wants to dance, Ma!" She hugged her arms around Jacks's middle, and they stepped haltingly together to the fiddle.

Black Vy sang:

All day and all night
Old Nick digs up stalks
My second deathbed
He falls over, he coughs
In my dreams
He goes before me
His soiled suit beseems
Death
I paid my debts
I bide my time
He licks his teeth and rolls his eyes

Jacks licked Clara's face and trotted to the thick of the crowd, his tail thumping the men's legs. Stanhope ended the tune. Eben Cooper called out, "Another reel!" Stanhope set the neck of his fiddle low, rested his chin on the cup, and drew his leg back, getting traction with the tip of his toe. He worked his strings to a lively whirl.

Hugh bowed before Hildy. He began the formal steps of the reel, advancing toward her then retreating. She lost the count of the steps, moved forward as he moved back. He stopped and called, "Hold!" Stanhope abruptly stopped on a discordant pull of his bow and rested his instrument on his knee, looking expectantly at Hugh.

"Oh, Ma, dance with Papa." Poppy edged her seat to a better view of the crowd, hugging herself, eyes bright.

They all stared keenly at Georgie. She rose and the fiddle started from the reel's first note. Georgie chose Isaac Coe, raised onto her toes, counted steps to the high strings. The crewmen shuffled roughly through the formal paces, clomping with heavy heels and toes. They stomped out the reel, galumphing a lively backwoods rendition, a dance they made their own because of so few women. Hugh had adopted the elegance of the dance because he always had women.

The crewmen, obliged to the wages of seasonal work in the outlying foothills, felt the lonesome sacrifice of camp life, of leaving their sweethearts behind in their fathers' homes. The men had been absent from their sisters and sweethearts for so long they couldn't remember whose sister was whose and which sweetheart belonged to which man, so they would turn their fireside talk to other women, chance women, never-spoken-to women, women traveling through on foot, skirts flying past on horseback, streaming through on boat, lurching by in the frame of a carriage window. Memories of these women were more detailed than the women they grew up with and to whom they pledged love and fidelity. These were the women the men asked each other to describe each night, not their sisters or darlings. The woman sloshing buckets at the Hudson headwaters. The woman grabbing a branch to bail from her boat before wrecking into white current. The woman with a rag over her mouth raking pearl ash from a kiln. The woman standing strong in the current wringing out her hair, bare feet hugging riverbed stones. The woman with the flintlock bloom across her nose shouldering a rifle, a bundle of jackrabbits, twined at their feet, bouncing against her hip. The woman carrying two bolts of cloth across Bagg's Square. The woman dragging a snare from the Mohawk so her boat could pass. The woman driving a runaway gig with her legs braced against the floor-board. The woman climbing a tree with a smoking sage bundle to dip her hand for honey. There had been fewer than ten sightings of women outside of family and neighbors for the crew of twenty-odd young men. These women had loomed unexpectedly in the streets, in the rivers, in the woods like fresh bald moons passing close, filling the men's skies, then receding, gone again, leaving the men riotously earthbound in their longing. The men were never able to draw the women close to share sublunary relief. The novelty of those visions would be retold among the men for the rest of their lives.

Georgie let Isaac bounce her about and did not correct him toward conventions of the dance. Hugh's eyes shone against the fires, his color high, his arms rising and falling. He performed the reel as Georgie had taught him. He engaged Hildy in the formal steps, locking arms, stepping sideways. Hugh turned his head to Georgie and said some-thing, but it was lost underneath the men's voices and the high fiddle music and Isaac turning her round; Georgie knew it was pride for Hildy, whatever he had said. He held Hildy closer than the dictates of the dance allowed and spoke a stream of observations into her hair. His breath would be rich with whiskey for the way his lips curdled around his words, that point in the evening when his spirits were highest, before they crashed down after one too many drinks. His hand closed over Hildy's. His legs drove and directed her steps. If anyone had stumbled into the group just then, Hugh might have introduced Hildy as his wife, ignoring Georgie for the complications of their arrangement.

They spread their arms low and wide, tiptoeing backward, chins tilted toward the dirt, displaying profiles to partners. Hildy clapped her hands with the music, casting about for eye contact with the rowdier men. She had stepped back from Hugh, the music overtaking her as she howled, and the men and Jacks chorused back. The dance did not end on the dignified posing of tradition. Stanhope revved his fiddle, discarding the stately final notes for a leap into a frenzied sawing tempo. Poppy covered her ears, and Clara knelt by Jacks, feeling his yowl erupt at the bottom of his ribs. Hugh and Black Vy swayed together. Hildy and the men tried to match the fiddle notes with their calls, throats breaking. Mr. Boorsma grabbed Black Vy's hand and led her to his tent. So Black Vy was the love that Georgie had heard Mr. Boorsma rhapsodize about at the tavern.

At the fringe of the dancing, Mr. Lipson and Dirch Maas and Cager Bullfinch staggered and threw slow, heavy, one-handed slugs at each other, spilling drink from the near-empty whiskey bottles they held.

"I will not dansh with 'nother man on tippy toes!" Mr. Lipson slurred, raising his whiskey bottle, the fire sparking a high shower of cinders. He pushed his way through the dancing men, lurching toward Georgie, but he tripped and fell face down and lay there still as a stone. The crowd parted around him, the fiddle stopped, and Hugh called an end to the evening. Mal Hitchens and Oepke Bonnema dragged Mr. Lipson toward a fire and curled his body there, tucking the whiskey bottle against his chest, lowering his hat over his eyes, the shadows of flames flickering across the brim. Jacks curled against his back.

The men dispersed, flopping to their tents, rousing fires, lighting pipes. The girls and Hildy swayed together, milking the last of the evening to the plinks of Stanhope wiping the strings of his fiddle.

Hugh pulled at Georgie's elbow. "Favor a bouse?"

They settled at the hearth, and Hugh tipped amber liquid into two glasses. Georgie basked in the fire at her back. Hugh raised his glass to her.

"To women." He held the sentiment long enough that Georgie sipped.

But he held up a finger. "To the culture of woman." He shook his head and tried again. "To a woman cultured in the wilds." He raised his glass, but stopped, fingered his lip. "To a woman who cultured the wildings." He was satisfied with this and drank. But he stood and wagged his finger back and forth. "To a woman with cultured talents," he toasted and sat with hard finality.

Georgie raised her glass and drank. She flicked her eyes to his demeanor to determine if Mr. Lipson had told him of her attack. Hugh's eyes were unfocused and glassy. She sipped her brandy, and the heat collected at the back of her throat, draped down her ribs.

"S' good to have you at home, Georgie."

She slumped from the fire's warmth; this was not a homecoming. Her eyes dipped heavy. "Did the men retrieve the horses and wagon? Have you heard word?"

"They found only a broken piece of leather. I will ask them to try again at daybreak." Her question sobered him, and she could hear the mean edge of the liquor crabbing up for air. He stabbed a finger at her. "You've allowed Clara to become even more contrary. She has no notion for the value of a horse and wagon. And she embroiders lies about where they are."

"She is a child." Georgie swirled her glass.

"Yet old enough to know honesty. But it's too late now for her to learn it."

"Allow her to follow you around all day to learn honest ways then."

"You may not understand your role here, but it's an important one as mother to my children. Now that you see my attachment to Hildy, I s'pect I shan't have to send you away again."

Georgie studied the legs of liquor trickling down her glass. She was to be a third-tier servant. "Might I return to the tavern? I quite proved my competence there."

"No. Jeremiah Van Rensseleer now assumes duties there."

She swallowed the last of her brandy. "I shan't swive you ever again."

He snorted. Then cast down his stare, stung. He sipped and smacked his lips. "Why were you alone on Mr. Lipson's land today?"

Georgie bristled and straightened. "I was in the river, not on land." Hugh had a way of accusing her when he felt slighted, and her mind acted trapped and reacted with half-lies.

"Mr. Lipson does not tell stories. He said he found you on your back with a man lying on top."

"I was clubbing for eel in the river, and the apples…" Georgie felt hot and snared. She could not begin a sensible narrative of what had happened.

"While you are in my house raising my daughters, you will not bed with any man."

"I was attacked."

Hugh sputtered and stood. "Likely. You invent stories. There is no such man. I know all the men in these woods. I em*ploy* the men from these parts. And if you did speak truth, these men cannot be expected to control themselves at all times. You are not to wander alone. You brought this dismay onto your careless person."

"You cannot control your men." She cowered, but her eyes flashed and her voice deepened with conviction.

Hugh grabbed her jaw to shut her mouth. She saw the recognition in his face for what she was about to say.

"Silas Andrus," she declared through the dig of his fingers.

Silas Andrus had been a crewman two seasons past, and when Hugh had caught him hoarding black powder in his tent, he did not whip the man. He secluded him from the others to think in isolation and to repent for his transgression. The other men were stunned when Hugh did not punish him proper. The men drafted one of their own to horse whip Silas. Hugh had been unable to witness, descending the cliffs and sitting on the river's slate bed, a few sharp cries echoing down the rock. Later that evening, Hugh joined the men by their fires in the yard and passed around whiskey. He styled himself as a leader of men, having inspired them to hatch justice and assert punishment, as if that had been his plan all along. The men begrudgingly drank the whiskey. Silas was still tied to the tree as the men sat and drank. The men had tied his back to the tree, so the front of his body—his shoulders, groin, hands bound in front—had borne the brunt of the blows.

The following morning, Noord Boorsma told Gideon Bell, Rye Syphur, and Jeremiah Schuyler to tie the peccant Silas to a horse and ride him north for several days to the High Peaks, dumping him at the source of the Hudson River with only his whip-torn, bloodied shirt. Mr. Boorsma did not consult Hugh. Once at the headwaters, the men had stripped off what was left of his breeches and took his boots to trade back down the mountain for supper. Hugh never docked the three men for the eight days' pay of their desertion and had cheerily ignored their absence and the extra burden this put on his other men, a load they unanimously bore without complaint or retribution upon the three men's return to work duties.

Georgie had expected mutiny and a similar flaying for Hugh by his own men. But it never happened. Hugh never regained more than a tenuous hold over his crew; the men stayed for lack of other work but also because they believed in the promise of the profitable future they were creating. The orders Hugh asserted henceforth were met with a series of glances between the men. A new, unspoken hierarchy had been established, one which Hugh was too proud and nervous to acknowledge.

Hugh stared into the fire over Georgie's shoulder. "Mr. Andrus was a thief. Thieves on this crew will be dealt with by the men. I am no sole arbiter of justice."

Georgie opened her mouth to speak, but Hugh's eyes burned in reproach before she could name the second man.

Hamilton Key. She bore a defiant look at Hugh.

Hugh poured more brandy and stared back into the flames.

Ham Key still worked the crew, the fingers of his right hand crushed stiff, twisted useless as horn candlesticks. After Silas's exile, the men had self-organized into two groups, the North Pocket and the South Pocket. They didn't tell Hugh. Hugh had surveyed the main clearing site, finding half his men absent. But Hugh figured it out after seeing Mr. Boorsma guide Black Vy's hand across a map, instructing her how to site her position with a pocket compass. She left the shanty after her chores with the compass in hand. Hugh had followed her, finding the North Pocket, the missing men, laboring in the area a mile north that Hugh had pegged to clear next season. Some men were resting after a productive morning of felling twenty trees. This was where Black Vy had navigated, to fry up a shared noonchine of bacon for her and Noord.

Three men double-jack drilled the rockface, the two men in rhythm with their sledgehammer blows as the third man turned the rod after each strike, adjusting his cap and hiking up his trousers after each snap-turn of his wrist. Hugh crowed that his decided leadership had inspired the men to unite, to innovate, to hasten the blasting plan.

The men had assigned Ham Key as trotter. On horseback he patrolled between North Pocket and South Pocket, keeping the narrow wagon trail clear and delivering communications back and forth. Ham had been loading brush into a cart, separated from the North Pocket to clear the path of a fallen tree for their return to camp. The South Pocket had gone ahead to town to pick up supplies. But Ham's horse got mired in the black muck. Frantic, it flopped onto its side, landing the cart askew, pinning Ham's hand underneath, trapped between a boulder and the cart's heavy wooden side. With each great flail of the horse, the cart's weight drove with more force onto Ham's hand. Ham had screamed for help, a relentless cry that had become so regular in the trees that Hugh ignored it for something feral dying. But after an hour or so, Hugh walked toward it.

He saw Ham and quailed. "You were to be with the others hauling back supplies."

Hugh reassured Ham of returning with help. But as Hugh walked back to the shanty, his mind blanked. He let it wander to a geometry problem of blasthole diameter and spacing that one of the men had presented him. Those linear relations and ratios preoccupied Hugh, shut out Ham in his distress except for a few fleeting moments after supper. Hugh felt overcome by not organizing men to right the dying mount and lift the cart off Ham.

Ham had restarted his cry later in the evening. His squall filtered through the women's chatter, and they shushed each other to listen. Hugh told them it was a dying catamount. But he had to sit as seams crimped his gut. He hoped the men would travel back through past Ham. And in fact, the men had much earlier in the day heard and found Ham. The men had pried Ham from underneath the cart, his horse dead from shock. Ham's cry in the evening was from pain as Cager Bullfinch picked clean Ham's hand and wrapped the crushed sack of it.

The men later derided the evidence of Hugh conducting his evening rituals as usual: on the porch, his polished boots and smudged brandy glass alongside the boot blacking and neat pile of split kindling. For days after, the men's eyes hung onto Hugh, their anger at flashpoint for Hugh abandoning a crewman in such dire straits. They told themselves again, they had no other means to earn wages, but they had the power to bear decency in what had become an execrable work environment. So the phrase *they had no other means* became winking, tacit code for working the long view, for one day making the blasting enterprise their own.

Before hired on to Hugh's crew, they had all worked the yeomanry of the Mohawk Valley, cutting and girdling trees, clearing the forest for farming. They cleared parcels that they did not own, nor would ever own. When Hugh came to them with the pledge and power of black powder blasting, they walked off their landlords' tracts. Hugh promised a cleared pathway for tourists to visit the spectacle of the falls and rattled off the jobs that would present themselves to the men: drivers, stable owners, water guides, joiners, carpenters, cutlers, farriers, gunsmiths, tavern keepers, wheel wrights, belly builders, preachers. The tourists would need food and drink and lodging. The tourists would need horses and guns and sturdy shoes. Bonesetters and bloodletters. Keepsakes to bring back to their city relations. Pianos and fiddles to express their joys in the evenings. The tourists would need their sins ministered and their carnal will-o'-the-wisps gratified. Hugh encouraged the men to think beyond tending to the fields of landowners for the rest of their days. The men came to this work avid and stout, hacking, cleaving the corridor, tearing out thickets of choke vines with barn-raising hands, felling cedar brakes, bracing their bellies against the thrum of the axe, wheeling scythes through coppices of root suckers, burning the axe-breaker stands of hickory, rags tied over their mouths like snavellers as the smoke billowed low and spread around their ankles as if they had thrown fog bombs to blot out their escape.

The men learned single- and double-jack drilling, hand chiseling to bore holes into rockfaces, their rods and sledgehammers ringing and chiming like sword blades. They set in those bore holes black powder bundles, careful as returning fallen baby birds to nests. They covered the holes with clay plugs and affixed wicks for lighting the charges within the rock. They felt for the rock's weak seams and built a hot fire beside. They gauged when to douse the rock with cold water to shock it apart. The work with Kettle was still fatiguing, but there was combustion and detonation and the promise of greater prospects. Overwinter, the men smoked and dreamed about doctoring the daughters of rich city tourist bankers and collecting stables of fine mounts.

Hugh drank off his brandy and fixed Georgie a look. "Fetch my daughters and go to bed." He turned to the door as if the others were still dancing and fighting outside. Then he remembered the evening was finished, that everyone had retired to their tents. He climbed above stairs, calling for Hildy.

Georgie tucked in the girls and drew the curtain closed. She hung her gown on a peg. Black Vy was in bed, back from Mr. Boorsma's tent. Above stairs, Hildy's hem swished and her bare feet padded across the sleeping garret. Georgie stood before the fire letting her thin shift absorb some heat. She felt woozy and sleepy from drink.

"You always dreaming, never in the room with others." Black Vy watched Georgie as she climbed into her side of the bed.

Georgie peered between the wallboards. The yard was awash in swirls of dust and smoke, and the men who were still conscious sat and drank, staring into the low-burning embers.

"You dream all day and all night, sister."

"How do you know I dream at night?"

" 'Cause you twitch. You dream of animals, yes?"

"Do I keep you awake?"

"No. I's already awake."

Hugh and Hildy had blown out the candle. They rustled, and a vigorous floorboard squeaking began. Georgie closed her eyes.

"How did Hugh acquire you?"

"What you say?"

"Where did he buy you?"

Black Vy rose to her elbow. The hearth glowed behind her, lighting the top of her head, spiked with coarse knots peeping from her head wrap. "He found me. In Boston. I is not no longer bought or sold by any man."

"He found you. How?"

"I worked for a man in Boston."

"Worked. In what capacity?"

Black Vy tightened her grip on the pelt.

But Georgie persisted. "How were you working? You are obviously a fled slave. Under what arrangement were you working for a man?"

"Woman, my life ain't for you to be twisting 'round."

"All I state is that *working* means a straightforward exchange of labor and recompense. Your status would surely mean having to provide any benefactor with extra incentive to not alert your master, is this not so?"

Black Vy did not answer. She was tired. "I is not no longer bought or sold by any man," she repeated. "Your husband be a good man, and say my place is here." She rolled toward the fire.

Black Vy had poured drinks for the menfolk playing the card tables at the Swelt Gentlewoman Tavern in Boston, owned by Clinton Bangs Bickford. He had Black Vy and women alike in his service. She did not have the patience to explain that her employer in Boston was a man Georgie knew, for Bickford had met Hugh and Georgie straight off the ship from England at Boston Harbor. Georgie would have remembered him as the tallest man in the crowd. He led Georgie and Hugh away from the teeming throng to a formal breakfast at his tavern. They stayed with him before they arranged a bateau for travel north on the Hudson. It was plain from their first night with Bickford that he operated a house of ill-repute, though patrons also picked up their mail, conducted court sessions, and ate family meals there after church. Farmers unloaded sacks of rye in the tavern's entryway, which bakers picked up hours later. Crofters tied sheep and goats to the posts outside, and butchers led them away for slaughtering. Hugh returned many times to Boston as a student of Bickford's business mind and magnanimous sway over the people of his town, the Swelt a hub for dealings of all kinds.

The people of Boston thought Bickford grew up wealthy, well fed. He carried himself with authority and the expectation for others to listen and obey. Any man with that ox-sized frame and self-possession must have chewed through beef at three meals each day since popping free of his mother's breast, the harbor masters said. He drank bowls of dark broth before glistening and gelatin-rich platters of beefy cuts were set before him, a kill-pile of brown-tipped bones curling upward from a bounty of shanks, the sailors said. His jacket cuffs were ever dark pink for having to daily wipe away juices from his chin or drag his sleeves through the mud-red bottom juice of platters, the worshippers at Old South Meetinghouse said. Sometimes if his belly was meat sore or sensitive before breakfast, he would break off a bone and suck the insides, the hunks of meat steaming pleasantly to his face but left uneaten, the aged Sons of Liberty said. This was the boyhood the people of Boston imagined for Bickford, for surely a man of his stature and assurance was spoilt with marbled riches at table provided by a sensible, monied father. But Bickford never spoke of a father, and he didn't correct the stories about his origins. From a young age, he learned to scrap and hustle for every mouthful, not a bite of it beef, but he grew to great proportions despite malnutrition. The people of Boston all but cheered as he walked the streets, greeting Bickford with hearty calls, men of civil authority tipping their hats and relinquishing way. For if there had to be a dockyard brothel, they preferred it overseen by a man like Bickford, ascribing his surfeit of brawn to respectable bloodlines and character.

He was not handsome. He had pale, dim eyes without the definition of lashes. His face was a sun-roughed hide that flaked off flat white growths like oyster salts. He dealt mainly with ship captains and resembled their tendency for scurvily loose teeth, blinking dry eyes of dehydration, and bouts of the same venereal disease resurfacing every few years to ravage his looks. He did not dress like a town father. He milled about the streets tipping a fine hat, but his overcoat was open to a night shirt underneath, and his boots were half-fastened, the disheveled way everyone in his house was clad because of so much undressing.

During Hugh's visits to the Swelt, Bickford talked freely about how he had obtained his troop of women, mostly from the circuit of ships outfitted for cabotage, transportation of goods along the coastal waters to nearby points. There were as many slumped pineapples onboard docked ships at Boston Harbor as there were escaped slave women from Virginia and even as far away as the Indies, Bickford had said. Bickford knew where to look, where the women hid themselves; he did not ask for permission from ship captains to board their vessels. He had marched belowdecks, lifted a tarp, and extended his gloved hand to Black Vy, who hungry and weak, eyes pinging along the length of his rangy height, took the hand without hesitation. They climbed onto the foredeck, her body tight against him, shivering in her coarse dress, and her head filling with the bustle and noise of the harbor, booming horns of promise. Bickford vowed protection for the women, and when they realized what they had to do for it, they didn't leave. It was better than what they had come from. Bickford told the women to work the men in his house for eighteen months, then promised to find them paying jobs as cooks and laundresses. That's what he arranged with all the women. Yet their assent made Hugh uneasy.

Two women had been gulled by their new households when they were delivered back to their old masters. The reward monies for returning slaves were substantial and spurred the new employers to profit. A third woman, Cleo, had been returned to her old master because the local magistrate, Cray Hyslop, had hard proof she was a fugitive and collected the five hundred dollar fine from the new employer who plead he didn't know when he hired her that she was already possessed labor. This frightened the women still under Bickford's agreement, causing many to stay in his brothel beyond eighteen months. Bickford allowed it, shrugged his shoulders, accepted the hazards of the dealings, stating that none of this was in his power to prevent. He regarded his actions as upright, for he found paid employment for former slaves, women no less.

One Southern master, John George Graves of Caroline County, Virginia, rode north to raid Bickford's tavern, charging inside with his escaped slave notice in hand, calling Bickford a thief. Bickford made no reply as he drank a crisp cider. The locals at his tables rose from their cards and suppers and drinking. They were the cordwainers, the haywrights, the fruit jobbers, the pewterers, the glovers, the joiners, the shipkeepers, the clothiers, the mariners, the saddlers, the sail makers, the varnishers, the surgeons, the wigmakers, the fishermen, the widows. They all risked being charged with offenses of profane cursing and breach of peace when they booted Graves out of the Swelt. The mob tied him and marched him to a frigate that sailed the tidewaters, wandering its course for months of supply hauling. When Graves did not return home to Caroline County, his slave-owning peers sent angry protesters north for an investigation. That's when Magistrate Hyslop seized Cleo and rode her back to the South.

Magistrate Hyslop would not apply the Fugitive Slave Act by seizing Bickford's whole house of women. He didn't agree with the law, fretted over the manpower to execute the captures, felt a bald dislike for the owners of the Southern plantations seeking to uphold their ways in his town. He had made Cleo, one woman from Bickford's string, an example and hoped his cooperation with the law would appease the outraged cries from the Southern gentlemen—keep them quiet. The magistrate did not intend to snag any more escaped slaves. Nor did he intend to allow another gang from his city to overpower a second slave owner. He hoped the like-for-like retaliation settled the matter.

Hugh often played cards and ninepin and stayed overnights at the Swelt. He became friendly with Black Vy as she poured drinks behind the bar. She learned to pour whiskey to his liking, adding a few drops of the house lemonade. Hugh had hoped to learn Bickford's business model but instead found himself wary of it. Bickford made a profit off these women when he could instead help them find legitimate employment without eighteen months' service to him. There was immediate need for household help, laundry, cooking, milking, in Boston households.

Black Vy got sick, all those men from near and far ports, traipsing through swamps and dirt streets and drinking water from this well and that trough, then sticking their bodies onto hers. She could not bed with them after a time. Then she got too shaky and ill to pour. And Hugh saw this, saw how Bickford about near had a fit every time she poured more whiskey onto his counter than into the glass. Hugh asked Black Vy if there was not a doctor in Boston to cure her shakes and ills. Bickford did employ a trusted doctor to care for the women in his brothel. He was a loyal cousin whose discretion meant he did not speak of his care for Bickford's women among the other doctors of the city. But his practice was busy, so he had limited time for Bickford's women, and his preferred treatment was laudanum, which had done little for Black Vy's shakes but mask them in a stupor. She got worse, grew skinny, and couldn't get her head clear from his medicines.

Hugh acted on a flicker of his higher intentions toward Black Vy. He found his good grace at the ready with her, this new acquaintance. He could start fresh with Black Vy when back home he had a string of personal failures behind him. His efforts to make amends with his wife and crewmen had not worked. Here was an opportunity to remake himself as man of character.

So Hugh said, "I will take that sickly skinny girl from you, Bickford, as a favor to your good name."

Bickford was ever cunning with a mind counting time owed him. "You don't like the dark, skinny ones, so what do you try to achieve, man? You try selling her back to her master? 'Cause I don't allow that."

Hugh said, "Allow me take her to the fresh air up north to cure her shakes, and when she's better, I will bring her back."

Bickford agreed, provided Hugh return her when recovered to complete her eighteen months of service. The men shook hands on it. Hugh and Black Vy left the next morning to travel north to the falls.

Black Vy did recover in the clean air of Buttermilk Falls, and one day when her shakes stopped, she asked Hugh when she would have to return to Bickford. She knew she was on loan. Hugh said she was not on loan, that she shan't never have to return, and he would fight off Bickford if he tried to make claim. Hugh pledged she had earned her place at the falls, in his family, as cook.

But Black Vy knew Bickford would come. He knew of Hugh's

settlement at the falls. And Hugh would advertise far away in all directions, farther than Boston, to Virginia even, for men of his kind to visit his new-built Buttermilk Falls Resort.

Georgie slept, her dreams saturated with the brine stench and inky darkness of the sea. In her dream, she was aboard the ship that had brought her from England to America. She lay below decks, looking through the timber hull, between the interstices in the planks, somehow transparent but watertight. The cavernous ocean was green-black. The ship's horn blasted, juddering the water, and a leak sprang at one of the plank breaches. Water sloshed in, soaking her nightdress and hair, swishing around the bed's bolted feet, but not overwhelming the ship to listing or sinking. The ship submerged many fathoms deep, and its momentum and pressurized air surged her deeper into her dream state. The silt from ocean floor vents bloomed from the depth; in the rising clouds, creatures floated toward the surface, propelling themselves in graceful thrusts of tentacles, bubbles streaming off eyeballs. She felt a profound sense of well-being, her blood thrumming from tip to tail as the bodies undulated. Suddenly, a pointed head tip sailed close, and a great eye stared at her, rising slowly between the hull's boards.

She startled awake, her eyes open to the crack between the wall-boards of the shanty where she saw a filter of breaking darkness, the last before dawn. She was soaked with sweat, reeking of camp smoke, feeling the vulnerability of being watched. She lay still for a long time, eyes darting for movement in the yard. But she saw nothing.

Black Vy slept, face heavily laid into the pillow. The embers glowed under ash, which Georgie brushed away, and the influx of oxygen sparked a flame. She laid pine shavings, the sticky, sappy pieces igniting instantly. She chucked an ironwood log onto the small flaming bundle. Behind the partition, her girls stirred underneath their shared pelt, but their eyes were closed.

She wrapped in a shawl and opened the front door. A faint dawn spread among the trees, the yard smoky from the night fires long burned out. No men stirred in the tents. They had all bedded down with heavy heads.

The porch was shadowy. A heap glistened on the steps. Another of Mr. Bell's spoilt muslins. She walked to retrieve it. Yet it was not muslin but fur. One of the tufted hog sires. No, it was Jacks. She knelt, patted the porch board. "Here, boy." He didn't move. She ran her hand along his neck, wet with blood. She startled, jerked back her hand. Then reached again for him. Her finger found the hole. His neck had been punctured, not slit. One swift downward jab. She staggered into the yard. Mr. Lipson curled, passed out, near one of the dead fires. Georgie shook him. No response, his breathing congested and deep.

She ran for the pushcart. Jacks was not yet rigid. She sunk both hands into his fur and dragged him bumping down the porch steps. Even for the fatal gash, there was not much blood. The animal had bled at its murdering spot or along the way to being dragged and dumped as a warning threat at Hugh's door. Georgie heaved Jacks's body, heavy and unwieldy as the innards sack of a bear, into the pushcart. She slid down the rocky path, wrestling the load past the swift shallows to the steady deep water, landing at the sandy strip where Hugh banked his canoe.

She rode downstream, the water full and swift, her paddle making hardly a difference to steering or forward motion. Water pooled at her feet; the hull's bark was dry and needed a good smear of waterproofing at the seams. Jacks's corpse shifted from the pitch of the bow, and the water inside the boat made his body buoyant and alive, paws and nose unnervingly animated. The blood caked on his fur dissolved in the sludge water. His body floated to her skirt hem then back toward the bow, sliding in a pink suspension.

She bailed water as it crept gelidly past her ankles. When the river became so shallow that the vessel scraped on the pebbles and became stuck, she stumbled out. The back end skated sideways, still caught in deep current. She lugged the boat along the pebbles. She spied the tree growing sideways out of the bank, the point where she had discovered the tin. She slung back into the boat and with all her might paddled for the bank. The current bumped the hull against the thick trunk, and she grabbed hold of the low limb. The boat pulled underneath her. It nearly slipped away in the current to leave her dangling from the branch, but she held fast, wedging the boat securely into the muddy bank. She tied her shawl around the lip in the aft and secured the other end to the branch. She climbed her way forward, stepping over Jacks, peering over the bow into the swirls. She dipped her arm and probed until a deep throb crept up her shoulder. She cursed and pinched her limb to warm it. It was bright pink, the tips of her fingers waxen. She plunged her dry arm, this time leaning over the boat to her armpit, the canoe tipping dangerously, her foot bracing Jacks's body from falling into the river.

A low growl boiled in her throat. She drew out her arm, frigid and dripping. The tin was no longer anchored there. She shook with cold.

She untied the shawl from the branch, and the current swept them back downriver. At the stone bridge, she steered to the steep bank and secured the boat. She kept her head low, grasping Jacks by the ruff and rump, heaving him up the high bank. His body rolled back toward the water but caught on a root. She leapt from the boat and climbed, sinking into the dirt as it eroded, spilling into the current. She hauled Jacks to the bridge.

The bridge was empty. The water shone on either side. She dragged Jacks into the woods, to the tree where the man with black hair and green eyes had pinned her. Black Vy's club and oilcloth were still piled at the base of the tree. She poised the club for striking and slung the oilcloth over her shoulder.

Jacks's limp form didn't make the threatening message she intended. His black fur made no contrast to the damp forest debris as if it were already decomposing into the earth. She tapped the air with the club, waiting out the man's return. She would take him on alone. Being smothered and destroyed by him as she fought would be more tolerable than her isolation at the shanty. She sat with her back to the tree, her blood whooshing in her ears along with the low tumble of the river. She was far enough into the woods to catch a blinding ribbon of the water. The astringency of cedar swirled in the back of her throat. Then a man's tobacco scent swept in and the backs of her hands bristled. A twig snapped.

His form—his dark breeches and white shirt and stone-picker hands—suddenly filled her field of vision. Then he shimmied aside, the flares from the water blinding, blotting out his face. She stood, one hand shielding the bright sun, deflecting any blows. She thrust the club in blind jabs. He caught the club and yanked it from her grip.

"You are easy to follow. I could have thrown cannon balls into the river and you not have noticed."

It was Mr. Bell. She fell on her bottom against the tree. She clutched two fistfuls of her skirt. Mr. Bell knelt, glancing at Jacks.

"You paddled behind me? Why are you not wet? I did not spy you, and I was turned around more than once by the current."

"From up high, on foot, walking along the bank."

"Whatever for? Why have you followed me?"

He smothered a smile, lowering his head to scratch his eyelid with the tip of his thumb. "I woke to great thumping and squeaking and saw you hauling a dog carcass and wheeling it off. I thought it might prove arresting to see where your errand led you. Next time you want to sneak off quiet like, grease the wheels of that cart."

It was still cool in the woods, but he had kept a steady pace to follow her; his shirt clung to him. His hair was wet, dark curls stuck to his ears. He ran a finger along his brow, mopping away sweat.

"You were all so rum soaked that not even a dog dragged through the yard and dumped on the porch in the night woke any of you."

He smiled in that way he had, of being impressed at what he was about to say before saying it. "How did you figure you were going to haul that heavy craft back upriver by yourself?"

"I was intent upon my errand. I would have managed the boat back."

"You were what? Say again? You have a fog of distraction about you at all times." He sat, rounding and stretching his back. "Did you murder the dog?"

"Me? No," she sputtered. "I found him. On the porch."

"Why drag him out here then? Why not leave him for Mr. Lipson to bury?"

"I'm replying to a message."

"I cannot understand you."

She repeated each word deliberately.

"A message? Whatever for? Do you not think that Mr. Lipson would not want you using his pet hunting hound as a message?"

"I did not start the communication." Yet she felt an uneasy wash of shame and wondered if Mr. Bell had seen her desperately searching the river. The loss of the coins was dismal, though she flushed for scrambling for such a beggarly sum.

He placed his hand on her arm as if to discipline a child. "You must tell your husband what this is about. He should be conducting this matter for you. No woman should venture out with darkness in her heart then dump it at a tree. You must learn your place."

She pulled free from him. "There is no need for familiarity. He is my husband in name only. He gave up duties of protection for me long ago."

"Are you in danger?"

"I do believe so. But I do not know why or from whom by name." Then she narrowed her eyes. "Did my husband pay you to follow me?"

"Say again?"

He was slowing her down. "Pay. Husband. Follow."

"No." But his voice was too quick, too high in reply.

Her resolve for completing her confrontation was weighed down by the ever-present impediment Mr. Bell had become.

"Grab the fore end," he instructed.

She grabbed Jacks's ruff while he lifted the hindquarters, and they carried the body between them.

"We'll put him in the canoe then carry the canoe together back through the woods. You see, your face is flushed with gratitude." He turned away. "I will let you blush privately." He walked toward the bank to retrieve the canoe.

She did not follow him, and when the dog dropped between them, pulled from his grasp, he stopped and turned.

"No, sir. I am to stay here to deliver my message as I intended."

"You cannot." He put his hands on his hips. "That is a vile action for a woman." He looked down to the dirt. "This is not your dog." He pointed at her. "You behave with cruelty." Dark scorn crossed his face, and he ran his palm over his mouth as if swabbing a dripping annoyance. "Do you not think that Mr. Lipson wanders the woods and calls for his Jacks even now?"

This made her pluck falter, but she spat out, "Go back to your tent to heal. You cannot handle this errand. I will return the dog myself."

He turned down the riverbank to drag the canoe up to the walking path, obeying the directive Hugh had given him to retrieve the boat and Georgie.

Any courage she had to face the black-haired, green-eyed man was spent, her words all bluster. She was too afraid to leave on her own, so she followed Mr. Bell.

They set down the boat. Mr. Bell's face was white from effort. He bore the heavier end with Jacks, the oilcloth and club in a heap. Georgie wiped her face with her shawl then retied it around her waist. They were not far along the wooded path back to the shanty.

"Perhaps we can leave the canoe then send two lads to come fetch it later," Georgie suggested.

"No to whatever you said. We will return directly with your husband's canoe and Mr. Lipson's dead dog."

"I only suggest an alternative to your back's burden."

Georgie reached for her end, and they both lifted and resumed walking.

Mr. Bell hummed a lively chantey, its measure thrown off by a gasp of pain. "A husband who has forsaken the job of protecting his wife should release her so that another man may take up the job." He started up his tune again.

"He would never do that for he likes me best as scullion."

"Is Miss Tepper fifteen then? Sixteen?" The crowning chorus of the chantey broke against his throat.

"Do you ask if my eldest is of age?"

Her tone cut short his song. They walked along as the path increased in elevation. A great boulder sat in the clearing. It stood taller than two men, if one stood on another's shoulders. It was Big Rock, and travelers through the area knew this as the spot parallel to the river where the water started its more placid flow. Just when Georgie thought Mr. Bell might stop and rub his back on Big Rock, she heard him stumble.

With a jolt to her shoulder, the back end of the boat lurched. Her front end dropped, yanking her off balance, the whole boat too heavy to maintain on her own. Mr. Bell was bent over, his hands on his knees, wheezing.

"Lord, have you become my errand for the day again?"

His breathing was rapid, his back rigid. He grimaced in pain.

"We must return you to camp. Whyfor leave your tent, sir?" She would not be able to support his weight on her own.

"I cannot lie without task all day." His words caught at the back of his throat as a fresh spasm seized him.

"Can you straighten?"

"No. Give me a moment." He inhaled through his nose, willing an uptake of strength. With a twist of his mouth and a stumble backward, he straightened, but almost immediately sagged against her. She bore his weight, keeping him upright.

"Bend your knees less," she said.

He stiffened then wobbled, staggering to sink against a fallen log. She untied her shawl and wrapped it around him.

"I will fetch a mount," she said.

"No. I cannot get astride it." His chest heaved. He reached out both hands to her. "Lean on you. Try again."

She grasped his forearms, drawing him upward. He secured a long arm around her shoulder and leaned his weight against her, hunching protectively as though she had landed a painful blow to his kidney. She started purposeful strides toward home. His shirt was damp; he would chill soon.

She looked over her shoulder to the canoe, sitting in the clearing as if floating down a stream of cedar needles.

"Forgive me, sir." She let go of Mr. Bell.

He swayed, flopping forward. She ran to the canoe, Jacks's body crumpled at the stern. She grabbed the sack and club and turned, catching at the edge of her vision a mound of boughs, a rough shelter. She looked closer and saw the litter of squash blossoms and rinds. A flash of movement in the trees. Her back prickled. She felt spied upon, certain the black-haired, green-eyed man had been watching them all along. Dragging the dead dog had been for nothing. She had intended to heap the carcass at his feet, to shame him for cruelty, to hold him to task for murdering this dog, to show him she could walk right up to him without fear, could occupy any space she liked, and because of what he had done to her, she would pin this monstrous deed of a dog's cut throat on him. But now she hunched. He was behind a tree. But which? She could not muster courage to move, to flush him out of hiding. Then the blood throbbed at her neck, and the trees blurred, and she fled. She ran to Mr. Bell, wrapped her arm around his waist, and only slowed her pace when his feet dragged.

As they limped farther away, Ida Tewatcon emerged from the trees. She stood on the cedar-needled path. Her skirt and bodice were a mix of pink calicoes, her cloak was of European trade material. These and her buckskin leggings were stained with blood. She watched the woman and the man clutch each other. When they were far enough away, she sheathed her knife, knelt to the boat, and parted the fur at the animal's neck. Her cut had been swift in the darkness after luring this dog away from its pack brothers, and she confirmed now in the daylight that it had been the merciful yet fatal slash she had intended.

The infant sleeping on her chest rustled beneath her cloak, and she moved the cloth aside to cover her son's head with her hand.

"Hush, Káhuk," she said in her native Oneida. She called him Goose.

She stood, gathering her thoughts, recalibrating her idea of Dewitt Otis Lipson now that he had sent this woman to convey his response over his slain dog. Who was this woman to Lipson? From her hiding place, Ida had not understood the English woman's words nor the limping man's, but felt the English woman was the mother-in-law of the limping man. She was a good mother-in-law, properly scolding yet carrying the burden of his injured body. Ida thought she was formidable and wondered how loyal the English woman was to Lipson.

Ida lived with her parents and grandparents a distance west that took her an entire night to walk to the falls. During the war, her family's land and home at Oriskany had been burned, abundant fields of squash, cucumbers, beans, corn, watermelons destroyed by soldiers who wrote in their diaries laments for obliterating such bounty. The soldiers had burned her family's winter stores too. Her family's ravaged, smoking black land would recover, but it was the split among their Iroquois kin that had made her family retreat. Most Iroquois tribes had fought for the British, but the Oneida and Tuscarora tribes had fought for the Americans. So the ties of support and reciprocity among the Iroquois tribes were broken. Her family had surrendered the certainties of their life, withdrawing from meditating with the spirit world, no longer gathering for ceremonies, hunting and fishing in smaller party numbers. Her grandfather had been a scout for the Americans; despite his war service, his land was taken. The State of New York after the war had parceled off the Natives' land to white men who grabbed up the coveted fertile plots. Ida's family sought refuge west while others of her tribe were pushed north. The devastation of their life had forced them west before Ida was born.

When Ida was a girl, her grandfather had signed a treaty with the U.S. government providing restitution for her people who had fought in the war. The treaty acknowledged wages never paid for war service and funds for land and possessions ruined. The treaty had promised money to rebuild a church, although it was still not erected. Ida's grandfather had submitted a list of items lost in the war: his blanket which he shed before battle and never recovered, his house with one stone chimney, two horses, a wagon, one sleigh, all burned by Loyalists or Iroquois allied with them. Her grandfather, along with others, received arrears in wages for service in the war and each year thereafter five yards of bolted calico cloth. Ida's family did not replace their horses or wagon or sleigh, for they mistrusted their new neighbors, could not understand local governance, and each year their new land shrank by bits.

The first time she walked to the falls, Ida had navigated by the landmarks her grandfather described, but the land was so changed since he had last traveled through that she became lost. She had returned to him, and he instructed her to travel at night, giving her directions by stars. This routing worked, and her habit became traveling by cover of night, exulting in the pricking sheen of constellations.

Before the war, Ida's family had also farmed land at the falls where they had a fishing spot and a hunting camp; though the shelter was in disrepair, she used it for cover on rainy nights. This was the land she traveled to visit, passing first through Oriskany. Since well before she joined with her husband, Charlot, and had her child, she would walk through the night to sit on that land, the old carucate of crops now overgrown with Lipson's except for the squash vines and blossoms curled among and laying heavy upon his blighted wheat. Her family's squash seeds had survived the old fires set by the Revolutionary soldiers. Ida watched Lipson hoe and hack the squash vines only to see them grow back season after season, making a hardy mixture with what he tried to cultivate. Ida did not take from Lipson's field until she had her son and carried him along. She gave Káhuk squash rinds to gum after their long nights of travel to supplement her breast milk until they returned home to her family's relocated plot, plentiful yields of pumpkins, strong stalks of corn and beans, though pressured from the family's diminished share of acreage. Her family talked about advancing farther west into Wisconsin, but it was just talk. Still, a sadness loomed, a separation of distance too far to travel overnights to visit her family lands.

So her trips had become more frequent to the falls. She sat protected in the trees, cloaked from a wandering bad spirit with green eyes. She sang to her son the story of her grandparents' work in these lands, anointed him with water and soil, and stayed days longer than she had on previous trips. On one of these extended days, she had heard sounds above her singing, a pack of dogs quarreling, a man and woman shouting, then a woman in distress. She had resumed singing more softly, Káhuk sun-warmed on her chest. A word of anguish from her own language thudded like a rock at her ears. She ran with Káhuk in her arms to the sound and crouched through the night outside the small homestead, beyond the detection of the dogs tethered in the yard. The woman yelled a mix of English and Oneida words. Then her voice cut silent. At daybreak, Dewitt Otis Lipson hitched his mare, untied one of the dogs, and rode off. Ida emerged from her hiding spot, ran past the remaining dogs straining against their ropes, and entered Lipson's door.

Pelts were piled in front of the hearth, scraps to form a bed. A kettle steamed, his breakfast stew rich with fish. She huddled against the warm stones and dipped a cup for the stew, sharing sips with her son who kept pursing his lips for more. The place was tidy, neat stacks of provisions, weapons and snare lines hung on the wall. There was no sign of disturbance. She had not heard the woman escape in the night.

Káhuk reached to pet the furs, kicked his legs to be let down. She unwrapped him from her chest. He sighed into the pile, rubbing his hands and cheek on a mound of silky rabbit trims. He lowered his bottom, his ears sinking, face first as if peering into water. He pulled up a lustrous beaver hide and handed it to her like a prize. He burrowed deeper, rolling like a marten in a black bog. He came up for air, babbling words of discovery, and went down again. He surfaced hugging the hind end of a black bear, teething on its snub tail. His legs were sunk into the furs, and he blinked, at the edge of snuggling into a warm nap. He shifted and swam, finding the right spot. She would let him rest, allow him to dip into sleep then nudge him right back awake, for they had stayed too long. As he waddled, a bright blue cloth twisted over his legs. Ida unwound it, tugged it free. It was a dress of trade cloth with porcupine quill embroidery at the hem. She lifted Káhuk from the bedding pile and ran from Lipson's house.

Later in the night, tucked beneath boughs outside Lipson's house, Ida dreamed that the lost woman lay next to the fur bedding. The lost woman raised her head. Her hair was undone, covering her face, and she cried her name, Talise Jollicoeur, pitiably. She crawled to her gown. Ida spoke words from their language to reassure her that she was not Lipson. Talise sat, brushed the hair from her face. She had the long nose of her mother's sisters, but Ida did not recognize her. Ida sat spellbound, beholding Talise's dream form. Was this what Talise had looked like when alive? Or was this what she looked like when dead?

"Can you walk?" Ida asked in their language, and as Talise stood, blood gushed down her legs, and she fainted to the floor. In her dream, Ida was stiff with fear, could not move to revive the woman. Ida woke at sunset and walked home to her family.

But she returned again to the falls, watching Lipson, her family scolding her for doing so. They were too bitter to go back, her grandparents too frail. They advised her to leave the white man for his own people. To Ida's family, the matter was settled.

Ida tried but could not concentrate on her work at home. She could only think of Lipson and Talise. Ida wrecked the beading of leggings, spilling loose beads then mashing them irretrievably into the sand. She bumped pots of soup, disrupting the contents. Her husband lost sleep because her limbs twitched all night. She overwatered the garden plots, flooding the brace roots. Her milk vinegared then dried up. When her mother suggested a wet nurse, Ida fled with Káhuk back to the falls, weaned him on the pulp of squash, which he mashed to his face with relish. He held fast to the rinds, clutching them in his small fists like the bones of a proud kill.

Ida dumped a sack of deer innards in front of Lipson's dogs. She spent the next several days winning the dogs' trust and favor by feasting them with the fattest trout and plumpest eel from the coldest part of the river near the stone bridge. It was then she had warned away the English woman with missiles of apples, watched the black-haired, green-eyed spirit pin her. Ida knew it was a spirit, not a man, for its eyes were iridescent and damaged as smudged moth wings. Ida had watched Lipson charge at Georgie and the spirit, yet Lipson had rushed as if the spirit were a man, a trespasser upon his land. As the spirit had retreated from Jacks, Ida ran in the opposite direction, unintentionally drawing Jacks at her heels.

How had Lipson and the English woman not noticed it was a spirit? The English woman had been blinded from panic, Lipson half-drunk. But the dog. How had the spirit beguiled an animal?

The spirit had power to appear in flesh-and-blood form, fooling even the dog as it held flesh in its bite. This had made Ida cower and run, for it was counter to how she had witnessed spirits called down by rites. They never loomed without being beckoned. And when they did, they were luminous, dispersive as melting lake ice. Ida's family performed the traditions irregularly and without the exacting intent her grandfather taught. Ida thought this lazy practice had caused the disruption—this spirit bold, a fugitive from convention, sly enough to trick a dog.

Hidden in Lipson's yard, she kept watchful, but never heard Talise's voice again. One night as the dogs watched with sleepy, full bellies, Ida painted two red stripes on the outside of his door with boiled berry juice. He opened his door in the morning, stumbled down the porch from the fright, stopped cold, gaped at the door, muttered words of disbelief. He loosed his dogs, scooted them in all directions to search the woods. They ran to her, nosing her and little Káhuk affectionately, then ran off again for the game scents they craved. While Lipson was out of his house, Ida entered, sprinkled dried flower powder onto his furs. That night, his face sunk into the minky down, and he dreamed and drooled and woke to wipe the wetness away, his lips dragging over the powder, and he smacked his lips from the slight bitterness and swallowed then fell back into dreaming. He would endure a worrying, though temporary, impotence for a few days: upon waking, even after gutter dreams, clutching a prematurely lain, soft-shelled egg between his legs. His hand groped to check through the afternoons and evenings only to find the same the lax sponge of it even as a pair of stockings ran through his mind on a clothesline, the legs of a different woman kicking through each pass.

On the night when the dogs didn't so much as whimper when she approached, she stood before the pack. Jacks slipped off his tether and followed her away from his brothers, understanding his sacrifice. She would use Jacks to send a threat to Lipson and a clear message to the other white men that Lipson was no good. She would lead the rest of the dogs back home with her, relocate with them in a few years to the promise of Wisconsin, to free the dogs far from this man. But before that, she would stay long enough at the falls for the dogs to show her where to dig for Talise's bones. She would carry those bones overland west, the dogs trotting behind. But for now, dread rooted her to stay alert outside his door, and she trenched down to see what he would do next. She intended to watch Lipson, and now she would watch the English woman too.

Georgie and Mr. Bell staggered into the yard. Poppy ran to them, and seeing Mr. Bell sag at the knees, helped her ma half drag him into his tent.

"Where is Mr. Lipson? Poppy, where is your sister?"

"He's gone looking for his pup. Clara searches for the dog too."

The women settled Mr. Bell onto the bear pelt.

"I will fetch a poultice." Georgie left the tent.

Poppy knelt. "Grab hold of my hand if it comforts, Mr. Bell."

He grasped her hand, closing his eyes.

Inside the shanty, Georgie dumped the oilcloth bag and club on the worktable as Black Vy skimmed fat from a boiling kettle. She nodded in acknowledgement of her returned goods, wiping her hands on her apron. "What trouble is there?"

"A poultice. Mr. Bell."

Black Vy thrust two rags and bread leftover from the morning meal into Georgie's hand, and Georgie ran outside for the spring box. She flung it open, lifting the slick bottle of milk, dribbling it over the muslin.

Mr. Bell had not moved from his stiff sideways posture. Poppy had heard her ma's approach and dropped his hand. Georgie stood over him, crouched for the height of the tent, and worked the bread into the cloth. She held the poultice out to Poppy. In the transfer, it dripped on his breeches, and Poppy quickly drew it away. Georgie lifted his shirt. Poppy saw the full glade of his hair. A scar broke across his low belly, a row of white unripe berries cutting through a dark thicket.

"We will have to roll you," Georgie said.

He drew aside one arm, and Poppy saw the fish belly white of his underarm and its tuft of hair.

"Behind me," he gasped.

Poppy reached across him, the poultice dripping on the tender spot below his ribs, and he curled his stomach inward. She tucked the cloth at his low back.

He nodded to the corner. "Fetch a man a dry shirt?"

Georgie laid this and a blanket over him.

From outside, they heard a distant call: "Ja-a-ck-s!" And the high call of Clara repeating Jacks's name after Mr. Lipson.

"I must find Mr. Lipson." Georgie left the tent.

Poppy stood over Mr. Bell.

"Would you stay for a bit?" He gripped her arm and drew his fingers down her wrist.

Poppy freed her wrist, drew her sleeve to cover it. She sat next to him.

"Are you in a great deal of pain, Mr. Bell?"

"Yes."

"Might I fetch a strong medicine from the house? I do not believe there to be laudanum, but Black Vy has whiskey."

"Do not trouble yourself." He reached for her hand again.

She tucked her hands into the folds of her skirt. Sunlight lit his eyes golden and cast warmth on his cheeks. He would not look away. His breathing was ragged. She tried to compose herself, hoped he was in too much pain to see she was flustered. She lived in the memory of having the courage to pile her hair and cast him a fetching look yet now could hardly meet his eyes. When she had been wedged underneath his armpit as they had carried him into camp, she had been cradled by his scent. She had remembered it ever since, the salted, smoked, sage-laced gamebird nip of him. Even though he and the other crewmen bathed only in summers—and then it was splashing without soap—his scent was clean. She tried to remember and inhale it at night as the smoke from his outdoor fire drifted toward the shanty. He was a man whose sweat was salty. He needed someone to notice, to clean up his whiskers.

He was pale, straining his face as though needing privacy. She shrunk back, not at the pain evident in his face. He had been centered on his pain, not her, and she felt foolish. She rose to leave, but he grabbed her hand. He squeezed. She sat, bearing his grasping fingernails as they dug into the spaces between her fingers. In the enclosed tent, his smell soured. He seized rigid as he had when they found him at the tree. The spasm released him. The relief made his eyes water, and he relaxed the grip on her hand but held it lightly.

"Thank you, miss, for staying with me."

"You will be well soon. What ails you? Did you seize before your back was injured?"

"No. The fits are brought on from the back pain."

He could not stay on if he were no use to the crew. The black powder blasting required a doubling down of manpower and after that, the cold weather would set in, time to hunker for the season. He had duties as the hired driver, but that was a temporary position until he healed, a deal

Hugh had offered to keep him in wages. Mr. Bell had asked how much
back strength it took to light a wick, but Hugh had answered that it was
strongman's work, and he could not be chief wick lightsman. Hugh told
him to take the winter to heal then to come back to wages and strapping
hard labor in the spring.

"The men will have to carry me on a board out of these woods." Mr.
Bell tried to lift off the bed but fell back. "The man who figures out
how to blast this sodden rock will command all of New York."

"You do have family to care for you?" Poppy asked.

"A sister in Little Falls. But she has small ones and cannot journey."

From outside once more: "Here boy! Hie boy! Come back!" Mr.
Lipson had circled back to the yard. His voice and Clara's called out
together. Her ma must have lost them.

Poppy kept blinking, the only way she could hold his gaze. She
pushed away thoughts of lying next to him, the curling of his body
against her back.

"I am sure Papa will want you next year. There is much clearing to
be done. His ambitions are many." Her face grew hot. She had reached
her limit of sitting so close to him. She needed space to consider his
words, their meaning. She might be blurting nonsense and not know it.
She bent over him, tucking the pelt about his shoulder. This was the last
advance she could properly make.

"I will allow you rest, sir. I must find Ma."

But he squeezed her hand. "Stay, miss."

Black Vy entered the tent, and Mr. Bell let go of Poppy's hand. At
this, Poppy startled, looking between Black Vy and the space where her
and Mr. Bell's hands had just been joined. He had held her hand for
more than comfort of his pain. Black Vy stared sternly at her, at him,
and without needing direction, Poppy followed her out of the tent.

Ezra Emmons and Noah Stiles had fetched the canoe with Jacks in it,
and when they laid Jacks down in the yard, Mr. Lipson lunged at them
as if to strike but sagged into their arms. He twirled round, his fists
bunched, sank to the dirt, and cradled Jacks. He didn't need to be told
that Ezra and Noah did not kill his dog.

Clara ran to Jacks and stopped short of Mr. Lipson. She wept at
his shoulder. Her parents scolded her to hush, that it wasn't her loss
and wasn't she ashamed to disrupt Mr. Lipson's grief. But Clara wailed,

rooted in the dirt when Hugh tried to carry her off, tears and exertion shining up her whole face. And the louder she wept, the tighter Mr. Lipson grasped Jacks, the lower he buried his head against his fur. Her parents commanded quiet, but through her sobs they heard her say she could not stop. And she wailed this phrase on repeat for awhile. "I cannot stop. I cannot stop." At the first cease, Hildy picked up Clara and carried her snuffling against her shoulder into the shanty.

The crew had returned to the yard to cook noonchine, and they sat with lowered heads eating pike fried in bacon drippings, listening to the whump and chink of Mr. Lipson's shovel as he dug a grave for Jacks in the stony dirt. He had asked Hugh if he might dig a grave for Jacks there, at the most elevated ground of the river. Georgie could not bear the scene, the silence of the usually lively men replaced by Mr. Lipson's digging.

Georgie walked to the rise that held Margaret's grave. The rest of Hugh's family, his mother's brothers and sisters and their parents, were in a family plot in Albany except for one sister. Margaret had determinedly said she would be buried alongside her cherished sister, who had died suddenly after contracting scarlet fever while visiting the falls. Her body had not been fit for transport, so it was buried a short walk from the shanty. But her grave had not been marked, and its exact location forgotten over the years. So the sisters lay in the ground at a distance from each other.

Yet even before her sister's death, Margaret planned for her own burial at the falls. She had a vision for her son's achievements. To Margaret, it was a foregone conclusion that Hugh would make Buttermilk Falls the tourist destination he said he would. He would garner security for his family, and the Tepper name would be known as one of enterprise. Margaret wanted her permanent mark on that estate, a headstone proclaiming her as the matriarch of what she imagined would be a successful family dynasty. The wealthy families from New York City and Boston would travel north to visit the falls, and they would stop briefly to view her grave, knowing the woman who had raised Hugh Tepper.

The burial plot was up a steep hill surrounded by cedars, studded with stones that had always been there and would be rolled into place then chiseled as each family member died. Yet Margaret had no headstone. Georgie sat, the light shafting down from the leafy gap in the trees. Margaret had been buried near the middle, or was it the south edge? There was no evidence of her burial, the mound of interment dirt obscured by strewn pine needles, branches collapsing in. An entire tree had fallen across the plot some time after Margaret's burial, but Georgie's memory of the burial layered falsely with the family having to tramp around the tree. She corrected the cloud of her memory and doubted the spot was even close to Margaret's resting place.

Hugh had grand plans to build wrought-iron gates to formalize the family plot. He intended a headstone for his mother once he had the funds, once the tourists started. He had written an inscription for the stone carver on birch bark: "Margaret Rosalie Wemple Tepper. Relict. Born 1720. Died 1789." In brutal shorthand, Hugh honored both his parents.

Samuel's body had not been buried. Georgie had heard the men's stories about the Oriskany battlefield, where none of the fallen men had been interred, their bones still scattered throughout the swamp between the wagon road and the Mohawk River. Hugh had not set aside space for his father in the family burial plot.

Before wrapping his mother's body in its burial shroud, Hugh had cut off his mother's thick white braid of hair. Georgie had tried to stop him, but he insisted, later hanging the braid alongside Amaranthus's bridle and lead rope. Sometimes the girls looked at the braid then stood behind Amaranthus and plaited her tail in the same pattern. Georgie envisioned Margaret's shorn, ragged locks beneath the needles and dirt. Margaret would not have wanted that.

The tree bower occluded the bright sky except for the strake shining down like a glass chimney. A promethea silkmoth crawled at Georgie's feet, dragging its wings across the needles, rotating its feathered antennae as it wobbled toward a fallen black cherry branch. Georgie lifted the diurnal creature. It was a giant, the wings extending past the width of her wrist. *Callosamia promethea.* Eyespots on each forewing. Bark-brown wings, so female. She set the moth down, and it picked its way crabwise into cover.

On the day of Margaret's burial, Hugh had crudely pegged a space alongside his grave for a wife, though the marker was now obscured. This would not be Georgie's final resting place. Hildy or some other woman would occupy it. Georgie imagined the pale stone atop Hildy's grave, her hair cut off, draped over the headstone, cascading pretty ringlets sweeping the copper pine needles.

The trees arched inward, a ceiling of protection and permanence that would have pleased Margaret a great deal.

Hildy carried Clara above stairs to the sleeping garret, laid her down, and curled alongside the child. She let Clara exhaust herself, stroking her hand until she fell quiet and dozed. Hildy closed her eyes, and in the silence, she slept. Clara woke after dipping into sleep. Hildy faced her, breathing softly through open lips. Her legs were curled, and the skirt of the blue embroidered dress billowed like a lake-oxen's rump. Both of Hildy's arms extended toward Clara, and Clara thought to gently lift her dead weight limbs and snuggle close. Hildy twitched in her dreams. Clara didn't want to wake her. Hildy jerked again, and Clara saw the cap sleeve of the dress ride up. The sleeve was too tight on Hildy. It left a red mark. The smash of Hildy's bosom rose and fell. Hildy was growing, Clara thought, and that was called getting fat in adulthood. One of the embroidered blue buds was fraying, a thread springing free.

The dress was dirtied and tatty from Hildy's wanderings in the yard and forest. She had a habit of trying to hug the pigs even though they would squeal in alarm and squeeze from her grip with a thrust of back legs. And this showed in rips and dark hoof streaks on the bodice. But Hildy had the impulse to throw her arms around everything, her spirit a poor match for the delicate chiffon layers, the dress a shabby version of what she had once fussed for. Hildy was not caring for the dress as Clara and Poppy would have. Clara's foul sadness returned.

Clara climbed down the steps, slipped outside, running to the fringes of the yard. She sat and watched the men, not talking, hunched over their chores, and this disruption in their mood and routine made her remember how awful the day was, and her lip trembled again. As she buried her head in her knees to let out the heave of sadness, she heard a high tinkling crash, like icicles falling onto themselves. She looked to the men. They had not heard it, for August Knecht stretched, bellowing out a yawn, and the other men were still. Clara saw a flicker of movement near the sugaring room. A woman wearing different shades of floral pinks ran deep into the trees. Clara followed, clomping after the billowing hood and skirt, a baby staring straight at her, strapped to a cradle board on the woman's back. The woman wore calicoes of different plant patterns: branches, buds in every shade of pink: salmon, sumac, autumn leaves, the warning sky of sunrise. The shapes in the calico rippled as the woman ran. A thistle popped back at Clara, then as the woman leapt right, a leaf-sprouting branch snapped behind. The striped boughs and spurs on her calico bodice and sleeves undulated with her driving arms. The heavy, bright border of her skirt sprouted rosy bog laurel, and the cloth hem swished the green undergrowth. She flew as she ran, her beaded leggings flashing like feathered raptor legs. The baby reached his arms out to Clara as if to encourage her to catch them. Clara was hindered by her big boots, then tripped, whumping onto her chest and palms. When she lifted her head, they were gone.

Clara wandered to the overturned tree. The gape in the ground left by the toppled roots had been dug out. Where before there had been a dusty layer of leaves in a shallow depression, there was now a black pit, deep enough to peer into. A cold rush hit her face like when she opened the shed door behind the tavern in springtime, the ice block from the pond just starting a watery drip onto its sawdust bed. She craned closer into the pit. Broken roots stuck out on the sides, creating a jagged maw. The pit was too deep and dark to see bottom. It was not wide enough for a horse to fall into, but she could. It was so wide she would not be able to grasp onto roots as she fell, even if her arms were outstretched. Had the men been working here to dig out the pit? She looked around. There were not dirt piles, no boot tracks. Had the dirt sunk from its own wet weight? She dropped a stone into the pit and waited several hammers of her heart before hearing a whumph. Not the plunk of a well or a privy, but a dry thud as if a bird slammed against a shutter.

Clara stood and knocked the overturned roots, sifting down clouds of dried mud. Couldn't Baron Saturday tell that she needed to see his horses? There were chatterings in the trees, a cauldron of crows diving to raid a nest in a cedar. The cedar's base was darker, and nearby trees were stained at the same height. Snags of limbs and leaves were entangled in some of the trees' crotches. The distant trees did not have the same water marks or knots of debris caught where their great limbs branched. There had been a flood, but where had the water come from? She picked a few stones from the dried-out roots of the overturned tree, throwing them into the opening, sending down a whir of hellos, as if knocking on Baron Saturday's roof.

There was no response. She turned for home and walked several minutes before she heard a faint cry behind her. In the scrim of branches, flashes of pink. The hooded woman was crouched, dumping from a clay jar a circle of what looked like black ash around the opening of the overturned tree. Clara returned to her. The woman stood, clapped the black dust off her hands. She spoke something stern in a language Clara did not understand. The baby was hidden on her back, shouting out, sensing Clara. Clara looked in dismay at the black ring around the opening. She recognized it as black powder. Her first thought was to throw her body across the opening to prevent the woman from lighting it on fire. But the woman gestured for Clara to approach the opening, and Clara thought she understood. Of course, fire would draw the devil to the surface. She then thought the woman impressive and wise. Clara obeyed, kneeling at the opening. The woman knocked stones together, sparking alight not the black powder but dried bundles of herbs tied with red string. The orange bits of flame burned out quickly, and the smoke poured off the bundles' ends. The woman knelt next to Clara, fanning the smoke across Clara's head. Clara directed the smoke to the opening, but the woman clutched Clara's hands and directed the smoke to Clara's heart. The woman released Clara's hands, closed her eyes, and floated smoke across her own heart. Then she cupped her hands and drew smoke over her head, and the smoke curled down her shoulders, wisping off the forehead and nose of the baby on her back. Clara imitated her, lifting smoke. The woman opened her eyes. Clara nodded to the opening.

Ida drew her lips tight. The girl did not understand. Ida had chosen this spot because it was important to the girl, a place where Ida had seen the girl come to make prayers. And of everyone, Ida saw the girl bear the loss of the dog most painfully. When dodging into the sugaring room to hide from the English woman, Ida had bumped the orderly rows of jars. They were the barrier to the boxes with the black powder, so the jars must hold strong medicine. The black powder was valuable to the white men, useful to honor the dog. She had hurried too much upon leaving, knocked over more jars in her haste not to be discovered. She had picked up a jar to set it back, but instead had fled with it.

"I cannot make the dog appear from the earth," Ida said in her language to the child. Ida smudged her finger on the black powder and drew a crude dog on the underside of birchbark.

"We honor with the black powder the dog's spirit and sacrifice." Ida set the drawing onto the opening.

But Clara took this to mean that the dead dog was now with the devil underground, and she felt another wave of grief rise.

Ida pulled smoke down the child's legs and sang songs of mourning and forgiveness. Ida held her hand on the girl's chest to slow her sobbing breath. Clara calmed, and breathed in the sweet grass smell, the smoke washing around her heart.

Clara trudged back to the sugaring room. Inside, clay jars were knocked over, bees hovering, buzzing from the disruption, the clattering over of their caves. One of the black powder boxes had been pried open, its lid askew. Bees crawled at the edge, dipping into the dry meal of the powder, drawn to its wood ash smell. Clara saw the sinkhole of a hand swipe. The woman had scooped a pouchful. Clara understood that the black powder meant something different to her than it did to Clara's papa and the other men.

It was a hot night, a night for the women to claim the fire room for washing. Hildy, Georgie, and Clara fetched water from the river. Poppy built the fire. Black Vy was the first to wash. She poured reheated water from the morning kettle into a porcelain bowl set within a crate. She sat, her haunches resting on the crate's edges, and opened her legs above the steaming bowl. She lifted her skirt to rest on her lap. She untied her stockings, rolled them down, tossed them hearthside out of splashing range. With a cloth, she duckbilled water onto her private parts, her wrist and forearm working up there a long time, her face lifted toward the fire. Poppy saw the tattoo inside Black Vy's leg, different from the one on her palm. Her leg was inked, her palm marked by fired metal. Poppy sat with clean rags and busied herself folding.

At the tavern, Poppy and her ma and sister had washed wearing their shifts, sitting in a tub, so their skins and shifts were washed at the same time. The washing between their legs happened under the soapy dark cover of the water. There was no tub at the shanty, just the wide porcelain bowl or the river for a few short weeks of high summer. When the men were around, the women closed themselves in the shanty and made it a bathhouse.

Black Vy stopped washing. The girl had thoughts. Black Vy closed her legs and wrung out the rag, felt the steam glaze up the backs of her calves, purl at the crooks of her knees. She lifted a dripping foot and reached to rag between her toes. She splashed her foot down and dredged up the other. The girl would not look at her. The girl was steadily crumbling in her avoidance and silence, eyes darting, fingers folding the rags over and again till she might shred holes. The girl had thoughts she could not harness, as if something unholy had flopped onto her dinner plate and she was obliged to preserve polite manners at the table. Black Vy knew the girl's thoughts. The girl thought Black Vy had been owned by more than one master, for what other past could two marks declare? Black Vy widened her legs and let the firelight play over her skin. She grasped and framed with her hands the inked flesh on her thigh. Poppy glanced over at the wad of flesh in Black Vy's hand, then looked away. Her mind altered the inked initials into a spray of purple violets.

Black Vy had inked the initials of her first born's father there when she was young, before she ever spoke a word to him. His name was

Barnaby. She had thought it was a safe place to inscribe the initials. But her master saw them before Barnaby. And her master punished her for effacing her body and for disloyalty. He tried to scrub the initials off with scalding water and a horse brush, but the ink was needled below her skin. He threatened to burn it off, but never did. When her master took her, that was the flesh he grabbed first, and sometimes she had bruises around Barnaby's initials, but the bruises faded and the initials remained.

"My Barnaby's." Black Vy's words choked off as Poppy looked away.

Poppy could not listen nor return Black Vy's gaze. She did not have a framework for an exchange of this kind. She tried to hear in those two words if Barnaby was a father or a son or a master or a husband or a brother. She decided he was a Valentine, but there was sadness and defiance that Poppy did not understand. A tremor rippled across her cheek and mouth. She was certain her ma would not approve of this talk, would shut it down, redirect the focus to the rigid checkpoints of bathing. Whenever Poppy had thought of the body parts Black Vy now displayed and handled, she had conjured with buoyant pleasure, and now Black Vy was mapping over these parts with a raw leaden fear. The gobbet of flesh was bulging. So Poppy did not listen. She stacked her rags. Her thoughts shilly-shallied. She saw the violets in her mind dissolve to the inked man's initials as Black Vy released her thigh. Neat, blocky letters. Poppy had never conceived of carving an emblem onto herself to decide a future with a man as to preordain it in stone. The gesture rang her heart like a tin angel.

The remembrance of her ma's burnt and stinking forearm never sharpened beyond the edges of Poppy's memory. She didn't allow it. She had told herself and Clara that her ma's brand was the welt of a chimney exploding its hot stones onto her flesh. Black Vy's ink was a revelation, upended the scorn of a man burning his mark.

Poppy knew she was expected to consider a lesson of rectitude after Black Vy showed her flesh. She understood Black Vy to mean the inside of the thigh was not the place for a man's initials. She gave Black Vy a practiced nod. Poppy handed Black Vy a clean rag and inwardly mapped her own body, striking out several possibilities until she landed on the inside of her upper arm, a space almost always covered by a shift and that could be drawn close to her ribs when changing or bathing. She knew to not ask Black Vy Gideon Bell's middle name.

Black Vy watched the girl avoid her. She lamented speaking Barnaby's

name, regretted any attempt of explanation to the girl, was surprised at
herself as the words came tumbling out, angry for expecting sympathy,
irritated with the girl for not giving any. She shook her head, the girl too
callow to understand. Black Vy pressed her lips together and lowered
her head with the sadness she had chosen this suckerel.

Black Vy peeled down her shift, the rag catching the scribbled scars.
She wiped down her armpits and neck and underneath her breasts. She
swished the cloth in the water, squeezed it out, then rose from the crate.
"Next."

Poppy tossed the old water to the yard. The others were returning,
breathless from the strain of the buckets, their skirts splashed with
dark stains as they switched hands to ease the carry. Poppy rinsed and
warmed the bowl with fresh water from the kettle. She straddled onto
the precarious edges of the crate.

Black Vy stood from the hearth and set the hot pan of biscuits on the
table. She took her seat at the head, opposite Hugh.

"Who wants to hunt weasel today?" Hildy asked, nudging Clara.

"Weasel?" Georgie asked. "Whatever for?"

Clara dropped her slice of pork, wiping both hands together, her
eyes wide, conscious not to betray too much excitement. "Yes, please.
May we, Ma?"

"I wish to go," said Poppy.

Georgie and Hugh responded over one another.

"Yes, you may," Hugh said.

"No, you may not. Black Vy needs help emptying ash from the
hearth," Georgie said.

"Poppy sha's stay behind for that chore," Hildy announced.

Hugh dipped his chin to his plate, pinched up ham.

Georgie and Poppy stopped eating and stared darkly at Hildy. Hugh
mopped his fingers across the juice on his plate and licked them clean,
nodding in assent toward Hildy. She clapped her hands.

Black Vy tore open a fresh biscuit, the steam rising. She nodded at
Poppy. "They's a bristle out back."

Clara mouthed the words, *May I leave from table, Papa?* but she answered
her own question by shaking her head and biting her slab of pork. She
was not to leave the table until she chewed and swallowed all her food.

Clara cleared the dishes to the hearth where Poppy wiped them clean with a rag. Georgie brought a handful of sand from the yard and vigorously scrubbed the pans. Black Vy stood at the window, counting the hogs in the yard. It was a slaughtering day.

Hildy daydreamed at the table. Clara wrapped her body around the chair back but could not get Hildy's attention. Clara tapped the chair with her black shoe. Hildy came to life.

"Let's to the weasel, little lamb." And they ran out the door.

Georgie watched as Hildy and Clara went hand in hand through the yard to the woods, Clara tripping a bit in her excitement and big black shoes, waving at each man cooking and eating by his fire. Georgie would have the morning for other tasks without having to braid or wipe down Hildy.

Black Vy stropped her butchering knife. "Folks'll take your children away by snatches if you allow it."

"What am I to do? And what do you know of it?" Georgie left the shanty, for there was not space of her own.

At the upturned tree, Hildy beat the roots with a stick.

Hildy knew this section of the forest, the one in which the men could not hew the fallen timbers because the trees grew twisted, the internal fibers coiling and ropy tough, repelling men's axes. The wind force that had shaped the trees' spiral growth had also toppled them down, one old giant breaking over, crashing the others with it. When young, the trees had bent riotously in the winds, the torsion forming their tough, spiral cores, their twisted heartwood and outermost layers. No one knew why the winds ravaged this grove. It was not situated on a high spot; in fact, the grove sagged a bit in a spongy depression. The new growth, mostly elm suckers, was already taking root, the shoots spreading laterally, fingering across the surface soil, beneath and around the crashed tree site, thirsty young growth that would thrive in the spring floods and soon mature to start a fresh generation of spun-hardened wood grain. The suckers cast a net of roots that would search and dive to the blackest, deepest waterworks of nutrients, penetrating toward bedrock, intending permanence.

"This is where he comes," Clara announced, spreading her arms wide.

Hildy smiled, looking around. "Who come? A man from the crew? Which 'un?"

Clara's eyes darkened, and she gave an impatient yank on the cape in reprimand. "No." She grimaced her mouth, unhappy Hildy did not understand. Clara became mired in thinking about explaining everything. Then she raised a stick.

"Come out, devil!" Clara called shrilly, brightening at the grand fun of directing an adult at the game. "Beat the roots!" She passed the cudgel to Hildy.

"Like so?" Hildy beat hard, knocking dirt, the spray hitting Clara's hem and shoes. "Do you think he sleeps curled up with the weasel like this?" Hildy closed her eyes and curled her fists to her chin, snuggling the stick against her cheek.

Clara imitated the pose. "Mayhaps he is sleepless with a squirming weasel!"

Clara tied Hildy to a tree. Hildy didn't seem to mind, but playfully shifted her shoulders to test the reach of her cape tether. Clara stopped abruptly as Hildy tested the cape, expecting her to simply break free and decide the cloud of Clara's command was over. Clara was losing stamina, hovering between the foul mood of having to convince someone older of the game of minding her rules and the delight of the adult obeying.

Clara made downward striking motions. "Beat the twisted roots." Clara grunted from her effort. "Then call him to come out."

Hildy beat the roots, and more dirt sprayed onto Clara. "Stand back, child. We must rouse him now."

"Come out, devil!" Clara touched her fingertips together in delight.

They waited, both eyeing the pit. Hildy untied herself and stepped closer, peering in. It was a windy morning. The treetops clattered and swayed. Dirt and leaves swirled at the edge of the pit. Rays of sunlight bounced into the pit as the riot of trees tilted. The pit was deep, no discernable bottom. A branch dropped, heavy as a sailor's arm, and they both jumped.

"I believe he waters his horses at Buttermilk Falls," Clara announced. "We cannot miss their morning drink. We must go there now."

"Oh?" Hildy looked back at Clara and dipped her toe in the pit as if to test a pool of water. Her eyes widened and her whole leg began to throttle in stiff spasm.

Clara gasped, both hands spread wide.

But Hildy laughed. "Oof! You thought he bit my toe! You did!" She withdrew her foot and playfully hopped up and down.

Hildy's hem had not been shredded by claws. The tattered chiffon was an old frock, and Clara saw that Hildy had not cared for this dress any more than the embroidered one. "Let me see your shoe."

Hildy lifted her skirt hem and pointed her toe. Clara confirmed it was unchewed. At the rim of the pit, a strip of dirt whispered, sank. Clara drew her focus to the deep hole, waiting for it to happen again.

Hildy turned around. "Oh, you got me! You tricked me back, lamb!"

The wind swept leaves across the opening, some of them swirling out of sight down the black pit.

"We are to go to Buttermilk Falls now. To the milky rock and see the fine horses."

Hildy sat on a fallen log. "Sha's we not stay here awhile and admire the fine sunlight?" She tipped her face to the bright morning light.

"No." Clara assumed her posture of authority. "Now to the falls."

"We sha's go when I say we go." Hildy lay back languorously, closing her eyes.

Clara grabbed fistfuls of Hildy's skirt. "The game is to skip to the falls!"

Hildy sat, slapping Clara's grip.

"You go now as I say!" Clara tore off the topmost layer of the front of Hildy's dress.

Hildy's face hardened. Clara stood with handfuls of the pearly material, realizing with shame and a fallen face what she had done.

"He will come out when ready." Hildy's mouth knitted a mean line. She dangled one leg over the pit, her arms tight to her sides. She tipped in headfirst, disappearing, the last sound the flap of her skirt hem.

There was no more sound from the pit, no thrashing, no bump of landing. The leaves swirled at Clara's feet.

Clara ran back to the shanty. There, she could not speak. She held the dress layer to Black Vy.

Black Vy tore to the blast site to alert the men.

The men searched the woods all afternoon. They indulged Clara's pleas by digging out the depression at the overturned tree. One of the men even murmured that the hole could have backfilled after Hildy fell in. Clara's insistence of the story was that convincing. They lowered a few men into the pit, scooping into its sides, then stopped for fear of collapse. They called through the woods, climbed trees to get a better sight of the whole area. At dusk, they regrouped in the shanty yard for lanterns, Hugh imploring them to continue searching.

Hildy returned to the yard, ambling through as the men's lamps swung halos of light. She was cheerful, called good evenings, carried a bundle of greengage plums wrapped in a white cloth. The men stared. She smiled and laughed and passed out a few plums.

Hildy embraced Hugh, who worked his hands all over her hair and face and whispered into her mouth. "Have you no thought for others' concern for you?"

Hildy said she had met up with the Coopers in the woods and they had invited her back for a tour of their orchard. "And now wouldn't good girls enjoy a plum?" She held out a plum for the girls to split.

Poppy accepted it and gave it to Clara. She brought the fruit to her nose, a smell of vines and sharp violets. It was soft, and the skin tore easily, smudged right off the flesh. The first bite would be juicy all down her front.

Hildy and Hugh climbed the stairs to the sleeping garret with a plum of their own. Black Vy and Georgie tucked in the girls, Black Vy with a plum already sunk in her front teeth, wiping the juices with the back of her hand.

From bed, Clara watched the bundle of leftover plums on the table, a round tumbled mass on the white cloth. She was pleased to think of herself as the only one who knew Hildy wasn't just badly behaved; Hildy knew where Baron Saturday kept his horses, and Hildy could fall and fly in and out of the pit like a plume of smoke on the wind.

Clara set off early in search of the orchard. Past the sleeping men, vines climbed the trees then crept the forest, fingering a path. She reckoned her way by following one bright tendrilled green patch to the next. She carried one of the plums Hildy had brought back the night before as if it were a ticket of admission to the orchard. She would share the plum with Baron Saturday, split it carefully along the stone, let him work a knife down the cleft in the skin. But she would hold a careful eye to keep him honest so he wouldn't split it unevenly and take the greedy half for himself.

There became fewer and fewer green patches from which to steer forward. She was soon surrounded by rock and faced with a sharp over-hang. She lowered to her belly and peered over. Water rushed through narrow crooks in the gully. On the far side was a grotto with a curtain of rain dripping off the rock. There was a man crumpled inside the rock shelter, lying on his side.

A rope bridge swayed over the river, the only way for her to reach him. She gripped a tight fist over the plum in her pocket. She reached for the rope, stood before its length, stared down its long sag in the middle and its upward slope at the other end. There were several wooden planks still attached, but some had rotted in the middle. She reached for the rope rail and stepped onto the first plank, the pitch of the bridge so sudden from her weight that she tucked her bottom under to regain balance. She shuffled, hands high on the rail for the whole length, the roar and mist of the water coolest as she sank at the low middle.

By the time she peered around the corner of the rock, the man was upright, though slumped. *You are Baron Saturday*, she decided. He was the same man from the tavern gangway, but his person was much deteriorated. Clara slid in the space between his legs, grasping his ankle to balance herself. She plopped down, tying the loose ribbons at his knees. His chest rose tight and shallow behind her. She made big bows and tied them securely. She had to redo one twice. When they were neat, tight bows, she looked at his face. He could not focus. Like Mrs. Peach's brand-new baby girl, he could not control his neck. She drew the plum from her pocket. He grimaced and shifted, his hands limply upturned at his sides. She thought herself wicked, her only thought that if he didn't gain strength, she would never see his horses. She set the plum in his palm, closing his fingers around it. She left him by the roaring water, tucked away in the grotto.

The next day, she balanced a place setting—plate, knife, mug—as she crossed the rope bridge. He must eat. He startled at the clatter as she sat between his legs. The plum was uneaten, so she set it upon the plate. She removed her shawl, wrapped it across his chest, tucked it to his chin.

"How did you fall into here? And why have you not flown out?" He was not bleeding, and his breathing pained him. He seemed more alert this time, his legs restless. He disrupted the supper setting, knocking over the mug and scraping the knife with the heel of his boot. His upturned hand bent at the wrist, fixed to the rock. The wrist twitched, tore away, and a pale-green spume flowed onto the rock, foaming like ham salad left out too long at a picnic. She checked his coat. It was different from the traveler's in the tavern gangway. His jawline was stronger too. Red in his skin and hair. This was a different man, but a familiar pale-green foam, what dripped off a tired horse's muzzle, leaking as though he were made of it. It was the same pale green she had seen streaked across the traveler's coat. And the same from a horse that grazed a bright patch of clover.

She knew then he had used up this body and would form a new one. He had played hard, his condition was too serious, and he had to let go but later return as a new figure. She took back the plum. He wheezed. His eyes widened. She scooted closer to him. He was in pain, still in this body, and she would wait with him.

She knew a person didn't have to be bleeding or crying to be in pain. When she had fallen off Glory, she could not hear, could not breathe, could only feel the star explosion of pain heating her tailbone, needling outward for all her limbs. When her hearing came splashing back, her papa's frantic question *Where does it hurt?* was the first thing she had heard, and she blinked, confused at how he could not know where, that it hurt her so bad everyone must know. She had looked down, clawing at her skirts to show them blood, but there was no blood, only pain without any proof, only the throbbing within her own body. Her ma had said, "She is fine. She is well. Just frightened." And Clara thought this is how the man must feel, so much pain but no blood, and how could he explain how bad it felt when it gripped him so, shutting off his regular speaking and pointing abilities?

"Your horse threw you. And I know how that is." Clara held his hand.

Glory's crooked back, her gracefully curving spine, made her gait twisted. Clara had practiced on Glory without a saddle, had gripped her legs against Glory's flanks for balance. Her father insisted that Clara ride astride, not sidesaddle, on a tricky mount like Glory.

"Heels down!" he had commanded.

But Clara had the habit of curling her toes inward to touch Glory's belly for balance. Astride Glory, she had the confusing sensation of Glory's great hind end being pulled by a watery current. But Glory had known what Clara meant by curling her toes against her hide. The girl meant to grip on for balance, like a baby to its mother, and when Clara had obeyed her father and dropped her heels, she lost balance, her outstretched arms flailing to catch handfuls of mane. Glory's pace quickened at the jolt of unsteadiness in the child. Glory had lowered her head in annoyance, brawing for a trot, bouncing Clara clean off. Clara had landed hard, the compact dirt terrible and disorienting. She had heard Glory's hooves close as the horse balked against the lead rein her father had quickly grabbed, the hooves striking, thudding soundly. All of Clara's bony points that had just ground against Glory's bony points, that pleasant grind had been disrupted. She had tried to breathe, but her bones folded onto themselves with each heaving breath.

She squeezed the man's hand, and this time he pressed back. "The horse that threw you must be wandering alone in the woods. I will find it, but you must tell me how to release the others from behind the rocks."

He did not respond.

She thought of her grandmother, how she had shuddered and focused unblinking on the rafters before dying. Clara had asked her ma what made her sick and her ma had answered, "Sometimes it is just time for a person to die." Clara pressed the man's upturned palm and said, "Sometimes it is just time for a person to die." She shrouded his form with the shawl and left him.

That evening at supper, Black Vy announced a shawl had gone missing. She only looked to Poppy. The next morning, when Clara went to retrieve the shawl, she could not rouse the man. The shawl had slipped off during the night. She wrapped it about herself and sat between his legs, untying the ribbons, pulling the bright silk out of his breeches.

The next evening at supper, Hildy eyed the ribbons tied at the nape of Clara's neck, ribbons unlike any scrap in the shanty. They shone like jewels peeping from behind Clara's ears. "Where did you find such fine ribbon?"

"The devil died in the grotto," Clara replied. "And now his horses are trapped in the rocks."

Hildy sat at the table, already combed and dressed. Poppy secured a cap into her hair. Hildy cradled Clara on her lap, who plucked at the blue embroidered flowers on Hildy's bodice. "There is less room here for me now." Clara laid her head against Hildy's bosom.

Hildy thrust the tambour and paper to Georgie. "He says you are to teach me the needle."

Georgie pushed up her sleeves. Hildy had found her embroidery patterns. Hugh had stacked the scenes of female supplication at the top, women kneeling alongside jugs of water in anticipation of washing prophets' feet; women threshing fields while nursing children; women full with child attending to cook fires. The patterns were not simple; they required several different colors of thread and weeks of knotting and tedious stitching. The only thread in the household was the white silk the men used to sew repairs on their own breeches and shirts. Georgie chose a crude reprint of a Francis Wheatley portrait: a mother stood amid hung laundry; three children and a husband slept in the background. A halfmoon shone through the home's window, conveying that the woman's chore extended deep into the nighttime.

Hildy drew another pattern from underneath her skirt, disrupting Clara from her lap. "Help your sister fetch water, lamb." Hildy patted Clara's bottom.

Clara and Poppy ran out, happy for a chore.

"I want this one." Three noblemen stood within a garden, one atop a ladder cutting the noose of a hung body.

"Whatever would you choose this for?"

Hildy smiled. "It has beautiful color. And that outland tree! Wherever can they be?"

"We don't have colored thread. It will all be one color."

"One color. Well, look how his coat flies in the wind!"

"Yes, that is a particularly tiresome and repetitive stitch." Georgie traced her finger along the folds of the material. "Do you see how there are four coats as such to stitch?"

"Three coats as such. The dead man wears only his shirt."

"Let us start, then, if this is what you choose. We begin with the running stitch." Georgie secured the muslin in the tambour. "Here is our starting point, at which we insert the needle through the backside of the fabric. Here, then, you take the needle and do as I instruct."

Hildy wove the needle in and out of the fabric. Georgie nodded approval. Hildy's first stitch was promisingly straight.

Several stitches on, Georgie dabbed a rag at the bloodied corn mattress; Hildy twirled about the house, the blood-streaked tambour sewn to her skirt and bouncing against her hip. It had simply been too much stillness for the girl.

"Stop." Georgie grabbed for the tambour. "Stop turning!"

But Hildy was insensible to her surroundings. The flurry of her skirt whooshed several paper patterns onto the fire, which Hildy rushed to save, only to upset one of the hanging kettles, which fell and displaced embers onto the floorboards then spattered up her front skirt hem, which smoldered and ignited. Georgie rushed over, sending a drying rack keeling into the hearth. The whole frame lit, laundry and all. The flames leapt out of the over-fueled hearth and climbed Hildy's back skirt hem to kindle the tambour still sewn to her waist.

Black Vy entered the house, wrestled Hildy to the floor, tore the tambour from her skirt, and padded out the flames on the embroidered dress. She heaved the flaming rack out of doors into a hog rut. Georgie doused the flames with dirt, stamping out the smoking heap. Black Vy waved her long apron, airing the shanty from the heavy smoke, checking inside for stray bits of orange ash that might ignite the bed or wallboards.

Hildy coughed as her blackened dress smoked. The dress had burned up to the smocked bodice, the blue embroidered flowers now dotted red as Hildy touched the flowers with her needle-stuck finger to count the buds still intact. The black overskirt hung in limp spikes around her hips. The underlayers were yellowed from smoke.

Black Vy grasped Hildy's bust to locate the source of the bleeding. Hildy broke free, ran, spitting into the dirt. She touched the tip of her tongue to staunch the bead of blood. Poppy and Clara entered the yard carrying a bucket between them. The dress smoked before their eyes.

The men had not recovered the wagon nor Balor and Brace. Hugh borrowed a cart and horse from Mr. Lipson and parked on the outskirts of the shanty yard, knowing when Clara heard the mare's nicker, she would come running from the house and follow him down the road through the woods. Hugh told Clara to walk alongside the cart. He would not let her ride on the seat until she told him the value of two horses and a wagon. For the first rods, she near exhausted herself howling and trying to climb into the cart. The cart did not move fast on the uneven road, but she could not find purchase on its swaying height, and she was not strong enough to haul herself up. After plodding many oxgangs, Hugh thought she might drop before telling him the value. She was quiet and kept pace walking with the cart's slow amble through the ruts. She walked alongside the mare's rear. The child had enough heft of spirit that the horse was not spooked. If she kept sight of the mare's front hooves as they lifted and pointed and flashed their triangular undersides, Clara was calm. Yet as Hugh craned back, he saw she was not grappling with the lesson. He grew scornful of her: so stubborn, so resistant to an inner morality she should have by now grown into.

Hugh had to relieve himself, had the urge for the last few rods, but was determined to outlast the child until she stated a reasoning of worth. He squirmed in his seat and bargained inwardly that if she provided a bare explanation by the next turn in the road, he would let her ride in the cart for home.

They came to a point in the road that Clara recognized, where she had followed Jeptha Buell and Isaac Coe, where they had stooped and picked up a piece of the harness. Clara stopped, and her papa told her to keep walking. She looked to the bog. She did not see a glint beneath the leaves this time. Hugh called for her to walk. But she kept looking at the stone dark surface of the bog.

He pulled the reins, stopped the cart. He yelled at her to catch up. He clucked and slapped the reins, and the horse started forward, but Clara did not move. Hugh called for her to follow, swung around flapping the reins, causing the mare to fuss at the bit and toss up her neck. Clara walked off the road, toward the bog, into the woods. He could no longer hold his bladder. He stopped the wagon, trammeled the driving lines, jumped down, and ran clutching and stumbling to the cover of trees. As he relieved himself, he called out to her not to wander far, he would be right back. If she explained the worth of horses and a wagon, they could head home to a fine dinner. He kept going, his bladder being very full, and he tried to speed the emptying, but the effort seemed only to find reserved bladders as full as his primary one, and the heavy water kept pouring from him. When the last piddle and drips hit the leaves, he leaned his forehead against the tree and let his shoulders down, did himself up, and walked back to the wagon. He watched for the snag that had tripped him on his walk in. He called to Clara: dinner awaited them, a delectable loin of venison, and couldn't she imagine licking the black cherry sauce off her fingers? He stepped onto the road, looked up. Clara sat on the cart seat. How had she climbed into the tub? He did not notice her dress had been changed. Yet he was overcome with an urgency to trot them out of the woods.

Poppy heard the cart stop at the edge of the yard. Clara stood on the seat, the dress hanging loose, its arms flopping long past her hands like a cleric's robes. Clara raised a finger to scratch her nose, and the sleeve peeled down, her hand exposed like when the minister raised one hand to bless the congregation, then tucked it back in the sleeve as if his hand were too potent, too sacrosanct to keep exposed for long. As her father hooked his hands into Clara's armpits and swung her down, Poppy saw the blue embroidery on Clara's dress.

Poppy ran to usher Clara inside. Her father unbuckled the harness, intent upon his work. Poppy hesitated behind her papa's back. Clara tugged at her hand.

Behind the partition, Poppy patted down her sister, turned her round, unfastened the small buttons, pulled the dress off. Poppy lifted Clara's hair off her neck, parted her legs, turned up her palms. Nothing. No bruises. No brands. There were rings of dirt around her wrists and ankles like always. Her belly protruded, relaxed. The folds of her rear and the backs of her legs were creased and flushed. From sitting on the wagon seat, Poppy told herself. A fine down of sweat clung at Clara's hairline and high color crimsoned her cheeks. Clara stared at the dress heaped at her feet.

The girls spread the dress on the mattress, searching for the catch of a note. Poppy's hand stopped on the snag of a pin, and they cleared away the skirt layers to find a torn fragment of paper. The remnant of the note contained no ink. The dress was identical to the first one, from the blue embroidered flowers to the sizing to the airy sheen of the layers, except for the long sleeves. The first dress that Hildy had claimed had modern, capped sleeves. Clara slipped her hand up the right sleeve. Another pin and note. It was a sketch of Clara. In a few gestured lines, it captured Clara unmistakably. The lilt of her nose, the storm of her eyes, her bulldog posture.

Poppy sat on the bed and cupped her sister's hand. "Does he harm you? You must tell me."

Clara's eyes seized, reflecting Poppy's fear. "No. Will he harm me?"

"You must not seek him out. Did Papa see him?"

"No. And don't you tell him. He will give away this dress too." Clara's voice started to rise.

Poppy drew her close and whispered, "Who is he? A man from the tavern?"

Clara furrowed her brow, disbelieving her sister was so slow. "The devil," she whispered back.

Poppy dropped Clara's hand, pushing her away. "No. That's not possible. Have you seen him before?"

"Yes, at the show when he rose from the cloud of smoke, then again behind the tavern. Then today at the bog when the leaves swirled in the wind."

"At the show? The one Ma took us to? That was an actor."

"It was him." Clara patted her face. "Who else is white and glowy?"

Poppy shushed her. She could not explain the tricks of the theater to her sister. "Makeup. Pearl powder," she whispered.

But Clara shook her head, confused. She did not know what that was. They were called for supper. Poppy wrapped one of her long aprons onto Clara, then Clara's own shawl on top of that.

Hugh watched Clara eat, the corners of her mouth stained jelly-dark from the cherry sauce and loin juices. She ate with gusto, as though in a feeding trance, always a strong appetite. She was well fed, a growing girl. His tooth hit a cherry pit, and he worried the meat around his mouth until he could work the pit free. The cart's tub and wheels were taller than a man. Clara always needed a boost and a steadying hand to manage the footstep up any cart or wagon. A pang of uneasiness swept over him as Clara poured more sauce on the meat, tined a bite into her mouth. She had not yet recited the value of horses and a wagon. He sighed and pulled the pit out of his mouth and resolved to carry on with the lesson the next day.

Each night, Hugh led the women and girls through prayer. They sat around the table as the water for washing heated in the kettle. Hugh cradled his prayer book and spoke one line at a time, and the others in unison echoed back.

"Abide with me! Fast falls the eventide."

"Abide with me. Fast falls the eventide." The women and girls recited in dull chant.

"The darkness deepens; Lord, with me abide!" Hugh's incantatory delivery marked the brief twilight between work and sleep.

"The darkness deepens; Lord, with me abide."

Hildy had to sit on her hands to concentrate. Black Vy muttered another prayer underneath each of Hugh's verses, her lips moving as Hugh paused with silent hard stops for emphasis.

"When other helpers fail and comforts flee…"

"When other helpers fail and comforts flee…"

Georgie held a fist in her lap and struck out another finger to mark one more section to finish. They repeated three rounds of the same prayer. Poppy and Clara held hands, Poppy squeezing to correct Clara's mistakes: "flail and fleas" and "eveningtoad."

"Help of the helpless, O abide with me! Amen."

"Help of the helpless, O abide with me. Amen."

"Again. Abide…" Hugh launched the next round.

Clara peeled one eye open. Her papa held his prayer book open, but recited from memory, his eyes closed. Everyone's eyes were closed except for Hildy, who watched the kettle. Steam rose from the kettle, the sign that prayers for the evening were almost finished. Clara closed her eyes, peaceful from the routine of ritual.

"The darkness deepens," bellowed her papa.

Baron Saturday climbed out of the hot kettle and stood glistening wet, listening to the table recite orison. He was quiet, his movements masked by the crackle of the fire, and the hiss of the rising steam, and the ticks of the kettle's pressure changing with the licking flames. Baron Saturday dripped a path to sit on the three-legged stool. He crossed his legs and tipped back his hat, watching the table. He eased into a hunch, pushed up his shirtsleeves, water spatting onto the floor. He was patient as a man waiting for a companion outside of a storefront.

You are the loudest, the baron thought of Hugh. *You speak from a drum inside your chest.*

The women and girls droned in reply of the man. The baron tried to guess which one was his wife and decided upon the English woman with her severe face. He picked out her voice from the group.

You are the dullest, the baron thought. *You speak from a sanded bowl inside your skull.*

The children held hands. Baron Saturday drew a tobacco paper from his pocket and poured a line of leafy threads onto the paper. The younger child heard the rustling, and he froze. He flew behind her before she cracked open her eyes. The elder sister had not heard. But the well-turned one had heard him. Hildy stared across the table at him. He motioned for Hildy to close her eyes. The elder sister squeezed her sister's hand. The younger child closed her eyes, and he melted and swept with celerity back to the stool, leaving a mop trail of dark water, but it would dry. The older sister was lovely with the blue of the plum on her. He cupped his ear to hear the older sister's refrain.

"Abide with me. Fast falls the eventide."

You are the softest, the baron thought. *You speak from reeds woven across your throat.*

He tamped the tobacco and licked the paper, wrapped it tight. He rose back to the fire and touched one end to the embers. He filled the pleated leathers of his lungs with his first draw of smoke, sank more comfortably onto the stool. One leg wobbled on the uneven floorboards. The younger child touched her knuckle to her nose, peeked open her eyes again. He vanished, frustrated at the child's interruptions. The elder sister pressed the child's hand again, and she focused once more on the chant. The baron reset upon the stool, leaning forward to prevent rocking. There was a murmuring underneath the primary prayer. The baron, as if staring directly at the sun, shielded his face from Black Vy who mumbled a different prayer after each line the man spoke.

You are the most booming, he thought as he shuddered at her conviction. *You speak from the sizzling grates of your belly that spit bacon fat.* He hugged himself.

The father drummed his fingers on the opened book of prayer, faltered his recitation, then shifted in his chair. He resumed the next line. "Help of the helpless, O abide with me! Amen." The baron saw the man's mouth angled toward the well-turned one. Of course, she was his wife, not the worn-out one. He listened as Hildy's voice played above the rest. *You are the tinkliest*, he thought. *You speak from the rope bobbing at the front of your gorge.*

The baron heard Margaret outside the shanty, murmuring along with them. *You speak from lungs swamped at their bottoms with droplets*, the baron said of the dead woman.

He listened to Clara. *You speak from the hairs wisping behind your ears.* No, that was not right. He looked above her to the portrait on the wall. He noted the artist had not captured her. The children in the portrait looked like wizened adult hags. He thought bitterly of Goya's renderings of his own form. Reduced to grinning monsters or wide-eyed animals, the drawings captured nothing of his male beauty. The baron traced his jaw then yawned. He was bored of staging events to injure men, his main occupation for the last twenty-five years. And he had lapsed in the practice of his secondary pursuit, the refurbishment and design of carriages, an unintended pastime he had stumbled upon after looting so many wrecked vehicles. It was time for a new interest. For he strove to be a man of the new century, protean, modern. He had yet to master a lifework *nobilis*. He looked again at the portrait, then at the child squeezing closed her eyes, clenching her sister's hand. His crude sketch of the girl had rendered something of her power, but he itched with ambition for a larger canvas and passel of oil paints to express the knots and nuance of her spirit. He decided his next chapter would be painting. He nodded and tapped his foot and determined he could be good at it. He would have to keep studying the younger daughter. Baron Saturday drew one last guzzle of smoke and left the shanty.

Clara smelled smoke; it was rooty, like dried apples gone bad in the cellar, not the crewmen's tobacco, not her papa's, nor Black Vy's. She thought she had heard tobacco paper rustling, but when she had opened her eyes, it was only the bubbles breaking open on the kettle's surface. Poppy kept pinching her hand to refocus her prayer, but Clara's thoughts flew to the woods, down the rock to the white rushing water, back to the woods, to the milky rock and the smaller waterfall that spilled over it.

"The darkness deepens; Lord, with me abide!"

The water dammed before its spill over the milky rock. The milky rock dried up. Clara stepped through the moss and marshy ground and removed her boots before wading into the shallow pool at the base of the suspended waterfall.

"When other helpers fail and comforts flee…"

She was ankle deep in the cold water and touched the milky rock, hearing the dammed-up water quiver above her head. The water had rubbed the rock smooth, and it shone like a curtain between the dark side sections of stone. Her hands searched for dimples or gouges or cut straight lines, any sign of a secret doorway to his horses. If the rock opened, it would flake, she reasoned, and show marks of hinging.

"Help of the helpless, O abide with me! Amen."

But she saw no hinges, no depressions in the rock, only sparkling crystals in the white. And she sagged her body onto the rock, hugging it, pressing her ear close, listening.

"Again. Abide with me! Fast falls the eventide."

She heard the water above straining against its dam. The water would break soon and rush back over the rock. She pressed her ear urgently against the rock. She could not hear pawing nor the jangling of bits and bridles nor the hammering of a blacksmith shoeing nor the rustling of bedding as the horses settled for the night. She slapped the rock and called, but there was no answer. She kicked the rock and bellowed to the devil, but he did not cry back. The water from above dribbled onto her head, and she shook it off.

"The darkness deepens; Lord, with me abide!"

The rock was warm, but her feet were numb, and she lifted each from the water and felt the pour of water from above drizzle down the rockface onto the front of her dress. The interior of the rock cavern would be lined with bright diamond crystals, bulging from the walls like stonified suds, the horses within rubbing their muzzles against the abrasion.

"Help of the helpless, O abide with me! Amen."

And she stepped back from the rock as the water flowed, overtaking its dam, and she said a prayer to the horses and to Jacks, "Amen, amen, amen," because that part of the prayer made her tremble most. Poppy led her to the kettle, dipped a rag, and wiped down Clara's hairline and behind her ears as the last rays of sun filtered through the smoke of the men's fires. Mr. Lipson's other dogs called downriver.

After everyone had gone to sleep, Poppy snuck to the spirits cupboard, retrieved the chaplet and silver coin, and slid them into her sister's side of their lumpen bed. In the morning, the second embroidered dress was still in a heap on the floor, but it had disintegrated to sludge like wafer paper left in the rain.

The next day, a man entered the yard. It was raining while sunshining, drops shining through boughs. The man's shoulders were stained wet, and he tipped his hat forward to spill off the water collected in its brim. Steam rose off the backs of his boots and trouser cuffs. The crewmen were in Utica, fetching supplies. The women and girls were fishing downriver. Hugh was inside the shanty, piling firewood. The door was open.

The stranger leaned against the doorframe. Hugh, bent at the hearth, stiffened and turned around.

"Might I come in for a dry off?" the stranger asked.

"Who's there, sir?" Hugh did not recognize him. In the shadow of the doorway with the sun bright behind, the man's face was obscured.

"I was out for an eel gig and with the rains found the river rising, so I climbed to this higher ground. Might I shelter till the rains cease? It won't be long now with the sun peeking through."

Hugh hesitated, making a quick assessment of the man. "Where is your fishing tackle?"

The man looked to both hips, patting them down. "Dropped them quick on the rocks, must have." The man blew on his hands as if for warmth. "That's a brisk river." He stepped one foot across the threshold.

"Yes, come through, please," said Hugh, though the man had already limped past him toward the hearth's low fire. "Are you traveling?"

The man sat on the stool beside the fire. "Yes."

The man had days' old beard growth. He was dark and thin. From the city. "Been sleeping rough? Do you have ties to these parts?"

"No. Yes," the visitor wheezed. "The wilderness draws me."

Hugh saw the leather bracer on the man's arm and the leather whip coiled at his hip. He thought the man foolish for over-accessorizing as if dressed for ancient battle though city people were oft costumed for trips to the woods. The man's trousers were of degraded wool, like the tatters of a long-buried corpse.

The man saw superiority rise in Hugh's face. He touched the leather bracer. "From when I fought the Scythians to dominate the Pontic steppe." He paused seriously before breaking into a grin.

Hugh eyed him and nodded uneasily.

"I have traveled extensively and collect odd treasures of skirmish. I find myself returning to this region. So much gloried, blood-soaked land to wander. If only there existed a rural resort to soak my skin and lay my head."

Hugh blinked. He strode forward to shake the man's hand. "Sir, I toil to make that reality."

The man wobbled to stand and returned the grip, looking into Hugh's lit eyes. "You are the man whose blasting I hear."

Hugh hooked his hands onto his hips. "How long have you been here? Been a long time since we've any dry weather for fuses to light. You favor a long stay, then?"

"Yes." He sat again on the stool and drew from his pocket a tobacco paper. "Where are the women and girls?" The stranger nodded toward the table, his eyes flicking to the portrait on the wall. He pinched a pugil of tobacco leaves from his breast pocket.

"Do I know you?"

"I seen a gaggle down at the river and thought when I saw the shanty they must belong to you." He lit his tobacco, and the dried apple smell filled the space between the men.

"Then why ask..." Hugh began but shook his head. He scooted another stool close to the man and sat. "Tell me, sir, do you have associates who know of these parts? Surely at your place of business you have told stories of the beauty of these woods and waters."

The man smiled at Hugh's enthusiasm. "Yes, I will tell them." His gaze relatched to the portrait.

"And you will tell them they are welcome here, that we have grand plans to accommodate?"

"Oh, I will tell them your doorway is welcoming, even permeable, sir. That you are most hospitable without barriers to your doorstep."

Hugh gripped the caller's knees. "That would be a kindness, sir."

The man savored one last draw of smoke. He flicked his tobacco stub into the embers and stood. "I have kept you long, so I must take leave back to my camp." He hobbled to the wall, peering close to the painting.

"Do you know portraiture, sir?"

"In truth, I dabble." The man turned around. "Quite an expressive brush stroke there." He ducked through the door frame and strode into the yard. Hugh followed him off the porch. The rain had stopped, and the sun warmed the air again.

The man looked back, tipped his hat. His eye caught something beyond Hugh's shoulder. Hugh turned as a swine crossed behind him, trotting across the porch.

The man nodded to the pig. "A happy life for you, sir."

Hugh beamed. "An old superstition. But true enough."

"Or a dire omen?" The man wiggled his fingertips to his lips like a child. "I can never remember which." He turned and walked away.

Hugh watched the man shuffle into the woods. A sourness filled his gut, a regret he had allowed the stranger inside. Yet he called out, "Visit again if you like."

Georgie lay in bed. Hugh's and Hildy's voices chirred down from their sleeping quarters. Black Vy was with the girls, telling them the story of the animal scenes printed on the cloth partition. Black Vy held the candle close to each dragonfly and farmer. Her face traveled the length of the cloth partition, silhouetted by the candle flicker.

Georgie turned toward the wall. The men's tents were lighted by lanterns. Their low voices carried across the yard. Black Vy blew out the candle and murmured to the girls. There was rustling as they scampered into bed and Black Vy drew the cloth partition behind her. She settled onto the ticking. All was dark from above in the sleeping garret; mercifully, Hugh only sometimes rutted Hildy in the nights. He mostly took her in the woods during the day.

"Did you have children?" Georgie whispered.

Black Vy did not respond.

"Will you go back for them? Someday try?"

Black Vy blinked her dark eyes.

"No, I reckon the danger would be too great," Georgie decided.

"Woman, you stop this yap and let me lie." Black Vy turned her back to Georgie.

The men's tents were dark, the smoke from their spent fires rising in time to the low, bright moon mounting the rim of the gorge.

Georgie woke to footsteps padding down the sleeping garret steps. Black Vy breathed evenly. Hildy's dress swished against the steps. Georgie lay still as Hildy soundlessly lifted the arm of the door and went outside. Through the wallboards, Georgie saw Hildy pause on the porch and take in the bright moon. She tiptoed through the yard, weaving between the men's tents. Hildy did not duck into one of them; instead, she veered toward the path to the river.

Black Vy stirred. "Attend to her 'afore she come to harm."

Georgie protested, but Black Vy snatched away the bear pelt.

Stepping into her skirt, Georgie tucked her knife into her pocket and hurried after Hildy.

The sawing of wings and mandibles worshipping the moon. Frogs throatily calling for it. The creaks of trees like the boards of a great ship under pressure from battering waves. But at the rim of the High Falls, the only sound was the rushing torrent. Georgie peered into the chasm, the water bright foam under the moonlight, and Hildy's white shift tucked into a small rock alcove. Hildy lay wedged there, perfectly still, glowing inside the enclave like a saint laid out for viewing, shining with opal softness. Georgie sat alternately watching below and looking over her shoulder. Would one of the men meet her? Hildy rose onto her knees, extending her arms as if to embrace someone. She smoothed her undone hair. She braced her body against the rock as if to shield someone. Hildy pantomimed a fantasy, herself the heroine. In the depths of the cataracts, so far below the homestead, her private amphitheater, she was possibly gravid with the first little president she would bear for Hugh.

Georgie's last happy day with Hugh was an Independence Day celebration during which he had raised his pistol skyward and fired amid the crowd as boats gathered along the harbor. The last time he sought her out in a crowd, to rush over to share a remark and grab her hand. Thereafter, a cold distraction and irritation at her presence.

If a man were coming to meet Hildy, he would have by now. Hildy lay motionless on the rock. The night sounds were different from the day, percussive crashes. Georgie gripped the knife in her pocket, mustered patience to wait out Hildy, in a Juliet stupor laid upon her death stone.

This insensible girl playacting on the rocks would have to work. They all would have to work. Legitimate labor this time. Not like before when Hugh had committed financial indiscretions—selling fraudulent fossils he purported to be from the falls, but which were instead cast-clay replicas of one actual fossil Hugh had found in the gorge. The family would now have to earn wages to keep paying the crewmen and Black Vy.

After Hugh had found one fossil, he had convinced his mother the gorge must be full of valuable prehistoric artifacts. Margaret had scoured the rubbly banks of the river, dove into the bracing depths of the kettles in August, brandishing a pickaxe in one hand, down stroking with the other. Georgie had watched Margaret from the riverbank, too pregnant to assist her. Hugh and Margaret never found another fossil as pristine and intact. They found worthless bits of shell and curled husks, broken-up petrifactions. They took out preemptive loans from local landowners, certain there must exist specialized tackle for locating

and extracting such treasures, yet their inquiries to makers went unan-
swered. Georgie had urged Margaret to use the loan money to purchase
linens and tables and cutlery. Margaret stored them, reserved ready
for when the tourists would come. Margaret assured Hugh they would
easily and quickly pay back the money after finding a cartload of fossils,
but they never did. And Georgie had believed Margaret's conviction.
So, Hugh cast crude clay imitations and sold twenty of them to the
cider-drunk revelers at the Oldenbarneveld summer fair. Then he cast
fifteen more and sold all of them to the same drunk crowd at the fall
festival. He touted the rarity and abundance of the fossils in their wild
crook of New York, which he bleated would be yet another draw for
tourists, and the townspeople cheered him, raising their clay casts into
the air. None of the townspeople questioned how a thing could be at
once rare yet abundant. They were unfettered by the details of Hugh's
promise. They were even optimistic. There would be lucrative prospects
for everyone in the settlement of Oldenbarneveld when the tourists
came, the townspeople had buzzed.

Yet Hugh and Margaret had made overeager estimates on the counterfeit fossil earnings. The numbers didn't add up. They had bungled the
math. Hugh stashed away the meager gains, defaulting on the loans. He
continued to use Georgie's family money to pay the crew wages. His fob
to generate income had not worked. Georgie told Hugh to admit the lie
to the townspeople, but neither he nor Margaret would, holding firm
to the gamble of the next money-making prospect, the cleared roadway
for tourists to a grand resort.

By early December, the residents of Oldenbarneveld, now sobered
by the bitter chill air, compared their fossils after Oliver Ellington had
accidentally crushed his fake fossil while showing it off to his relatives
visiting from Boston. It had burst in his hand into a cloud of dust as
he gripped it with excitement, hailing it as a primordial gem, the slate
ravines of the falls its ancient seedbed. He knew slate did not crush
so easily, and when the clay broke apart, he saw that the replica was
surface deep, not embedded. When the people compared their artifacts,
they were identical. They were outraged—they knew God created even
primitive beasts of the same kind with variances of size and shape.
The townspeople confirmed that the fossils lining their mantels were
not in fact bona fide shale but were a mix of clay and ash. Instead
of organizing a witch-hunt, Oliver took his case directly to Minster
and Constable Beers, demanding charges of fraud be brought against

Hugh. Ellington claimed Hugh had embroidered the idea that their land holdings were more valuable because of the fossils. The townspeople had bought more than counterfeit artifacts; Hugh had sold them the illusion of profitable futures, for the influx of tourists would surely come north, right to their doorsteps clamoring for singular fossils.

When Minister and Constable Beers balked, saying a claim against a man such as Hugh, a man who was trying to improve the community, could not be true, the residents gathered at the cross creeks in town and smashed the fake fossils against the embankment in protest. The clay casts dissolved in the current, the articulated thoraxes of each trilobite melting away at the furrows, the dust and fragments drowning in the swirling eddies. Beers and his housekeeper, Mrs. Fothergill, rode that afternoon to arrest Hugh.

At the shanty, they had not found all the profits from the sale of the fake fossils; Hugh had buried small amounts at different spots high along the river though the officials did seize enough coinage from a concealed tin to think they had found all the money. And they seized the cast that Hugh had used to create the fake relics. Hugh was contrite, and Beers and his matron softened against arresting him. They did not pursue prosecution for any charges. Hugh convinced them to allow his efforts to blast away the wilderness. Beers made a show for the villagers, destroying the cast, setting it to burn upon the farrier's trough of raised coals. The defaulted loans were redrawn with new terms, increasing the pay back according to the promise of tourism. The villagers of Olden-barneveld were forgiving but wary. They would hold Hugh to the new loan terms and the promise to bring in tourists.

Hugh's hope for Margaret before she died had been for servants to bring her trays of iced tea and cakes as she rocked on the porch of his grand hotel as paying guests busied the entrance. Since his father's death in the war, he and his mother had been trying to acquire land. She had made hasty promises, a necessity for their hardscrabble existence, made convincing by her bluster and natural authority, but without any knowledge of business transactions and formal channels. She had built a life on a principle of entitlement and deception, which to her was simply a birthright as an American.

Georgie yawned, rubbed her face awake. When she looked down, Hildy was no longer in the enclave. Her white nightdress starkly reflected in the water—she had gained a foothold and started to scramble and climb back. Georgie heard above the water the scattering of loose rocks and the muffled crashes against the current. Hildy was young, so lost in fantasy, but she was surefooted, had decided who she was and who she would be. Georgie stood, made way back to the house, crept through the yard. She climbed into bed. The girls were silent behind the partition, sleeping the hard sleep of children. Black Vy was awake, propped up in bed smoking. Georgie nodded to the door to indicate Hildy was near. Georgie peeped through the wall crack to watch Hildy walk to the porch.

Would Hildy stop at one of the men's tents? She lingered in the yard, looking to the moon, in no hurry to get back into Hugh's bed. None of the men would attach to her. The men had their own code of conduct, one which took the high road even when there was bad blood or eruptions of disagreement. Yet she swayed in the moonlight. Perhaps Hildy would settle on Hugh when she was with child. Until then, her head was a cloud of romance. Her youth and temperament compelled her to creep into the night like a mink slipping headlong underwater.

Hildy at last climbed the stairs to the sleeping garret.

"You don't sleep well, do you?" Black Vy whispered. "You tell me what you dream, then I throw the bones for you in the morning."

Georgie turned away. "Those bones are twaddle." But she lay on top of the pelt, exposed to the night air, to keep herself from dreaming. She was tired and grew nettlesome.

Black Vy rolled the bones around and around inside of her hand. Georgie could not fight sleep.

Georgie awoke irritable, sweeping damp hair off her temples. She had twitched and dreamt on top of the pelt. Through the gaps in the shanty wall, she saw Black Vy crouched in the yard. She had already cast the bones and thoughtfully sucked on her pipe studying their pattern. Georgie dressed.

"I shan't tell you of my dream. I don't believe in magic, and those bones stink." Georgie addressed Black Vy's back. The scattered grid of bones radiated in the dirt above Black Vy's head like a shooting crown of thorns.

Black Vy did not look back at her.

"I have no time for foolish folk games."

Black Vy held her hands over the bones but did not touch them, cupping her hands as if to warm them.

Georgie wrapped her shawl about herself against the morning chill. "Are the bones warm?"

"No, they are cold. Like the river rocks. Like you."

Georgie went inside the house.

As Hugh came down the stairs, he paused halfway as he saw Georgie's hands folded on her lap, waiting for him. "Hildy awaits you," he said.

Georgie stood and whispered, "She ventured last night past the men sleeping in the yard to play out a burlesque on the rocks."

Hugh motioned to follow him onto the porch. "I know. She is one for pageantry and antics."

"You know of it? And you allow it?"

"Yes. She has asked me to join, but…"

"You require your rest." Georgie shook her head.

Hugh hesitated. "Pray, would you be so kind as to…"

"No."

"If you would only humor her. Create a drama for her to engage with, not too much danger. I fear life here at the shanty is not enough to keep her stimulated."

"Make her with child. That will engage her."

Hugh drew his lips tight. "I have tried." He lowered his head then pleaded with her. "Put on some of the theatricals you and your maids used to perform."

"I don't feel like mirth-making any more."

"Then see to your laundry." His voice heated. "It could be pleasant for you too. Lift that hard, sour face you wear."

"I will watch over her," Georgie conceded. "But I am not a circus performer."

"That is all I ask, that you keep watch for her spirit."

Georgie nodded and lamented inwardly. She was to continue tending a grown fool.

A young sow nosed a flap of moss, its conformation wild-bred, sparsely haired. Its neck fluttered, and Georgie saw the budding tuft of mane. Like a warthog. She reached for the sow, but it squealed in outrage, faced her down with a stamp of pasterns, scampered off.

Clara wandered onto the game trail that cut through the bright ferns. This was the path the woman and baby had fled to the overturned tree. Clara brushed her hands along the tops of the ferns, rustling them as the woman's skirt had. The black powder still ringed the opening at the overturned tree. But there was a break as if something had emerged from or entered the hole, dragging a foot or a cape or a tail across the black powder. Clara patted the powder. It was damp. She knocked two rocks together as she had seen the woman do. The sparks fell flat on the sodden powder. She cleared a few heavy top wet grains and struck together the stones again, sparks chipping down. This time, a small clump of the powder ignited, but the brief combustion did not catch fire to create the flaming circle she hoped for. She dropped the rocks, sat on her heels. There had to be another way to call up the baron. She would not waste the powder, and thinking it could be dried like coffee grounds brewed once to be used again, she pinched up the black powder, stowing it in her apron pocket.

She was overcome by a pinprick at her neck of being watched. She didn't raise her head. She scooted her knees over, working round the circle, plucked up the black grains. Yet the bore hole pierced the back of her neck. Her vision closed in. He was behind her. Her hands trembled, and she quickened her effort to gather all the powder. She concentrated her task to impress him, prove herself useful. He measured the sincerity of her effort. She shivered her hide like a dog, confused if this lock of submission and toil was of her own will or his.

There was no wind. She had not heard leaves crunching, nor heard anyone's approach. The birds and fly hordes and squirrels were silent, but when had their chirps and drones and scutters stopped? She stamped her knees around the black powder circle, her pocket loaded as a baby's hipping. She would soon be sidelong to him. She clicked her eyes over, but there was nothing in the trees. Had he simply walked off?

She stood and followed the direction he had been a moment ago. Then she smelled it. A florid scent of apple blossoms wafting down upon her head. She had been sensing the wrong vantage point. He was above her. In the trees. She cuffed the back of her neck as if to slap away a dart shot from a hunter's blow-pipe. She cowered, and fear shed its waters through her. The apple smell was enfeebling. She dropped to the ground. It was meant to make her drowsy. But she staggered for balance and looked overhead. She was overcome with dizziness, but there was his blurred, dark form in the gnarled spray of apple limbs. Her long-held list of questions bobbed at the backs of her eyes, but she was upended by another smell: the blossoms soured to the stink of a bad well. She fell, wavering on all fours as the sinkhole at the overturned tree overflowed with water. The water seeped and spread, swamping her hands and wrists, her knees, and the tips of her black boots. She gasped at the cold. Her thoughts must be running amok as her grandmother's had before dying.

The water filled between trees and floated the loose material of the forest, needles and leaves and branches coursing, riding the spill. But she stood bold, staggering from the tug of swift, cold water rising past her ankles, lifting her dress hem. She removed her boots, lacing them around her neck. She woozily burped, could not focus her eyes, yet she warbled up to him, "I am here! And I shall meet your horses." His form dropped with a splash, swirled in the brisk eddies. The water receded and whirlpooled back down the hole, leaving muddy flowers and fronds clinging to her feet and legs. Dark water marks stained upside the trees' wide bases. She regained steady balance and clear sight. Her hem was dry, her skin clean. She ran to the base of the apple tree where he had fallen. A tent of caterpillars, thrashing in their gauze.

"Then what of the man's back? If he plans to stay, he's to work. If he is only well enough to sit upright, then he must travel back." Hugh spit in the dirt.

"I do believe Mr. Bell would like to stay on as a driver," Georgie began.

"He cannot."

From the porch, Poppy called, "Mama, where is Clara?"

Georgie turned to the shanty. "In the privy."

"No, I just checked there."

"Check again." Georgie turned her attention back to Hugh.

"His injury has cost me two horses and a wagon. I have no use for the man. There is no room for a supernumerary on this crew. I need fellers and ostlers and whifflers and way-makers. Any one of those can assume a secondary position as driver."

Noord Boorsma stood alongside Black Vy. He considered Hugh's words, but made no reply.

"Let him descend the rocks. At the bottom, he's to hoist one stone to his shoulder and climb back up with it. If he succeeds, he can stay on. You take him down to test his strength," Hugh instructed Noord.

Noord took Black Vy's hand and with Georgie they walked to find Mr. Bell.

"Hugh's running out of wages and uses a weak man as an excuse to save costs," muttered Georgie. "Mr. Bell's been hard working and loyal as any man."

"I don't believe Mr. Hugh has it in his heart to let any of us go," said Black Vy. "He will find another way."

Georgie and Noord exchanged grim looks.

&

The four peered over the ridge. "He wants me to climb down there? Mayn't I do a jig instead?" Mr. Bell pumped his arms and lifted his toes.

"He was quite specific about you climbing down the declivity and carting up one stone if you are to stay on the crew working," Georgie replied.

They walked the path to the steep rock, Black Vy and Noord hanging back. At the last boulder before the steep descent, Gideon rubbed his back up and down against the boulder. Georgie averted her gaze as he squatted deeply.

"Were you one of the men who drove Silas Andrus to the headwaters of the Hudson?"

"I were, yes."

"Did you think of him after you left him on your ride home? Did you wonder his fate?"

"Say again?"

"I know you understand me, sir, so stop." Georgie repeated her question.

"Not much. I don't expect a man like that to survive long on his own."

"If you knew he would die soon, why ride him so far away? Whyfor not just murder him here?"

"To give a man a chance, that's not murder."

"But you said a man like him wouldn't survive."

"Still, to give a man a chance and at the same time ride him far enough away to drive home the point that he was no longer part of the crew, to ride him away from any folk he might have know'd. He deserved that punishment. But any man deserves a chance, and we gave him that. That part was up to him. We left him a'tween a den and the river, and it was up to his mind and will whether he took the den as his home and what lived inside as his dinner or if he became a rot pile of bones."

Noord held Black Vy's arm, guiding her down the path.

"And his boots. You left the man bereft of boots so he could not walk back," said Georgie.

"They were a fine boot that bought us a smacking pork and whiskey supper at the headwaters tavern. He had stole them off a dead man who had stole them off a Hessian. Silas knew how to care for a boot. And he knew to steal from men who cared for their belongings to begin with."

"Do you think his brothers could seek revenge for his fate?"

"No. You seen someone?" His eyes tried to search hers, but she lowered her head. He looked at Georgie's neck. "No, I know the brothers Andrus. They are not the wreakful kind. Could be any number of man traveling through the outskirts of camp."

They reached the flat, graduated slabs lining the gorge bed, the water level low enough that one of the great slabs was bleached dry from the air and sun.

Gideon lay on his back and closed his eyes. "It's warm." He ground his back against the slate.

Georgie nodded to a hefty, basket-sized rock. She and Noord lifted the stone as Gideon followed them back up the trail. Georgie and Noord shifted the weight between them, looking to Black Vy to help.

Yet Black Vy hung back. "Ain't what Mr. Hugh asked of you." She carried nothing but her skirt hem the whole climb.

Black Vy had not intended to escape from the plantation in Fairfax County, Virginia. Tuesdays, when fresh wagonloads of tidewater oysters filled the markets, she accompanied her master's young daughter, Addie Maude, to town. Black Vy had a note of permission pinned to her sleeve, hand-written by the master himself, stating when she left the property, where she was going and for what purpose, and when she was expected to return. Anyone in town who requested to read the letter would have recognized the sprawling signature at the bottom: Benjamin P. Breedlove. If someone in town had not yet formalized a contract or barter with Breedlove or received a letter of reprimand from him condemning a messy yard or riotous animals, then all the townspeople had seen the authority of Breedlove's signature scrawled and set in the cornerstone of the courthouse. Breedlove liked for Addie Maude to have small errands of responsibility. The towns-people were used to seeing Black Vy waiting outside the shops and strolling the market stalls.

Black Vy had been off the plantation many times over the years; she had never attempted escape. Each time Addie Maude and Black Vy would walk to town, they passed the men working the rice field. The men's sung verses boomed below the high-pitched choruses of Black Vy's daughters who beat laundry against field rocks. Breedlove would follow Black Vy, singing along to mimic the piping of her daughters' voices, his falsetto notes straining above the rest of the outdoor hands' singing. Breedlove's voice pierced considerable distance into her walk to town. Black Vy learned the quickest route to and from town, learned efficiency, keeping Addie Maude focused on the task. She always returned Addie Maude with clean gloves, a spark in her eyes, a happy story to tell her father. Black Vy's head thumped during each outing until she and Addie Maude were on the path toward home, sweating until she could run her hands across her daughters' shoulders. They had been safe from him because Black Vy did not cry out or fight when Breedlove took her body.

On the day she disappeared, Black Vy had been dressed in new spring clothes: a blue Kersey petticoat and white apron and hat. All the indoor and outdoor hands had been provided new clothes that day. Black Vy held Addie Maude's hand. Their errand was to purchase a clyster pipe and several hanks of sewing silk.

With Black Vy's coaching, Addie Maude had developed a clear and commanding speaking voice from an early age. Outside the mercantile this day, Black Vy encouraged her to ask loud for the clyster pipe and hanks of silk. Addie Maude marched to the shopkeeper, bore the shilling from her child's purse onto the counter. As Black Vy waited outside, customers exiting the shop proclaimed the girl a natural orator. Addie Maude busted outside, her cheek fat with hard candy, a treat for being a clever girl. Black Vy carried the wrapped items, plucked Addie Maude's collar so she wouldn't run with the candy in her mouth. Black Vy's heart quieted as they left the townspeople behind, the errand complete. The heat of the day hazed over the tall grass. She drifted her free hand over the bristly tips. She would help her daughters try on their new clothes that evening.

This day had been warm and golden, and Black Vy walked taller in her new spring clothes. The slaves would never be fresh like this again until next year when the cotton would be near rags and the master would replace them. With her old skirt, she would make a baptismal sack for her new baby girl, a snug sack that drew closed at her toes like a purse. One to keep her tightly warm like how she loved to be swaddled in a blanket. So when the minister dribbled and rubbed hot holy oil over her ears and eyelids and brows and flower petal lip and greased the fat little rolls on her arms, she could get warm again before being carried around the church three times to ward off the devil himself. Black Vy had tipped her face to the sunlight, smiled down at Addie Maude. The baptism would happen that Sunday. Her older girls would wear their new clothes. How pretty their skins would shine in the light of the church, their faces at the ledge of the baptismal font, watching the anointing.

It was not customary for her master to keep the children of the slaves he owned. He had rented twelve children in the past year to plantations farther south where there was demand for tobacco labor. This had not been his father's practice. His father had encouraged marriage among his slaves, exhorting to his son this kept them docile. After his father died, Breedlove took his seat next to other land and slave owners who for generations had rented their slave holdings according to financial need. Breedlove liked his cash, and he reasoned only so many positions for slaves on his property before the work became too divided and what he called ease set in among the workers. When his slaves began aging, he would retain their children to one day replace aging parents. But that was years off.

Black Vy had prayed and pinned Bible pages inside her girls' work smocks. So far, that had worked; they had not yet been rented away, but Black Vy wept, each dawn rising like bad waters. Black Vy had known her daughters' fates as soon as their fingers developed fine movement for sewing and cutting. There was not enough work on Breedlove's plantation to keep the girls useful. They were more valuable to him rented out to other masters until they could bear children to add to Breedlove's holdings. Once gone, she would not know where her girls were, if they were together, or how to find them even if she could get herself free. She wished to smack the pretty off them, wished the small-pox to bubble their skins because for her that had meant quarantine without him messing with her for a time. Until her girls were rented, she could offer her body to Breedlove in place of theirs. Black Vy never intended to escape Breedlove's plantation.

Black Vy and Addie Maude had already walked back a mile when the bright gold grass grew black. Black Vy's field of vision had shrunk to a pinhole, and she dropped. Black Vy awoke in wet grass. She grabbed for Addie Maude, but she was not there. Black Vy stopped herself from calling out. She struggled to sit, her new clothes weighted, sodden from rain. Her note of permission and the wrapped clyster pipe and hanks of sewing silk were not around her. Over the tall steaming grass, she saw the dark void of town. It was nighttime, long past the hour when the street lanterns burned out, yet Black Vy ran toward the buildings. The streets were deep mud. No wagons stood. No windows were lit. She heaved in panic. She knew what this looked like, but her first thought was to run through the night, back to the plantation and beg for forgive-ness, explain her fainting spell. The longer she waited, the worse her punishment would be. She slumped. It was already too late. At dusk, her master had probably made his decision; the dogs waited for her; her daughters pulled from their beds, the easy and immediate targets as the other slaves were woken and called to witness. Her returning now would never take that away or make things better. She panted with confusion.

Why had Addie Maude left her? Had someone taken her? She lurched toward the path home. She flailed in the dark, losing the path, caught in the lashings of tall grass when she stopped still, startled like a colt. She tore away, running for the opposite direction of the plantation.

As the dark fainting spell had overtaken her hours before, so had the compulsion to run. She had never been this unattended or farther away from her master and his dogs. She leapt through the darkness, chucking thoughts of how to protect her daughters, how to keep Addie Maude clean and safe, pitching these worries like a caravan of wagons wrecking into a gulch. A force greater than herself obliged her to run, and she did not fight it.

She made her escape without prior planning. She ran deep into the swamps, took shelter at the base of a smooth, giant tree, and slept fitfully from heat and mosquitoes during the days, for she was certain she was not yet clear of the area where men on horses would search for her. She had never seen a map, had no skills for dead reckoning or navigating by the stars. Her night sky at the plantation changed with the seasons—this she could tell from the slivers between roof cracks, from her bed at the top level of the sleeping shed. She had never before seen a complete night sky. In the swamp, the bright cap of clouds crowning the sky's center, the whirling dipper shapes, and the shooting streaks filled her with strength to keep trekking. Her people fleeing toward freedom before her had followed these listing heavens, so she would, too, even if she could not sense her bearings, untethered from land for never being told how to read its sky. She drifted along with the tilting of the nighttime.

She walked deeper into the swamps, ankles and shins dragging mud. Tree roots hard as iron tangled around her. The gnarled roots curled above the swale, as if lifting their skirts clear of the muck. She climbed over the roots on her hands, the only way to proceed forward. She slept on top of the roots, suspended above the black water. Upon waking to splashes and slithers, she tugged at her sleeve, which had shrunken after drying. She ran her hand along the seam of her skirt, the cotton tough and withered. She reckoned months' worth of wear already from sleeping two days with the swamp water lapping up. Her feet were shriveled—she had no shoes. Brambles, briars in all directions. She climbed on all fours across the welter like a cat. On the second day, it rained, and she licked drops off her skin.

It was slow going. The fastest she had ever traveled was riding in a runaway wagon pulled by two horses. The wagon had bumped and sailed upward from the ground, flying then crashing, busting apart like a dropped melon, with her in the wreckage. She had never been permitted in a boat. But she had stood in strong current, imagining being taken by it and whipping like a ribbon in a boat downstream.

She shut her mind against the darting and scattering of reptiles, grasped the smooth, warm root bark. In the spaces between overlapping roots, the sun shone on the patches of water, illuminating bugs skating on the surface and shadows propelling in the depths. Her sweat broke drips onto the surface, things from below biting as if her sweat droplets were bait. She held her head above the splash as her paddling hands and feet touched many hard things and many fleeing things in the black water.

She had been hungry before. She had eaten raw things before. When she foundered from hunger, she grabbed for any live pest nesting against wet tree bark and ate it. A few bit or stung before she could crush them down her throat. She kept swimming, kept crawling.

Over the years, a few men had escaped from the plantation, never to be heard from again. There was speculation about what happened. The master said they were all caught and hanged. But Black Vy heard from other slaves in town and those visiting the house about the Great Dismal, a swampland of escape where men made free lives. On the third day of her escape, Black Vy knew she had reached the Great Dismal as other noises rose above her own breath. It was men singing work songs. Songs she knew. She sputtered and sang in reply out of habit and sheer shock, then stopped and drew low in the water. There was shouting and digging. There was what looked like firm ground ahead, so she swam silently to it, tried to walk the ankle-sucking mud. There was metal clinking. She crawled partway up a tree, the water slinging off her legs and skirt.

White men stood in their shirtsleeves, wiping their faces, swatting at the air, yelling orders. A crew of Black men were digging a canal, their low, mournful singing a steady hum beneath the sharp commands. The white men were slave catchers digging their way into the Great Dismal to capture runaways. They had made progress on the canal: it snaked as far as she could see from her high tree perch. There was no smoke in the expanse. Maybe the settlers had heard the digging and fled.

She hid. She could not stay there. There would be more white men coming, white men with dogs, white men with guns and rope, piking their boats down the canal, hauling men out. The crewmen sang into the night. On the fourth night of her escape, a man grabbed her awake, covered her mouth, told her to stay quiet. It was a Black hand, one of the digger slaves risking his life to help her. He pressed a pouch of dried venison and a water jug into her hand. "Follow the flow of water. Track with it till you reach the bight. There be a ship at the coast. Get aboard the *Star*, get belowdecks."

She fled that night, so startled by human contact. At daybreak, she reckoned her travels by the pull of water. This forced her back to black water, swimming, crawling. At midday, she smelled fire. The water became muck then stable ground. She was loud and stumbling in her approach, too dazed and hungry and scared to be quiet. She wept at being free from the jumble of hard roots, water, and sucking mud. She collapsed onto hard sand, the arches of her feet stiff. The sand bristled against her feet, softened to thick moss, an open expanse of land, tall grass crushed flat from animals or people or both. A Native mounted on a white horse waited for her; as she neared, he yipped a cry of warning. He had no saddle, no shoes. His dark smock was baggy at the armpits and wrists. He wheeled his horse around and sped into the distance of the flat plain. He turned toward her, his smock flapping tight like sails with the speed of the horse, his feet and knees pressed against the hide, gripping the mount's belly.

He stopped the horse before her, holding his long spear, ready to drive it through her breast. He jerked his head toward the roots and water. His golden-brown eyes probed her completely. His chin kept tipping up, a command to retreat from his camp. His black hair fell past his shoulders, lifting in the breeze, lifting with the mare's mane. He studied her, his body relaxed, a wrist crossed over the other resting on the mare's neck, his feet gone slack.

Black Vy stood defiantly; she would not go back through the water. He tensed, prodding his mount forward, pinning Black Vy between his horse's chest and the black water behind her. He jabbed the spear above her right breast, but she caught the rod below the tip so it only penetrated her first layer of skin. They each struggled to control the spear. She fought against it, the tip of the blade dancing, ripping the fabric of her bodice, bloody red scribbles blooming onto the fabric across her breast and shoulder. She found unexpected purchase in her grasp, and he for a moment lost balance. This surprised the mare so that she backed up a few steps. But he pressed forward. Black Vy could not duck away. She caught the animal's shoulder with her free hand, and like her master Breedlove's ponies, this one responded to her firm pressure, backing up. But the Native barked into the mare's ear, and in that awful moment right before her strength gave out and the blade pierced a notch deeper, she mustered enough fight to jerk the spear away.

She fell against the edge of the water as the horse in irritation at her cry skittered back. Black Vy sat, panting. The Native glared dispassionately at her, the sunlight slanting into his eyes, gold menace. She let out another desperate cry, held up her raw palms, lifting her cut feet, gesturing back over her shoulder to the expanse of roots, and buried her face in her lap. He clucked his tongue, disgusted at her weakness or being seated in his presence or simply refusing to obey his command to leave.

A group of his people emerged behind him, and he dismounted and heaved his spear onto the moss. It was a woman and children. They exchanged words with the man. She wore a long skirt and a shawl wrapped around her shoulders like an Englishwoman. But she had two thick black lines drawn from each corner of her mouth to her ears. The woman walked off.

The man studied the side of Black Vy's face. Did her color confuse him? A look of distaste pulled down the corners of his mouth. Her smallpox scars were highlighted in the sun as his deep golden eyes were lit a moment ago. He brutally rushed forward, grabbing her arm. He eyed the pits up close, his breath warm and grassy. He followed the pit tracks from her cheeks down her neck, tearing away the bloody rips of her bodice to confirm the scars spread over the tops of her breasts. Had he seen anything like her scars before? Did he know about the sickness? He sniffed the blood trickling down her chest, his nose tilting toward her underarm to detect if she was still ill. His eyes met hers again, the impatience replaced with confusion and wariness. He pressed the flesh of her forearms, determining how she was still alive. He called to the woman who had walked off.

The man distrusted her, worse than his initial irritation at her intrusion upon their camp. She laid her hand onto the spear cuts over her breast. She knew how to doctor a fresh brand mark or the neat slit of a knife wound, but not this mess. More hot, hopeless tears welled up. Her journey would not end here at the border of swamp roots, bleeding down the front of herself.

The woman came running back with a rotted log in her arms. She solemnly presented it to Black Vy. Black Vy needed both arms to bear its considerable weight. A rustling inside, the sound so like the whisper of termites as they had eaten through the wall of her sleeping shed, dropping in clumps to her mattress. Repulsed, she dropped the log, and it broke open, a ball of stark white grubs wriggling in the pine shards. The Natives were not pleased at this. A boy child with a smock but no pants crouched at the grubs and fisted them into his mouth. His father crouched and scooped several handfuls into the pouch slung over his shoulder. She was meant to eat them. The log was a food store. The flailing grubs scurried to find cover from the light. The father thrust a handful of grubs at Black Vy, and she accepted them, ate them right there in front of him, which eased the tension on their faces considerably. The woman spoke in a language Black Vy did not understand, her tone commanding, and the father scooped as many grubs as he could while the half-naked little boy squatted at the broken log, the tip of his penis stamping little wells in the dirt as his fingers picked through shards of sodden wood, separating the fat white grubs, dropping them into his mouth like wax drippings.

The woman motioned for Black Vy to remove her clothes. She dropped a woolen blanket and a belt studded with shells at Black Vy's feet. Black Vy stepped out of her skirt, and the Natives stared at her dark skin. She stood tall and fought any indignity as the woman first pressed moss to her chest to staunch the bleeding then smeared a golden paste onto her wounds. Black Vy seized then spit up from the pain, and her eyes watered at the sharpness of the paste's vapors. The woman pressed a bouquet of soft yellow flowers on long green stems into Black Vy's hand.

The woman folded Black Vy's new spring clothing, stuck fresh moss over the paste, and wrapped the blanket about Black Vy's shoulders. The man packed two handfuls of grubs into another log and pointed at it. They left, the horse trailing. Black Vy followed, but the man pointed sternly to the crossways direction, a path that skirted the field of tangled tree roots. Black Vy started her own course, watched them walk off, her new spring clothes tucked in a wadded bundle underneath the Native woman's arm. In mere days, her new set of clothes from her master had been soaked and ripped and bloodied beyond wear and now stolen. She had no chance to return to Master Breedlove. She had known other slaves who had lost ears for ruining the clothes on their backs without leaving the plantation.

That night, the grubs rustled, noisy as if they had wings, their black mandibles working nonstop. She looked to the trees, to the moon, and fingered the shells on her new belt. She resolved to keep going the next morning, to leave these woods, to find her way to the coast as the man in the night had told her. She would leave the nest of grubs in their putrid log, leave them to fatten up. They would overwinter there, chew the log into splintered litter, molt to beetles, burrow under leaves, walk about the forest. She blinked as she saw them fat as pigeons nesting in the trees, and she worried for how hungry she was. She forced a handful down her throat.

Her daughters by now would think her dead. How would she find them, three daughters split up at separate plantations? It was more likely that Breedlove would brutalize them with her absence, keep them near. A thread of loss wound through Black Vy, gathered terror, spooled its pile in her gut. She gathered the skirt of her blanket dress in her arms and pressed it to her heart. In her new blanket dress and belt, she would move forward in the morning. She would walk to the coast, to the *Star*. She vowed to not run from the plantation any longer; she would travel toward a new life. She pressed the inside of a shell's curl, anchoring to this thought.

The next day, she walked into Georgetown, hungry, cold. Without Northern bearing or speech, no money, no food, nothing but coarse and dirty clothing. She smelled the sea grass and the sharp salt of the Potomac, heard the distant bells of the docked ships and their creaking hulls. She would hide away in the *Star's* decks, burrow underneath cargo layers, hide until the ship made way to a distant island or northern port, hugging the American coast, to free country.

There were watchmen on all the ships. But they were a drunk and careless lot, and during a pissing match, two watchmen hooted and arced their streams into the river, their backs facing away from the docks. She could not read the bold names on the hulls but figured correctly that these men's star tattoos were tribute to their ship. Black Vy slipped quietly aboard the *Star* and spent the day and one night above decks wrapped and hidden in the rigging of the foremast, piled in folds on the bow. Before dawn, she slipped from underneath the heavy canvas, crouching along the curved interior of the hull. She hid behind the great mast until the hatch bounced open and a throng of sleepy men clambered up, slamming flat the hatch. After the last man climbed out, she hurried below decks, reaching the hold without any man seeing her. She dodged blocks and cordage, slipped shivering underneath a tarp, alert to rustling all around, too frightened at the possibilities of other stowaways or rats. She dreamt of the ship lurching from the harbor, taking off for a distant port.

She startled awake as the movement in her dreams became the swaying of her body. She was tilting with the rock and sway of the sloop. There was a small porthole that shone light into the folds of her space. She saw sky then water, sky then water, the ship rocking against swells even here at its dock. High tide. And had the dock been stained fresh in the night? No, it was a new dock! They had departed in the night. She rested upon coils of rope, and ballast water churned nearby. The ship did not depart that day. She spent one more night aboard the *Star*. On the second morning, she heard heavy boots enter. She peeked from underneath the tarp and met the eyes of three other women scattered about the hold, emerging from underneath rope and canvas. They had been there the whole time. Two were dark like her, one was light-skinned. They looked hungrily at the man.

"I told you women 'no' last week," a man chuckled dismissively. "You." He looked to Black Vy. "Stand up."

Black Vy stood and curtsied to him. His expression softened, but he held his arms crossed.

"Quickly, pretty black pearl, how much weak to strong in a sling?"

Black Vy croaked an answer immediately. "Three dash sweet to four finger whiskey."

He reached his hand to her. She hesitated. "Come then, black pearl." Clinton Bangs Bickford led her above decks, striding past the crowd of men, past the captain fishing off a cannon for breakfast. He did not stop at the men's greetings, but clapped their shoulders, bellowing back "good day." He did not remove her hand from his arm or make her walk behind him. They walked the muddy hill to a large building.

Black Vy looked back to the ship. "Do you own that ship?"

"No, but I own the tavern. So I own the men."

The bar was crowded, so Bickford ordered her to work without changing. But Black Vy suspected this first night was a test, that she wouldn't be awarded a clean uniform before first proving competent. Black Vy poured fifty-five stiffeners and bracers that night and wiped out as many glasses. Her blanket dress and shell belt sparked many curious remarks from patrons. In the wee hours, Bickford led her upstairs to a hallway full of women. He escorted her into a small room, pointed to the bed, to the bowl of water, to a clean linen and a jar of honey. He nodded. "For tonight." He closed the door and locked it from the outside. She did not sleep for the bumps and ruckus in the other women's rooms and men's voices coming up the stairway then down through the hours. In the morning, she cleaned her face, winced picking moss out of her neck and shoulder wounds, made her bed, sniffed at the honey, and sat waiting, looking out the window to the people in the street below. Herds of pigs grunted and ate garbage then moved along in packs out of sight. People of all kinds and dress filled the streets, moving with purpose. She felt a flicker of hopeful obscurity. She could blend into this place.

He did not knock, but there was enough clatter in the lock from the key that she sat straighter and faced the door. He held a plate of ham and beans.

Black Vy stared grimly at the food. She was hungry. She set the tray on the bed. The room felt warm though it was still early. He stood in the open doorway, women bustling back and forth behind him, linens draped over their bare arms, passing cakes of soap to each other.

He looked beyond her, to the bed, and gave an uptilt of his head. She approached him and mechanically reached to undo the laces of his breeches.

He flinched and instinctively drew his arms downward, securing his waistband. He stepped backward into the hallway, bumping into the flow of women. He shook his head no, then nodded toward the tray. "Breakfast's getting cold."

Black Vy had balked when he flinched, confused. The parade of women streamed behind him, the sloshing of pitchers in their arms and the swishing of skirts along the floorboards.

Bickford gripped the lapels of his waistcoat. "Starting tomorrow, you are to eat in the dining hall with the other women. Be prompt at seven. You shan't be locked in here again. You will sleep in the common room. If there be more men that need service than women are free, you will accommodate the gentlemen. Supper's no later than two-fifteen. Today is wash-up day—bodies, laundry."

"Yessir."

His eyes skimmed her cheek, tracing over the rough scars on her face, down her neck. She drew her hand to her throat. Her face was not pretty enough, that was it, pitted as it was, her one cheek and neckside the most raggedy. And now the yellowing, stinking spear cuts winding over the old scars. Her neck, before the Native's spear, was so ruined that it made men's thoughts travel to beneath her clothes and imagine the spoiling down her whole body, she knew. Bickford had a fine house of women with smooth, pretty skins. She saw him judging what marks were freshly laid open and what would heal and how Black Vy would present after recovery.

He entered the room. "You must care for your wounds and cover them." He opened the jar of honey and extended his hand toward her, allowed her to step forward to meet his dripping fingers. He swabbed long strokes of honey back and forth across her collar bones. He smeared more honey on her chest and shoulder gashes. She drew sharp breaths from the pain. He pressed the linen to the honey, and she staggered back. "These fester if we don't attend to them." He peered closer. "Mere tracings, not deep." He capped the honey. "A fighter you are."

She wiped her eyes from the clench of the honey on her skin.

"Mabel will bring you a fresh dress, cap, and apron. Don those before going downstairs to prepare the bar." He looked at her blanket dress and shell belt. "You may give me your old rags."

Black Vy gave a little bow. "Nossir. I hold onto these. To sleep in."

He tilted his head in curiosity and left the room.

She shook out her skirts, sat on the bed, and ate for the first time in many days.

Gideon Bell dipped a ladle into the water bucket and drank, watching Poppy cross the yard. Her hair was wet, and her feet were bare, and she held a cask against her hip which caught part of her skirt and made it ride up to show the back meat of her leg. She smiled, and he lowered his head and wet his hair and dragged his hand down his face to gather off the drips.

She bowed without setting down her cask. "Good day, Mr. Bell. How fares your back?"

A twig stuck in her hair, tucked underneath a fine green ribbon. "Were you swimming? You have a bit of something."

She shifted the cask to her other hip, and her skirt fell. Her fingers searched her temple. She did not shy when he stepped close.

He picked through her hair, the stick being well worked in. He tried to catch her eye, but she would not look at him. He sifted through her wet locks, undid the knot at the back of her neck, leaning closer, fingering the plush ribbon. She tensed, the cords in her neck tight. The stick dropped. He reached for the cask and found her wrist, the cords rigid there too. He unburdened her of the cask, and she locked her arms to her sides. He took her hand. It was damp, and her skin through her gown was damp too.

"Meet me again." He pressed the ribbon into her hand.

She hefted her cask and ran to the shanty.

Once inside, curtained in her sleeping space, Poppy drew off her bodice and shift, both soaked. She had thought that being touched and whispered to by a man would be like the first time she had tasted bread and butter and pork together, all her concentration on the ecstasy points, the juices filling her mouth then flaring down to the notch between her legs, wadded like hot laundry. As she had taken another bite, then another bite more, and biting once again, her cords and strings had ignited. The rest of the family at the table had not noticed, it being a holiday with liquors and stories. She had climbed out of bed in the night after everyone was long asleep to taste the butter, and the bread, and the pork together again, to tempt the response of her body. It had happened as before, the transport to rapture, and alone at the table in the dark and cold this time, she had allowed herself a few pleasurable grunts out loud.

But Gideon Bell's hand, like the worn flap of a saddle where the rider's thigh fit, and his pressing nearness were not like that. She was sweating all over and could not contain her shame, did not want him close. She thought of Barnaby's raised initials on Black Vy's thigh, their crude exaggeration when Black Vy had pushed forward the flesh. Barnaby's initials had been distorted as if carved in weeping rock. It was happening too fast. She could not be near Gideon Bell so often. She peeled her upper arm off her ribs and with her finger traced the rest of Gideon Bell's initials there, imagining them darkened and countersunk like floor nails, a permanence too difficult to remove.

In the morning, the girls whispered and tracked their fingers across the pictures on the bed curtains. Sunlight hit the indigo ink, brightened the linen fibers. A hummingbird poised ready to dip into a deep-throated flower. A man brandished a long pole, driving a pair of yoked oxen, the tip of the pole flicking above the near oxen's ear. The forward shoulder stance and lowered heads suggesting the brunt of the oxen's load and the heavy clay soil through which they ploughed. The moment right before the oxen were to receive the pole to their heads and jolt forward with all their might to pry loose the sunken wheel. A maid dumped a bucket, pitching its contents into a trough, the tip of the liquid suspended in the air, held above the splash point. Clara dreamed of a pony's velvet mouth, its whiskers flicking in anticipation before her fingers stroked it. The steam rising off her morning porridge, her spoon hung before stirring into the mush and disrupting the heat cloud rising onto her cheeks.

Yesterday morning, her papa had tried again to blast the rock. She had held her hands over her ears as he held a lit rag to the wick, and the wick sparked and blackened, burning fast toward the rock, toward the bundle of black powder he had stuffed into the rocks. And there had been the awful moment when the orange flame at the end of the wick had met the rock, but the black powder had not exploded. She had expected the blast right away, but there was only a terrible hissing silence, doom hanging in the air. That moment had lasted a full minute, then hours. All the men had cautiously risen from their ditches, their backs hunched and tense, climbing out like dogs that have to go but cannot go, looking toward the black powder bundle, toward her papa. The strain had lasted all through the men's supper break as they shoveled beans anxiously into their mouths, twitching at every snap from the woods, into the evening when sounds they all normally enjoyed crept in, and all night as their ears echoed black water in their beds.

Now it was morning. There had been no blast overnight, no deafening boom. Clara had lain awake through the night waiting for the blast to go off, imagining rock breaking open and the devil's horses flying out. Sound had been whinging through the trees since her return. Its deep echo whorled below the constant rush of falling river. It was not wind clacking the trees. It was not the high whine of night beetles clinging and molting and singing and dropping to the earth. It was not the settling, crackling, hissing of the many spent fires in the yard. It was not the high howl of wolves and the cracking answers of barking dogs. It was not the drone of frogs, for that would have lullabyed her to sleep. Was it the charges inside the rocks, so many set and abandoned by the men, that they now throbbed within and glowed a weak life of their own? Was it the pawing and pacing of the horses pent up in the rocks, it being far too long since they were exercised? Was it Balor and Brace, lost and wandering, braying to find acceptance to the baron's pack?

Georgie had listened all night to the restless men shift and swear outside in their tents. They had given up hours before dusk of any delayed explosion. The impotence of the black powder worried them. The rock held too much water and when they had drilled shallowly into its surface and set a clay plug over the black powder, water had saturated it. The black powder would not fire if wet. Water trickled through and from the rock in many places; sometimes it sprung like a fountain from flat rock faces. Sometimes it poured from cracks like tears, leaving dark blots. The soil and rock covered huge tracts of underground springs, and when the trees and soil soaked up their fill of the water, the overflow seeped through the porous rock. Hugh had not anticipated the rock being so wet that the black powder would not combust. They had all banked so much on blasting away huge sections at a time.

The men were up early. Hugh demonstrated a new method of ignition: he held an oily rag in one hand and a pine bough in the other, touching it to Cotter Wilkens's spent cook fire embers. The bough lit and crackled, and Hugh swept the rag through the flaming needles; he jumped back from the whoosh of the oiled rag, flung it down, a desperate show for the men. They would not figure out a way to set off the black powder before the snow, and they would have to wait out an entire season before starting again, hoping the new season was a dry one.

The unexploded charge had the crew still on edge, each man's jumpiness compounding the jitters of the next man. They braced for the looming moment before explosion, yet hopeful for the demolition of rock. None of the men liked to be caught off guard. They were a hair-trigger lot, able to sense impending blows or malice through the fine hairs on the backs of their necks. They spooked at the clanging of pots from inside the shanty or any upswish of wind that masked the rush of the river, mistaking it for the vacuum of sound before a great percussive boom. They all skulked about with impatience and twitching, the baleful chroma of camp intolerable. They had no way to expend the energy they expected to use on hauling away loads of blasted rubble. They would soon be fighting each other and drinking away their whiskey rations.

Hildy loved the suspense. After breakfast, Georgie led her through the rocky shallows downstream from the blast site, Poppy and Clara behind, lifting Hildy's cape train. Hildy insisted Georgie play aegis by wielding her knife high like a torch. Hildy commanded Georgie to twist the knife this way then that to see its point glint in the sunshine, a beacon of warning for any marauders. The smoke from the distant burning of wicks drifted to settle above the water, sucked low, caught suspended above the current, carried for a ways downstream. Their immediacy to the blasting made Georgie nervous, but Hildy insisted on being close enough for when the blast took hold so she could finally feel the fine spray of pebbles rain down.

Black Vy had conceded a branch of trust to Georgie, allowing her to dress out fish and fowl, though not yet wood birds or hogs. Georgie slit open trout bellies on the porch, collecting the spill of roe in one pan and discarding entrails to another. Hildy tilted her head, eyes closed. The sun cast a shadow on her face, a stark mottle of leaf-light spilling across her high cheek and upper lip. Poppy combed through Hildy's hair, loosening the neat braid. Clara pushed in and began a clumsy hairdressing, chunkily rebraiding Hildy's locks. Poppy set a crown of grapevine on Hildy's head. Clara batted her hands against the layers of Hildy's dress, and Poppy clasped Clara's hands to stop.

The fish catch had been plentiful, and Georgie watched the eyes cloud of the ones she had yet to clean. "There are more filleting knives inside," Georgie said to Hildy.

Hildy looked away. "We sha's find pretty buds in our forest. Come, girls, we sha's search for them."

Georgie pricked the tail of the fish curled in her hand then turned her knife sideways up its white belly.

Hildy and the girls scampered off the porch collecting themselves into a rehearsed formal procession. Clara led the way, carrying a stick in defense of Queen Hildy. Poppy draped the makeshift cape across Hildy's shoulders. Hildy strutted in her royal garb. Poppy hurried to catch the train trailing in the dirt, and Hildy beamed a smile, arms outstretched. The sky was an azure dome, a bluebird's cap.

In the woods, Hildy dug up a tin and took two coins from it. She told the girls that Mother Daphne told her where to find coins buried at different spots in the woods, and Mother Daphne was never wrong. The girls asked who that was, and Hildy answered they would meet her soon. Hildy said she had desired for a long time the money to afford a fortune telling from Mother Daphne and brought her some dried turkey, but Mother Daphne had refused it. She drew Hildy a map to find the coins, instructing her to bring those to pay for the reading of her lot. Hildy said the tins had sprouted when the skunk weed unfurled. She was just that lucky.

Clara reverted to her position of command, picking up the points of Hildy's cape. She steadied her mount sternly. "Whoa, girl."

Hildy obeyed, craning her neck as Clara pulled the cape taut with all her strength. Hildy grabbed the ends around her neck to secure the cape.

Clara gave the cape some slack. "On, girl," she urged Hildy.

Hildy pranced ahead gathering her gait spiritedly, then let Clara rein her back.

They reached the sound and spray of Buttermilk Falls, the trail mucky. They drew nearer, the rock bright beneath the falling water, a white glow through the brush. They hugged the steep bank to get close to the flow, their backs darkening from the seeping hillside.

Clara reached the falling water first. "Ladies do not bathe in furs." She pointed high, where the water fell over the precipice. "The water blurbles from up there. From the ground. From where we cannot see."

"She repeats what Ma told us," Poppy explained.

But Clara struck the wet earth to reclaim her authority. "And men do not undress ladies!"

Poppy and Hildy laughed, and a small smile crept over Clara's face. She leaned her face into the spray. She gripped her stick, warming up for a good strike. Clara beat the rock, splashing water in all directions, trying to rouse the baron's horses.

"A man keeps horses behind these rocks, and I must coax them out so I can practice my riding skills."

Hildy played along. "They be wild and snorting and pawing, pent up behind rocks all the time."

Clara's speech quickened. "Yes, if I can handle these ponies then I will be able to hold any mount. Ride and leap and fly on their backs, holding onto their manes, my feet and nightgown streaming back in the wind like a flower stem."

Hildy was amused. She liked stories. Hildy looked over Clara's shoes. Clara wore the shoes their ma had found in the woods by Buttermilk Falls, the pair the lady had left in the woods. On Clara, the shoes were still too big, too black.

"Mayn't you start with smaller, gentler ponies?" Hildy crouched to the milky rock and touched her fingers to the spill.

Clara took her wrist and moved her fingers out from the water. "Be careful. The horses could come crashing out."

Hildy flinched back. She stood, drying her fingers on her skirt and looked around. "It's chilly, girls. We sha's move ahead."

"We have one more thing to show you."

Clara lifted the train of Hildy's cape, fluttered it to encourage Hildy to giddyup.

Hildy let out a high whinny and reared with clawed hands. This delighted Clara, whose face flushed bright. She lost her footing in the rocky shallows, catching herself with both hands as she fell forward into the white foaming spill. Her feet slipped and teetered on the uneven stones. She lifted her head, sputtering from the tumble of water. She tried to push upright, but her hands gripped a flat panel. She tugged to free the board, but it stuck from the pressure of falling water, driven into the sucking mud beneath. Poppy and Hildy ran to help her, for it appeared as though she couldn't free herself from the water's spill and churn. Hildy pulled her up by the hair, and Clara choked out water.

Hildy lifted Clara's wet face. "You's safe, lamb. See how you breathe with your strong lungs."

Clara cried out and sank her hands below the water. "The door! His door is underwater. Help me open it!" She grabbed Hildy's wrist and plunged her hand under the water, moving it over the panel.

Hildy craned her face from the spray and felt for how large the panel was. There was a latch on it. She yanked, but the water's force was too great, and the handle snapped off. She held it up. Clara gasped and clutched for the latch, golden and hammered to a thin curve that fit her hand. Poppy knelt in the water, searching the edges of the door, which were framed with molding. She and Hildy pried the door free of the mud. Hildy held it dripping to the light. They all stood and staggered back from where the door had been planted, looking for anything to fly out from the water. Nothing came.

Hildy set down the object, and they panted and stared.

"What is it?" Poppy asked.

"It's too small to be a door. He could not drive horses through there." Clara was disappointed.

Hildy studied the ornate marquetry. "It be a thing of beauty. And look, hinges. It was part of something larger. I not seen such fancy work. Can it been part of a carriage?"

"Yes! His carriage! It broke apart when he was driving his horses from the rock." Clara shuffled her hands through the water, hoping to uncover more wreckage from the baron's travels.

"I seen this afore, but in a drawing." Hildy studied the inlaid whorls, an intricate pattern of thistles. "Come on, we sha's move ahead." They left the panel upright alongside the falling water. Clara still held the latch in her tight fist. She started walking the path back. But Hildy called from behind.

"Hildy must visit Mother Daphne. Mother Daphne has fortunes to tell." The girls followed as Hildy ran for a new part of the woods.

Ida had heard the girls shouting and splashing but kept out of sight downriver. When she was certain the girls were gone, she waded through a shallow neck to where they had been at the waterfall. The blue of the morning had faded. The wedge of sky parted by the river was a silver dome, her grandmother's tea strainer.

Ida was not scouting for the English woman or Dewitt Otis Lipson. He and the English woman had not seen each other after he had buried his dog, so Ida had not watched the English woman for long. And when Ida had spied, she often had to look away, rankled by the isolated drone of the English woman's habits. Ida had continued to watch Lipson. He doddered about his chores or ran to the river to plunge his head to quell his rages, like a self-satisfied penance for murdering Talise Jollicoeur. A disquiet urged Ida to wander to find Talise's bones. Ida scouted long days, searching for remains, circling back to Buttermilk Falls to drink and rest on the cool rocks.

At this warm noon hour, Káhuk squealed, strapped to her back. She unfastened his cradle to help him squat by the stream to drink, but as soon as he was free, he crawled toward the water falling over the rocks. Káhuk shrilled and pointed. A door was propped upright, its varnish shimmering. Ida caught her son, swept him up, draped a hand over his head. He fussed and craned around to see the door. Ida knelt, tipping the edge of the door away from the rock. Above the roar of the water, voices rolled, cries of men. She flinched back, the door toppling into the spill. The rock was stained dark where the door had leaned. From inside the rock came bleating—English, Oneida, and Seneca words. Yet she did not hear a woman's voice.

Ida rebundled her son. After the long trek home to her family, she lamented Talise's body as irretrievable, drowned in the wasteland of slaughtered soldiers.

The chimney smoked white. Tall bright ferns filled the clearing, shrouding the tree stumps. Mother Daphne waited at the door, waving them in with her apron. She lived in one room. Hanging from the rafters were whole pike, trout, and salmon all mounted as if swimming toward stuffed owls, herons, hawks, and blue jays, also suspended, some in full wingspan as if about to wrap their prey within attack dives. Predators of water and sky pitted against each other. The hearth was as large as the elevated pulpit in the Fort Herkimer church. Three kettles boiled inside. Turtle shells of all sizes lined one wall with stacks upon stacks of books against the other walls. Mother Daphne sat at a table. She motioned for them to sit. She arranged a shabby but once delicate cape that topped her shoulders and fell longer in the back. Her dress sleeves peeked out from the cape, many layers of flounce and ruffle and coral pink ribbon tied at the elbow. Her white chest was exposed; a scoop of satin hugged her bosom. Her hair was brushed into a wide, curly halo, and fatter curls hung down her shoulders. There were tight rows of sheep's head curls at her temples, a few pearls and turkey quills tucked between them. Her cheeks were smooth and painted, and she blotted the back of her plump hand to cool them. When her thoughts paused, her fingers fanned and pointed skyward. When her thoughts spun forward, she sometimes wrote the words with a finger on the air.

"Are you a queen?" Clara's eyes strained over the complications of bows and sleeves and flounces.

Mother Daphne laughed. "Does a queen boil her own supper? I am Mother Daphne." The kettles roiled behind her.

"Where are your children?" Poppy looked around but saw no crib.

At this, both Hildy and Mother Daphne laughed. Then Mother Daphne composed her face, motioning for the girls to stop asking questions.

Mother Daphne closed her eyes and smoothed an embroidery pattern, tracing the outlines of a man and woman homesteading in high mountain peaks. Mother Daphne cocked one eye open and gestured to an empty saucer. Hildy plinked coins into the saucer. At Mother Daphne's elbow was a fine china plate with golden pollen grains. Cups of weak-looking tea were alongside, half drunk and cold. Mother Daphne's finger stopped on the breast of the woman in the embroidery pattern.

"You call to enquire about your fortune. Now ask your question."

"How many sons sha's I bear for Hugh?"

Mother Daphne circled her finger over the woman's form in the pattern. She opened her eyes. "What happened to that fine dress you once wore? With the embroidered buds?"

Hildy hugged herself. "It burn up."

The woman's eyes glittered. "I could tell your fortune better if you wore that dress. You must take off the dress you wear now. I cannot relay your fortune when you wear this tattered thing."

Hildy stepped out of the gown, laid it in Clara's lap. Hildy chattered more questions. How many of her sons would be president? Is there a room in the capitol for mothers of presidents?

Mother Daphne closed her eyes and traced the pattern. Her eyes shot open to the dress. "Who allows such a fine dress to burn?"

Hildy opened her mouth to protest but knew better and tapped another coin into the saucer.

Clara sat quiet and hid her closed fist in Hildy's old dress.

Mother Daphne sighed and pushed away the pattern. She addressed Poppy. "You must take that dress out of doors."

Poppy did as she was told. Mother Daphne snorted a snuff of pollen grains then tapped the edge of her nostril clean. She shook her head to clear the rush and sniffed. Hildy reached for the spoon to inhale a share of the pollen, but Mother Daphne snatched it away, dumping the remaining grains into a teacup and swallowing it down.

"Does that help you see his horses?" Clara asked.

Mother Daphne closed her mouth. She stared at the child, slowly set down her teacup as if she might give away more of herself if she were not careful. "What do you know of his horses?"

"They are behind the milky rock..." Clara began.

Mother Daphne shot an angry glare at Hildy. "How dare you. He is mine."

Hildy avowed innocence. "No, she knew'd. *She* shewed *me*."

Mother Daphne reached forward to take Clara's hand, but Clara drew her closed fist behind her back.

"What do you hold in your hand, child?"

"We wants to ask you about that, Mother Daphne," Hildy said. "Mayn't we see your picture book? The moth-fretten one."

Mother Daphne nodded. "One moment and you may look." Then to Clara, "Answer me."

Clara slouched in her seat, tucking her chin to her chest.

Mother Daphne grabbed Clara's arm but shrank when Clara didn't break her stare or shy away. "If you cannot make civil words with me, then you won't be able to with anyone."

Clara flinched, believing it.

"She hold a little blue-green crawdiddy husk she find under the rocks. Leave her be." Hildy walked to the stack of books and drew the largest one from the pile.

"Why do the turtles walk the wall?" Clara asked. The shells graduated in size from tiny, globose eggs at the bottom to freshly hatched babies to white-spined adolescents to painterly adults to grandfatherly giants nosing the roof joists.

"Do you know what a charm is? My turtles keep and defend. That whole north wall is protected as if lined with the Virgin Mother's golden teeth." Mother Daphne drew from her skirt pocket a leathery turtle claw, touched the points of its long nails. She watched Clara stare at the tiny eggs. "Those would not work for you any more than dead stones. You must dream on what animal is strong for you. It might not be the turtle. The turtle is mine."

Hildy opened the book onto their laps. Clara raised her side of the book and looked at the title, *Modèles de voitures d'époque Louis XV.*

"What does it say?" Clara asked.

Hildy paged through the illustrations. "Look, they be carriage types and parts."

"A king owned them," said Mother Daphne. "They are models of the old school."

There were different types of carriages drawn in opulent detail, some with open tops, some like wheelbarrows, some large enough to carry four people, some closed on top and on all sides. They were baroque, lavishly detailed, not at all like the plain wood planks of the wagons in which Clara had ridden. Some drawings had smaller parts superimposed above the larger image to call attention to the fine workmanship: a folding seat, a reinforcing strip of metal, a trunk to hold belongings, a dust screen, a small plate upon which to step the foot to easily climb aboard. This confused Clara because the parts were the same size as the carriages. But Hildy pointed to where each part fit onto the carriage, and Clara was made to understand the notion of scale. Clara clutched the latch in her hand, recognizing its fine style in these drawings. Hildy paged to a four-paneled carriage. Each panel had a different pattern of inlay. Clara laid her finger on the page as she recognized the thistles and molding from the panel at the falling water. In the drawing, the attached panels made up one side of the carriage; their designs were cleverly in the same family of shapes. Clara pressed the latch against her palm.

"I knew I seen it," Hildy murmured, and underneath the book she closed her hand over Clara's fist.

"Did you draw these?" Clara asked Mother Daphne.

"No, child. These were drawn many years ago in another country across the great ocean."

"Did you build his carriage by looking at these drawings?"

Mother Daphne's eyes filled black, the pupils spooling malevolence. "What do you know of his carriage?"

Clara shouted back, "What do *you* know of his carriage?"

Mother Daphne dabbed the sweat at her bosom. "What do you know of him, child?"

"That he keeps fine horses. That I should like to see, to mayhaps ride, those horses. What do you know of him?"

"That he likes to playact as an injured man, for that's when men reveal their true character, having to rescue the injured, to care for them, to make room for this act in their daily habits. Now does he sound like a friend you would want to have?" Mother Daphne shook her head to indicate how Clara should answer.

Clara did not answer. Hildy had flipped to the back pages of the book and nudged Clara's attention to illustrations of injured men and wrecked carriages. Men had Xs for eyes, their limbs broken backward. All kinds of injuries were drawn in detail like the details of the carriages, enlarged. The back wheel of a noble's carriage ran over the midsection of a market stall proprietor, long stems of onions scattered about the cobblestones. The driver held his whip, long as a fishing pole, and looked away. The lord peeked out the window from inside the carriage. Hildy flipped more pages: horses careened off cliffs, passengers and luggage suspended in the air. A woman lay outside of a wrecked carriage that had run into a fence, her wig knocked off.

"Is this one you?" Clara asked.

Mother Daphne spat, "You have a hard green seed. On your liver. A splinter that you hardly notice now. But as you grow, it will blossom black and soft and grow heavy in you like a burdensome wet fungus."

"You jealous of the child. There ain't call for cursing her." Hildy closed the book and drew Clara behind her. "I paid coin for you to tell my fortune, now you sha's tell it."

Mother Daphne dropped the coins from the saucer into her apron. "You shan't bear him any young ones. You will have your troubles with these two milksops." Mother Daphne nodded to the porch. "That older one obeys." Then she squinted at Clara. "This one is hard-nolled. That older one is pliant even when she feels something isn't right." Mother Daphne closed her eyes. "She frets out on that porch even now but won't come back inside until she's told." Mother Daphne opened her eyes and narrowed them on Hildy. "That could be useful to you. Do you hear me?"

But Hildy had stopped listening after the statement of her barren future, her face clouded and locked. Clara peeked from behind Hildy's skirts. "How many horses does he have? What colors?"

Hildy snapped alert, catching Clara from stepping out further.

Mother Daphne reached behind to the hearth, her hand clanking the hanging utensils. But Hildy was quick and hurried Clara out the door before the ladle of scalding water hit them. Mother Daphne shouted baneful pledges of their futures, but she did not chase them as they whipped past the ferns.

Hildy stopped, brushed at Clara's dress as if slapping away biting flies. "That woman have no power to curse you. She full of nonsense. She a fool woman who the men don't want to lay with no more. She don't got powers over you." Yet Hildy ran her hand over Clara's head and tapped her fingertip under Clara's nose to clear away the curse. They heard Mother Daphne rage inside. They were far enough away that Hildy shouted, "Grimalkin!" and the girls startled back at the force and bellow of her voice.

Hildy nodded to Poppy to make haste. Clara, emboldened by Hildy, craned her head and shouted: "How many? What colors? Which rocks? Where are they hidden?"

After a distance, they slowed, leaving the deep woods, passing again by the upturned tree.

Hildy wrapped each girl in a corner of her cape. "Come, lambs, we sha's see iffen your pa has busted rock today."

Clara climbed piggyback onto Hildy, chattering about fried pork for dinner and all its crispy edges. Her big black shoes knocked against Hildy's hips as they walked. Hildy slid them off and handed them to Poppy, who wore them on her hands like gloves.

The charges that day had not exploded. The men wandered around the falls, swimming naked in the cold water, arms outstretched, thighs bounding through the swift current. Standing, their skin turned waxen from the chill, their elbows tight to their ribs, but it was the warmest it would be all year. They sunned on the flat slate, rowdily holding court with their stories, smoking, laughing, shivering, scrubbing their hides in anticipation of Captain Lewis's upcoming visit.

On July 30, President Jefferson had traveled by carriage from Washington to Monticello. He ambitioned to find the shortest route, so he counted the wheel revolutions, the monotony of which was frequently interrupted by bad road. It became muddy at Little's Lane, and as the horses balked and the wheels stuck in the mire, his driver and postilion jumped down to heave the landau free. The men slopped the mud off the rough road, and Mr. Jefferson stood outside the carriage daydreaming on one of many letters he had written the day before his departure. He had written congratulations to the artist Charles Willson Peale who had recently purchased bones from a farmer named Hugh Masten south of Albany. Masten had found mammoth bones in his pond. With a great wheel of buckets and a crew of men, Peale drained Masten's pond and displaced much of its dirt and found a few more bones, then uncovered a partially complete skeleton nearby. Mr. Jefferson promised in his letter to send a pump and tents, resources he hoped would support Peale's unearthing and packing of the incognitum bones for eventual display. Mr. Jefferson expressed his conviction that the American mammoth must still be living west on the vast and unplumbed territory beyond the Missouri.

Mr. Jefferson's postilion opened and closed the private gates along the route to Monticello so the carriage could pass. Mr. Jefferson ticked through the pecuniary needs of a westward expedition counterpoised against the frugal spending that his inaugural speech had promised. He dreamed a list of all the animal, vegetable, and mineral discoveries yet to be found. For even his daydreams were productive. The carriage pulled forward. Then, bah! More sludge on the road. Another stop. He thought to Ledyard's arrest in Russia and Michaux's bungled diplomacy, both men's expeditions impeded years ago. He thought hopefully still for the right man to break open the continent. The carriage was free, and as it pulled forward, his daydream dried up. He resumed counting wheel revolutions.

Captain Lewis, President Jefferson's newly appointed secretary, had been in Philadelphia on July 20 to see the *George Washington* sail with a diminished crew for the contentious Mediterranean waters. Lewis bade the ship's Captain Bainbridge courage, for his voyage earlier that year had resulted in extortion by pirates, the attack of which Bainbridge had protested, but under threat of fire was forced to obey. Yet Captain Bainbridge had returned his ship to American shores. Lewis shook the captain's hand and stood stoically on the dock as Bainbridge shouted commands for the frigate to again leave harbor. Lewis's heart pumped for the men who hoisted sails on three masts, and he watched as the ship was pulled by the outgoing tide toward open water. With his president at Monticello for August and September, Lewis could not resist traveling farther north to Newburg, New York, to inspect Mr. Peale's mammoth bones.

Once at Newburg, Lewis shook Peale's hand and assured him of Mr. Jefferson's promise to send supplies. Lewis did not hold eye contact with Peale longer than good manners dictated. He felt restless after congratulating Bainbridge and Peale on their bold ventures. Lewis pocketed a flake of mammoth cartilage then swung onto his horse. Mr. Peale had gifted him a dried cake of venison and a crock of butter, of which Mr. Peale boasted his game and cows were doused and happy on the richest grasses. Captain Lewis headed north to attend to a nagging errand and while there would call upon his longtime friend Hugh Tepper, the man breaking open the Adirondack foothills, and his fetching wife who by now must be tired of him.

In the afternoon, they heard the approaching hooves, the heavy clomping trot. It was Captain Lewis wearing buckskins with fringe on the sleeves and sides that bounced limply with his mount's gait. He carried a rolled buffalo hide on his saddle. Hugh rushed outdoors to greet him. Lewis did not return Hugh's broad smile, but he embraced Hugh tightly, and Hugh thumped him heartily, drawing back and cupping his roughly bearded cheeks. The men strode toward the house, Hugh's arm around Lewis, Hugh besieging a flurry of questions.

Georgie had met Lewis once before when Lewis answered President Washington's command to quell the Whiskey Insurrection. Even though Hugh and Lewis had defended opposite sides of the conflict, they had formed a friendship; both men had lost their fathers in the Revolution. After hearing of the government's plot, Georgie, Hugh, and Margaret traveled to Pennsylvania to help the rebels whip, tar, and feather the tax collectors. Hugh had distilled whiskey for a few seasons with surplus corn and traded the liquor as currency, one of many short-lived endeavors to sidestep cash. And Margaret had wanted to stop the tax from spreading north to New York, her hackles high as it reminded her of the taxation they had fought against during the Revolutionary skirmishes.

At the Whiskey Insurrection, Georgie had watched Lewis closely: his horsemanship, his table manners, the way he held listeners in his eyes as he spoke. His face was comely, his profile angular. In camp, he had shaved twice a day, a personal discipline not shared by his fellow soldiers; in the hours between, Georgie had watched the black nubs of his whiskers darken. No matter how much sun he took, he retained a downy white cast on his fresh-shaven jaw. He was very much a gentlemen, as all Virginian men were said to be. She had not met a man of such manners and mind since leaving England. He had a highborn upbringing, but his comportment was of the woods, not the drawing room. He was tall and bowlegged and ungainly, though sincere. At times, he could have a dark edge, a sudden remote manner, cutting off short those around him. He had delicate blue-gray eyes that would lock in a celestine stare then gulf with sadness. But when he set his gaze on Georgie, his eyes livened, sharpened. She had found herself in his warm gaze often. She boldly entered his tent one night only to find she had misread his fixed regard when she was met with the naked back of a woman sprouting upright in his bedsheets, her spine flexing in the candlelight, on top of him. They never spoke of it, but Lewis later wrote to Georgie saying he regretted the circumstances at Parkinson's Ferry and if he had felt worthy of her, he would have swayed the events of that evening elsewise.

As the men strode toward the house, she saw Lewis was rougher, a hard, hot wire running through him. All the lore and miles spattered over his regal bearing. They had heard of his recent service in the wilds of the southern Great Lakes against the Miami Natives. Lewis had written to Hugh about his new appointment as secretary to President Jefferson.

She tucked back her curls, wrapped her shawl about her shoulders, and first sat on the bed, then rose and took a stool near the hearth.

The door burst open, and Lewis's eyes glittered in recognition at her. He clamped shut his mouth, which had been ready-pursed to bite back to Hugh's wit. Captain Lewis was disarmed, overtaken by a rush of feeling that he was determined to control. He nodded then bowed. She rose and bowed then went to approach him, but Hugh steered him to the table. This was where the two men's sensibilities broke apart: Lewis was unable to enter a room without formally greeting a lady. Stiffly, he let his host lead him toward the table while Hugh did not so much as look in Georgie's direction. Instead of protesting, Lewis continued to hold Georgie's gaze, the black irritation of his eyes softening to the shared amusement over Hugh's rough manners. Then his face faltered again, shy not at her beauty because it wasn't foremost, but her spirit, open as he remembered.

"Did you find the blue-eyed Indians, man?" Hugh straddled a chair and poured ale.

"No. None in the Lake Erie tribes. Perhaps farther west." Lewis drank a long pull from his cup.

"Farther west than the Northwest Territory? But how is that possible?"

"There is talk of planning a westward route to the far edge of the continent."

"Well, that is talk. With two failed attempts already. Let me tell you of our progress thus here at Buttermilk Falls. Perhaps there are spare Republican funds for my venture. For I have already started, the men assembled and productive, a portion of the rock already cleared."

Lewis stared around the room, a disinterest that normally Hugh would flatten by proceeding to explain at length despite his guest's indifference. Hugh instead tried to regain Lewis's attention by diverting the subject back to their shared military adventures.

"Many long years since we first made your acquaintance during the insurrection at Pennsylvania. And your adventures since your triumph with the battle at Lake Erie. We thought you had been overtaken by the Indians or starved or kidnapped by the British. And here you are before us. You must tell us everything."

Lewis drew one arm across his chest and clasped his wrist. "I've had a long time of it."

"Yes! Of course. You will stay for supper and rest. The men are aching to hear your tales. We will fill your dry well. And we will spar in the yard until you bleed, man." Hugh playfully cuffed Lewis's chin.

Lewis stiffened and shot Hugh a warning look. Hugh tensed, held his ground long enough that it looked like he would pounce. Lewis scudded back his chair. Hugh flinched against the hearth, pointed his finger at Lewis. "Ever quick, captain." Hugh bounced on his toes, shrugged his shoulders, his hands limp, winding up for the evening's events.

Lewis downed another cupful of ale. He looked to Georgie. "And what of you, mistress? How have you fared since last we visited? You are a true wife of the north woods by now, yes?" He withdrew the crock of butter from his coat and set it on the table. "A contribution to our supper. I'm told the cows of Newburgh produce a fine quality butter. Indeed, I beheld a store of it. Butter by the hundredweight. The stuff of dreams."

Georgie straightened and began to address Lewis, but Hildy came rushing down the stairs. She was done up fancily, large curls at her cheeks. She curtsied shortly to Lewis. He bowed crisply, without words, nodding back and forth between the women.

"Stars, is Mr. Jefferson in the yard?" Hildy teased. "Surely, sir, you got important work for the president? Whatever could bring you this far north to us folk?" She sat upon Hugh's knee, and Lewis averted his gaze.

"What business does find you in New York, man?" Hugh asked.

"I witnessed the *George Washington* sail for Málaga to reach Algiers with God's help against the pirates. Mr. Jefferson entreated me to bid aid and comfort to the good Captain Bainbridge with his small crew. Much trouble with the Barbary corsairs."

At "Málaga," the fiddle roused from outside, and Hildy jumped off Hugh's lap to the yard.

"It sailed from New York Harbor?" Hugh asked.

"Philadelphia."

"Philadelphia? That's quite a journey. Might you have other interests here in New York? Might Mr. Jefferson have caught wind of our development plans here at the falls?" Hugh persisted.

Lewis touched his hand to his coat. "I do have the errand of returning your book, man." He withdrew a slim hardback: *Buffon's Natural History, Volume II.*

Hugh placed one hand underneath and one on top. "It made the journey, to and from Lake Erie with you?"

Lewis nodded.

"There be the many miles of dust and air upon it?" Hugh lifted the book, inhaled. He cracked it open, intent upon being hit in the face with a whiff of myth and smoke. But he only sagged slightly in the shoulders. "You bastard. The spine is broken." He laughed, and Lewis smiled for the first time.

"It had much use, passed from man to man, and myself leafing through." He took the book from Hugh and thumbed it open to the cover plate.

Hugh touched the page and read aloud: "Mr. Hugh Tepper so considerately lent me this book May 1794. It has since been ferried by me to Lake Erie by inland way of the Northwest, and I, his friend Meriwether Lewis, now reconvey to him, Buttermilk Falls, early August 1801."

Hugh read the entire inscription once more silently. "Did you find the irregular winds of his description? The caverns, the clefts? The land changed to sea and sea into land?"

"No. Nothing of my journey was reflected in those pages. But I clung to the order and certainty of his cataloging like a book of prayer."

"Was Lake Erie the forty leagues surmised?"

"I did not survey the waters. But some mornings it seemed as though I stood before a sea whose curve I could ride to penetrate the tropics."

"Sir, now you have your own natural history to write," Georgie said, her voice rough from not having spoken in so long. "Your own catalog of the northwest journey."

Lewis nodded and drank. He did not look away from her as Hugh paged through the book.

"I assure you that the book is in fair condition save for one spill into the river at the Wyandot village. Though it was tied in oilcloth."

Hugh jabbed his finger onto a page. "Yet, here, here a spot of grease from a meal of Great Lakes bear?" A translucent circlet on the page made the letters from the back of the paper show through the front. Hugh held the page close to his nose. "The smell of far waters and all of the molds that collected to the damp pages on the ride back east." He closed his eyes in rapture as he snapped shut the book.

Lewis's gaze moved past Georgie, locking onto the fire.

"We have had grand business here while you were shooting your rifle." Hugh tried again to commandeer the topic to his blasting. He rubbed the tops of his legs briskly, clenching his shoulders, and bracing for the long wind-up to impressing his guest.

Having downed a sufficient quantity of ale, Lewis submitted to listening. He nodded toward the yard. "A crew you have here? For what purpose? They labor at a quarry it would seem."

"Joseph Bonaparte will have my back on this, friend. The King of It-Lee will put funds toward developing the New World. We will blast away the rock and overgrowth and build grand escapes for the rich to make their summer destination. We have started with family funds and expect those to continue." He didn't look at Georgie as she gathered a handful of her skirt and cocked her fist to her hip.

Lewis listened, flitting his gaze between Hugh and Georgie. "The world is no longer impenetrable. All men of this age will pry open a small piece of their place in it. As I said, Mr. Jefferson proposes an expedition west. We will see what comes of his planning this time with government funds."

Hugh clamped his hand on Lewis's shoulder. "Yes, so you said." He leaned back and settled his boots atop the back of an empty chair.

Lewis glanced sideways at Hugh's boots, which were now level with his face. Georgie covered her mouth with her shawl.

"Might Mr. Jefferson direct some of those funds to efforts here?" Hugh pressed.

Lewis would never raise his boots above his head while visiting, and he drew a breath to ground himself in the bond of his Virginian manners. He backtracked his comments: "There is the nation's debt to be scaled back and the belief in men to hasten enterprise for the good of the country by their own means. Any funds approved to search for navigable courses west would surely be modest, without surplus to direct to small-scale tourist development."

"Indeed, I have demonstrated enterprise by securing private funding through family connections overseas." Hugh nodded to Georgie. "Surely, this could persuade the president to the worthiness of the work I undertake here?"

"Have you made recent progress with your blasting?"

Hugh refreshed the mugs of ale. "The season has been wet is all."

"Do you hear of Peale's dig at Newburgh? He and scores of men toil with a turnspit large as a courthouse, men trudging inside to power its rotation. Good God, the line of buckets wheeling in and out of the water. The sludge! With men below in the pit hauling up mud by hand. They have found a mammoth skeleton and pick and ply at each part to transport and reassemble the whole so it can be examined and exhibited and further the understanding of this nation's treasure of great land beings." Lewis retrieved the flint of sinew from his pocket and offered it to Hugh.

Hugh turned the artifact over in his palm. "We had a few fossils here at the falls." He glanced at Lewis to gauge if he had heard of the deception.

"And Peale prepares sketches to depict the scene on a grand canvas. He is a most enterprising and energetic fellow." If Lewis had heard of Hugh's forgery, he was politely sidestepping. Lewis stood and addressed Georgie. "May I have the pleasure of dancing with the most elegant lady of the north woods this evening?" He bowed and offered his hand to escort Georgie outside, and Hugh withered in his seat as he lost the last word on convincing Captain Lewis of his mettle.

After supper, there were fires all about the yard, the men rousing and pushing each other, the usual build-up before the nightly fight, but with a louder cadence at the excitement of Lewis, the center of talk and stories. Lewis was flushed, deep in a bout of inebriety, his face greasy in the firelight after devouring crackled pigs' ears, his fingers licked clean.

Georgie hung back, seated on the porch. Black Vy leaned on the railing, watching with amusement. The girls lay with a young pig, picking over its skin for ticks. Georgie stared at Lewis's open way with the men. Her mind spun to his journey, of nights with the men he led down the Ohio. She did not try to conceal watching him even under Black Vy's heed.

Lewis had been giving Hugh dark looks after supper as Hugh recited a steady cataloguing of Lewis's accomplishments: his fluency with Algonquin languages, his knowledge of botany, his marksmanship, his prowess for hand-to-hand combat. And now, Hugh announced, Mr. Jefferson was refining the man with a focus on arts and crafts and sciences. Hugh's trumpeting irritated Lewis, for it was a barrier to getting acquainted with the men, and Lewis could not abide a man whose own worth depended upon the achievements of his acquaintances.

Hugh addressed the men lecture-style, gesturing toward Lewis as if he were a pug on display, speaking a high discourse on the freedoms of men and the liberty of expansion, laying the mantle of responsibility on Captain Lewis for ousting the British from the Maumee in the Battle of Fallen Timbers, thus clearing the Natives farther west. At this,

Lewis's face reddened, then darkened. A silvery pink flash of pig flank skirted through. Hugh worked to a fever pitch of oration, tilting his head for emphasis, laboring to foment the men's passions. Hugh began the speech in English, transitioned to German to highlight his main points, peaked to Latin for natural science oration, his speech eventually unfolding in three different languages. Lewis muttered, leering at Hugh as the men, mostly uneducated, frowned into their mugs or spit into the dirt.

Hugh, who normally was not one to respond to intended slights because he would never think a man justified in doing so, did react rather hurtfully to losing Lewis's attention. When shouting in Latin directly at Lewis did not work, Hugh stopped and asked in English, "Were the beaver seven foot tall, man?"

The men leaned forward to hear Lewis's response.

Without moving his eyes or expression, Lewis answered, "Not that I saw."

Hugh forced a laugh. He raised both arms, gesturing for the men to rise; it was time for sparring. The men dispersed, knowing none of them were to be tonight's opponent. They pulled on the brims of their caps, eager, eyes bright. Charles Boudinot rested his elbow companionably on Noah Stiles's shoulder, and there was an intent exchange of words and an expectant nod from both toward Lewis. Before Hugh's lecture, Lewis had walked into the crowd of men, shook hands, and visited with a few. They had immediately liked him, had told Lewis the story of Hugh nearly drowning and calling him Kettle, and they had all laughed. They had bestowed upon Lewis a marten head, their preferred charm that season. Lewis had admired the heads slung about all their waists, praising this totem of brotherhood. Lewis had encouraged bets on the fight, boasting he would trounce Hugh, and the men had pooled their coins and amulets into a cloth sack, tucking the wager pot into Quill Stibbens's sleeping pelt.

Hugh removed his shirt, and Lewis followed. They stood glowing bare-chested in their trousers and boots, bare-knuckled. Lewis was solidly muscled across his chest and shoulders and arms, and he stood a couple inches taller than Hugh.

Hugh angled his stance to address the crowd as if to say more about his opponent. Jeptha Buell, overeager, shouted, "Hook that pretty jaw!" which Lewis took to signal the start of the fight. Hugh was unprepared as Lewis drew back his arm and drove a jab with such force that it knocked Hugh cold, a formidable blow to the side of his face. Hugh spun flat to the ground from sheer physical impact. The men gasped. Georgie and Black Vy hid their faces in their aprons, and the girls blinked at the sight, their hands resting on the pig's belly. Hildy ran to the fore of the crowd. "Stand up! Knock 'im back!" she yelled.

Hugh lay motionless as seconds ticked onto a minute. Finally, he stirred, shaking his head clear as he drew to his hands and knees. He lurched and swayed upright but had to shake his head clear before he stood all the way. Derk Arendshorst rushed forward to splash cider on his face. Hugh spluttered and wiped at his eyes, gained a stronger foothold and steadier gaze on Lewis. Lewis braced to receive another round. Hugh revived to his old showmanship and grand gestures, raising an arm and a smile to the men who gave a few encouraging shouts back.

Hugh touched a fingertip to his empurpled eye, swollen to a slit as though bee-stung. There was a murmuring dissension in the crowd; the men expected a certain order to these fights, and Cotter Wilkens dashed to clang a go signal. Hugh began his quick jabbing movements, his strategy each night to encourage the fight to peak energy, but the effect was confusing after the bruising power of Lewis's initial blow which seemed to make the crowd somewhat restrained and let down. Hugh usually shouted playful banter during these warm-up jabs, but his mouth closed in a grim line. There was a shout from the crowd, and this propelled Hugh to speed the circling of his fists and the fleetness of his darting steps. He feinted a jab to Lewis's solar plexus, danced backward on his toes, his eyes merry with the thought of the damage he could have done if he had wanted. He aimed a stomacher at Lewis's low ribs, but Lewis dodged clear. Hugh aimed high for a muzzler, but Lewis avoided that too. Clara rushed toward the men, and they stumbled off balance, trying to prevent knocking her over. Clara latched onto her father's pant cuff as he gulped breath. Jantjen Meijer lifted her from the fray, raised her onto his shoulders at the circle of the onlookers.

As the men braced their stances, Cotter re-clanged the pot. In one swift and powerful lurch, Lewis clocked Hugh in the head, sending him reeling to the dirt. August Knecht this time rushed forward to spill cider on Hugh's face, but Hugh curled up, coughing. Sweat beaded on Lewis's back and abdomen, amber in the firelight.

It took several minutes for Hugh to stand from the leveller, both eyes swollen, one cut and bloodied. Jeremiah Schuyler gave Lewis a full mug of ale, the reward for first blood, from which Lewis drank long and deep until it was drained, and Jeremiah raised Lewis's arm in victory. There was a smattering of whistles and cheers from the men.

"Quite a sport, Kettle. Quite a relaxing pastime," Lewis said, shaking Hugh's hand. "I could easily learn to look forward to this frolic every evening."

Hugh did his best to stay upright, nodding blindly in the direction of Lewis's voice, his gaze off from where Lewis stood. He burned at being called Kettle and knew from the men's titters they had told Lewis of his near drowning.

After the contest, Poppy slipped inside to Black Vy's worktable. Captain Lewis's gift crock of butter sat in a pool of pink pork juices beside green grapes and their leaves and yellow apples. Black-masked songbirds lay with their feet curled, not yet plucked or dressed out, eyes veiled over as if with white stockings. The cat had padded through the feast, for a string of crayfish spilled halfway to the floor and a bowl of walnut husks tipped strewn across the table, and the cat sat near the hearth lapping her face. There was enough butter leftover for Poppy to smear onto bread, scraping out the last pale curls to make two sandwiches. She tucked fatty pork slices between the hunks of buttered bread and nipped a bite. She bundled up both sandwiches and went outside to Gideon Bell's tent.

At the flapping canvas, she lost her nerve, ground her toe in the dirt. She stood aside from the entrance, set down the sandwiches, smoothed her hair, securing the knot of the green ribbon woven in, flipping its frayed end to fall across her shoulder. Gideon Bell had been inside of his tent for awhile, not in attendance of the fight, his back again poorly. She shook her head and turned to go, then remembered a few days back when she had run by him in the rain, the downpour sudden and cold, her clothing tight to her skin, her lungs sucked dry of air at the sight of him. He had asked if she needed an umbrella, and she had asked if he had one. He had said no, rain sheeting down his face and soaking his shirt. The cold rain had been bracing, had made him gleeful. It had been the most hopeful *no* she had ever heard. She took another bite of the sandwich.

When she entered the tent, his eyes were closed and he picked his teeth and sang softly. His naval showed, his breeches unbuttoned, his hand tucked against his stomach. It had been a rich supper. Poppy sat on the low stool and set one of the sandwiches near his hand. She lifted her sandwich and chomped its middle. She chewed and nodded at his sandwich. She swallowed roughly and bit another thick mouthful. She coughed a little.

"Chew," he said.

She slowed her munching, and the rapture started to boil across her cheeks and down her neck. Gideon Bell lifted the bread of his sandwich and groaned at the smear of butter and the thick ham slice. He pushed the sandwich away.

"I'm not hungry." He lay back and burped as Poppy crammed another bite. He cupped his distended belly with his hand. "I's full up on venison, eel, crawdiddies, pike, apples. Thank you most kind, but I will save it for later after more drink and rest."

Poppy swallowed hard the last of her sandwich, coughing again. She brushed crumbs from her mouth and apron. He drew his hat over his eyes and let his fingers tent upon his chest. She leaned forward and tugged on his boot toe.

"Hmm?" He didn't move.

"But by then mine will have worn off," she said.

"Huh?"

A hot flame spread across her chest.

He peeked from underneath his hat. "Are you well? You look unwell." Her face and chest were red. He sat. "Do you have the fever-and-ague?"

She shook her head. Her breath was shallow. The heat rhapsodized and spun in her chest, and flared, and sunk lower. He studied the intent on her face. He reached for her, pulled on the tether of her hair ribbon, drew her onto the cot. She straddled his lap. It was not unlike crashing down upon the spindle or splat of an overturned chair. He winced from the surprise. She leaned away, but he held her there. She arched back again.

"No, you must stay." And he opened his mouth onto her neck.

The heat burnt at the inside edges of her bottom as his hand felt down her back and wedged in the cleft. She flailed back again, this time reaching the edge of the bed, grabbing for his tossed aside sandwich. She lifted the sandwich to her mouth, and biting down, she sprawled onto him again and offered her neck to his mouth.

⇗

Kit Stanhope Smith slept with his fiddle every night, cradled her, plucked her strings drifting off to sleep on nights he couldn't bear to pack her away in her case. He slipped his fingers into the F-holes looping about her waist, drew her upper and lower bouts close to his ribs, and woke each morn to red marks on his cheeks, embroidered by her tuning pegs as he slept. He heard her finely flamed maple back shift and crack during the cold nights, expand and sigh when warm winds blew in. In this uncommon wet season, her cracks had swelled shut, mellowing the brittle edge of her tone. In the sagging humidity, the camber of her bow had warped some, skipping across the strings, muting some notes.

No one was allowed to play her except for him. No, he did not give lessons. No, he did not take requests. No, he did not want to learn Quebecois tunes nor Dutch folk melodies. No, he did not want accompaniment with the men's spoons or mouth harps. No, she did not need varnish. Each night, he used a soft square of flannel to brush the rosin dust from her body and strings, careful not to press the dust into her wood on those nights when the wet air mopped at his lungs and the rosin threatened to leech into her like mildew.

In the dawn hour after Hugh had fought Captain Lewis, Chute Littlejohn crept inside Stanhope's tent. Mal Hitchens and Dirch Maas and Gideon Bell stood watch outside, their belts at the ready. Chute held his breath and, silent as a cat, lifted the fiddle from Stanhope's embrace. Chute ran out of the tent as the other men ran in, tying a bewildered Stanhope to his cot with their belts. Stanhope yelled and thrashed. Dirch stood outside the tent, twankling a spritely Dutch jig on the fiddle. On her. Stanhope cursed threats of murder.

The men ran for the shanty where Poppy stood on the porch waiting for them as planned. Gideon grabbed her hand, and they all ran to the river, crashing through the woods. Dirch leapt and kept playing. Gideon did not release Poppy's hand. The sky brightened with orange-bottomed clouds. They stopped to catch their breath at the rapids. Dirch laid down the fiddle on a bed of moss, and the men bounded down the steep river-bank to the water, rolling logs toward the white, narrow strip of sand. Gideon guided Poppy down the steep bank, and she stumbled and slid toward the men. The men straddled the logs, ready to push off into the rapids. Dirch clamped Poppy's arm for her to climb on behind him, but she balked. Gideon towed her back, his arm securing low about her stomach, drawing her into his embrace. They stayed onshore as the men jumped astride the logs, pushed off into the water, coasting and bucking along the rapids.

Gideon and Poppy scrambled the steep bank and ran along the river as the men bumped and whooped. Gideon held Poppy's hand as they raced high above the men.

Chute caught sight of them. "Holla!" he cried. He bellowed the first line of a sea chantey.

Over the roar of the water and the wind surging in her ears, Poppy could only make out "Poppy on the shore." The other men hollered back the lines in vigorous response.

Gideon stopped running. "They salute you, miss!" And he kissed her long and deep.

They watched the men bail from their logs, stumble to free themselves of the current, cheer and raise their arms as they watched the logs break apart and jam in the violent white waves banging upside tall stones that rooted in the river. Gideon and Poppy beckoned to the men, and they waved back as they hauled their soaked skins back up the wooded path.

Clara walked off with the chaplet around her neck and Black Vy's bones wrapped in a muslin. The silver coin was wrapped with the bones. She knelt at the rock and pleaded prayerfully for entrance, untying the bones and the coin, exposing them as offerings. And this time, he came, but not from within the rock. He reached a hand down from where the water spilled. He held a torch close to his face. He arced the light in the direction of where she should climb, and she scrambled upward, taking his hand for the last steep strides. She caught her breath and followed him, his torch held low. It lit the pathway of water spilling toward the fall. Tiny springs of water bubbled from the ground. He led them uphill, his breath rasping. The path became drier. From a small cabin, orange beacons pricked through log walls, the cabin aglow against the slate and trees, a nimbus of light in the forest. There were no sounds or smells of horses.

He set her alongside the hearth, arranging her hands, one on top of the other. He was not well, had the stale breath of an ill person. His breath bubbled in rales. His limp caused him to stumble. His shoulder afflicted him, and when he reached painfully upward to stretch his arms, she saw he had only one wing, white ratty feathers that sprung the length of his arm and top ribs, then folded undetectably back in place when he lowered his limb.

There was a table piled with carriage doors alongside a heap of dusty gemstones. He saw her looking. "An old interest in restoration and design that I never mastered. And supplies are always at a shortfall in these nethermost moose-yards. You are a smart child. Perhaps you could earn a place as my assistant."

"Don't you have sons?"

He sighed. "Here and there. They are occupied elsewise."

He shambled to an easel propped in the corner and dipped a brush in water, making long, shaky swipes onto the canvas. His palette was dried over with bright droppings of old paint. He scraped away a small section to squeeze out fresh, wet paint. The first worm of color was her pale straw hair. She could not see his brush contact the canvas, but he was painting her, for his concentration lifted from the canvas, to her, back to the canvas.

He swiped his brush onto the wall to test the color, and after awhile the wall showed a proximity of what he created on the canvas, the array of hue and composition. The wall version looked like her as a large woman swimming sprawl-limbed in a blue-green pond. The layers of previous paint testing caked his walls. Clara lifted her hand to the chaplet around her neck, instinctively emphasizing it. But he walked to her in his labored gait and lowered her hand on top of the other one. As he walked back to the easel, she lifted her hand to touch the chaplet. They engaged in a few rounds of this, and finally he relented, too tired to keep pacing, and she raised her chin willfully, hand resting on the chaplet. He had rearranged her hands as he had wanted them enough to compose their form in his mind, to render them that way on the canvas. She wouldn't know until after he finished the painting. But the sheer endurance of clutching the berries made her yield and drop her hand after some time. She hoped he would capture a noble, fierce look. She caught herself wondering at how long this would take. She felt stifled from not being able to shift about, worried he would capture a vacant, tired look in her, a look forever locked onto the canvas, a sad scowl of waiting for the sitting to be over with. She mustered a brief arrangement of her face into a ferocious strength, like the whir of bitterns locked in battle. But she soon became tired again and her muscles slackened. She drifted, disappeared to the waterfall, to the rocks, mapping all the places she had searched with her fingers for signs of a door.

He glowered, threw his brush, sneered at the painting. With a vigor that belied his limping and wheezing, he slashed a knife through the canvas. Clara jumped. He paced the room, slumped against a wall, nodded to the wardrobe. She walked to it, her boots clumping. He shrunk irritably from the sound. She opened the door to a row of white dresses with blue embroidered flowers.

"It never fit me," she protested.

He nodded to her boots. "It's time for you to dress in proper garments."

There were different sizes of the dress in the wardrobe, and she drew one out. In the gap created, her old service dress lay in a heap, the dress he had changed her out of the night before she and her sister and ma had left the tavern. She hesitated before undressing. He lifted a fresh canvas onto the easel, blocked the view of her, and wet the canvas in preparation. She changed into the new dress and sat at the hearth with rekindled energy, her hand posed on the chaplet, the folds of the white dress stark in the firelight. Hours passed. He slashed two more attempts, two more canvasses. She was weary, as if climbing a hill for a very long time. When her attention wavered, he was shaken from his trance of fixation on her image.

"I cannot paint if you sit there watching for me to be finished." He gripped the sides of the canvas.

He moved the easel closer to her, and they became so intent upon each other they mimicked each other's tics: she sniffed, he sniffed; she blinked, he blinked; he yawned, she yawned; her eyes watered, his eyes watered; he sprang goose flesh, she sprang goose flesh. Her eyes darted in frustration with the stalled painting, for his eyes darted over the canvas, and her, and the hearth, and the fire, and the spiky walls of the house. She scratched as if she had caught fleas from him. He reached to stop her fidgeting, but she could not stop. He grasped the knife to slash the fourth attempt.

She held his wrist. "Please. I know you will succeed with this one."

She cocked her head the quarter turn he preferred and made her expression regal though she was tired. His eyes reddened and watered but did not spill tears. He poised his brush over the canvas. His face broke one time, dropping into his hand, because he was dying and he doubted his ability to create. So she wept with him for a moment, composed herself, and he collected himself. They settled into sitting and painting for a calm stretch of time, interrupted only by the snap of a log on the fire and the embers spraying out to the floor and needing to be stamped out.

When he released his brush and she rose stiffly and staggered to see her portrait, she gasped. She was not in front of a hearth, but outdoors with woods all around. She stood with her legs in a triumphant stance, a drum between them, her dress falling off one shoulder. She lifted one arm holding a drumstick to the sky, her other hand slung low to beat the drum. She wore red shoes, a magical shoe she had never before seen. Light blue tips of mountains rose in the distance off her wild, uncapped hair. "But we are not there, and I do not do those things, and I do not wear those shoes," she protested, but she saw herself and no one else in the painting.

He lifted the canvas and wheeled minuetto steps around the damp room.

"May I ride one of your horses?" she mustered politely.

He slumped on the stool, energy spent. "Bring me a marten head, and you may ride one."

"I'll bring you a marten, and I'll ride your horse, but you'll also tell me the value of two horses and a wagon," Clara responded.

Baron Saturday nodded in agreement and tapped his pocket for tobacco.

On the second night of Captain Lewis's visit, the men stayed hunkered. The fiddle played, but Kit Stanhope Smith glowered. His temper had cooled only after the men returned his fiddle unharmed but for one clutch of moss hanging to her chin cup. The men had also offered Stanhope the pooled gambling stakes from the fight the night before. Still, Stanhope performed unrelenting waltzes, stewing in his resentment. The men stared into the fires awhile, avoiding Hugh as his face and knuckles were at the height of swelling from the sport the night before.

Captain Lewis walked toward Georgie. He sat on the porch, and she handed him a fresh mug of cider. He stared into the crowd, at Hildy looping her arms around Hugh's neck and swaying with him. Hugh shuffled through the steps to be a good sport, and the men relaxed a little, starting their evening conversations that would eventually rise to whoops and palming each other's faces.

Lewis was quiet and watchful of the crowd, his knees splayed open and nearly up to his chin as he sat. Georgie walked from him toward Black Vy, meditative and puffing on her pipe. Lewis reacted right away to her absence, looking after her and fidgeting. She glanced over a few times to Lewis and reluctantly walked back to him.

He boldly claimed her hand but immediately gave it back. She tucked the hand into her shawl.

"Do you have such a low opinion of me?" The triumph he had felt at whipping Hugh in front of his men the night before was now faded.

"What did you see out there?"

"Great things, wonderful things." He had not looked at her all evening this close; she had been across the table, across the room, across the scattered fires in the yard. Now the height of dancing and shouting and laughing rose, a shield for any brash looks he could give her, the men's and Hugh's attentions elsewhere, jesting and carousing.

"Do you still have that gown with golden stays? The one you wore at Pennsylvania? With the charming bows at either side?"

"Do you normally shun entire groups of men by embarrassing their leader so?"

He glanced with mischief to the crowd. "Tell Hugh the honorable thing is to let those men go so they can find other work before the snow."

"I hold no sway with Hugh."

"You must." His eyes traced her mouth and the curve of her cheek up to her ear.

"No."

He clenched and unclenched his hand, the knuckles tight with cracked scabs. He reached for her skirt and hung onto a fold of it. There were too many men around for her to draw him to her bosom or to slap his face for being a brute or to shush him like a child, all of which she felt the urge to do. She would have been much more flustered had Black Vy not been standing nearby. She drew the inch of cloth from his fingers. He noticeably crumpled, tightened his small mouth. A mouth that occupied so little space on his face. If she had any less propriety, she would have palped a finger along its well-curved top edge. He had never married, yet never had to face rejection from women. His grip on her hand, on her skirt, was his broken way of trying to express what he could not, all of the terrible weight of the army and expectations he had trailed on his way back home.

"Did you bring this sadness home with you, Captain Lewis?"

"Yes, I'm afraid so. I dug up earth and valleys on the way back with the increased weight of it."

He abruptly stood and said good night, walking off into the darkness.

Black Vy drew hard on her pipe, gave Georgie a sidelong glance, and went after Captain Lewis.

She followed his tobacco through the trees. Birds scattered at her skirts, startled from their settling spots, their ground nests for sleeping. He walked toward the precipice overlooking the High Falls, and as she drew near the beat and rush of the water filled her ears. He hiked a leg along the rocky edge and leaned into the view. He relit his pipe with the end of a cinder he stowed in a bit of leather. She let him inhale a few draws before edging alongside him. He was not startled. The water coursed darkly over the slate rock in the twilight, the sky a luminous patch where the trees parted down the length of the river, the last shaft of deep blue.

She drew on her pipe, the cake of tobacco still aglow. He stood rigid, distaste in his grimace. There was a point in each day when every man she knew stole away to stew in his bitter-most thoughts, and she had caught him in this privacy.

"Is it your presumption to stand beside me in companionship smoking?" he asked.

"This here my favored spot in the evenings. That blue-black sky."

"Are you not to be behind the shanty with the hogs?" He did not say this cruelly. He opened his body to hers, appraised her curiously.

At this her eyes narrowed. She offended his notion of mixing station. She gathered dry needles, heaped them upon a blackened ring of embers, tipped her pipe to spark them alight.

"Here, I choose where my feet is to be. I stand with the hogs only when one's upon my worktable as I work off its hide with my blade." She rooted her heels and blew flames to life.

His composure and steel crumbled as she, right there before him, became something more than a woman or a slave. He shifted to leave, having no immediate response to her breach.

"Why you here? Long way to ride to return a book and make pretty hands with the mistress." She settled before the fire and gestured an invitation for him to sit.

He regained his cool, remained standing. "I suspect you got yourself into trouble that you do not know how to handle. But you can make it right. Surely you will have to give up your easy life as a fugitive, but you cannot choose to keep yourself away. Somewhere in Benjamin Breedlove's cabinet there is a bill of sale for you with a date and dollar amount for which now Hugh Tepper is beholden."

"How you acquainted with Master Breedlove?"

"I know of the man. We have sat at auction together, nodded across hands raised high for bidding."

"Maybe one time you saw my man at the sale block? He like a pipe too. He tall, dark, strong. Name of Barnaby."

"I was never at the sale block. My slave holdings were passed down from my father. I meant livestock auction." He turned dismissively.

But she pressed harder. "He have gold flecks in his eyes especially when he laugh; he hook his thumbs to his chin when he thoughtful. He superstitious as not to ride a horse through water that could touch the bottoms of his feet. He can imitate most any man, white or dark, with such peculiar sameness that if you close your eyes, you guess the right man."

Lewis was dry and impassive. "There would not be occasion for me to know these habits."

Black Vy puffed her pipe, touching its bowl and flaring open her fingers. In the firelight, Lewis caught sight of the brand.

"Who owned him? What name was his master?" Lewis offered.

Black Vy set her mouth.

"Ah, he was a runner? You won't tell me his master's name?" Lewis livened as he had before knocking Hugh to the ground. "I bid you tell me. I can arrange some men to track him. But if you think the purpose to be reunion, you are mistaken. He is rightful property of a Virginian, and as that man's brother, it is my duty to deliver him and you back to rightful sorts."

"I has my employ here with Mr. Hugh."

"Indeed, you have. If I were to have a freed man as my servant in my employ, I would purchase him from his master so that the master could recoup his investment, make back his shillings. Even if I found the man as a fugitive. Hugh Tepper will soon not have enough money to employ you much less settle fairly the price of your purchase with your Master Breedlove."

"You make stories to try to scare me." But Black Vy's stomach churned. The blasting had progressed so slowly.

"I do not create stories. I speak truth. We as Southern men of business cannot allow men of the North like Hugh Tepper to steal from our well."

"But he did not steal. I came to him previous by a Mr. Clinton Bangs Bickford. I were his barmaid. Mr. Hugh show me a mercy bringing me here to the falls."

"Then two men owe Breedlove fees. Do you not see the wake of dishonesty that taints your so-called legitimate employment? Hugh Tepper must be stopped now before his delusions of mercy set precedent for harboring more fugitives. He must pay dues to men who do right by the law."

Black Vy huddled to the crackling flames.

Lewis sat at her fire. "Now come to mind your man, mayhaps. I knew a slave who would naught mount a pony at high water. Mind he was a criminal, charged with the crime of refusal, and cuffed by each wrist and bound to other men, one a thiever, t'other of a mean disposition. They were tied to each other, a bound chain of prisoners. The men were led to be shot, and when the balls hit their bodies, they each jerked different ways, the forceful yank of the chains pulling them on top of each other. Your man was at the bottom, and he survived the shooting with enough strength that when the shooters lifted the dead men's bodies off his own crumpled form, he was able to control his breath so he didn't gulp for relief of the bodies' dead weight. He lay face-down in the dirt but had a shallow pocket of air between the earth and his chin that kept him conscious, must have. One of the gunmen began to drag away a body, and your man must have felt the awful pull on the rope, for he was still tied to the dead. The other shooter shouted to stop dragging, and the man's knife sawed the rope that bound the bodies together. Our blades had been overworked of late and neglected—"

Black Vy interrupted. "*Our blades*. So you was there?"

Lewis hesitated. "Well, yes. I was there."

" 'Cause at the start of you tellin', you make as though you tellin' another man's story. But then you sidestep into bein' there youself."

"As I was saying, our blades were dull, so it took some muscle to hack through those bindings. Your man burst up like a demon, face ashy from the dirt. And he quick threw dirt in our faces, and we were stunned because a dead man had just risen before us. I cleared my eyes, and my last sight of him was running with those chains and ropes dangling. The ball must have glanced his clavicle, sprung a superficial wound, or he was drenched from the blood of the other men's mortal wounds to vital organs. For blood soaked your man. The dogs never found him. Strong and cunning."

"He be strong and cunning." Black Vy puffed smoke out the side of her mouth. But any man she knew—any girl she knew—could likely pull the same tricks and make such an escape. She did not say this out loud. "Was your dogs tired that day?"

"Yes, they had been run hard hunting the week 'afore."

"And he rose up scaring you like an avenging angel?"

"Yes, I had the fright of brimstone before me. Now, woman, go rest. To bed. There is nothing more to discuss this evening, and your day comes early enough. There is a price on you, so you naught be outdoors."

"I's not tired." Her voice gained strength. "Up here in this country, you cannot go off haulin' whoever back to wherever a' cause of person-al bitterness. A person travels far enough away, she this person, earn her freedoms." She scoffed. "Is you to raid my master's cabinet o' bidniss papers and come back, pinning it to my chest and riding me off back south?"

"There is the Fugitive Slave Act. Yes."

"But this here free country. This ain't your South."

"But you started running in slave country. As a slave. It does not matter where you end up. And there exists this." Out of his pocket, he withdrew a newspaper clipping. He held it close to the firelight. She could not read but recognized the lettering and border ink of a runaway slave notice.

"I traveled this far, as you say, to retrieve one of my slaves, a woman your age who may well lurk in the wilds of upper New York for she oft spoke of the great waters here. And before seeing off Captain Bainbridge at Philadelphia, I gathered this notice."

Lewis read aloud:

> Alexandria Advertiser and Commercial Intelligencer. Twenty Dollars Reward. Negro Wench, by trade a cook, ran away yesterday before candle-lighting. Will answer to Black Vy. Sometimes called Violet Crush Harding. About twenty-three years of age, very black face, pitted with the smallpox. Well-made with a lusty temper. Cunning. Prone to fits when questioned or reprimanded. Branded inside her leg and upside one palm. Black, black eyes. Not afraid to stare men and women down. She had on a new-that-day blue Kersey petticoat and apron. I am fully insensible to the cause of her desertion and so suspect she fell prey to an artful villain, whom, if apprehended, will be prosecuted to the utmost extent of the law. All masters of vessels and others are forewarned at their peril not to harbor her or take her upriver. A reward of twenty Spanish-milled dollars shall be paid whenceupon she is delivered to any gaoler and I get her.
> Benjamin P. Breedlove, Fairfax County, Virginia

Captain Lewis folded the paper and tucked it into his pocket. "This is you by name and by description of person. Now you have already admitted your master to be Mr. Breedlove. All's I need now is proof of his identifying initials branded on your leg."

"You ain't get that, sir. You not in Virginnie no more." Black Vy kicked dirt to snuff the fire. She walked until she was sure she was out of his sight, then shook as she ran.

☙

Georgie awoke when Black Vy crawled into bed.

"Back so soon?" Georgie sleepily chuckled. "Whiskey-soft?" She meant Noord Boorsma, not Captain Lewis.

Black Vy said nothing and undressed.

Georgie sat upright. "What is it?"

Black Vy put a finger to her mouth and peered through the wall crack. Captain Lewis returned to the yard. He flopped bedding onto the dirt, settled underneath a buffalo robe. Black Vy pressed her thumb into the brand on her palm. Georgie sat back on her heels, then wrapped the pelt around Black Vy. The women did not sleep.

At dawn, Lewis shook out his animal hides. His horse had walked into the yard during the night, having loosened its tether. The horse exhaled long and deep, breathing into Lewis's hand for grain or to offer warmth. There was the heavy whump of the hides onto the mare's back and the slight flinch in her back hooves as she swung her rump and pranced to prepare for Lewis's long body to mount. There was the creak of leather bridle and the chink of metal as the bit hit the mare's back teeth and she chewed it into position. Georgie tensed. Not to flee the bed, not to fly from the shanty in her night chemise, not to rush out to Lewis and jump onto his mare, not to ride away with him. Black Vy fretted next to her. Captain Lewis had been, only the evening prior, a means for Georgie to escape. She had told herself that she could leave her daughters. Just until she could secure a better life. But now Georgie rooted alongside Black Vy, waiting for Lewis to rush in and take Black Vy like a sack of eels, ride with her captive back to Virginia. Hugh would not help her. Georgie lay braced.

Lewis cleared his throat so suddenly near the wall cracks that Georgie jumped. Lewis's noises outside were exaggerated, invitation for Georgie to come away with him. He wasn't going to snatch Black Vy. He was waiting for Georgie. It was early. The men and Hugh would be too sleepy to respond to any flashes of nightdress they spied in the yard. Georgie slowly drew back the pelt, gathering the will to bolt. Black Vy reached for Georgie's shoulder. Georgie sank back down. No, she would not bounce behind a reckless, sad soldier. Lewis walked away. With a huff, he mounted swiftly, reined his mare in the direction of worn track, and rode off. The women heard the clop of hooves for several minutes. Black Vy drew her face to Georgie's back and wept.

Captain Lewis would travel from home to home in Oldenbarneveld that day, inquiring. It was only a matter of time before someone in Oldenbarneveld would claim to know Black Vy and alert authorities. Lewis did not want the reward money. He was a Virginian landowner with the interests of his culture and brotherhood to protect. He aimed to stir up the local citizenry, school them according to the Fugitive Slave Act. He would preach vigilance, urge forthright wariness when questioning Black men and women who suddenly appeared in their communities. He would expect fellow citizens to do the same for him, to return property that was rightfully his. He would explain the great cost slave owners expended in the absence of and search for a fugitive. Lewis knew that Hugh had swindled the townspeople before. They would be eager to take from Hugh whether they held principle with the Fugitive Slave Act or not. After all this, Captain Lewis would forget Georgie, set his mind to mapping the terrain and figuring the pace for the day's ride to return to Mr. Peale's dig site by dusk. Lewis fancied pocketing another chip of mastodon bone, for his flagging spirit required a holy-stone.

Who et the last of the butter?" Black Vy's shout was directed at no one in particular. Her voice filled the shanty. The sounds in the household quieted: Hugh and Hildy above stairs, Georgie brushing her hair on the porch, the girls dressing behind the curtain. Black Vy leaned against her worktable and thumped the crock. "I say again: Who et the last of the butter?"

Poppy stepped from behind the curtain. "I ets it, madam." She wore only her shift.

"Step here, child. Have you injured yourself?" Black Vy held Poppy at the elbow and picked at undoing the small knot of muslin tied around Poppy's arm.

Poppy wrenched her arm free. "It's nothing to fret over. It's a bite. From the cat. I been keeping it clean. I used the butter to smear over since we had no bear grease."

"You said you ets the butter."

"I did ets the butter. On one sandwich. Then used the rest for the bite."

"How did the cat come to bite you that far up the arm?"

Hugh bounded down the stairs. "What's this? A bite? How many days whence?"

"It's healing. It's not a thing to fret over. It causes me no pain." Poppy went behind the curtain to don her dress.

Black Vy was stern. "Not your place to take the last of the butter for eating or for salving."

Hugh agreed. "You are to ask before taking the last of anything in this house. That was a gift of a rare occasion. And a fine quality butter. We don't have butter yet in snatches. And only when good folk visit with generous hearts. You girls are to learn the value of things."

"Yes, sir."

Georgie spoke: "Come out from behind the curtain so I can see your wound."

Poppy drew back the curtain. She had already pulled on her bodice but not yet laced it. Georgie stripped down the sleeves.

Poppy held the bodice in place. "Papa, please."

Hugh turned.

Georgie untied the muslin, and Black Vy stared at the red slash line. Poppy could not meet Black Vy's eyes.

"And? Is the wound festering? Or has the butter helped?" Hugh asked, hands on his hips.

The wound was dry, not greased. The scrawl was open and watery. Georgie caught the drip of ooze by pressing the muslin against the skin.

"Who has done this upon you?" Georgie asked.

Hugh turned around.

"No one," Poppy answered. "The cat."

"It is a straight-like line for a cat swipe," said Black Vy.

"It was a bite. I said a bite," Poppy persisted.

"She has done this to herself," Black Vy said in disgust. And she left the shanty.

From outside the shanty, Clara heard her ma talking with another woman, but it wasn't Black Vy. Her ma was laughing, so the woman couldn't be Hildy. Clara stopped. Maybe it was not her ma because her ma did not laugh. Did her papa have new women in the house? Clara walked into the shanty. Her ma and Mother Daphne were laughing at the table, laughing so hard they could not breathe. Clara had never seen her ma in this state before, her face red, her eyes wet, her shoulders slumped, helpless with mirth. Clara sat by the hearth, her heart pounding from seeing her ma's fit and the upset of Mother Daphne seated at their table.

The women tried to collect themselves and quiet down, but this ruptured a fresh round of hysterics. They grabbed each other's hands, each in her own grip of laughter, yet clenching the other in the shared understanding that one's laughter infected the other, and this contagion could continue for awhile. The women both choked out the words, "In his hair," and this phrase proved so risible that Mother Daphne flopped her chest and cheek upon the table, stamping rouge upon the wood. Her wig rose and fell against the table, drifting down sprinkles of powder, and the only sound for a minute was the scrape of her wig jewels against the tabletop and the hiccups of their laughter.

"What's so funny?" Clara asked.

The women looked at her and were seized again by open-mouthed, silent bouts of hilarity.

"One of the crewmen had a tick," her ma began, tears streaming, "in his hair." And this phrase pitched both women back into throes of heaving laughter. Her ma snorted, and this made the fits worse.

Her ma caught her breath. "And he had to burn the tick off. In his hair."

"That's not funny," said Clara.

Both women calmed. Her ma's hair was falling loose. The women were red-faced and shiny as pony trick riders.

"Look at miss sober-sides," said her ma, wiping her eyes.

Mother Daphne's fingertips circled over the rim of her teacup. She lifted one finger from the cup and pointed at Clara. Had Mother Daphne dosed her ma's tea with pollen grains?

"In his *hair*," said Mother Daphne.

But Clara did not understand, and her ma squeezed Mother Daphne's hand and shook her head.

"Do you know each other?" Clara asked.

"No, yet do we not seem the best of companions already?" exclaimed her ma.

"I knew your grandmother," said Mother Daphne.

"How Margaret kept you from me, never had us acquainted, I will never understand."

Mother Daphne shrugged.

Her ma held out her hand to Clara. "Come, greet Mother Daphne. She's been asking all kinds of questions about you and Poppy."

Clara did not move from the hearth.

"Welcome the woman. Mind your manners. And take that wild thing off your neck." Her ma lifted off the chaplet of red Hobblebush berries from Clara's neck.

Clara was pushed to the table. She curtsied before Mother Daphne. "Good day, madam."

Mother Daphne nodded appraisingly. "A pretty girl. Yet with a fine, strong form. Does she know music? Do you sing, child? The men in these parts will always seek a musical wife."

Clara stared at Mother Daphne, making no response.

Her ma thrust a fife into Clara's hands. "Go on, play the lady your tune, Clara."

Clara hesitated, lifted the fife to her lips, blew a couple practice breaths into the mouth hole and braced the fife with her thumb and pinky. She covered the finger holes and blew her first note, a dissonant peal. She stopped. "I am not in practice. But I can find things in the woods. Shall I bring back something from the woods?"

"No," replied her ma. "That is not what ladies do for other ladies."

"The last child that wandered the woods was fatally scalded by maple syrup," declared Mother Daphne.

"Sit down, Clara. Recite the story of the turtle to Mother Daphne."

Miserably, Clara sat in the chair opposite Mother Daphne. Her ma closed away the chaplet in the spirits cupboard, out of sight.

The nights were cold. Georgie and Black Vy stood with armloads of moss as Hugh re-chinked the cracks of the shanty's wallboards.

"I cannot do anything to persuade the townspeople to mind their business." Hugh measured an arm-length from Black Vy's moss heap and cut a narrow strip.

Georgie persisted. "If you would write to Captain Lewis, explain that Black Vy is under your protection."

"You write to him," Hugh shot back. "You hold sway with the man." The moss fell through to the other side. He sheared off a larger piece. "I assay to build back goodwill with the townspeople, and that effort takes time."

Georgie dropped her armload. "You make no attempts with the townspeople. Because you know you have lost their trust forever. You cannot pay back their loans. A man like Captain Lewis can persuade them to uphold a law or not."

"Captain Lewis has a desk full of letters to answer for President Jefferson. Your nonsense vexes me when grief is all I have now that the blasting is stalled." He turned to Black Vy. "You have become more trouble than you are worth."

At Black Vy's look of betrayal, he recanted. "No, no. That is not what I meant. I will of course defend you if man or mob crosses onto my property. You have my word. Yet men obey laws. It is not my affair. I cannot further ruin alliances with other men in town by trying to preempt their notions." Hugh nodded to undergird his words, searched her eyes, clasped her shoulder, decided that her faith in him was restored. He left to help the North Pocket clear away the morning's felling of timber.

The women warily eyed the woods and kept busy with chores, scrounging the cellar for last-season squash and other roots for a warming stew. They restocked the cellar with pumpkins, stacked like small skulls. The cold was coming. It kept them alert.

At night in bed, they waited until the girls fell asleep then whispered the possible scenarios: who among the villagers was most likely to give up Black Vy for the reward or for the principle of returning property to its owner. Or out of spite for Hugh. Yet others might keep quiet for a disdain of slavery. But Black Vy knew reward money to be a powerful motivator. The two women bantered quietly in the dark, Georgie politely deceiving Black Vy with optimism for the outcome. Until Black Vy could bear it no more.

"You a helpless ninny," Black Vy hissed.

Georgie sputtered. "Whatever could I do to help, a woman without influence or means in the wilderness?"

"You a white woman married to a white landowner."

"Who has a ruined state of marriage, status as a foreigner, a servile role within my former household."

Black Vy calmed, ending the quarrel. "Yes, you helpless for improving your own condition, much less my own. You no help." She rolled to the far side of the bed.

The women did not discuss how Black Vy prepared to defend herself and make a quick escape into the woods. Yet Georgie knew. Black Vy had not been using her butchering knives for a few days, instead, dismembering the pigs' shoulders and back meat with her bare hands. She had hidden the blades, sewn them into the hem of her skirt. The front hem bumped heavily against Black Vy's shins.

Each escape route Georgie imagined led to capture or death, outright failure. The women had no resources, but for a few kitchen blades. The men had strength in their ranks and numbers and had horses and pistols. The crewmen had protection, speed. They had authoritative voices for bartering, skilled hands for trade work along any route. Their gender provided entitlement to travel unaccompanied. Georgie could not ask one of the crewmen to escort her to the New York harbors. Helping a woman escape her husband would risk the man imprisonment. Noord Boorsma had offered to ride Black Vy north, keep her hidden. But she had refused that life, not wanting to live in isolation near icy headwaters, waiting for a lawman to seize Noord for harboring a slave.

Georgie woke shivering, the sting of cold on the bedding. She had wintered at the falls before. She rolled onto her back, the steady breathing of Black Vy next to her. She looked to the sleeping garret, remembering mornings up there with Hugh, hoar frost thick and spiky on the nails coming through the roof, grown fast like mold. And the window on the main level so loosely framed that snow would drift in, creating long wreaths on the floorboards.

Georgie stirred the embers. She cracked through the ice skin on the water pail with a heavy spoon. The half-loaf of bread was block-hard frozen. She set it on the hearth to thaw. The cider in the dugout cellar was surely frozen, and she told herself to fetch it, but a sleepy inertia settled over her. Black Vy sat in bed, inhaling, her eyes a little wild at realizing the drastic change in temperature. She clasped a shawl and swung her legs to the floor. She gave Georgie her no-nonsense look—it was time to work and survive. Georgie willed herself to activity, fighting every impulse to hunker and hide by the fire. The girls were difficult to rouse, stubbornly clung to the hearth, desultory from Black Vy's edict that winter would mean even more chores. Black Vy scolded them to show resolve and keep busy but brightened them when she said the weather would be unpredictable for next several weeks, with a few warm, wet days before the real cold settled.

The girls dressed and went outdoors. Poppy carried a hot coal on a shovel in case any of the men's fires had extinguished overnight, chirping "good morning" to the closed tents. Clara wandered off and found the hard freeze had made the boggy places walkable and the nests, dens, burrows, lodges, blinds, and lairs she had observed from afar for weeks within reach. But the ice was a thin skein, and her foot broke through to the watery cold. She leapt back, sloshing, and sat to remove her black boots and hold her painful feet in her jacket. A pair of marten busted out of the trees. They were snarling, entwined in battle. They rolled and parted, leapt at each other, twining limbs and sinking teeth. They looped their dark bodies through the snow, creating tracks around Clara and picking up the snow from the ground onto their fur as if rolling a snowman.

As the men's fires were high and their breakfasts steaming, and they shivered in their long underwear and coats, taking the first warm bites, Clara entered the yard with two martens strung around her neck.

Georgie rushed from the house. "How did you get these?" Snow-caked fur clung to her daughter's jacket.

"With the snares the men use." Clara held out her palms, wet and stuck with fur. Clara clutched the cord in place so her ma would not remove the animals.

But Georgie recoiled from the limp necks. "You will wash at once." She led Clara into the house. After much scolding, Clara allowed her to lift the cord of martens only if she promised to give back the chaplet of red Hobblebush berries. Georgie threw the martens outdoors. Clara waited until her next outside chore, burying the strung bodies in the sedge thicket at the woodrow.

Poppy skipped to Gideon Bell. She stopped short at the clink of spikes, the sight of his deflated tent. He was packing. He didn't look up. She clasped her hands, elbows locked. He was going away for good. He pushed past her to load his packs.

"How will you walk out of here? The condition of your back, I mean."

"'Tis no concern. I'm packing out with a couple of the other men."

"But I thought—" she began.

He spat to the dirt and cut her off. "I'm to work the church spire."

She closed her mouth. He snapped the tent, fluttering off the dirt. He met each tent corner in a neat fold. There was a drag mark over the empty space where the tent had been. Her throat narrowed, her insides so in love and pliable that she bore his rejection, stood there as it knobbed upon her shoulders. She felt her knees go slack as she searched for ways to make him change his mind, to take her with him. The words she wanted to express were locked away. She was not strong enough to override his indifference, or to tell him he was wrong, or to simply pack up herself and go along. She dug the posts of his indifference in the deepest gravel of her heart, and she walked off.

Gideon Bell chewed on tobacco for the walk out and loathed himself for leaving her. But there was a spire to rebuild at Schenectady and Lorna with her crescent thighs nearby in Little Falls. And, as Black Vy had advised him, it was best not to take on a young, unstable wife.

The Bible lay open, Poppy's punishment from her papa for not knowing the value of a gift crock of butter. She hunched over the pages. Clara rocked Poppy's chair. "Come with me to his horses?"

Poppy lifted her face. She had been crying. "I cannot play games today." Poppy buried her head to the verses.

Clara lay the martens at Buttermilk Falls. The water fell steady and cold. She pressed her ear to the rock and beat her palm against it. The burble of the fall's flow was disrupted. She looked up. He held his hand down for her, the water coursing sideways from the obstruction of his body. She lifted the martens to his grasp. He threw them over his shoulder, lifted her over the water. She followed him, slipping on the rock. He dropped into a narrow slot and called out for her. When she landed, the interior of his cave was lit, smelled of the underside of logs, and was stuffed with wagon parts.

She sat at the hearth as he sifted through piles and piles of paperwork.

"What are those?" Clara asked.

"Claims for lost goods and property submitted by the Oneida after the war. Ah, here it is." He brought a crinkled note close to his face and read aloud. "From 1794." He muttered calculations. "Seven years hence. Round down or up for lowered inflation rates?" He frowned. "Yet the dollar has since gained ground." He sighed. "When this claim was submitted, the value of two fine bay horses was seventy-two pounds currency. The wagon fifteen pounds." He fretted over the sums, scribbled a figure onto paper, underlined it twice, and handed it to Clara. "The value of two horses and a wagon, as you requested."

Clara clutched it in her fist. Over the paper crumple, a horse nickered. He shifted a stack of papers to mask the noise, but it nickered again. Clara ran to the spiked wall, pounded on the paint. Before he could stop her, a panel clicked open to a stairwell.

Down a narrow hallway, a whiff of hay and horses. His stable was connected to his cabin underground. The stalls were orderly, the hay fresh. She had imagined a more splendid interior, but it was dark, the tack plain, not ornate. He had more mounts than she thought he would, the row of stalls extending into a darkness beyond. The horses blew from their nostrils in greeting. Balor and Brace were not among the horses sticking their heads over the stalls' half doors.

"Why is one not saddled and ready?" Clara asked.

"Because you are to do one more thing for me," he replied.

"That wasn't the agreement."

"Yes, but you added to our arrangement, and so shall I." He leaned against a stall door, and a young mare twisted her lip to tickle his fingertip. "If you bring me a dead dog next time, you will find this beauty saddled, geared up for you to ride." He opened the stall and coaxed out the mare. She stood in the hall, nuzzling his pockets.

"But I wish to ride her now." Clara's voice rose, and the mare's ears folded back.

Baron Saturday slapped the mare's rump, her hind legs buckled, and she burst to the end of the row, clacking hooves in the darkness.

The next morning, Clara followed the men out to the rock wall. Her papa squinted at the rock from a distance, fighting the rising glare. He held out his thumb, squatted, extended his thumb again toward the rock. He rose and shouted, "It's moved!"

The men crowded around Hugh's thumb, taking turns to squint over the curve of his nail.

"I reckon it's shifted, if only slightly."

There were murmured affirmations as the men drew out their handwritten logs and Gunter's chains.

"Do you see how there rise four pine boughs above the leftmost jagged peak when yesterday only three boughs rose?"

Clara saw it, the whole rock ledge, great shoulders slumped down. The men rushed to measure, but Clara pushed through their legs, picked up one of their shovels, and beat the rock face. One of the men gently lifted her out of the crowd. She pushed her way back to her papa, grabbing his leg. She drew a slip of paper from her apron.

"Papa, I know the value of horses and a wagon."

The other men crushed her against her papa's leg. She stumbled, disrupting the rod and pin at her papa's feet. The chainman grumbled and picked up the chain to restart the measurement.

Hugh lifted Clara and walked her to the outskirt of men. "Now you are to stay back." He bent low, holding one finger before her face. "Hear my words."

Clara retucked the paper into her apron and walked back to the shanty.

Several nights passed. No one had come to claim Black Vy. Georgie disclosed to Black Vy the content of her aunt's letter. And the women soberly figured the ledger numbers: Hugh's funds for wages were depleted. Black Vy clung to loyalty for Hugh, claimed Hugh would keep her safe and employed even though he had spouted off angry words. He had been a good man to take her away from Boston, and good men struggle but do the right thing in the end. Georgie did not agree. *I will do her the kindness of remaining quiet*, she thought.

Hildy crept down the sleeping garret stairs. They both feigned sleep, heard the arm lift and the door open, close. Georgie turned toward the wall and dug out chinking to spy into the yard. Hildy was headed to the rim again.

"Lord, have mercy on us," Black Vy muttered. "She lose all sense? There be ice down at that water last morning."

Georgie rose from bed, wrapping on a shawl and stepping into her heavy skirt. She pulled her blade from the straw tick. "She has not gone down to the water in several days. Whatever is she after in this cold?"

"Only one thing get me to rise out the bed of a warm man," Black Vy answered. "And that be another man. But no man get me to meet on a freezing rock. Lest he churn fire in his belly. And that man come only from one place."

"Yet I have none time seen a man with her there. She goes alone with her thoughts."

"You scratch sticks together enough times, you conjure sparks. She best be careful with that play acting. Him left up there alone. What iffin he wakes? What then?"

"Hugh knows." Georgie opened the door to the night and followed after Hildy.

She peered over the rim. Hildy was tucked into her usual alcove, lying in her death stance, an interlude lasting several minutes, so Georgie sat, huddling against the cold. She looked skyward. The night was remarkably clear, pricked with arcing stars. She lay back, felt the cold slate against her, her blood slowing. She could freeze against the rock, could die sleepily on top of it. She did not have to fall from it or be bashed against it. It held enough cold within to freeze the flutters and expansions and contractions within her body. She flung her arms wide and inhaled to send up a call to spook Hildy.

But a disturbance in the drum of water rushing in her ears made her rise. She could not locate Hildy's bright dress. Had she started the climb back to the rim already? She scanned the slope, but saw nothing. Georgie had memorized the pantomime, and Hildy still had to defend her love against the invaders, to twirl in her woe and grasp her breast, to lie in supplication on the altar of their lovemaking. In the alcove, a dark shape moved, and Hildy's dress blinked on and off like someone passing his hand over a faraway lantern. The white dress floated away in the current, ribboning around the boulders. At the alcove, the dark shape was now a large white shape. A man's shirt hovering over Hildy's white luminous body. There were shouts and cries. But they were distorted by the current rising from the depths of the canyon. Georgie gripped her knife handle. Hildy stood, her hair loose, bouncing against her waist, and she staggered backward into the current, then climbed back onto the rock of the alcove. The man drew his shirt over his head and lassoed Hildy with it, drawing her close. Hildy tossed the man's white shirt. It floated downstream, stuck on a boulder, wriggling with her nightdress like a pair of illuminated trout. Hildy climbed on top of the man and ground onto him, the meat of her calf flexing above the pistoning arch of her foot. She planted her hands on his chest. This was not a woman being taken by force. Georgie looked away. She slid herself into a rock crag. A few stars blinked brilliantly.

The tryst did not last long. Georgie looked to the alcove. It was empty. In the dim, the tops of two heads bobbed. They were climbing back. Georgie hesitated, scampered to hide, shot back to her first crouching spot. And in only those few moments, Hildy and the man had scaled high enough to see her. Georgie's motion had called her out, white sleeves flashing.

The man locked eyes with Georgie. His eyes glittered, stark against his black and shining form as if he had crawled through an underground mudway. He dug spread fingers into Hildy's waist, at which she gasped, reignited. Hildy did not see Georgie. Hildy dragged her nails down his muddy forefront as if shredding off leathers. He cocked his head to Georgie, an invitation. Hildy danced him toward an acclivity. A rock under his foot gave way. He lost balance. They crashed backward down the rock slope, entwined. Georgie heard the spill of loose rock, their tumbling bodies, the thud of impact above the roar of the water.

❧

Hugh carried Hildy's bruised and battered body up the rocky slope. Ham Key and Eben Cooper hauled up the man as the other crewmen held lanterns to light the rescue path. The man and Hildy were both unconscious, the man's face so bloody and swollen that no one recognized him. A marten head slung about his waist, and Hugh recognized it as the talisman that all crew men currently wore. Hugh cried, "He's one of the crew."

Hildy's lip was split, her nose was broken, and her scalp oozed a caked veil of blood over her forehead and eyes. Her shoulder dangled, loosely disconnected from its joint.

Before wrapping her in blankets by the fire, Hugh examined her, scanning her bruises, touching each lightly. He took her hand and kissed it. She did not grasp back, her hand cold and heavy. Her mouth hung open. Hugh grasped her chin, as if the pressure would wake her. When he withdrew his hand, her mouth would not stay closed.

"Is she poisoned? Drugged? How is it that she will not respond?" he asked.

"No, but badly banged about the head," Georgie said.

"God, she has been brutalized by this man." Hugh trembled and collapsed upon the stool.

Black Vy came down the sleeping garret stairs, having secured the girls in Hugh and Hildy's bed away from the sight of injured bodies. She soaked a rag in the kettle water and cleaned the blood from Hildy's face. "Where is the man?"

"On the porch with Ham and Eben," Georgie answered.

"Will he live?" Black Vy asked.

Hugh punched his fist against the ceiling boards. Clara's and Poppy's eyes blinked large through the cracks.

"To bed!"

The girls retreated, scampering to the mattress.

"There's no telling. The man scarcely has breath," Georgie said.

Hildy lay unconscious through the night. At dawn, she stirred awake. Georgie was at her side. Hildy's gaze was fixed, her mouth parting slackly. Georgie held a spoonful of whiskey to her lips. It all dribbled down her chin and neck.

Hugh slept on the straw tick.

❧

At noon, Black Vy lay her head on the man's chest. A slight rise and fall. "He's still alive," she announced.

Ham and Eben had kept him warm on the porch overnight. His face was caved in, crushed. His mouth would not stop bleeding, and his abdomen was rigid, his fingers curled and broken, but he slept unawares in a deep coma. Ham and Eben had mopped at the deep cut in his upper gums, and a bloody heap of rags lay nearby. Ham ran his finger inside the man's mouth; the back molars sat low and square, but the rest had been splintered off or knocked clean out.

The man's features were so mutilated from the fall that no one recognized him. Hugh wanted to know who the man was. He hadn't the presence of mind the night before to perform a formal roll call. "We will keep him here until he heals, if he lives. When we know him, we will decide his fate."

The man had black hair. Georgie had elbowed past Ham and Eben in the early morning light to pry open the man's eyes, but they were entirely bloodshot, impossibly reddened. She had jumped back at the brutality of his broken teeth, noted the marten at his waist but only to reaffirm what Hugh had called out, that this man was a crew member. The martens Clara had snared scuttled at the edge of Georgie's thoughts. Yet those thoughts dispersed as the crewmen gathered around the porch. Kit Stanhope Smith stared grimly from the front. Georgie silently counted the men. There were roughly twenty-five men on the crew. But a few—Mal Hitchens, Wiley West, Noah Stiles—had returned home after Captain Lewis's departure. Jeremiah Schuyler and Eldridge Gary whispered back and forth, a sober exchange as they regarded the injured man's clothing, nothing about it distinguishable from what the other crew men wore beyond caked mud. Jeremiah suggested lifting the marten head off the man's waist, insisting it was bad luck for the man. But Eldridge stopped him. The marten head could be the one thing keeping him alive. Noord Boorsma stood alongside Black Vy. They both agreed with Eldridge. Several more men had ridden north to hunt and bring back meat. So her count faltered. She couldn't keep track of who had stayed since the work had become so disjointed and unpredictable and the season was closing.

"Papa." Clara had snuck into the crowd. "You must figure a way to blast the rock. They are trapped inside and he died."

Hugh sat her on the stoop. "Hush. He is not dead. He is sleeping."

Clara pushed past pant legs to stare at the injured man. He cracked one eye open. She looked at the others, but they did not see. *It's you,* she thought. Baron Saturday. He made up new scrapes each time. At the bridge, the injuries had mostly been inside his body. She studied the cuts and bruises upon this man's face before her, a face so different from the other man's he had been. As different as frostwork from separate winter mornings. What feature was his own? She could not tell. Her eyes landed on the marten tied at his waist. She understood he must go. He was only trouble. For the first time, she worried about his horses.

That night, as Ham and Eben slept on the porch, the injured man rose, a bit stiff from not having moved in a couple days. He shook off dust and bloody rags, dropped the blanket, and walked into the woods. The men in their tents did not rouse. In the morning, Hugh and all the men searched, walked the woods, the trails, the wagon road, but there was no sign of the injured man.

In the morning, Noord Boorsma packed his gear. He was done. He wrote an inventory of the supplies left, the black powder, the wad packing, the rods, and axes. The other men watched him, working their minds up to leaving too. Hugh stayed inside the shanty. The only things Noord would pack out were his bedding, the clothes on his back, and the cloth bag of wicks.

Clara saw him make ready to leave. "Stay on as foreman. I know how to blast the rock."

"How will you pay wages, little miss?"

"The clay jars. They keep the powder and the wads dry."

"Do you know how delinquent your pa is? Men must work for wages. You are a child with a poor example of that fact." He cupped the cloth sack of wicks, a lightweight, thread-boned kitten.

"Leave the wicks behind with me," she said.

He slipped the sack into his coat. The stockpile of black powder was useless without the wicks. "What do you need them for? Even if you was to blast rock, who will cart it away? These men will soon leave this failed mission." He patted her head, but she swatted it away. He walked off toward the woods.

"You'll be back. One day I will pay your wages," Clara shouted after him.

Hildy woke with the ability to speak. "I's was raped," was her first, flat statement to Georgie. "Tell Hugh."

Georgie sat in the corner, fingering her neck scar, watching Hildy. Georgie sniffed sharply, her shoulders rigid. She had been recalling the black-haired green-eyed man pinning her, his rank scent, the stab of his whiskers. The attack replayed once more. Her toes pressed into the floor. Had Hildy sent the man to attack her?

Hildy slapped the side of the bed to shake Georgie out of her silence. "You hear what I say?"

But Georgie stayed inward, glaring at Hildy. Had the black-haired green-eyed attacker been a man? Samuel had never warned Georgie of other spirits. Both her attacker and the man with Hildy in the alcove had moved with the brawny grace of real men. Though that was how Georgie had always known Samuel. Georgie's thoughts knotted with confusion.

Hildy clucked impatiently for Georgie to speak. Georgie's attention snapped to the truth of what she had seen, a willing union between Hildy and the man. Georgie sputtered to correct Hildy.

Hildy interrupted. "Tell Hugh," she insisted. "*Raped*."

But Hugh entered the room. He had heard Hildy and knelt to her bedside.

"Yes, love, can you believe what happen to me?"

Hugh grasped her hands and kissed them. He lightly palmed her stomach, broke into weeping.

Hildy touched the top of his bowed head. "But I's fine. Please do not cry. I can nots bear you crying. It is over with. I have snugly forgotten it."

Hugh cried open-mouthed against the sheets. Hildy lay back against the pillows. Her eyes darted from Georgie to Hugh.

"He worries for your health as a woman," Georgie said. "I will have to care for you, dab you with sour milk in case he has passed you the Louis Veneri. We don't have mercury."

"No." Hildy clamped her legs together.

"Yes, we must do this right away or the pox will take hold."

"No." Hildy gripped the blanket down as a barrier.

Hugh lifted his head. "Yes," he urged. "Please do what you must."

"No. I could tell he ain't got nothing by his look. He got clear eyes and clean fingers and his beard trimmed all neat."

"Georgie, please, tend to her." Hugh drew off the blankets.

Hildy's legs were splayed, her nightdress twisted about her thighs. Her knee and ankle were battered and puffy.

"So many contusions. All up and down." Hugh buckled in a fresh bout of weeping.

Georgie lifted Hildy's nightdress to above her waist and spread her knees. "We'll start with the worst of it." Georgie dabbed the rag between Hildy's legs. Hildy was indeed slightly swollen shut from either the trauma of falling or her vigorous ride. Georgie took her by both ankles and straightened her legs back against the bed.

Hugh crouched by Hildy's side, fretting her hand in his. "Is it bad?"

"Some swelling and a bad bruise up the flank. But I cannot see any cuts or bleeding. Nor lesions. Yet."

Hildy had a look of calm dread, her eyes weary and heavy since regaining full consciousness. She braced for Georgie at any moment to betray her secret to Hugh. But Hugh could not bear the scene any longer. He dropped Hildy's hand and left the shanty.

A few of the men had gone with Hugh to watch the hanging on Whitesboro Hill. Hugh witnessed at the back of the crowd as the hangman slipped the cord around the murderer's neck then fixed the end to the gibbet. The Reverend and Constable Beers sat with the condemned man singing verses. He jumped off the cart the moment before the executioner slapped the rump of the horse and the cart pulled from under the prisoner. Hugh slipped away from the crowd as the condemned man flailed his legs for many minutes, still alive as the crewmen helped his wife and children tug at his feet to speed his death. After the body was cut from its ligature and shrouded for the messenger to carry it away for dissection, the crewmen waited for Hugh. "You seen Kettle?" No one had seen Hugh leave.

The crewmen returned to the shanty yard, conferred briefly with the other men, and decided as a group to leave. They all scribbled written accounts of the remaining stores of black powder and other supplies, like Noord had. It was not to discourage any man from sneaking back to steal. Instead, the notes were to make plans to take up the endeavor again, to note what they had left behind so they could purchase additional materials after they had all grown fat on other wages. Each man would become a shareholder to restart the blasting effort.

Clara milled about the men as they wrote their notations, advising each man to reduce his amounts by one-third, the volume she figured she would need to blast the rock to free the baron's horses. The men dismissed her, some irritable at her disruption of their weighing and counting, others amused at her gibbering. August Knecht lit one last pile of powder for her, sparking a small show, but instead of her usual delight, she upbraided him for wasting the supply.

The men shook hands and agreed to return, to take over the site as their own. They walked out of the yard, scattered across the Adirondacks and Mohawk Valley for other work. Black Vy draped a clean towel over Hugh's supper, for she believed he would come back, and he liked his supper fresh.

Clara watched Mr. Lipson's dogs sleep. They slept in a mass, like the fruiting body of a broad fungus. She could not imagine picking one dog from the pack for Baron Saturday. She recalled the force that had made her squeeze the martens. She did not feel this force now strongly, yet there was a nagging chain link of it as Clara pressed her lower rib. She knew things could lie quiet and hidden for a time, stored away. If she pressed this spot on her rib enough times, the energy could change, like when she poked an apple to bruise and soften it before her ma screwed it through the cider press. She could use this energy to get a dog for Baron Saturday, but she had dreams of her own, and they played out in the frame of her painted image, ever heroic. In her dreams, the dogs ran with her, barking along to her drumming.

Clara walked back to the shanty. With the cold, Black Vy had been serving different suppers, less meat. The night Clara had returned home from being painted by Baron Saturday, she had been aware that everyone at the table watched her. She had been wearing the embroidered dress. But they had not noticed. They were expecting her to spoil supper by protesting a lack of meat. Their eyes were not on her dress but on her spoon as she stirred it through her bowl of stewed pumpkin, searching for bits of pork. Her family sat watchful for a tantrum, the steam from their bowls shining up their faces. They anxiously rubbed their spoons, delaying enjoyment of their meal lest it be disrupted by Clara's choler.

"Eat," Black Vy had urged, not one to be put off her supper by a child. "The child don't need so much meat. And she learn not to wail about it."

Clara, positive and chirpy from having seen herself painted so heroically, had hardly noticed. But as she walked back home from seeing Mr. Lipson's dogs, she recognized how her family had braced for her behavior. She had plucked up a slice of pumpkin, skinned it, tipped her head back, scoffed it like the sweet tail of a trout. She had asked for more, please. And her family had relaxed, finally spooning up their suppers.

Clara's throat was hot with shame. She made others flinchy. Would her family ever see the new portrait of her, and if not, how would they ever not think of her as a bawler? Clara's heart dumped a flood of charged waters.

❧

Black Vy and Georgie had been counting pigs in the woods, spreading mash to keep them close before the slaughter. The women returned to the shanty cold from the damp, walked into the fire room to what looked like a box of fine European frippery. Black Vy drew a frightened breath.

"A man rode in," Clara announced. "But it was not Captain Lewis."

Clara and Poppy sat at the worktable, tracing their fingers on the wide satin ribbon tied around the paper box. "He brought this. There is a letter with it, Ma. But we know'd not to open or read it."

"Look at how pretty, Ma. Whatever could be inside? You must open the letter right away so we know who it is from," said Poppy.

Georgie broke the seal of the folded letter and scanned the words. Black Vy pulled the ribbon loose, lifted the stiff lid to reveal a puff of creamy ivory paper. She parted the folds, but Georgie grabbed her arm.

"It's from Mr. Van Dijk in the village." Georgie read from the note. "The dress is for you, Black Vy."

"Whatfor send me a dress?"

"He has invited you to dine."

The girls peered into the depths of the box. Black Vy dug through the paper and lifted a silken saffron-yellow bodice with fine coral beading at the low neckline. Georgie rumpled around the paper and found the smooth burden of a puddingy skirt. There were pointed slippers and a pin, a dark garnet that Clara held to Black Vy's hair wrap.

Black Vy and Georgie looked at each other. It was a trap.

"Ma, a cap." Poppy ran her finger down the length of the scarlet silk ribbons and traced the pleated rosettes at each ear.

"A man with shipping connections. French or possibly Dutch imports. Mr. Van Dijk, the man who builds the big house." Georgie had not seen such finery since her days back home; there was not enough silk of this quality nor the workmanship to fashion it in the whole of upper New York.

"A man who sends this intends you to be his jewel." Poppy held the shimmery red cap to Black Vy's pretty chestnut face.

"There's to be much skin showing." Black Vy traced the bumpy coral neckline.

Georgie urged the girls outside. Their hands searched the papers of the box for more treasures before they scamped to the yard.

Black Vy sat heavily at the table.

Georgie began hopefully. "He is a man of means. He brought his fortune with him. Dutch with no loyalties to slaveowners in this country. He has a large family of daughters. He may have lost his cook and seeks a new one."

"Whyfor send a fine gown if I's to tend fires and butcher meats?" Black Vy answered.

"You are right. You dursn't go."

"But if I was to step into the man's trap halfway to see what he intend, at least I could name the danger."

"Not if it means you are to be captured back to enslavement." Georgie read the rest of the note. "He claims to know the whereabouts of your daughters."

Black Vy grabbed the note. "How he know where they at?"

Georgie shook her head.

Black Vy waited for her to speak. "What do it say? Read it again."

"What am I to do? I cannot parse the man's intentions."

Black Vy abruptly closed the box. "If they's a threat to my freedom, I need to face it. I see that be on my own. If my daughters, if they on his lips, on his pen, I will know why."

Georgie unlaced Black Vy's work frock. The two women dressed Black Vy for her journey into town.

Georgie was quiet. Hugh had foreseen this, his timing seamless for leaving without having to confront the townspeople's trap.

The wind was picking up. The bonnet straps hit her face, the soft silk lifting and sticking against her mouth. She brushed particles off the fine material: insects caught helpless in the gale and collided against her bodice; the cotton from trees floated, then stuck with their spines like brooches into her hem; the upswirl of fine, dark dust all around. Her hand raked across the slip and butter of the silk dress.

A bright hard carpet of winter moss spread across the clearing. She was near. She picked up her heavy skirts and ran. The Van Dijk's first home sat at the confluence of the Steuben and Cincinnati Creeks, the garden between the water and the house now gone to seed with a few bright gourds curling in the dirt. She crossed the bridge, where the darker Steuben water met the clear, swift Cincinnati. The whirlpools dug away at Van Dijk's high lot.

Van Dijk's new house under construction was set farther away from
the water. Mr. Van Dijk had named the new house Braam Hall for the
blackberry trellises he intended to cordon the property. He was a man
who needed many great rooms to compose his thoughts and house his
books. The tarp covering the hole where the roof was yet to be raised
had torn from one corner, and it tipped in the wind like a giant bird's
wing in a slow, upward flap, the heavy graceful weight of it dropping as
the wind eased, like the powerful thrust of flight. The walls might lift
skyward, jump off the foundation, gnash back down, knocked askew.
The wind gusted again, and more lashings tore loose. The tarp shot
skyward as if blasted from an inferno, wavering tautly like a blue flame.
The creeks surged as the wind wafted higher. Spatters of the first rain
hit the dusty street.

She did not hear the dog trot up behind her. She felt a wet nudge
at her fingertips at which she startled and yelped, and the dog yipped
and drew its head low, growling at her fright. An aproned woman came
rushing out of the smaller Van Dijk house, broom bristles against the
dog's backside. Black Vy was hurried along inside the white one-and-a-
half story house, a dwarf alongside the Braam sprawl. The vacuum of
silence as the door slammed behind her. The wind sealed from her ears.
The creaking of the windows hung loosely on their sashes, rattling from
the disturbance outdoors. Voices in the next room. No time to pick her
dress clean or arrange the ribbons of her bonnet before she was ushered
to the dining table, standing before already-seated guests, one of them
a gentleman rising to his feet. He was Clinton Bangs Bickford bowing
to her. Another man she did not recognize was seated next to Bickford.
He had already started drinking from his wine and spirits glasses. The
man had not removed his weather-mantle and was overprideful of his
hair. He would not look at her. "I am only here to drive the team," he
said overly loud, already inebriated.

Mr. Van Dijk ordered her to sit before a centerpiece, silver urns filled
with swamp reeds, feathers, and candlesticks as if she were seated in a
blind for hunting fowl. Her place setting: three glasses filled with light
and dark spirits, enough cutlery for several suppers. A wreath of metal
and glass.

A man servant dipped low a steaming plate of meat and gravy, two
long silver handles sticking out for her to portion a slice of the joint.
She set a hunk onto her plate, wiping her palm on the fine linen napkin.
She had no intention of eating. The host's daughters craned around the

hunting blind and directed outrage at the meaty smudge on her napkin. Bickford took the silver handles, deftly skewered a slab.

"You will not take me by force," she said, her voice low and interrupting Mr. Van Dijk's lip smacking, his anticipation of the pork's succulence.

Bickford adjusted the stock at his neck, and he glanced at his host. "Of course, I would never. I only intend to honor our agreement."

Black Vy had not rehearsed what she would say. Now words came spilling out. "I has freedom. Free employ here. A living, a life. I has earned a life. I's recovered. My palsy, yes. But you has no claim on me. I's not to be tossed between the services of men's fancies."

Mr. Van Dijk, offended at having been interrupted at his own dinner table, was deaf with irritation at her table manners, his eyes rounding the points between her filthy napkin to her greedy choice of the rarest slice to the disorderly fan of her cutlery displaced from a nervous bump of her forearm.

There had been too many glances between the men. They had already made some agreement with Lewis about returning her to Breedlove's plantation. Her thoughts, rattled from Mr. Van Dijk's claim to know her daughters' whereabouts, were now swamped with Bickford at this table. Her resolve faltered, and with it, coherent expression on her own behalf.

Mr. Van Dijk stood from his chair. "Why have you arrived unaccompanied? Who speaks for you?"

"I speak for her," said Bickford.

Bickford's drunken companion pointed to Bickford. "He speaks. I am not here completely under my own will." The man pointed at himself. "Although the law states plain." He thumped his chest. "I am the law." He stood and introduced himself as Magistrate Hyslop. "I do not condone this."

"Where my daughters at?" Black Vy asked.

Mr. Van Dijk scoffed, confused.

"They are at my tavern in Boston," said Bickford. "They ask for you. Return with me to be reunited with them."

Black Vy bolted out of her seat. "You will not take me back."

Magistrate Hyslop sat and drained another glass. "I am here to rein the horses. No more, no less."

Black Vy marched out of the dining room, but Bickford caught her. She threw off his grip and dashed for the door. He snared her wrists.

"Stop. You show disrespect to your host. Sit." Bickford's voice was low in her ear.

Black Vy lashed out with the knife she had taken from the table and nicked his cheek, the sting knocking him back. She screeched to such a pitch that it brought in the kitchen servants. The daughters stood from the table and went to the cooks' sides, each cook draping a towel over a daughter's shoulders in protection.

Mr. Van Dijk seized her like a grain sack, and when she kicked her legs, Bickford held them. The men carried her screaming up the stairs to the half level.

"They do not need me, she being so very small," yelled Hyslop. He held up his hands. "You see I do not bring chains with me. I do not help this along."

Van Dijk shoved her inside a small bedroom, and she heard a key scraping from the outside, the tiny clicks of the lock. Bickford spoke through the door. "You owe me labor and time working at my house. Now when you calm down, you will understand this."

She paced. There was one tiny circular window. She looked toward the great half-built house across the road. It was raining now, steady drops pelting the tarp and staining the dirt, then began a heavy downpour, the tarp filling quickly, gravid and sagging inside the interior wall. She sat on the bed. Her throat closed hotly. She would not be a prisoner in this room. She knew being confined by walls, doors, dirt, stone, an upturned wagon. In a cellar, a stall, a privy, an icehouse. The longer she had been kept, the more convinced she had become it was her place. The feeling of being confined built on itself, and that was the true trap. She studied the intricate door lock, weeping vines raised in the metal. Her prisons at the plantation had been bare.

She seized a heavy stoneware basin and bashed her way through the locked door, wood splintering with each blow. There were shouts from the lower level, and between strikes, men's boots clobbered the stairs. She stepped through the split middle of the door, wood shards framing her shoulders at odd kinking angles like the hackles of a swooping bird. Bickford and Van Dijk stepped to seize her. She brandished the basin high.

"You not to keep me." Her voice thundered, the draw of a thousand prayers breaking for air.

The men flattened against the walls. They froze their gazes upon her, recalibrating her strength. Bickford's fingertips drummed the plaster. The men did not peel their backs away as she ran down the stairs.

Van Dijk loosened his neckcloth. "I don't need this trouble."

Bickford shouted for Hyslop. There was no response. "Go on, run," Bickford called after her. "But the law'll find you."

She ran out to the street, to the astonishment of the Van Dijk daughters and servants. Hyslop, who had never risen from the dining table, dropped his head into his hands as if to remove himself as witness to these events.

Black Vy ran, the icy rain hitting her skin and staining the silk. Rain was sheeting into Braam Hall, and the rainwater poured a steady wash over the dirt road, rushing over the bridge, spilling into the current.

She flung the basin into the creek swirl, and it rode there awhile, tossing and rising. The creeks were overflowing, spilling whirlpools ankle deep into the woods. She ran splashing across the bridge, past the meadow, to the trees. Fallen logs and all the forest litter buoyed up, floating and coursing, the cold current wrapping through the trees. She could not walk through it. She hunkered down; she would wait it out then climb back to the shanty. The waters bassooned around her. A fallen tree was carried by the heft of the current, bumping against other trees like a bull. Its overturned roots caught in the narrow space between two trees, the force tearing them down. There was a dam of wreckage, and the waters pooled higher. The water was swift, pulling icily at her ankles. The floodwaters crashed, the wild current streaming between her knees and crashing broadside against her thighs. She had to move or be run down. She clung onto trees, pulled her way through the current toward higher ground, free from the cold, quick water.

When she burst open the shanty door, drenched, the silk dress puckering, she bellowed for Georgie. "God damn you. Take the dress off."

And Georgie knew it was for letting her go alone. They tore the dress off Black Vy and wrapped her in dry pelts and listened to the storm rage all night long.

For a few days, Clara had spent each afternoon watching Mr. Lipson's dogs from the cover of a tree. The dogs huddled together in the cold, gathered around the post that held their tethers. It took them awhile to settle each time she sat behind the tree and peeked out. The lead dog jumped, strangled back from her leash, and barked warning. The other dogs yipped to underscore her cry. They nipped each other's ears, lay back down, fitting together, noses curved onto backsides. Mr. Lipson had looked out his door a few times but had not seen Clara. The dogs were rowdy and sent up many bouts of barking each day. Clara thought of the pack as one big blanket she longed to cuddle up in. One dog would fix his eye on her, blink, doze, and she would catch another dog blinking sleepily at her, curling its nose into its paws until the whole pack was asleep, their ears pricked toward her even when they napped. This made her sleep, and when she woke, they would be intent upon her, whimpering for an ear scratch. She knew not to get close. Not yet.

On the fourth day, she woke but the dogs were not watching her. They sat with their bodies sideways to Clara, looking ahead. Clara turned in the direction they were fixed upon. The hooded woman stared at her, unblinking. There was a hump underneath her cape, the baby at her breast. The dogs whined and licked their chops. The woman pointed for Clara to leave, retreat into the woods. Clara stayed where she was. The woman tossed scraps to the dogs, and as they piled onto each other devouring the bones, Ida slipped fast from the brush and lifted their tethers from the post. She grabbed the scruff of the lead dog and walked her out of the yard. The other dogs followed. They made no noise except for the crunch of cold leaves underfoot.

Clara ran after them, sprinting through the open yard. Ida wheeled around, her cape flapping open, spilling cold onto Káhuk. He startled awake, howled sharply. Clara stopped at the dark edge of trees, craning back to see if Mr. Lipson heard. The dog nearest to Clara growled, and Clara drew back, tucking her arms. The dog leapt and bit her arm. It was a quick bite, but blood gushed instantly down her forearm, coating her wrist and hand, and the dog clamped its jaws on Clara again to hold her in place. Ida rushed through the dogs, and Káhuk's cries squealed higher. Ida slapped the dog's muzzle, and it released Clara's arm. Mr. Lipson's door slammed open, and he ran for them. Ida fled into the woods, and the dogs followed her. Clara fell to her knees at the sight of them disappearing. Mr. Lipson scooped her up and ran all the way with her in his arms to the shanty.

When Clara woke, she was in bed nestled in Hildy's arms. A rag was tied about her arm. Her arm throbbed. She sputtered, trying to speak. Hildy clutched her tighter, but Clara pushed away, getting on all fours.

"I know how to blast the rock," Clara mumbled.

Hildy leaned toward her. "Hush, lamb."

"I know how to blast the rock," she said more clearly.

"But your pa's gone. Wait for him to comes back."

"Where did he go?" Clara pressed her pocket for the paper with the written sum of the value of two horses and wagon. It was still there.

"He say he was going to the hanging on Whitesboro Hill, but that was days ago."

"We don't need him. I know how to blast the rock."

"We sha's wait for him."

"The clay jars. They are dry enough to light powder. To keep the packing and the wicks dry too."

"You mus' rest."

Clara grasped her old service dress she had taken back from Baron Saturday's wardrobe. "No. Tear this into strips. Thin like wicks."

Clara climbed off the bed, weak. She scooted on her bottom down each step. At the hearth, she set the paper from her pocket onto the fire. She would not see her papa for a long time. The sum of value underlined twice on the paper would be outdated by the time her papa returned, and besides, these details cluttered the simplicity of her real purpose now, to blast the rock and free the baron's horses. She watched the sides of the paper blacken, its middle crumple, and she felt free of the burden of the lesson. She closed her eyes and listened to the sizzle of the wood, her will gathering strength, and she knew her energy would soon repair.

Georgie drew tentatively on Black Vy's pipe. The tobacco cake had lost its ember, so she knelt at the hearth, pricked a coal to it, puffing on the pipe stem. It crackled, and her mouth filled with a sweet whorl of

smoke. She heard creaking. Outside, Poppy and Hildy were pulling fat
turnips from the dirt. The noise was coming from upstairs. She paused
at the stairs, the noise rhythmic, some force making the floorboards
bow slightly at the center of the ceiling.

It was Clara, rocking with steady determination on a hobbyhorse.
Her stockinged feet were rigid, her heels downturned in the stirrups.
The horse had a real mane: blond and silken with a fine wave. Its back
legs were cast wide to fit the rocker rails, its tail raised high, the length of
it falling to the floor, the pale tips swishing against the wood grain. Its
hooves were shiny black, and as Clara rocked, the horse's black eyes and
hooves shone at intervals from the window's light. The tail was raised
high like a show pony with aromatics shoved up its puckered crevices.
The hide was real: camel-colored splotches on white, a skewbald pinto,
with long white stockings up its legs. Clara held the reins, and the bit
creaked mechanically in the beast's mouth.

Tucked under her bandaged arm, Clara pressed a short black whip
and cracked it every other pitch forward against the mottled flank. It
was Captain Lewis's crop.

Hugh had dragged the hobbyhorse from the wardrobe before leaving. It had been hidden away as a Christmas present. Clara held her
other arm firm against her side, holding what looked like a map.

"Where did you get that?" Georgie's voice rose above the grinding
of the rocker rails.

"It appeared," came Clara's short reply, her eyes intent out the
window, her rocking a steady pace toward an imagined path. She
hunched her shoulders and flared out her elbows as if to prepare to
clear a water hazard or wall jump.

Georgie grabbed the horse's nose to make it stop. "I meant the whip
and map, Clara. Surely Captain Lewis did not give those to you."

"No. I took them so he will come back for me."

Georgie grabbed the whip out of Clara's hand. "You wicked girl."

"He has no other reason to come back except for his whip. And
when he returns, he will see what a 'ccomplished horsewoman I have
become. But if he does not come, I will trace his path with this map."

"He will not come back. How would he know it was here? He will
think it lost along his travels deep in the woods or fallen into the water."

"No. He will come. He will take me west as his squaw."

"He will not return. Get off that toy and stop these stories at once."

"No!" Clara tried to sway the horse back into its rhythm.

But Georgie lifted her daughter off the horse and carried her downstairs. Clara cried, clutching her ma's puffed sleeves.

"Hush! You have overtired yourself." Georgie set her down at the hearth. "Now there are pigs' feet on the boil. Listen for the bones to drop. Do as I say, Clara."

Clara sat at the hearth. Her snuffling settled. But her breath caught low in her belly, and Georgie saw the wheels of her heart revving again, driven by nonsense. Clara moved closer to the hot kettle, close enough to hear when the bones dropped from the meat. Her ma climbed the stairs to the sleeping garret.

Georgie unfolded the map onto Hugh's bed. It was of the Mohawk Valley, the thick and thin veins a complex web of rivers and waterways showing how deep into the wilderness they really were. Captain Lewis had circled the top of an offshoot from the Mohawk River and written in "Buttermilk Falls." It was right there before her, the orienting pinpoint she needed to escape.

The map showed the fan of creeks and streams that overlapped and lead to nowhere. She traced her finger from Lewis's hand scrawled "Buttermilk Falls," down West Canada Creek, and held her breath as it connected to the thicker Mohawk River which met up with the Hudson, its endpoint emptying into the great ocean. There was a route, though a long one, from the falls to the great Hudson to the ship harbors at its southernmost mouth. Georgie folded Captain Lewis's map and tucked it into her apron.

Clara trawled the bones out of the kettle with Black Vy's long spoon, spread them at the lip of the hearth to dry and wrapped them steaming into a muslin. She carried the bundle outdoors down the path the men had walked each morning to the wall of rock they drilled and stuffed but could not explode. At the base of the rock wall, she rolled the bones. They struck the rock and scattered. She collected them and again threw the bones against the rock. A third time she spit on them and threw overhand with a grunt. They clattered, and bounced, and flew back over her head. She dusted them off and rebundled them in the muslin. She approached the rock, peering one eye into a hole the men had drilled. She looked for the horses. There was only the black wad of burned up powder and wick. She ran her hand along the rock face, feeling for any natural hinge. She pressed her ear to the rock and heard the horses within chewing their metal bits.

Ida led Lipson's dogs back to her family. The pack was wary as the lead bitch gave birth to three weak pups soon after arrival. Ida's parents lamented the burden of the white man's dogs, the yipping and snarling. Her family continued to talk about migrating west, but they made no preparations. Ida was restless. She had never found Talise Jollicoeur's bones. Before returning to her family with Lipson's dogs, Ida had scoured the woods for a grave, waded through swampy patches, climbed down ravines. She had stumbled upon a wolf pressing its paw onto bright flesh, its teeth skinning flaps of tawny hide, but it had been a white-tailed doe.

Reunited with her husband, Ida stopped sleeping. At night, she fretted in exhaustion. Each hour before dawn, Charlot woke, dropped his knee between her legs, covered her body with his, tried to soothe her. But she would doze into a nightmare, trapped in black water, grabbing at a snow-lipped edge. In these dreams, she was Talise Jollicoeur, unable to lift herself from deep cold water to ice. Ida would half-wake, Charlot rolling away, frustrated.

One night, Ida left Káhuk in the arms of his sleeping father. She crept out the door, the pack of dogs huddled watchful outside of the common dwelling. One of the new pups bounded for her. It was young, not yet weaned. Ida froze as its mother growled, slinking forward. The mother nipped the pup's scruff and dragged it back. Ida ran before anyone woke.

Before dawn, Ida neared Lipson's yard. He was awake, drunk, his outdoor fire leaping. He ranted and danced alone. He swung at an invisible opponent, cursed, stared despondently into the fire. He stumbled inside his cabin. This was Lipson without the comfort of his dogs. Ida panted with satisfaction.

He had left his outdoor fire raging, but the sparking high brush pile did not ignite nearby trees. One errant flare could overtake Lipson's cabin. She could sit and watch it burn. His neighbors and the English woman would think it a careless accident. But the flames diminished, and when the crackling heat quieted, Ida heard Lipson inside snoring. That he slept when she quivered from sleeplessness enraged her. She pried free his axe from its stump. She would dismantle his house, chop away bits each night until it collapsed upon him. One cracking break per night, no louder than a falling branch. She swung for the lowest log of the cabin's foundation, the strike clamorous.

"Who s'ere?" Lipson slurred from inside.

The swing against the house had broken the axe. Ida wrung her hands. She would have this strong house for her own. She pried away chinking between the wall boards to spy on Lipson, who was underneath the mound of pelts, glowing in the hearth's light. She would have his pretty pelts too. She waited until she heard Lipson snoring again, let down her hair, and skulked inside.

She stripped pelts from his long body. He slept on his back, his face turned to one side, a deep rhythmic snore inflating his neck and cheek. She slid onto his sleeping form, straddled the rise and fall of his torso, the velvety furs churning like wash. She leaned forward to whisper in his ear. He gagged awake, turned his face toward the familiar Oneida words. He reached for the silk of her hair, tugged her closer. He shifted and hardened, pressing against her calico skirt. He was in a bliss dream, in the time before he had killed Talise Jollicoeur. He thought he reached for Talise now.

Ida squeezed her thumb against his windpipe. "You murdered her."

He did not understand this Oneida phrase, but knew the music of the language. He jolted awake. He thrashed, bucking Ida, thinking her Talise's ghost. Ida knelt, rooted in the bedding, shrieking for him to leave. He ran from his cabin.

Ida built up the hearth fire, settled into the pelts, and slept. In the morning, she repaired Lipson's snares, swept the porch, reheated his stew. In a few days, her husband would appear in the yard carrying Káhuk, the one surviving pup and older dogs trotting alongside. Ida and Charlot would claim this cabin as their home, bring Ida's parents and grandparents to live there. On their old land, the elders would fold to rapid, peaceful deaths. Charlot would build biers in the trees, wrap their corpses, and Ida would build low fires to send up prayers to their elevated bodies. Before dying, Ida's grandfather would warn her against picking up coins from the old battlefield. Best to keep them on the ground, he would say, for they had been luckless totems.

The rest of Ida's family would set off for Wisconsin in a few years. Charlot would reason with Ida to relocate with them or further splinter the clan. But Ida would say let them go. She was bound to the falls, would spend years fortifying the soil and practicing the old rituals. Eventually, Ida hoped, the bad spirits would siphon away.

The bundle of bones and silver coin that Clara had offered at the falls had been lifted by the flood, the knot of the muslin unfurled. The bones tumbled downstream to settle at the bottom of a boggy watershed, as if a swine had fallen under, the boot heels of its spinal vertebrae landing scattered in such a long, gracefully sinuous pattern that a diver might have thought it the incomplete spine of a racehorse. The coin, being heavy, had not carried far with the swift waters. It was dull as a leaf among silt-covered flood debris, yet a traveler spied it, wiped it clean on the skirt of his coat, and presented it to Fortune C. White at the dry goods in Utica who examined the silver piece, wiped his thumb over the Russian ruble's imprint of Queen Anna Ioannovna's profile, and blinked his eyes at the double-headed eagle flaring tongues on the flip side. White declared the coin's value equal to threepence. The traveler accepted this, taking in exchange a half loaf of bread. White later that day used the same coin as fee for the use of Seth Capron's very handsome gelding to ride to Philadelphia to behold a live elephant on display in a well-lighted room. Capron plinked the coin into petty cash for his glass factory business, passing the coin to Eri Post at the packet boat where Capron was charged freight. Post paid his son Ezra wages with this coin, whereby the coin was soon tossed into the Mohawk River by Ezra's sweetheart Mary after she set upon it a flurry of wishes. Ezra soon after retrieved the coin by lantern and the good fortune of low waters for fear that his girl's wish would prematurely doom him to fatherhood. It did not. A fact which he celebrated quietly at the tavern, leaving the coin for the barkeep who passed it into the bank as part of the nightly deposit. The coin circulated around businesses in Utica, downriver to Albany, back upriver, until foreign currency was withdrawn fifty years later. The coin became a curio in a velvet case, its power never more great than when Ida Tewatcon's Seneca grandfather dropped it on the Oriskany battlefield and Margaret picked it up, heaping upon it hopes for the family's future prospects.

The men and Hugh were gone. Hugh was not coming back. Georgie did not have to hide Captain Lewis's map. It held such power that she kept putting it out of sight. Then retrieved it for study, tracing the route again and again as if mentally rehearsing a tricky hazard for a horse to clear before urging the animal to leap it. Balor and Brace had never been found, and she feared them a terrible fate in the crashing flood and hoped they had been found by a valley farmer before the storm. Margaret's grave was to be solitary. After being uprooted, the girls' prospects for marriage in England would be poor. The intended Tepper burial sites would continue to choke with growth. No one would know it had been a family plot with the matriarch already buried. Margaret would lie forever alone, a forgotten litter of bones beneath the heap of wild forest pressing down. Georgie thought of digging up her body. But it would not do. Best to leave her amid the withered hopes of her son's abandoned efforts.

Smoke from Black Vy's smothered hog-curing fires rose to the treetops. The yard was now tamped black earth, empty of tents, pitted from the wood-swine. The flood had spared the yard, their homestead being high ground. As Georgie set out to inspect the damage to the low ground, one of the boars stepped out of the woods. The wild sire foraged for mast. He followed her as if he had been afraid to scout the aftermath alone. He was wary, kept his distance, tramping through the marshier areas, rubbing his chin bristles against smooth-barked tree trunks, trotting and grunting through the fallen leaves, the swing of his heavy belly hitting the swales of the forest floor. She heard his relentless rooting, a metal chink. One of the crewmen had fixed a ring in his snout to inhibit deep foraging of their prized mushroom honeyholes.

Georgie reached the worst of the flooding. Hugh's wagon—missing a side—swirled in the water among other debris. Hugh's boat was gone, like the man. But the flood had carried in a new boat, wedged between rocks. The boar ran ahead, snorted in the reeds. His nose ring rang and clinked. Georgie parted the reeds. Two bodies. Men. The boar snuffled his snout ring over the coat buttons of the one man still alive.

The women dragged the injured man away from the dead man. Black Vy lay a sheet over the dead man and tucked the corners under his dead weight. The river would rise that night, lick at the sheet, float his hand off the stone, then in a plunge of cold, freeze it to the clotted riverbank ice as the center of the river ran swift.

"We c'ain't move him." Black Vy pointed to the injured man.

"We must. The cold. And the river may rise." Georgie squinted the steep path. They would drag the injured man up and build him a fire in the shanty yard.

Black Vy surveyed the boat on the riverbank. It was undamaged from the flood. She secured it in brush.

Georgie stared down the river. "We must take passage back to England. I have my family. We could assume you to be my maid."

"How we steal aboard a ship? What about them little girls?"

"We cannot be four stowaways. If we were discovered, they would be brutalized. We must go ourselves and send for the girls when we have means to buy them proper passage. Hildy will care for them here." Her voice faltered as she watched the water course around the first bend. The winter would be long and killing.

"How we get out this woods all the way to the harbor?"

Georgie pulled the map from her skirt pocket. "Clara pilfered through Captain Lewis's saddle bag and stole this."

Georgie spread the map on the stones and traced her finger from the top of West Canada Creek down to the Mohawk River, sharply eastward toward the Hudson.

Black Vy leaned in and traced southward down the wide Hudson. "The Hudson River to the harbor. That be our route." But she looked doubtful. "What about Mr. Hugh? How it look to him if I up and leave? He to return 'cause he knowd I need his help."

"He's not coming back," Georgie snapped. "At least not by the time another villager attempts to help capture you."

Black Vy slumped. "We c'ain't travel without a man."

Georgie nodded to the injured man. "I found a compass on his person. We will take him along and hope he recovers sufficiently to be of use, for navigation and protection. We will bring him to medical help." Georgie had also found a letter in his coat addressed to her aunt Emmeline stating they had seen no evidence of blasting progress and were heading back to Virginia. The return trip of the Virginian inspectors had been interrupted by the flood. The letter to Emmeline unsent.

"How you pay a man to physick another man? I keep those books. They ain't no spare funds. You c'ain't dump a man at the door of a city doctor. He won't treat a man without coin."

"We pray someone shows mercy to women who bear an injured man."

Black Vy closed her eyes to shut off tears. "You trust Hildy to care for your girls?"

Georgie shrugged. "I must." She rose and pocketed the papers.

"Where you going?"

"There is one man who may help."

Georgie had asked Hugh several weeks ago if he had seen his father, Samuel.

"Once," Hugh had replied, and this resounded through Georgie's head as she picked her way through the flood-flattened vines and grasses along the creek toward the Universalist church where Samuel had banished himself to gaol. Samuel had made the Reverend and Constable Wayland Beers and Mrs. Fothergill see him in the flesh and believe he was a criminal.

"I give myself up for hideous crimes, for I am fearsome," Samuel had said, surrendering as he dropped to the feet of the minister and the matron.

The Reverend and Constable Beers had bound his wrists, and this tether had given Samuel a peaceful grounding, for he had been flying farther and farther from his family and wanted to stay close by.

The minister had perpended the gravity of Samuel's criminal admission, securing his village by rigidly not allowing Samuel visitation. Hugh had gone, though, having heard of the curiosity of a stranger giving himself up. When Hugh had recognized his father, the two men had argued hotly. Hugh had demanded an explanation for his father's resurrection. Samuel had ordered his son to double-down on the blasting effort, chiding him for failing. The matron Mrs. Fothergill who had been carrying water to clean Samuel had discovered Hugh. She had startled, flung the water on Hugh, and began screaming. Hugh had been sternly admonished by Reverend and Constable Beers the next day when Beers rode into the shanty yard and threw his hat in furious display as he warned Hugh against sneaking to see his prisoner and frightening his housekeeper. And Hugh had rushed forward to pull the man off his saddle but stopped short as Beers hooked his horse around and fled. Beers didn't know Samuel was Hugh's father. His father had been gone that long.

Hugh wanted his father's spirit gone forever, had no use for him reincarnating and making demands, so Hugh had ridden his horse down the wagon trail to the Oriskany Battlefield, to the bones in great numbers, flaked and scattered still decades after the massacre at the edge of the swamp. If he could bury a piece of his father, even one of the bones as an emblem, perhaps Samuel would leave. Hugh had cursed his mother for not doing the job herself after he had fallen. And he had cursed the relief column that had ridden through the stinking aftermath and kept riding without stopping. But Hugh had seen the bones in such number and the thick woods on either side of the road, the boggy sinks beyond. And he might have left the dead unburied himself decades ago to escape the terrible hand of that defeat. He had walked over the ground, twisted with tree roots, thick as an iron cage that no shovel or axe could break apart. And he had left without burying anything.

Georgie would have to sneak into the church. The path opened to the bridge, and she watched the two rivers merge at the confluence as she walked toward the Van Dijk house but cut the other way toward Braam Hall. The workmen did not tip their caps or even raise their heads to acknowledge her as she weaved through their wagon loads of lumber and stone. A few heaved stones as the base of the back foundation; they shouted and mixed lime mortar and reckoned level lines with squinted eyes. They knew any mortar would not set now in the cold, so precise leveling did not matter, for they would tear apart this section in the spring to redo the cracked stone and grout, one of many dallying decisions after working for a man with money. The workmen shook out a tarpaulin, wet from the storm. The back portion of the house was now established and sound, but it had rained, and men broomed out the water. There was much mud in the adjacent lot, and the men shoveled it onto carts, would use it to fill the spaces between stone walls and plaster.

The church was at the edge of the Braam Hall lot. A piece of newsprint was tacked to the door. It was rain-streaked, but Georgie recognized it as the slave notice Black Vy had told her about. So Lewis had nailed it here before leaving town. She ripped down the paper and stuffed it into her bodice. One shutter on the second level was flung open. Georgie entered the church.

It was quiet and dim. Reverend Beers stood at the altar, setting out folded linens. "Do ye seek salvation, mistress?"

"No, indeed. I simply seek a godly refuge in which to reflect and quiet my heart."

His face darkened dubiously at her English way of speaking. Or perhaps at her "no."

"If your heart seeks God, I am here to minister its way forward."

Georgie sat on a bench and pulled a veil over her cap, knotting it at her throat. "My heart requires repose." She intensified the English of her words, it having the usual effect of making the other person move away. The minister's boots stepped heavily downstairs to the cellar.

There was silence, the flickering of candles, and her heart relaxed, but she startled at a construction load dumped outside. The echoes quieted, and the men's shouts dissipated. She heard scraping or mopping from above on the second floor. She waited. Outside, there was the muffled jangle of a wagon pulling out, and she used its noisy cover to run along the pews and climb the back staircase.

The stairs were narrow and steep, and dust rose in the shaft of sunlight. At the top were several closed doors. She pushed open the nearest, entering a blindingly lit chamber. He sagged against the wall, his face toward it to shield the glare. He turned his head to her, blinking in disbelief. His hands were bound together with rope above his head, pegged on a hook bolted into the plaster.

"Samuel," she whispered.

His eyes watered at the sight of her, and his legs swam restlessly against the floor—the mopping sound she had heard from below. He could not help but move them; he was tensed and cramped. His legs could kick freely, but his arms were rigid so he could not stand, a moth pinned by its forelegs. His hands hung limply over the rope that bound his wrists. The bright slant of sunlight shone on his freshly slicked hair. His face was pink and cleanly shaven. His neck was whiskered yet, and there stood a steaming bowl of water alongside him and a chair. Mrs. Fothergill had just been here, shaving him, and would soon return to finish his sudsy neck.

He rubbed his legs against the wood floor, his eyes settling in calm resignation. Georgie glanced at the steaming bowl of water, the swirls of soapy foam along its rim.

"Margaret," he whispered. "How fares my Margaret?"

He never remembered. Or even as a dead man, Samuel could not face his wife's death. "She fares quite poorly."

"Georgie, are you well, my dear?"

"No."

He gripped her hand with his dead fingers. An empty chamber pot was beside him.

"And you? Do they mistreat you?"

"They keep me clean and fed, one meal a day, and release me an hour or two from these wrist binds." He kept his voice low. "She will return soon. You must not be found. I should not want any complications to disrupt. Anyone caught here will be gaoled too."

"No, I shan't be caught."

"How fares the blasting? Mind, I cannot hear any progress over the crash of house construction outside. How many furlongs has he progressed? One? Perhaps two?"

Georgie shook her head.

Samuel squinted. "Pray, stand at the window to block that glare."

Georgie did, and he closed his eyes in relief as her form blocked the relentless light.

"I must tell you Hugh will never have the funds. The rock is too wet. The powder will not alight."

"No, you speak with confusion. That cannot be. Hugh was to blast away rock. Build the family name here."

Georgie tried to interrupt him, but Samuel would not have it.

"No, he must. He must figure this one thing out on his own. Is he not to figure this problem out himself?"

"The men have left. There are no more wages—"

Samuel cut her off. "There is no more time. Leave me now."

Georgie rushed back to his side, the harsh light once more on him. She slipped her knife into the laces of his leggings. "You are to escape here. Go to the unfinished part of Braam Hall. You can hide there. Van Dijik will never know. You will have to dart about so that the workers do not seal you into the walls. They will send search parties to Hugh's shanty, throughout the grottoes, but they shan't think to look this close. Do this for a few days. They will give up their search. I will come back, take you to the shanty and introduce you as an old family friend. You must meet me in the thicket past the confluence of waters over the bridge. Come to the shanty to watch over the girls. I have figured a mapped route to the harbors. I must leave, Samuel."

He looked doubtful. He kept checking the door for the matron's return. "And what of Margaret? Is she well to travel?"

Georgie hung her head. His confusion was worsening. "Yes, she will be there." She didn't blink. "You cannot stay here. I bid you protect the girls. This is why I came to you, Samuel."

"But Hugh, does he make this journey with you? And your children?

Are the young girls journeying as well?" He glared with uncertainty, barely able to suss out her intention of leaving her position as wife and mother.

"No. Please hang onto this world long enough to watch over the girls until I can send passage for them." They tightened their hands together as they heard movement below. Georgie leapt toward the door. She held up three fingers to indicate when she would return, and Samuel nodded. She fled down the staircase.

She tucked onto a bench seat, hearing the matron climb the stairs. Her heart hammered. She rose and tipped a lighted candle to spark the candle beside it and set the slave notice onto the row of flames. She prayed for the courage to walk out of the church.

eorgie returned three mornings later and waited. Samuel was not there. She stomped the flattened grasses, called to him softly, crossed the bridge to Braam Hall. The stone getters and masons had made considerable progress: the wagon beds were unloaded of rock, and the men stood lashing long strokes, slathering mortar to seal the finished south wall. They had even plastered some interior walls and were filling with mud the spaces between the exterior stone and inner walls. Samuel did not appear. She waited as long as she could and left to meet Black Vy.

It had been fortunate for Samuel that the Reverend Beers was also Constable Beers. The man possessed two appellations, thus performing two duties under the church's one roof. The jail housed prisoners on the church's second floor, though Samuel was the lone inmate. Samuel had been tormented by demons—even more so in recent years for reasons he did not understand. He could not bear it. He had acquiesced to being bound as a prisoner, free of the demons in so holy a place, yet forsaking his freedom to roam, to ascend or to descend, to decide a final fate. He feared he had waited too long to be claimed in either direction, and the approaching demons were deciding for him. Their mad blethering had filled his head, made him delirious, senile. In the church as a prisoner, their voices had subsided, and Samuel hoped to regain mental fortitude chained to the wall. He asked the reverend daily to pray with him and felt a stern devotion to God rush through the reverend's hand to his own.

Samuel had been bold in life, never one to cower. Yet, following Georgie's instructions, slitting his bindings and fleeing the church, the voices had assaulted him. He ran for cover in the partially built walls of Braam Hall. He endured a long night of head-pressing jeers. In the morning, the masons had filled the space between the stone and plaster with mud and straw, unknowingly entombing Samuel. At first, he choked like he had as he lifted his face from the shallow water at Oriskany after being fatally shot. Then he relaxed inside the wall, voluptuously encased. He felt a sublime peace, as if floating in a warm tank of salty water, the density of materials dulling the gibbering taunts. He soon forgot Georgie's request, did not recall his granddaughters. Margaret shrouded his thoughts as he hung suspended. This was the closest sensation since death of being held in her arms. He would never leave the embrace of that mud and straw.

Hildy wrapped her arms around Poppy and Clara. They huddled in shawls and mittens, the frost burned away, yet their faces chapped in the chill. Clara wore the chaplet around her neck. Georgie had given it back that morning. The red Hobblebush berries made for a festive send-off, as if they all stood at a real harbor waving goodbye, a rainstorm of wreaths and bouquets thrown up by the bystanders at the dock. Yet Clara clutched the chaplet, only the white smoke of their breath rising. They stood atop the embankment looking down as Black Vy and Georgie loaded the injured man into the boat. They had carried the injured man on a litter down the helical pathway to the water, but even with his body prone and supported, the pain had knocked him out. Georgie and Black Vy were getting a late start, having spent the night and dawn hours salting and packing as much hog meat as they could for the girls and Hildy to survive the winter.

"Hugh sha's come back. He gone off to figure another way. This time sha's work." Hildy rocked on her heels.

"I will send for the girls as soon as I make contact with my family." Georgie waved up to them. She sprinted the embankment, solid from the night's freeze, and embraced them once more, crushing the chaplet against Clara, knocking off a few dried berries.

The chaplet would become mouse-nibbled, dusty, stored away again in the same spirits cabinet. Clara would take to stringing animal heads and tails and feet and found objects about her waist after the practice of the crewmen, testing her luck with varying success, looping creatures of all kinds. The one constant on her cord would be the carriage latch.

"Keep your boots oiled," Georgie told Clara. "From the mink's glands like I showed you. When you grow into them, they'll still be sound."

Clara nodded and kissed her ma. Her ma sported small sacks of pork fastened around her waist, and Clara gripped one. "Are these for luck on your journey?"

"No. These will keep us fed until we reach the harbor. You have a supply to get you through winter."

Clara would grow into the boots. The blisters that pained her now from too-large boots rubbing against her tender insteps and bony sides would become worn to tough flaps. She would keep the boots oiled, would sew up a long crack in the sole, would rejigger the rotted laces with grape vine. She would jump into Avalanche Lake in the High Peaks of the Adirondacks wearing the boots to save her drowning young husband, at first becoming bogged down by the boots and her skirt, heavy as storm-soaked sailcloth. She would wrest out of the skirt, swallow much water, kick off the boots, flail in the windy chop, pull long strokes to the last point where she saw her husband's head go under. She would reach him before the boots landed on the fallen timber at the lake bottom, her lungs afire from the panic of almost losing him.

"The girls will need warm things on the ship passage. So keep their skirts and boots in good order," Georgie told Hildy.

"Hugh sha's want to keep the girls here where they's born. He sha's make this pros'pers, make it his sons' one day." Hildy cradled her low belly.

"Hugh will not return. His blasting venture is insolvent. Do you know what that means? He cannot pay back his loans to the townspeople nor my family. Nor pay men wages."

"He sha's return. We have a life here." Hildy drew the girls nearer. "He asked me to see after the girls 'afore he left."

"Did he now. And now I ask of you the same. Please care for my girls, sister."

Georgie cupped Poppy's face. "Dear girl, you have been weepy for days. You must stop. Forget your father. I shall soon send for you. You shall be in the arms of family."

Poppy gripped her ma's wrist. "Is there a church spire in England? That Mr. Bell could work on after he finishes Schenectady?"

"Yes, my girl. There are many." Georgie kissed Poppy's forehead.

Georgie reached for the sack perched on a stone behind Clara. Yet it was too lightweight. "What is this?" She untied the sack's neck. "We have no need for black powder nor rags. Where is the food?"

Clara retied the sack.

"Don't let them mess with the powder," Georgie scolded Hildy. "It's not to be disturbed. The men will return for it."

"It be time for you to go. You's holding up our day." Hildy lifted the sack of black powder onto the dry stone. "We has work to do."

"Yes, you shall have to work now, shan't you?" Georgie kissed each girl again, wiped at the black smudge on Clara's hand. Georgie slung the bulging sack of gruel over her shoulder. She slid down the embankment, hefted the gruel sack into the boat. The sack made a thunk. She dragged the bow into the water. Black Vy sat astern, her skirt hem piling heavily with the weight of the sewn-in blades. The women paddled into the downstream current. The injured man lay unconscious between them.

The man regained consciousness as the current slowed and slabs of ice hit the hull of the boat.

"Who are you, sir?" Georgie asked.

The sunlight hit his amber eyes. The whites were clear. His head turned against the boat's bottom, realizing he was afloat. He must have felt the cold water flush against his whole backside. He rolled his eyes upward in the direction of Black Vy's paddle sounds. He thrashed when Black Vy's paddle hit an ice hunk floating past. He blinked at the unrelenting sunlight. He drew breath to speak, craning his neck toward Georgie. Choked sounds came forth. He closed his mouth and sank his head, an unintelligible stridor stopping up his words. Georgie nudged his foot with her own. She opened the leather flap of a pouch and withdrew a mahogany box. Its hinges creaked, and the man's eyes shot to the glint.

Georgie tapped the glass of his compass. "You are to navigate us with your tool, sir. Otherwise we will dead end in the reeds. We must go south, east, and south again to reach the harbor."

He glared at her, and she mustered patience, for he was in pain and held against his will. He winced each time the boat rocked, shifting his weight to favor one side, for several ribs were tender. In the distance, the river split into two branches. She thrust the compass and map at him.

"Do your duty, sir." She pointed to a spot on the map. "We are roughly here."

He didn't move to reach for the tools; one finger snaked out from underneath his blanket and traced a line along his neck, his eyes on the raised scar on her neck.

She scanned his eyes once more. Amber, not green. It could not be him.

He touched his finger to his lip, indicating Georgie's bruised and split mouth from Hildy's blow. Georgie said nothing but swallowed heavily. Her tooth throbbed. She spit a pink gob into the river. Her lip was sealed with a tight scab and swollen. After Hildy had recovered some strength, she had thrown a mean-spirited swipe at Georgie for making such a show in front of Hugh for being spoiled from the attack. Georgie had not struck back, and there had been no exchange of words between the women. Yet the dispute didn't linger, Hildy's jab having settled unspoken misgivings.

There was malevolence in his face, the swelling of the trauma going down a bit to reveal deep hollows under his eyes and cheeks. He would leap on her if he had the strength. She gripped each side of the hull and rocked the boat with her weight. He doubled up in pain, eyes wide, choking out a ragged breath.

"You know who he is?" Black Vy asked. "You know this man?"

"The day I lost the club and sack and my neck..." Georgie began.

Black Vy poised her paddle over his head as if she were going to spear him. Icy water dripped onto his forehead, and he thrashed his face from side to side to avoid it. The boat floated underneath a low branch. The filtered light from the leaves played over his face, and as white runnels of reflected water trickled across his eyes, they shifted from brown to green to black.

"This the man who bite your neck?"

Georgie watched him. "No. He cannot be."

Black Vy huffed. "Why he in my boat?" She ruddered her paddle to turn them toward shore.

"It's not him. I found a letter on his person. He is the Virginian, come to inspect Hugh's blasting. We must keep him. We have nothing but his compass and his ability to use it. Stop!" She lurched to grab the paddle from Black Vy, but fell back as the boat tipped unsteadily.

"But I know how to use..." Black Vy began. "What are you doing? Don't do that."

Georgie rummaged for a length of rope. She bound the man's wrists, his hands cupped like a thistle pod at his crotch.

Black Vy stroked hard to avoid the shallows. "You don't think we can get to the harbor on ourn own?"

"We have but one chance and must be sure of direction. There are many tributaries, and we cannot travel as women alone. And we will take him to medical care once he proves his use." Georgie stubbornly held to her reasoning. "Sir, if you kindly steer us to the harbor, we will carry you to the door of a fine city doctor."

"You c'ain't leave a man's hands bound in this cold. They freeze off," said Black Vy.

"How do you know?" But Georgie saw the man's hands had already paled waxen against the pink of his skin above the rope.

Black Vy didn't answer but rubbed her wrists. She pled again to untie him. "He c'ain't move anyhow."

"What happens when he can? He shan't make threats to me again." Georgie touched the scar at her throat. "He will be grateful to us for the surgeon we deliver him to."

"What happen when he leap up, healed, and hold both our heads underwater?" Both Black Vy and the man stared hard at Georgie.

"He won't do that, for I have his whip." Georgie drew the leather coil from her skirt.

The man blinked once, the glitter gone out of his stare. Georgie tapped the glass of the compass. She held the map to him, reoriented him to where they were. She set the compass level with his heart. He indicated with a tilt of his chin to continue steering downstream, veering to the right tributary.

The injured man woke on his back, stiff and cold. His body rocked with the boat, and upon his chest sat the wooden compass box, its brass needle clicking. The night sky was sparkling powder, flowing swift as the river. He lifted his upper body, grabbed the gunwales for balance in the unsteady perch of the boat, half on sand, half in water. The oars were not in the boat. He stowed the compass in the bow. On shore, the women slept close to a near-spent fire. He sprang out of the boat but landed ankle-deep in the stinging cold river, stumbled from the shock. He dripped a circle around the sleeping women. Built up their fire. Warmed himself a bit. The English woman tensed awake but lay still. He snared the whip within the folds of her skirts, drew it out by ynces. She recoiled, rolled upright, her face and torso firelit, the pouches encircling her waist jouncing like bladders. He shrank from the amulet sacks, dropped the whip handle. The dark woman stirred behind him, the blades in her skirt clacking. He closed his eyes as she drew to her full height, wielding the oar to strike. But it was the amulets that made him retreat. He slunk from the women, from the warm fire, hauled the boat more securely onto the bank, and sank back into his sleeping cradle.

He woke before dawn, morning stars rising as radiant crosses. The low belly of the moon's illuminated crescent flanked by Spica, Venus rising in the haze. The fire sparked, but low as if the women had rekindled it hours ago. The women hunched on the sand, watching him spring out of the boat. They scrambled upright, sand whispering off their skirts. The amulets at the English woman's waist joggled. He stopped advancing then edged low to pluck an ember from their fire. The women brandished the oars, but did not strike out, the uncertain squeak of sand underfoot as they hesitated. He dragged off their sack of meal. He walked downstream to kindle his own fire, clawed open the sack, spilling a great quantity of the grains as he pulled out a serving platter stuffed at the bottom. A platter of respectable workmanship. It would do for a cooking vessel.

As he shivered by the fire, gingerly working his mouth around the hot grain, the ground shook, a barely perceptible roll. A distant rumbling like cannons trundling overland to a battle theater. He caught his balance on the fingertips of one hand. At the rim of the treetops, an orange glow arced. The sounds reminded him of the early warning shakes and spews before the volcano had exploded apart at Thera. He had been twenty miles away across a bay but had still felt and heard the blast, watched as the sky flamed bright. The sky had darkened for weeks with ash and pumice.

The orange plume brightened. It was dawn. *I was mistaken*, he thought, *to think it was a blast*. Yet a flutter of uneasiness passed through him. He scooped more gruel, ate the whole hot tray himself, saving not a bite for the women, and let the bottom of the porcelain blacken and crack on the flames. He opened his coat to the fire until his bloody undershirt began to smolder. He startled at a rasping on the sand—the dark woman dragging her oar to sit fireside. Behind her, the English woman closed in. There was only the snap of logs. He wheeled around, the sounds of Oriskany quelled. The women had taken him too far downriver, out of range of the dead soldiers' cries. He was overcome with urgency to return home as if he had forgotten candles burning.

In his haste, he would leave the compass, not remember it until he was several rods away. Then he would crow with spite, leaving them a tool they certainly could not know how to use. He would slink away, for his injuries would take time to heal and he would never keep warm with these women.

Black Vy shivered

"Are you quite well?"

"Yes." But Black Vy dipped her face to her shawl.

"We can return."

"We c'ain't." Black Vy stood, surveyed the ransacked food supply. She scooped sand-spoilt gruel, tied the torn cloth secure.

On the river, ice had rebuilt overnight, and it bumped past.

The first portage would be near Little Falls where they would drag the boat onto shore before anyone saw them bereft of male support and protection. They would hide in the woods, avoiding the well-worn shoreline path, carrying the boat over the wet rocks in the night.

Georgie kicked sand onto both fires, dragged the boat to meet the river, held the stern as Black Vy climbed to the bow. They pushed off, paddled hard to meet the current. Georgie scanned the shore. The sun played between trees as the current carried them away. The man was not there. He was not darting after them.

The sun rose higher, and the ice on the water thinned. Black Vy unlatched the wooden compass box, unfolded a wing of the map. The sunlight flared across the compass glass, the needle bobbing. She held it level on her lap as Noord had taught her, poised to navigate the day's first fork.

ACKNOWLEDGMENTS

I'd like to express gratitude to Darrin Doyle for being an early and enduring champion of the manuscript and advising me to stick to the integrity of the narrative's vision. Matt Plavnick devoted months to writing insightful feedback, and this story's publication happened because of his editing. Dave Byrne and Eric Howell supplied encouragement on the whole and essential feedback for the music elements of the story. Victoria Carroll read with her eagle eye and asked critical and useful questions. Corey Holstrom and Maria Mercado-Bravo gave staunch encouragement from early in the writing process as I wrote the first pages of the book longhand on a road trip to their house. My husband Michael provided love and support for over a decade as I worked on this book. My writing teachers, Stu Dybek, the late Herb Scott, and Jaimy Gordon, were invaluable mentors who inspired and affirmed a belief in the artistic process and showed a way to funnel vision and invention onto the page. My heartfelt thanks to you all.